# Miss Moriarty, I Presume?

## Sherry Thomas

BERKLEY
*New York*

BERKLEY
An imprint of Penguin Random House LLC
penguinrandomhouse.com

Copyright © 2021 by Sherry Thomas
Penguin Random House supports copyright. Copyright fuels creativity, encourages
diverse voices, promotes free speech, and creates a vibrant culture. Thank you for buying
an authorized edition of this book and for complying with copyright laws by not
reproducing, scanning, or distributing any part of it in any form without permission.
You are supporting writers and allowing Penguin Random House to continue
to publish books for every reader.

BERKLEY and the BERKLEY & B colophon are registered trademarks of
Penguin Random House LLC.

Library of Congress Cataloging-in-Publication Data

Names: Thomas, Sherry (Sherry M.), author.
Title: Miss Moriarty, I presume? / Sherry Thomas.
Description: First edition. | New York: Berkley, 2021. |
Series: The Lady Sherlock series
Identifiers: LCCN 2021020963 (print) | LCCN 2021020964 (ebook) |
ISBN 9780593200582 (trade paperback) | ISBN 9780593200599 (ebook)
Subjects: GSAFD: Mystery fiction. | LCGFT: Detective and mystery fiction. | Novels.
Classification: LCC PS3620.H6426 M57 2021 (print) |
LCC PS3620.H6426 (ebook) | DDC 813/.6—dc23
LC record available at https://lccn.loc.gov/2021020963
LC ebook record available at https://lccn.loc.gov/2021020964

First Edition: November 2021

Printed in the United States of America
2nd Printing

This is a work of fiction. Names, characters, places, and incidents either are the product
of the author's imagination or are used fictitiously, and any resemblance to actual persons,
living or dead, business establishments, events, or locales is entirely coincidental.

*To Kathy and Heather, my fellow members of the Washi Coven, thank you for making Saturday mornings fun again——magical, really. We never get enough writing done, but I say pawing over one another's collections of decorative stickers and wax seal stamps is one of life's greatest pleasures.*

# Prologue

FEBRUARY 1887

A lain de Lacey sprang up from his chair. "What did you say?"
He had not been de Lacey very long. At his immense mahogany desk, flanked by eighteenth-century oil portraits, sometimes
he felt as if he had been reborn into the household of a manufac-
turer wealthy enough to buy a viscount for a son-in-law. And on
most days, the sight of his secretary at the door, relaying the latest
news with deference, only reinforced the impression that he had succeeded beyond his wildest dreams.

Today, however, he broke into a sweat.

"Mr. Baxter is coming to Britain, sir," repeated his secretary.
"And he wants you to make an appointment for him to call on
Sherlock Holmes."

So he'd heard correctly the first time. But didn't Mr. Baxter usually visit Britain in summer? It was only February.

And Sherlock Holmes—or Charlotte Holmes, rather—had
been under surveillance since Christmas. If anything, de Lacey
would have thought that Mr. Baxter wished to get rid of the woman,
not to undertake a formal visit.

An interview followed by a bullet or a strangling? But that was not de Lacey's concern. Visits to Britain typically did not please Mr. Baxter. De Lacey needed to check everything he'd done since becoming de Lacey to make sure he hadn't made any mistakes that would bring down Mr. Baxter's wrath.

He took a deep breath and waved away the secretary. "Very well. Go prepare for Mr. Baxter's arrival, and I will have Sherlock Holmes ready to receive him."

# One

Dear Ash,

Allow me to set the scene.

The day is cold and drizzly. A fire crackles in the grate. I am seated at the desk in my room, a cup of hot cocoa to my left, and a plate of still-warm plum cake to my right.

I've portrayed my usual sybaritic setting, you say? Why, patience, my old friend.

For what do I see when I look down but enough lace and frill to astonish Louis XIV himself, an eruption of white foam upon a wildly pink sea. Yes, I am wearing my very first tea gown, which you kindly gifted me at Christmas.

Alas, I had to put on a dressing gown over this fuchsia splendor. Even with a fire in the room, the tea gown by itself is still too insubstantial a garment for this time of the year.

Now that you can picture me, let me relay some news.

It has been three weeks since we eliminated both milk and bread from my sister Bernadine's diet. Not only does she no longer curl up into a ball after her meals, holding her innards in pain, she has gained five pounds. Madame Gascoigne remains astonished. Earlier she was convinced that nothing could be more wholesome than milk and bread. But I've long suspected that it must be some very common foodstuff that caused Bernadine's perennial gastrointestinal distress. At home I couldn't persuade my parents to agree to a scientific trial, but here I was able to put my ideas to the test.

I would have liked to give Livia a thorough account of Bernadine's improvement. Unfortunately, what with the sums I remitted home last December for the family's upkeep, my parents have become much more interested in the contents of the post and Livia can no longer count on always being the first person to examine incoming letters. In the end I conveyed my news in a small notice in the paper.

But in a small notice, there is no room to describe Bernadine's new peacefulness or the beginning of a healthy blush to her complexion. Similarly, I can assure Livia that Sherlock Holmes flourishes, but must wait for a future moment to let her know that Mrs. Watson and I solved five cases in the past three days and that my esteemed partner levied from one client an exorbitant seven pounds eleven shillings for our trouble. Mrs. Watson can always smell those who will be happier with the services they receive if they are charged more, a valuable skill too seldom taught to young ladies such as my former self.

Ahem. Are you impatiently scanning this rambling letter, my friend? Well, skim no more, for here is where I at last thank you for the lovely, lovely microscope I received for Valentine's Day.

I have heard of elaborate Valentine's Day cards that can conceal a watch or some other small valuable items inside, but I must be the first person of my acquaintance to find a Valentine's Day card amidst the scattered straws of a packing crate.

I digress. But what a shining beauty. What a perfect apparatus. After the unboxing, I sat and admired the microscope for a solid quarter hour before opening the instructional manual you'd so thoughtfully sent along.

After learning the controls, I quickly went through the dry-mount slides that had been supplied alongside the telescope. This past week saw me invade the kitchen on numerous occasions, to Madame Gascoigne's wry amusement, to borrow bits of vegetable matter that I then sliced with a scalpel to make my own wet-mount slides.

I'll spare you a full treatise of what I've learned about dyeing the specimens and illuminating them for maximum clarity and resolution, as this letter is running long. But allow me to express my gratitude once again. I adore the microscope and I can't say enough good things about it.

Yours,
Holmes

P.S. But the letter isn't so long that I can't append a postscript or two. Apologies for using my own shorthand from this point forward as I answer the questions you posed in your letter. No, since you last inquired, I have not heard from either of the gentlemen in question. Our erstwhile companion in mischief has been silent since his abrupt departure last December. And my kin, after his brief but welcome message in the papers early in January, has also abstained from further communication.

P.P.S. I do worry a little about Livia. Granted, the swift acceptance of her Sherlock Holmes story for publication in Beeton's Christmas Annual put her in a state of euphoria. But euphoria never lasts long in the Holmes household and she has been stuck there too long without a respite.

P.P.P.S. The surveillance has been more or less the same. I wonder what will come next.

P.P.P.P.S. Were you beginning to believe, my friend, that I would never arrive at addressing your other *Valentine's Day* gift?

I am wearing them now, those very pink silk stockings and the no less frou-frou suspenders, beneath my tea gown. For a moment I marveled at how you managed to locate the exact same fabric as the one used in the tea gown, only to realize that the entire ensemble had been conceived and executed at the same time, but given to me in two installments.

I am amazed, Ash.

It warms the cockles of my heart, knowing that to an already scandalous tea gown, you chose to add an even more outrageous pair of stockings. One of these days you must recount for me what passed between you and the dressmaker. I hope she was appalled——and secretly titillated, of course.

And now we come at last to the reason that I am replying to you only now, after the passage of an entire week: I needed time to compose a suitable response to your extraordinary gift. It is in the smaller, waxed-sealed envelope. I hope, with every fiber of my being, that it will achieve its intended effect.

⊰⊱

Dear Charlotte,

I have marvelous news. Mrs. Newell, our beloved Mrs. Newell, has invited me for a visit. A fortnight away from home!

Of course, part of me bemoans the fact that we shall be in the dreariest stretch of the year, the last bitter dregs of winter. I'm tempted to reimagine this visit at the height of summer, with the sun all warm and liquid——or at least warmer and more liquid——and myself in muslin, strolling the parklands for days on end.

But I'm grateful. Oh so grateful to be given this reprieve. I will not describe for you the latest scenes of domestic strife in the Holmes household. Suffice it to say that whatever good cheer our parents derived from the funds you provided——and from being temporarily away from each other——evaporated after they were once again reunited under the same roof. In fact, they loathe each other more after an absence.

But let me waste no more ink on them.

Now that I have expounded sufficiently on this latest development in my life, allow me to at last thank you for the wonderful typewriter. (And how clever of you to have hidden it inside a box of painted pebbles from

Bernadine's "institution." Neither Mamma nor Papa displayed the least interest and I was able to whisk the box away to my room.)

For weeks after I received my news, I smiled until my cheeks hurt: I am no longer a mere scribbler, but a scribbler for whose words publishers—or at least one publisher—would part with real pounds sterling.

And I can't thank you enough—you, Mrs. Watson, and especially Miss Redmayne—for finding the chap who would lend me his name for this story. I do chafe a little at the thought of this deception, at the contortions I must perform and the credit I must sacrifice. But then I think of you, you whose very perceptiveness and audacity inspired the story. I think of the rigmarole you go through in order to make a living and tell myself that if you can put up with it, so can I.

But your genius is incontrovertible. Whereas my story has yet to face its true test. What if everyone who opens a copy of the Christmas Annual simply skips over my tale? Or what if everyone does read it but loathes it? I usually manage to keep such thoughts to the side, but sometimes, when Mamma is in an ill humor—

Let me not speak any more about that. Instead let me thank you again for your generous present and your even more generous note. You are right that I would be unlikely to use this typewriter, for as long as I live under our parents' roof, for fear of attracting their attention. But I held your note close to my heart and imagined, as you asked me to, the day when I would be free. When I can dash up and down staircases, saunter from room to room, and, my goodness, even pound upon the stubborn keys of a new typewriter without incurring anyone's disdain and wrath.

Here's to that day. Here's to us.

Eternally yours,
Livia

P.S. I am all right. I miss our young friend and I worry about him. But I understand that it may be a long time before we can do anything and I am determined to be patient. And to be useful, when the day comes.

❈

Dear Holmes,

I met Miss Olivia yesterday afternoon——a happy surprise I had not anticipated when I'd accepted Mrs. Newell's invitation to tea.

The three of us passed a very pleasant time. Afterward Miss Olivia and I took a walk by ourselves in Mrs. Newell's gardens. There I was at last able to congratulate her on the upcoming publication, albeit not for some months yet, of her novel. She was flustered——very nearly giddy. It took me a moment to realize that although she had written to you, this must be the first time she had been able to celebrate that achievement in person with anyone.

We parted ways with promises of many meetings during her time in Derbyshire, even though I suspect that Mrs. Newell plans to surprise her with a trip to London instead.

I haven't told you this, but the previous time I saw Mrs. Newell, she pulled me aside and asked whether I had news of you. With great care I related that according to Inspector Treadles, who had met you during the course of the investigation at Stern Hollow, you seemed to be faring surprisingly well. Mrs. Newell responded rather archly that she thought I'd have more direct news. When I equivocated, she sighed and said, "Of course I understand. You needn't say more, my dear."

She is far from the only person, by the way, who had approached me in the months since your departure from Society, whether in person or by post, and inquired after your well-being. I have become expert at deflecting questions about you, especially from those who simply desire to gossip or, worse, entertain themselves at your expense. But it does make me wistful that I also cannot answer the ones who are sincerely concerned.

I barely know some of the individuals. But over the years they have benefited from your perspicacity in one way or another. It comforts me that despite your public disgrace they have not forgotten your generosity. Some of the inquiries come with heartfelt offers of help attached. Yours, Holmes, has been an existence that has made a material difference in the lives of many.

*In other news—*

*In other news*, my letter-writing was interrupted by the post, which brought new correspondence from you. Upon opening the seal of the inner envelope and seeing that it was written entirely in your own shorthand, my heart fell, fearing news of the most unwelcome sort from our adversary.

Imagine my utter disorientation, then, when I realized that it was not the literary equivalent of a beacon lit in alarm.

I am flabbergasted—flabbergasted—Holmes, by what you saw fit to transmit by post. Did you for a moment think of all those who had labored to revolutionize our system of letter delivery, eliminating abuse and corruption and instituting efficient modern methods so that we may send a letter anywhere in the United Kingdom for all of one penny?

Or were you smiling to yourself at how much smut you could convey in half an ounce of ink and paper? No, no, I'm sure your face remained impassive throughout, but dear God—in my stupefaction I have now profaned in writing for the first time in my life. But dear God—I might as well repeat the offense now—how can one penny ferry this much epistolary prurience to my doorstep?

You shoved a stone's worth of obscenity into a small, defenseless envelope. And then affixed our sovereign's blameless visage upon the entire enterprise to give it a gloss of respectability, so that it may safely pass through many pairs of trusting hands before landing with an inaudible exhalation of sulfur upon my desk.

As soon as I finished reading, I glanced at the window to make sure there wasn't a rain of fire and brimstone outside. I then sent a prayer of thanksgiving heavenward that your erotic tale was composed entirely in shorthand. Even if twice I was brought up short by what the man was doing with his "crock"—and laughed out loud the second time—it did not lessen my gratitude that I needed not fear this tale's discovery by an overeager servant or my unwary descendants.

*And then I paced. And occasionally rested my forehead against the cold glass panes of the window, as if that could restore clarity of thinking and purpose of action. I hope you are happy to learn that I shall be completely useless the rest of the day and very likely half of tomorrow as well.*

*Oh, Holmes, what have you done?*

*Your bewildered servant,*
*Ash*

*P.S. To at last finish that previously abandoned train of thought, in other news I still have not managed to speak to the children about my impending divorce.*

*Every night, unprompted, they pray for their mother. They pray for her good health, her happiness, and her safe return without expecting their wishes to be granted in the near or even the intermediate future.*

*About her continued absence they are wistful, rather than forlorn. It is but a condition of their existence now. Some children stutter. Some are frail and sickly. And Lucinda and Carlisle have a mother who no longer lives with them.*

*I admire the resilience with which they have borne this great change to their lives. At the same time, I suspect that what I see, this seeming equanimity, is but a steadfast patience: They can endure her absence because they believe deeply and unquestioningly in the certainty of her return.*

*To take away that certainty—in fact, to inform them that we will never again live together as a family—I fear their serenity will crumble. And so night after night, after their bedtime stories, I say only good night and nothing else.*

*P.P.S. When I met Miss Olivia, we spoke briefly about our young friend. Though I could sense her inner disturbance, she remained stoic. She has often been a pessimist in the past, but this time it appears she has opted for hope. It both gladdens me and makes my chest pull taut. Hers—and ours,* too—is a most slender hope, as frail as the single hair holding up the sword of Damocles.

P.P.P.S. To help me pass this long evening, I have now sat at my desk and copied out, in my own dreadfully legible longhand, the entirety of your salacious tale.

—⚬—

*My dear, dear Ash,*

*I would set the scene for you again except I am wearing thoroughly sensible garments and it is too early in the day for my next slice of cake—it says something about your letter that I cannot wait to reply.*

*I adore the portrayal of your pure and unblemished self sputtering like an altar flame when the church door flings open on a dark and stormy night. Would you have dropped to your couch in a dead faint, to the panic of your house steward, if my almost-innocent little story had not simply featured a man watching a woman undress, but physical contact?*

*You play the abstemious gentleman perfectly. Someone who reads only your letter would never guess the very provocative role you played in the matter. Indeed, sometimes even I wonder whether I have hallucinated those fuchsia stockings.*

*Is there an equally scandalous item of clothing a woman may gift a man? I have become familiar with a gentleman's wardrobe, from having dressed as one numerous times, yet I have no answer to that question. Which leads me to ponder*

———

*Dear Ash,*
Mrs. Watson knocked on my door some minutes ago. As soon as I opened the door she thrust a letter into my hand. "This came for Sherlock Holmes."

Below I reproduce this letter in its entirety.

*Dear Mr. Holmes,*

*I would like to arrange for a meeting with you at the earliest possible date, to discuss a matter of great importance.*

*Most sincerely,*
*Alain de Lacey*

The letter was written on De Lacey Industries stationery. I need not remind you to whom that particular enterprise belongs. When I looked up from the letter, Mrs. Watson had her fist in her mouth. I pulled her hand down and saw teeth marks around her knuckles.

"What should we do?" she asked, her eyes so wide I could see a rim of white around each pupil. "I have a thousand pounds in cash and two satchels already packed. Has the time come for us to run?"

I also have ready banknotes, though an order of magnitude fewer. In that moment, I calculated how long eleven hundred pounds would last us, if we took only Bernadine as opposed to if we took Mrs. Watson's entire household.

No, not too excessive a reaction when a representative of Moriarty declares his intention to call.

But when I spoke, I said only, "If Moriarty wishes to endanger us, he need not send a note first."

Mrs. Watson swallowed. "You said something similar on New Year's Eve, my dear, when you told me that we were under surveillance and would be for the foreseeable future. Then, too, you said that we need not worry for our safety. But the situation has clearly escalated, has it not? First he sent people to watch us. Now he's sending someone to interrogate us. How long would it be before we are whisked away somewhere like Château Vaudrieu's dungeons?"

"Let me say the same thing now that I said to you then, ma'am," I answered. "Moriarty needs to watch us and speak to us because he doesn't

*know what we have done. He has suspicions but no firm evidence. If we
run, however, it will be an unequivocal admission of guilt."*

Mrs. Watson said nothing.

I walked to the window. No one lingered outside in the rain, but then
again, no one needed to. Moriarty's underlings have taken two flats
nearby, one diagonally across from 18 Upper Baker Street, the other a
mansard on Allsop Place, high enough that its view of the back of Mrs.
Watson's house is not obstructed by the mews.

I turned back to Mrs. Watson, who now held on to a bedpost with
both hands. "Since you usually reply to clients, ma'am, may I ask that you
offer Mr. de Lacey an appointment late in the day tomorrow?"

"What if he's going to ask you about——"

"Then there is even less chance for us to escape undetected." I took
Mrs. Watson's hands. "Let us listen to de Lacey and find out what he
knows and what he wants. And then we will make our decisions as to
what to do."

Mrs. Watson took some convincing. But in the end she agreed to reply
to de Lacey. I asked for a plate of cake, consumed all the slices, and
doubted myself with every bite. Even now I am not sure whether I haven't
placed everyone in greater jeopardy by not fleeing immediately.

But my choice has been made and I will meet with Moriarty's
lieutenant.

Yours,
Holmes

Ma'am, miss, Lord Ingram called while you were out," said Mr. Mears, the butler, as he welcomed Mrs. Watson and Charlotte back into the house.

It was tea time the next day and the ladies had returned from another successful small case. For the services rendered, Mrs. Watson had collected two pounds and twelve and a half shillings. The amount was no pittance: During Charlotte's time as a runaway, that much money would have lasted her a month, if she didn't eat very much. But she estimated that Mrs. Watson could have demanded another half crown and the grateful client would still have considered their fees eminently reasonable.

Mrs. Watson had been badly distracted.

"Lord Ingram is in town? Thank goodness!" Mrs. Watson closed her eyes and exhaled.

His lordship's arrival came as no surprise to Charlotte. If he *hadn't* rushed to London after receiving her letter, she would have been astonished—and perplexed. But now that he was here, she exhaled, too, a great tension leaving the muscles of her neck and shoulders, making her realize that all day she'd held herself stiffly.

"When he heard that you were out, his lordship asked for the key to number 18," said Mr. Mears.

18 Upper Baker Street served as Charlotte's office. It was where she met those who came seeking her "brother" Sherlock Holmes's help, and informed them that the consulting detective was unwell and needed his sister to serve as both his eyes and ears and the oracle via whom he dispensed his great insight.

Mrs. Watson settled her black velvet toque back on her head. "Thank you, Mr. Mears. Let's go see him, Miss Charlotte."

Mr. Mears, always prepared, held out a covered rattan basket. "For your tea, ladies."

Charlotte inclined her head. She had not eaten much this day and looked forward to an extravagant tea. She hooked the basket over one arm, Mrs. Watson took her other arm, and they exited the house.

According to the calendar, March was less than a week away. But there was no hint of spring in the wind that cut Charlotte's cheeks, the cold that seeped in beneath her clothes, or the sky above that remained a resolute grey.

"Did you write Lord Ingram, my dear?" asked Mrs. Watson in a low voice. "I wanted to ask you to write him—oh, how I wanted to. But I couldn't bring myself to do it."

"Because he has children to think of?" murmured Charlotte. "True, but he would have been extremely upset if we'd kept him out of the matter."

She sounded unhesitating, but before writing him she had wavered for twenty minutes, a long time for an otherwise decisive woman. She was not inclined to withhold the truth from those to whom it mattered. But if she could predict how someone would react upon receiving a particular piece of information, then in relaying that information was she letting a grown man make his own choice, or had she already taken away every choice except one?

He did have his children to think of. With their mother in exile, his safety was of paramount importance to their well-being. And de Lacey's impending visit was no ordinary peril.

In the end, she had arrived at her decision as she had arrived at the decision to meet Moriarty's representative: by relying on both the coldest logic and a rather shocking amount of intuition. It was the same problem, and needed precisely the same calculation of how much danger they faced at this specific moment in time.

And now, the fate of those who mattered the most to her rested on the accuracy of her assessment.

"It will be all right," she said as they stopped before their destination.

"Yes," replied Mrs. Watson a little too fast, almost as if she'd been holding her breath, waiting for this exact reassurance.

The stucco exterior of 18 Upper Baker Street had been mended and cleaned, the front door given a new coat of black lacquer. The renovation had been Mrs. Watson's idea: If the ladies were seen outside directing masons and painters, then they must not be thinking of running away from Moriarty.

Charlotte had no way of knowing whether their act of feathering the nest convinced anyone of anything, but the door itself, freshly lacquered, certainly gleamed. The lunette window above the door was lit, as were the parlor on the next floor where Charlotte and Mrs. Watson received their clients and the adjacent room that served as Sherlock Holmes's "convalescent" chamber.

Her heart beat a little faster. Ash. They hadn't seen each other since Christmas. She wished she had worn something better. Her grey jacket-and-skirt set was perfectly serviceable, but hardly had the impact of the velvet day dress she'd had made recently, in a similarly overpowering pink as her tea gown.

The next moment she had her hand on Mrs. Watson's sleeve. "Don't look anymore, ma'am."

She'd never prohibited Mrs. Watson from paying attention to either of the flats taken by Moriarty's minions, but she did not want the dear lady to betray too much agitation. Their attitude toward this "unearned" surveillance should be one of bemusement and disapproval, not trembling fear.

Mrs. Watson barely took her eyes off the Upper Baker Street flat today, and just now she was again about to turn around and look.

"Right, right," muttered her partner, her key scratching the lock a few times before she managed to open the front door.

"Is that you, Holmes?" came the question immediately—from the direction of the basement.

"Yes, and Mrs. Watson, too," answered Charlotte.

Footsteps. Soon Lord Ingram, in his shirtsleeves and gold-flecked waistcoat, emerged from the door that led to the domestic offices belowstairs.

He looked . . . healthy. He looked like exactly who he was, a country squire who rode and walked daily, rain or shine. She could almost smell the fresh Derbyshire air still clinging to his skin and hair, this lithe, strapping young man striding toward her, the lupine grace of his gait made more lethal by the fact that he was still rolling down his sleeves over his shapely forearms.

Mrs. Watson threw herself at him. "Oh, thank goodness you're here!"

He stilled in surprise before wrapping his arms around her, too, enfolding her in his embrace. "Of course I'm here. Where else would I be?"

He spoke to Mrs. Watson but looked at Charlotte. The letter from de Lacey must have struck him hard; the concern in his eyes, however, was not for himself, but for her.

She inclined her head. She was not fearful by nature, and the threat of Moriarty was not a new one. Moreover, short of fleeing, they had already made every preparation. Mrs. Watson still agonized over all the dire possibilities that they had not anticipated, but Charlotte's mind was focused on the upcoming meeting.

De Lacey might have been sent to interrogate her, but in speaking to him Charlotte would also gain valuable intelligence to guide her next step.

She said to Lord Ingram only, "What were you doing in the basement, my lord?"

"Washing my hands."

Mrs. Watson stepped aside so he could offer his hand to Charlotte to shake. Charlotte slid her still-gloved thumb across the back of his hand. He turned their joined hands so that her palm faced down. She wasn't sure how he did it, but as he let go, this man who had protested so vociferously at her only *somewhat* erotic missive, his fingertips brushed the inside of her wrist, that sliver of skin just above the cuff of her glove, concealed by the belling of her sleeve.

The water with which he'd washed must have been glacial melt, for his fingertips were ice-cold. And yet she felt only heat at their contact, as if sparks from the grate had landed directly on her skin.

"But surely we have washbasins upstairs," puzzled Mrs. Watson. "And are you not cold, my dear, without your jacket?"

Charlotte had already noticed the slight sheen of perspiration near his hairline. "I imagine Lord Ingram took off his jacket because he was warm."

No fires had been lit in the house earlier, as Charlotte and Mrs. Watson had been out all day—Mrs. Watson, having come from modest beginnings, did not believe in wasting coal in unoccupied rooms. Lord Ingram, who saw to his own comfort very well, would have laid fires after his arrival. But it seemed unlikely for him to have built such blazes that he needed to remove his jacket.

"Were you at some physical exertion?" asked Mrs. Watson.

"You could say so," he answered lightly.

"There's a dark spot on your elbow," Charlotte pointed out. "It looks to be a grease stain. Lubricating oil?"

Up close he did not carry with him the scent of a pristine countryside but a whiff of machinery.

"Correct again."

Charlotte looked at him askance. "Don't tell me you were assembling a Maxim gun upstairs."

"A *what?*" Mrs. Watson's startled cry echoed against the walls.

"You've heard of a Gatling gun, perhaps, ma'am?" said Lord Ingram to her, very gently.

"That—that American rapid-fire weapon?" answered Mrs. Watson in a whisper.

"One hand cranks a Gatling gun," explained Lord Ingram, "but a Maxim gun is recoil-operated. The rounds feed automatically."

Mrs. Watson stared at their visitor, and then at Charlotte, who said, "Do we have enough room upstairs for a Maxim gun?"

"Not precisely. But come and see."

He led the way. Charlotte, her attention snagged by the sight of him heading up the staircase—without his jacket she could almost perceive the contours of his posterior through his trousers—barely remembered to tug at Mrs. Watson, still rooted in place, to follow them to the parlor.

The parlor had been refreshed, too. A beige-and-gold Aubusson rug, full of blooming roses on stylized cartouches, now covered much of the floor. The formerly subdued armchairs had been reupholstered in a leafy chintz that reflected the summery themes of the carpet.

The space still smelled distinctly of tonics and tinctures, which served as a reminder to visitors that the unseen savant in the adjacent bedroom was a patient who could not meet with his petitioners face-to-face because of his never-specified conditions.

The bedroom, of course, was perennially empty, except when Charlotte entered to seek her "brother's" sage advice, or when her companions wanted to listen in on a particular client's story. But it, too, was fully furnished, with neatly folded pajamas and nightgowns in the wardrobe, a black shawl left on the headboard, a pair of slippers by the side of the bed, and even a bedpan hidden in the nightstand.

Now, however, in the space between the bed and the wall, there stood something that looked faintly like a camera on a tripod, except for the slender, foot-long metal tube that protruded from its front.

"It's much smaller than I expected. Did it come in that?" Charlotte pointed to a barrel-stave trunk that had been pushed to the far side of the bed.

Lord Ingram nodded, shrugging back into his jacket. "With the weight of the trunk, everything comes to about four and a half stones. Not easy for one person to move but doable."

Charlotte approached the apparatus and examined it more closely. "Excellent—it has a universal pivot. Where are the cartridges?"

He pointed to a smaller suitcase. "There, in long belts. I'll load them later."

Mrs. Watson held on to a finial on the headboard, her grip so tight the tendons of her wrist stood out. "So you did bring a machine gun," she said, her voice quavering.

"I didn't know what we would face," said Lord Ingram.

"Probably not a machine gun on the part of Moriarty's minions," said Charlotte quietly.

"Given our current uncertainties, I prefer to err on the side of caution. If the Maxim gun turns out to be comically unnecessary, I can always pack it away."

His tone was light, yet firm.

Mrs. Watson glanced again at the Maxim gun. "I think—I'd better see to our tea."

Charlotte, too, headed for the parlor—the contents of the basket she'd brought beckoned. As she passed Lord Ingram, she settled a hand at the small of his back. "I like it, your miniaturized Maxim gun."

He looked down at her, a barely perceptible smile about his lips. "I thought you would."

Said the man who knew all about her enjoyment of Patent Office catalogues.

"I might feature it in a story," she murmured.

"I see you plan to instill the fear of God in me yet," said he, his low voice sounding not at all afraid.

She laughed on the inside but kept her face impassive, since he had written in his letter that was how he imagined she'd looked, scribbling away at her small scene of seduction. "You've worked hard, sir. Come have some tea."

❧

"Her latest letter was full of musings on the human condition—or rather, the human apparel," said Mrs. Watson, of her beloved niece Miss Redmayne, a medical student in Paris. "After having attended two childbirths, an appendectomy, and a funeral all in one week, she wondered whether we are so insistent on good clothes because the body, in the end, is unmistakably animal. A human childbirth is shockingly messy, a human split open is just organs and intestines, and a decomposing human is no different from any other piece of meat left out too long."

Neither Lord Ingram nor Charlotte said anything. Charlotte had nothing to add. As for Lord Ingram, perhaps his sense of delicacy prevented him from furthering the conversation. But more importantly, they both knew that Mrs. Watson was reaching for things to say, meandering on to delay the inevitable.

Which could not be delayed much longer.

Charlotte rose and went to the window seat, where a pot of narcissus bloomed, all snow-white petals and bright yellow centers. It had been given to Sherlock Holmes by a horticulturally inclined client, alongside a handwritten booklet on its proper care and feeding. Charlotte's favorite part of the instruction concerned the sousing of the bulbs, an addition of spirits so that the stalks would not grow too tall and bend over.

She was decanting a spoonful of whisky into the footed bowl when Lord Ingram said, "Holmes, I take it your plan is still to wait and see?"

Putting aside the whisky, she picked up a piece of soft linen and wiped particles of dust from the slender green stems. "Officially, yes. But we also have Bernadine already sedated and placed inside Mrs. Watson's coach, alongside some essential luggage. Mrs. Watson and I currently carry a dizzying number of banknotes, plus two firearms apiece. And Lawson is to bring the carriage around the back of number 18 a little after the arrival of Moriarty's representatives."

Silence.

Charlotte continued with her task of keeping the narcissus pristine but gazed out of the bow window. Streetlamps had been lit, their glow hazy at this twilight hour. No pedestrians lingered. Heads bent, shoulders hunched, they hastened forward. Even the paperboy seemed to be in a rush.

"In other words," said Lord Ingram slowly, "all you needed was the addition of a miniaturized Maxim gun to mow down anyone standing between you and your coach."

Someone snorted. Mrs. Watson.

Charlotte smiled slightly. "Indeed."

Silence again. Lord Ingram left his seat to retrieve the whisky from the bow window, next to where Charlotte sat. He poured for both Mrs. Watson and himself. They drank without clinking glasses, and without speaking.

When their glasses had been drained, Lord Ingram said to Mrs. Watson, "I might as well load the cartridge belt into the Maxim gun. Would you assist me, ma'am?"

Mrs. Watson winced but agreed.

Alone in the parlor, Charlotte returned to the tea table and picked up one of Madame Gascoigne's dangerously delicious éclairs. The clicking and grinding from the installation of the cartridge belt lasted only seconds—as she'd thought, Lord Ingram had not needed any real help with that. But through the open bedroom door, Mrs. Watson looked very much in need of his renewed embrace. She clung to him, her arms banded hard around his middle, her fingers gripping on to the Harris tweed of his jacket.

Charlotte took a slow bite of her éclair. She was very likely endangering these two. But by how much? And was there a loss of Moriarty's that he could pin directly on Charlotte?

Her discovery that Lady Ingram was a Moriarty minion could be argued as Lord Ingram finding out the truth on his own. The public disclosure of Moriarty's name in the wake of the Stern Hollow affair? Lady Ingram had taken the initiative, when she'd turned against her former master. Ending Moriarty's thieving, via De Lacey Industries, from Cousins Manufacturing? Sherlock Holmes had merely been helping a friend suspected of murders he did not commit.

Of far larger concern were the great many items Charlotte and company had raided this past December from a hidden safe in Château Vaudrieu, Moriarty's lair outside Paris. But that grand larceny had taken place at a masquerade ball, where their faces and identities had been hidden. And really, they hadn't even known they would be dealing with him when they'd set out for the château to recover letters for a client suffering from blackmail.

Overall, from the point of view of an external observer, Sherlock Holmes had been but a coincidental inconvenience to Moriarty, never an intentional adversary.

This last was true even from Charlotte's own point of view.

In the bedroom, Lord Ingram and Mrs. Watson had moved to the window. They now stood side by side, his arm around her, her head on his shoulder.

Waiting.

Unfortunately, it did not matter what Charlotte knew or believed, but what Moriarty did. What *did* he believe? And what if he knew more than Charlotte suspected?

She glanced again at the two people at the bedroom window, then down to the dangerously delicious éclair of which she'd taken only one bite.

"A carriage!" cried Mrs. Watson. "A carriage has stopped before our door!"

— ❈ —

Livia Holmes had disliked London. It was too crowded, too dirty, too insalubrious—and too directly associated with her long-standing failure at matrimony. "Eight Seasons and not a single proposal!" was an expletive her mother hurled at her at the slightest provocation, or sometimes even out of the blue.

But these days, London had come to symbolize escape—and hope. London was where Charlotte had established a thriving practice as Sherlock Holmes, consulting detective. London was where she had formed a close-knit group of friends who warmly embraced Livia as one of their own. And London was where Livia planned to be, should she ever win the freedom to leave her parents.

All of which had made Mrs. Newell's surprise announcement the night before deliriously welcome. Mrs. Newell, cousin to Sir Henry, Livia's father, had always been sympathetic toward Livia's desire to be away from home. Livia was already profoundly grateful that she'd invited Livia to her place in the country; she almost could not believe her good fortune that Mrs. Newell had planned a trip to London.

At their hotel, they were put up in a large, luxurious suite reminiscent of a private house, with its own door to the street that did not necessitate passing through the hotel's foyer.

"Ah, but I've had enough of moving around today," said Mrs. Newell. "These old bones love a soft chair more than they love adventure these days."

"You must truly love a soft chair, as you are still one of the most adventurous women I know," said Livia with a fond smile.

Mrs. Newell chortled. "In spirit, perhaps. But now I shall have a nice long soak and then read magazines while I dine in bed."

"That sounds enviable."

"Then you should do the same. Now shoo, young lady, so I may at long last remove this accursed corset."

Livia laughed and bade Mrs. Newell good evening, understanding that she would not need to attend to the older woman again before morning. Mrs. Newell's maid asked after Livia's comfort, but Livia made it clear that she required no looking after. She would sit for some time in the hotel's reading room and then unpack her own luggage, see to her own bath, and order her own supper.

Five minutes later, she was outside the hotel. A one-mile walk to the north on pedestrian-clogged pavements brought her to Mrs. Watson's front door.

Oh, how she loved ringing Mrs. Watson's front door, especially unannounced.

She certainly surprised Mrs. Watson's butler. "Why, Miss Olivia, welcome!" cried Mr. Mears. "Do please come in."

He smiled. Livia, however, did not miss the strain in his eyes. She tensed. "Is everything all right, Mr. Mears? Is everyone all right?"

"Everyone is fine," said Mr. Mears, closing the door. Though they were alone in the entry, he looked around and lowered his voice. "Mrs. Watson and Miss Charlotte left for number 18 not long ago. Lord Ingram is there, too."

Lord Ingram? But she'd had tea with him just the other day—in Derbyshire. What was he doing in London all of a sudden when at their meeting he'd been full of plans to show her around Stern Hollow?

"That is—that is—what is going on?"

Mr. Mears chewed the inside of his cheek. When he spoke again, his voice was barely audible. "I have not been given express permission to discuss this with anyone, but I believe the ladies would not mind if you knew: They will be meeting with someone representing Moriarty."

Livia sucked in a breath—and could not exhale again.

"Some cognac, miss? Or whisky?" said Mr. Mears immediately.

Livia waved a hand, even though she desperately wanted a chair and a drop of something potent. "What does Moriarty want?"

"That is what they hope to find out this evening."

Livia swallowed. "I must go to number 18 then."

"You might be too late, miss. Moriarty's man is expected as we speak."

The air became thin. Livia braced her hand against a console table. "I'll take my chances."

Mr. Mears took another look at her and said, "Let me give you the key to the back door then."

Leaving Mrs. Watson's, Livia felt neither the key in her hand nor the icy wind that flapped her cloak. An entire doomsday unfolded in her mind, dark visions of Charlotte and Mrs. Watson, and perhaps even Lord Ingram, in some rank, horrible dungeon on the Continent.

Would they find Mr. Marbleton already there, Mr. Marbleton who could no longer outrun Moriarty?

Several times she nearly turned around to flee. But somehow, though her knees buckled with every step, she kept moving forward, Mr. Mears's words echoing in her ear.

*You might be too late.*

*You might be too late.*

She did not want to be too late.

A carriage slowed and came to a stop before number 18. Had it brought Moriarty's minions? She froze in place, before opening her reticule and, with shaking hands, rooting around inside as if she'd forgotten something and only now remembered to search for it.

Two men descended from the carriage. One she didn't recognize, but the other . . . He glanced up at the bow window of number 18's parlor, his profile both startlingly familiar and completely out of place. An eternity passed before she realized she was looking at Mr. Marbleton.

The man she loved.

# Three

I t's Mr. Marbleton!" cried Mrs. Watson. "What—what—"
Charlotte, who had been determined not to rise from the tea table until someone rang the doorbell, was at the bow window the next instant.

Two men had alit from the carriage, but only one looked up, his clear eyes meeting Charlotte's. Her astonishment was silent, accompanied by not even an exhalation of breath, only an ominous vibration inside her chest.

Very few people knew of Mr. Marbleton's involvement with them, and none of them had any reason to disclose that to Moriarty. Why was he here?

"Miss Charlotte," Mrs. Watson's urgent voice rose again, this time from directly behind her, "is that not Miss Olivia in the direction of the park?"

It was indeed Livia, looking as if she'd seen a ghost.

The doorbell rang.

Charlotte's stomach tightened. She turned around. "Mrs. Watson, a change of plans. Since Moriarty has long known that there is no Sherlock Holmes, before him there is no need for you to act the part of the consulting detective's landlady or caretaker. Let us head down together. You will please conceal yourself and I will open the door. Once I have shown our callers up, will you go out and retrieve my sister?"

Mrs. Watson nodded, two quick, jerky motions of her head. "All right."

The doorbell jangled again.

Mrs. Watson made to move but Lord Ingram stayed her with a hand on her arm. He faced Charlotte, his gaze solemn. "Holmes, are you saying that the man who came with Mr. Marbleton is not de Lacey but Moriarty himself?"

That the appointment had been made for Moriarty had occurred to Charlotte before, but she had not considered it particularly likely. Mr. Marbleton's presence, however, changed things: She could think of no good reason why he would be made to accompany de Lacey. "Yes, I believe Moriarty has come to take my measure."

She took Mrs. Watson by the elbow. "Let's go now, ma'am. My sister will have need of you."

The older woman swallowed, but nodded and followed Charlotte out of the parlor.

At the bottom of the staircase, Mrs. Watson gave Charlotte a swift, hard hug before she secreted herself in the caretaker's room. Charlotte stood in place a moment, then went forward and opened the door.

The man who stood in front of her—she had seen his face once before, two months ago, at a disrupted ball in what had once been and was now once again his château in the Parisian countryside. That night he had been shabbily dressed, his face lean, his eyes hard. Now he had put on some weight, some very fine day attire, and an affable smile that crinkled the corners of his eyes.

Had she never seen him coldly scanning the crowd at the château, would she have given more credence to this kindly expression?

Mr. Marbleton, standing behind Moriarty, was thinner than she remembered, his brown eyes appearing larger and more deep-set. She allowed herself a flicker of interest, as if she were intrigued by the appearance of this sweet-faced young man.

And only then did she return Moriarty's smile. "Good evening, gentlemen."

"Good evening. James and Stephen Baxter at your service, miss. We have an appointment with Mr. Sherlock Holmes."

Baxter. She had come across this name in her prior investigations, a name closely associated with that of de Lacey.

"Do please come in," she said, stepping back from the door. She shook hands with the men as they entered and introduced herself as Miss Holmes, omitting the pretense about being Sherlock Holmes's sister and oracle.

At her indication, the men preceded her up the staircase.

"I take it that you are Mr. de Lacey's representatives, gentlemen?" she asked, climbing up behind them.

This part of the pretense still needed to be kept.

"I would say, rather, that Mr. de Lacey is our representative," said Moriarty.

"Is that so?" Charlotte murmured politely.

"Indeed, De Lacey Industries is one of my holdings and Mr. de Lacey a valued lieutenant."

At the top of the stairs, to Moriarty, who very correctly stood to the side waiting for her, she said, "That would make you one of the most exalted clients we've ever had the pleasure of meeting, Mr. Baxter."

Moriarty's smile conveyed an unjaded enjoyment, as if it still pleased him to be reminded that he'd reached a high-and-mighty place in life. There was an openness to his expression that hinted at an unspoiled nature and a generosity of spirit.

Charlotte once again felt that ominous tremor inside her chest. How did this man, whose soul must be pockmarked by cruelty and a singular thirst for power, manage such a fluent yet subtle portrayal of nobility of character?

Beside him, Stephen Marbleton glanced about, as if he'd never before seen the interior of 18 Upper Baker Street. What role was he playing today, he who had been forced to reunite with Moriarty, his natural father, after a lifetime fleeing that very fate?

He didn't look delighted or comfortable. He looked like a young man accompanying his elder out of obligation, rather than enthusiasm. And that was perhaps the correct balance to strike—Moriarty would not believe him to be truly content, but neither would he tolerate an open display of misery.

In the parlor, after stoking the fire in the grate, Charlotte engaged in her usual tea-making ritual. Moriarty observed her closely, as if there were something to be gleaned from the way she warmed the teapot and measured tea leaves to steep. Mr. Marbleton continued his imitation of a youngster brought along on an errand the nature of which was a little opaque to him. He regarded Charlotte only briefly and spent more time looking around at the books on the shelves and the bric-a-brac on the mantelpiece.

His presence, as much as Moriarty's, boded ill. He had been deep in their confidence, especially with regard to the ball at Château Vaudrieu. If a confession had been compelled from him, then even a Maxim gun would not be enough to save everyone.

Where were Mrs. Watson and Livia? Where was Bernadine? And the carriage that should be pulling up to the back of number 18—was it, too, under Moriarty's control now?

But if he had come to seal her fate, even if he had enough self-control not to display any smugness, shouldn't she at least detect some regret on Mr. Marbleton's part?

She held the teapot steady and poured for everyone, filling each cup to just the right level. If they had not been compromised, then she must not betray any signs of guilt or undue agitation. And however desperate she was to find out whether Livia, Bernadine, and Mrs. Watson remained safe, she must act unconcerned.

"I hope your crossing was smooth, gentlemen?" she murmured.

Moriarty raised a brow. "Our crossing?"

"Yes, you crossed the Channel very recently, I take it. Possibly today?"

The two men stared at Charlotte, then down at themselves, as if searching for what clues they might have unknowingly displayed on their persons.

They did not glance at each other.

"How did you come to know of our crossing, Miss Holmes?" asked Stephen Marbleton. He seemed simply another first-time client taken aback by Sherlock Holmes's deductive prowess, marvel and disbelief writ across his countenance.

She put on a small, satisfied smile. "You were looking about the room just now, sir. Your gaze paused at the grandfather clock. After a moment of reflection, you took out your pocket watch, glanced at the clock again, and changed the time on the watch. Not a minor adjustment, for it required several turns of the crown, which implied that the difference between the time on your watch and the time on my clock was close to an hour, if not more.

"You have a fine timepiece, one I expect to be accurate. And since you didn't wind it, but only changed the time, this large discrepancy is best explained by rapid travel. You didn't travel alone, or you would have been obliged to match your watch to local times much sooner. Since you came with Mr. Baxter, it stands to reason that the two of you journeyed together. Only now, having arrived at your destination, were you reminded that you hadn't adjusted the time yet—and proceeded to do so."

Mr. Marbleton blinked. "That is remarkable reasoning."

Moriarty shook his head. "Astounding. Absolutely astounding."

Unlike Mr. Marbleton, who gave off an air of slight distraction, as if he had other things on his mind, Moriarty was fully present. And he regarded Charlotte with such genuine amazement that for a moment she felt as she had as a child, when her father cupped her face in his palms, called her his lovely poppet, and told her that she was the most extraordinary girl he had ever met.

She adjusted the cuffs of her sleeves and proceeded to bask, indeed preen, in Moriarty's attention. "May I also venture that you gentlemen didn't come from Paris, which has only a ten-minute time difference with London, but from somewhere further afield?"

Mr. Marbleton bowed his head, as if wary of giving unauthorized answers, but Moriarty said, "Indeed, we began our journey further east. What magnificent logic you possess, Miss Holmes."

He gave no geographic specifics, but Charlotte smiled broadly, as if his compliment was all that she wanted. "One does pick up a trick or two, serving as Sherlock Holmes's oracle. Are you familiar with my brother's condition, by any chance, Messieurs Baxter?"

"Yes, we have heard of his unfortunate state of health and have nothing but the most profound wishes for his recovery. But in the meanwhile, we shall be happy to work with you, Miss Holmes."

Such an easy sincerity to his words, too. And he meant it: No pretenses necessary. He was fully aware that Sherlock Holmes was a woman and fully accepting of that fact.

She handed around plates of baked goods. Mr. Marbleton declined everything but Moriarty accepted an éclair and ate it with obvious appreciation.

Seeing others enjoy their food usually buoyed Charlotte's own appetite. Moriarty's relish, however, did not have the same effect on her. She had seen his true face, cold and pitiless. Her brother's life was in danger because of him. And here was Mr. Marbleton, who, despite his effort to appear normal, obviously felt suffocated.

Should Moriarty discount everything else Charlotte might know about him, he must still take into consideration that Lady Ingram had publicly declared him a murderer, the culprit in the Stern Hollow affair. He knew Charlotte would be on guard. Why then was he taking the trouble to appear blameless?

Did he think that by calling himself Mr. Baxter she wouldn't know who he was?

She looked away from the refreshments on the tea table without making a selection. There was, however, nowhere else for her gaze to settle except on Moriarty's intelligent and empathetic face.

With a sinking feeling, she said, "I am honored by your trust, sir. May I ask why you wish to work with us? Mr. de Lacey, in his letter, gave no hint."

Moriarty looked up from his éclair. "Do you not know, Miss Holmes, why I am here today?"

His eyes were a pale blue, the shade at the edge of an English sky. They were slightly bloodshot, which served only to emphasize the gentleness of his expression. His voice held a hint of reproach, but it was a benign, forgiving disapproval.

Instantly her mind leaped to the list of "wrongs" she had perpetrated against him, especially that of the wholesale theft of his secrets at Château Vaudrieu. *Please understand, dear sir, that it was all a series of coincidences and misunderstandings. We never set out to interfere in your dealings and we have no wish, now or ever, to cause you even the smallest inconvenience.*

At the periphery of her view, Mr. Marbleton scuffed the bottom of his shoe against her lovely new Aubusson carpet.

Intellectually she understood that Mr. Marbleton was her canary in the mine, his reaction a sharp prod to her to remain alert and vigilant. Still, she found herself wanting to explain. To confess and explain.

A vein throbbed at the side of her temple—a strange sensation that she'd never known before, her heartbeat reverberating so far up, and so loudly and insistently, that she could not think.

Had a minute passed, or a second? Or no time at all?

She was still gazing into Moriarty's pale, fathomless eyes, still transfixed by the humanity and understanding he evinced, and still very much inclined to tell him everything and apologize for all the problems and difficulties she'd unwittingly caused.

*Your late—but still alive—wife approached me. Your former minion Lady Ingram approached me. Your blackmail victim, knowing nothing about you, ap-*

*proached me. Mrs. Treadles, fearful for her husband's life, approached me. In every instance all I did was agree to be gallant to a damsel in distress, albeit one with the means to afford my fees. Surely you see that, dear sir?*

Vaguely she became aware of her own face moving. Had she done something? Raised a quizzical brow?

"You did hear me correctly, Miss Holmes, but I'll repeat my question," murmured Moriarty. "Do you really have no idea why I am here today?"

———— ✳ ————

When Livia had learned of the impending visit by Moriarty's minions, everything around her had gone eerily dim. The sky. The air. The streetlamps, weak and sputtering, as if they were the Little Match Girl's final attempts to keep darkness at bay.

But all she saw now, as Mr. Marbleton turned his head toward her, were bright, vivid colors. The emerald ring on his right hand, the glint of silver atop his slender malacca cane, the flash of deep scarlet as a gale reversed the hem of his long black cape.

She had thought she would see him only in dreams for years upon years. But here he was, separated from her by nothing more than a few feet of air that suddenly smelled sweetly of roasted chestnuts.

He looked away as if he'd seen nothing more remarkable than a lamppost.

Her heart tore in two. Had he already forgotten her?

But the next instant, the same instinct that had her pretend to rummage through her reticule earlier made her yank shut the drawstring on the still-open reticule and spin around, as if she'd come to the conclusion that she'd indeed forgotten something important and must go back for its retrieval.

As soon as she turned, she felt the force of unfriendly attention on her back. She walked, shoving her feet down hard against the pavement so as not to break into a run. He hadn't come alone. There was another man. Who was he? Had he seen her looking at Mr.

Marbleton with her heart in her eyes? Had she exposed herself? Worse, had she exposed in Mr. Marbleton a hitherto unknown weakness that his captors could use to their advantage?

She didn't stop until she reached the sharply angled intersection between Upper Baker Street and Allsop Place, where she hid behind the end of a row of houses.

She peered around the corner. The carriage was still there, but no one was left on the pavement before number 18.

Her knees shook. But she bit her lower lip and headed back out: She still had to get to the rear of number 18. She would simply take a different route.

Someone took hold of her arm. A bloodcurdling shriek was about to leave her throat when she saw that it was Mrs. Watson. She threw her arms around the older woman. "Oh, Mrs. Watson. Mrs. Watson, what is going on?"

Mrs. Watson rubbed her on her back. "Come along. I'll tell you."

The tightness of her voice made Livia feel as if she were falling down a long chute. Was she about to tell Livia that Mr. Marbleton had thrown in his lot with Moriarty? Was that why he was now trusted enough to be Moriarty's representative?

She swallowed and walked faster, holding on to Mrs. Watson's arm with both hands. Without any reminders from her to avoid going too close to the carriage, in case any observers remained behind, Mrs. Watson headed north on Upper Baker Street, in the opposite direction.

They made three turns and entered the alley behind number 18.

"According to Miss Charlotte, that was Moriarty himself," said Mrs. Watson, who had been silent all this time.

Livia stared at her. Mr. Marbleton might be related to Moriarty, but he was most certainly not—

She emitted a strangled cry. Mrs. Watson meant the other man, the one who had come with Mr. Marbleton.

Moriarty. She'd always believed—fervently hoped—that he

would remain a distant threat. He was not supposed to materialize on Upper Baker Street, fewer than thirty feet from her. And Charlotte, dear God, was she speaking to him face-to-face, forced to put on a smile and offer him tea and biscuits?

"My—my sister—"

She didn't dare say it aloud, but why else would Moriarty be here, if not to demand that Charlotte return to him what she'd taken from Château Vaudrieu? And he could never have learned of it unless—unless Mr. Marbleton had informed him.

"I thought Lord Ingram had grossly overreacted when he brought a miniaturized Maxim gun," said Mrs. Watson with a grim satisfaction. "Now I wish he'd brought some proper artillery."

"What—" Livia almost could not ask the question. "What do we do if Mr. Marbleton—if he—?"

Mrs. Watson's voice was full of uncertainty. "I don't know. I don't think Miss Charlotte knows either."

Terror. Anguish. Livia thought she'd known plenty of both. But as it turned out, she'd never had a taste of either until this moment. She felt like a straw target at an archery practice, pierced through and through.

Blindly she followed Mrs. Watson and almost bumped into the latter when she stopped. When had they entered number 18, or climbed a flight of steps? Yet here they were, squeezed inside a service stairwell, on a landing that was barely big enough for their skirts.

"When Miss Charlotte receives gentlemen callers, the parlor door is usually left open. We should be able to hear them from here," whispered Mrs. Watson. "But we must make sure not to be heard."

Livia nodded. She felt as if she were moving inside a vat of glue.

Slowly, Mrs. Watson opened the door to a corridor.

Charlotte's voice came almost immediately. ". . . ask why you wish to work with us? Mr. de Lacey, in his letter, gave no hint."

Livia exhaled. At least Charlotte still sounded completely herself, cool and detached.

A man said, "Do you not know, Miss Holmes, why I am here today?"

His voice was deep, its timbre rich and slightly raspy, the kind of voice that would float beautifully, reading aloud in a cozy parlor with family and friends gathered around the fire.

Moriarty? But his question didn't sound sinister or brutish, only . . . reasonable. He put Livia in mind of a cherished friend coming to call after a long absence, or a beloved uncle freshly returned from abroad, posing his inquiry with goodwill and a quiet intensity.

She blinked.

Beside her, Mrs. Watson looked not so much confounded as wary.

But as they exchanged a glance, the questions in their eyes were the same. Was that Moriarty? If so, why were they not quaking in their walking boots?

Had Charlotte made a mistake? Mrs. Watson had said, *According to Miss Charlotte, that was Moriarty himself.* Which meant that Mrs. Watson didn't know for certain and Charlotte, too, had ventured only an opinion.

The fact that Charlotte had never in her life offered a frivolous opinion didn't seem to matter too much at the moment.

Thoughts spun in Livia's head. This man could be a timely ally Mr. Marbleton had encountered, a man who had Moriarty's trust but was secretly working against him. This must be why Mr. Marbleton had agreed to come along. With this man's help, he might yet slip away and disappear into the crowd.

Maybe—just maybe—Livia could have a word with Mr. Marbleton before he escaped to greater freedom. He knew she was nearby. He must know she would come into the house. A few minutes alone could be arranged without inconveniencing anyone.

"You did hear me correctly, Miss Holmes, but I'll repeat my question," murmured the man. "Do you really have no idea why I am here today?"

Livia did. He had brought Mr. Marbleton back to them.

A hand locked on to her upper arm. Livia glanced down at the hand, then up at Mrs. Watson's shocked face.

*Where are you going?* mouthed Mrs. Watson.

Livia looked down again. She had opened the door more widely and was about to step into the corridor.

Mrs. Watson's expression of exaggerated disbelief would have been comical if Livia weren't suddenly covered in a cold sweat.

Gingerly, she took a step back, but the impact of her heel on the floorboard sounded like an anvil crashing. She grimaced, retreated another step, and leaned against the wall, panting.

What had happened? She wasn't even sure what she had meant to do by rushing forward. She simply wanted to do something. To give the man an answer.

And to thank him for bringing back her beloved.

When she'd been told, in no uncertain terms, that the man was *Moriarty.*

# Four

Hypnotic.

In this age of the occult, with everyone's cousin having attended a séance, Charlotte had heard that word much bandied about. Once, it had even been applied to her own gaze by an eager swain, trying to explain her effect on him. But in every prior instance in her experience, its use had been figurative.

Not here.

She felt it, the slipping of her own volition into a state of dormancy, and the corresponding ascendancy of Moriarty's will. Remarkable, what he was able to accomplish, without a pendulum in sight—or her consent in the exercise, for that matter.

Earlier she had seen a parallel between Moriarty and her father. It had been an unlovely lesson, to learn that her father had prized her only for the novelty she had been as a little girl and had no use for the idiosyncratic woman she later became. Moriarty, too, saw her as a diversion, a woman winsome enough and clever enough to be entertaining for a while.

A good thing that she, too, had been aiming in that direction, offering deductions unprompted and giving every appearance of wallowing in his praise and admiration.

She continued to gaze into his eyes. She did possess a strong enough mind to break free of his cavalier attempt at imposing control, but did not want to give the appearance of doing so. It would be better for him to stop on his own, either because he lost interest in toying with her or because his focus shifted to something else.

She smiled. She even laughed a little, her laughter soft and breathless. "I do have some idea as to the purpose of your visit today, sir."

"Oh?" said Moriarty, sounding profoundly interested.

*Did you know, Mr. Baxter, that Mrs. Watson and I were about to take a trip to Paris? She to see her niece, and I to call on those fascinating items that we purloined from your château? Yes, I was planning to take them out of the bank vault where they have been stowed and spend quite a bit of time studying them. I thought I would have a greater appreciation for the photographs in the collection, now that we have learned something of your modus operandi.*

Under the belling of her sleeve, she dug her middle and ring fingers into the center of her palm and concentrated on the discomfort.

Raising her other hand, she waved an index finger, an airy, careless gesture. "I believe, Mr. Baxter, that you did not come with a problem about your enterprise—for that, a visit from Mr. de Lacey or one of his lieutenants would have sufficed. Am I correct?"

"Very much so."

She waggled her brows and hoped she looked supremely pleased with herself, rather than deranged. "Aha, as I thought. Well, then, since it is not business, it must be personal."

"Again, exactly on the mark. Tell me more," said Moriarty, his voice a siren song.

*Do you wonder who it was that stole your secrets? Do these secrets matter very much to you, or do you have so many secrets that you can barely keep track of them?*

Her nails again sank into the soft center of her palm. Her willpower was not the only thing in danger of wilting. Her eyelids felt heavy; her head did, too.

Still not daring to look away from his eyes, she said, "I do not believe this personal matter concerns you yourself—you, sir, do not appear to need help. It must then have to do with someone else. For you to have traveled so far—from a locale with a similar longitude to Berlin, perhaps even Vienna—this someone must be of great importance. A family member, most likely. A female family member."

Something flitted across Moriarty's face. "Indeed?"

"Indeed. It is much easier to go to the police with difficulties concerning a man than with those concerning a woman. Ergo, the need for a discreet consulting detective."

She was speaking more slowly. An enormous lethargy had settled over her, the cost of not actively resisting his mesmerism. A part of her was sincerely terrified, but the rest of her, perhaps most of her, could not seem to care.

A bead of perspiration rolled down between her breasts. She forced herself to carry on, slurring her words a little, yet at the same time injecting a measure of amateurish coquettishness. "I would not guess the difficulties to involve a lady . . . in a spousal position to yourself. You came such a long way, sir, which makes me think that this family member resides not with you in Berlin or Vienna or where have you, but right here in Britain. A distance spanning half a continent suggests that the person on the other side is a grown child, rather than a . . . domestic companion."

Moriarty, who until this moment had leaned forward in his chair, moved back. He tilted his face up slightly and studied Charlotte.

The foundation of Charlotte's reasoning rested on the fact that he was a man with bigger problems. It was only recently that his loyalist had freed him from others in his organization who had overthrown and imprisoned him. Compared to a successful coup and traitors in his own ranks, Sherlock Holmes & Co. could not amount to more than a minor annoyance, a fly that buzzed in a corner of a house that had very nearly burned to the ground. Obviously Moriarty, the owner of this damaged edifice, had instructed his underlings to keep an eye on Charlotte, in case she grew into a greater threat, but for him to have suddenly come to her in person?

If she were right, then she did not merit this kind of personal attention. Not yet, in any case. His presence could be explained only if he *happened* to be in Britain and happened to be in need of a discreet female investigator.

If she were right. If Lady Ingram had not been caught and interrogated. If Mr. Marbleton had not betrayed them, willingly or unwillingly. If Moriarty still didn't know who stole his treasures from Château Vaudrieu.

If he hadn't guessed the truth while looking directly into the very depths of Charlotte's mind.

Moriarty continued to consider her with avuncular beneficence. There was nothing intimidating in his conduct, which appeared merely to be that of a confounded man who didn't know where to begin his response. Still, she felt like a small creature in a glass vivarium, with no place to run and no place to hide.

Fortunately, it was not the same hypnotic scrutiny from earlier. Perhaps the effort had wearied him. Or perhaps she had at last distracted him with her deductions.

The sensation of no longer being stuck under a hundred-pound blanket, however, did not lessen her exhaustion. To the contrary, she felt even more depleted—and hungry and thirsty besides. But she only blinked a few times, as if coming out of a particularly absorbing reverie, and tucked a nonexistent strand of loose hair behind her ear.

"I must account myself impressed with your deductions, Miss Holmes," said Moriarty. "I have indeed come to see you about my daughter."

Beneath her skirts, Charlotte's limbs quaked.

So they were still safe.

For the moment.

She forced herself to hold still and glanced out of the corners of her eyes at Mr. Marbleton. He sat with his gaze downcast, seemingly uninterested in the goings-on. Instead of scuffing one sole on her carpet, he was now pulling in both heels, his gleaming black Oxford shoes inching over a spread of dusky rose petals.

Was he calmer, compared to a few minutes ago?

Calmer, perhaps, but not more relaxed.

Charlotte had decided, early on, that she wanted Moriarty to underestimate her. Sherlock Holmes's reputation of cleverness was well established, so she would not seek to misrepresent herself in that regard. Rather, she would distort her temperament, throwing in vanity, braggadocio, and a need for approval, especially from powerful older men.

"As I thought," she said with a trace of smugness, putting more water to boil over the spirit lamp for a fresh pot of tea. "Please, I'm all ears."

Moriarty sighed. All at once, he radiated fatigue and defeat. And she, who had struggled to understand human emotions as a child, and who still, from what she could gather, experienced fewer and less intense emotions than did most others, felt the depth of his loss.

Was this why Mr. Marbleton had not relaxed? Because Moriarty's gifts extended beyond mesmerism? The pain and anguish he manifested, real or not, were flames that beguiled unwary moths.

So she had better play the part of an unwary moth. Thankfully, she always brought a notebook to client meetings. She rarely used the notebook, but transcribing Moriarty's words gave her a valid excuse not to look directly at him.

At the flames that sought to burn her wings.

"The first Mrs. Baxter died in childbirth, a tragedy for which I've still not completely forgiven myself," he began, the faintest catch to his voice. "The infant survived, but the attending physician did not believe she would live to see her first birthday. Having lost Mrs. Baxter, I did not wish to love and lose someone else. So I allowed my daughter's maternal grandmother to take charge of her upbringing.

"She proved to be made of sterner material, my child. Not only did she reach her first birthday, she sailed past subsequent ones without any regard to predictions of her early demise. I, on the other hand, made the mistake of hesitating year after year, wondering whether she was only meant to flourish under her grandmother's care. Whether if I were to bring her back into my life, Fate would immediately intervene and seize her from me."

Charlotte, who had placed an éclair on her plate, proceeded to ignore it, transcribing his story with the earnestness of an apprentice secretary.

"She was ten when she at last came to live with me, after her grandmother passed away. I thought we'd get along very well and we did, but we never grew close. She missed her old life and always wished to return to England and live in the house in which she grew up—and which had been bequeathed to her in her grandmother's will.

"When she was twenty-one, she did just that, moving to England and taking up residence in the old house. But she did not stay there for long. Some months later, I learned that she'd packed up her worldly goods and joined a group of Hermetists who had formed their own community in Cornwall."

Charlotte had no choice but to look up in surprise. "By Hermetists, you mean those who follow the teachings of Hermes Trismegistus, as found in the *Corpus Hermeticum*?"

"Correct. It is difficult for me to acknowledge that I have a daughter who is an occultist, but there it is."

To Charlotte, the occult was but a religion that had yet to muster an army and anoint a king. But she nodded sympathetically before resuming her shorthand note-taking.

"I was . . . vexed. The next time I met with her, I expressed that vexation. She replied that she was both of age and no longer dependent on my support. Therefore she was free to follow the dictates of her own will. And if it pleased her to live among occultists, for a while or forever, then that was what she would do.

"Her response further infuriated me. But after a while, I realized that I could not change her mind. Time was the only thing that could change it—time and the actual experience of living among those people she considered her friends and supporters. So I relented and she was able to have her way."

He paused. "I believe your water has boiled, Miss Holmes."

Charlotte was aware of that but had wanted him to be the one to point it out to her. "Oh, you are right. My apologies, I was so absorbed in your account, I didn't even notice."

She turned off the spirit burner, warmed the teapot anew, and measured more tea leaves to steep. "I had better pay more attention to my tea-making, or we'll be drinking a bitter brew. But if you don't mind, Mr. Baxter, do please tell me how long it took you to relent and what Miss Baxter had to do to bring about this change of heart on your part."

A needier and more conceited Charlotte Holmes should still be able to detect an omission in the story.

"Ah, I see my attempt at eliding a few things did not go unnoticed," said Moriarty quietly. "Very well, I threatened to burn the commune to the ground and she came home with me. But in the fifteen months that followed, she became engaged to no fewer than six unsuitable men—and I assure you, Miss Holmes, hers had not been an existence into which unsuitable men were granted entrée willy-nilly."

Amazing how he managed to infuse that particular piece of information with such pathos. What would have been comedy recounted by another became a lament for a father's thwarted love.

Charlotte was in awe of Miss Baxter. She ought to have tried something similar, perhaps, when her own father had reneged on his promise to sponsor her education. Not to mention, she didn't know what kind of men Moriarty considered unsuitable, but to have won over so many of them in such a short time was a testament to Miss Baxter's charm and determination.

"Indeed, she demonstrated that what I had originally believed to be an intolerable choice was, in fact, the lesser evil. I could have continued to exercise parental authority and restricted her to such circumstances as to guarantee that she would not meet any man, but I did not wish to become her jailer."

It took some effort for Charlotte not to look at Mr. Marbleton. Moriarty clearly had no trouble becoming *his* jailer.

"She returned to the commune under certain conditions. She was to write once a week. I or my representatives would meet with her once every six months. She could donate money to the commune, for her own and its upkeep, up to the entirety of her annual income, but she was not allowed to touch the principal sum from which her income is derived.

"I did not think these were onerous conditions, and she agreed. For close to five years she kept to her end of the bargain and I mine. But of late, things have changed."

He fell silent.

"When did you first notice?" Charlotte was obliged to ask.

"Too late, I'm afraid. There was upheaval in my own life in the second half of last year. I was, shall we say, indisposed for months on end."

His voice changed. Until now it had put her in mind of a bassoon or a cello, an instrument that produced low yet beautiful notes. But all of a sudden the music left his words, and without it those words seethed with anger.

The coup that saw him overthrown—the thought of it still enraged him, so much so that it caused a stumble in his otherwise perfect performance. So much so that Mr. Marbleton shrank into himself.

Moriarty, too, must have noticed, for he stopped speaking. When he resumed, his voice became, if possible, even more mellifluous. "While my indisposition lasted, those around me failed to pay attention to her. Some subordinates did not know about her existence, and many others had forgotten. The solicitor who usually visited her passed away. Her letters lay unread in a private postal box in Switzerland because no one collected them.

"I was not able to look after my own affairs again until the very end of last year. It took considerable time and energy to put my house in order, so to speak. I'm ashamed to admit it, but since her return to the commune, my daughter had led a quiet life, and I'd grown accustomed to not thinking of her as someone in need of my attention."

A relief for Miss Baxter, no doubt.

"It was not until last month that I appointed another solicitor to visit her," Moriarty went on. "To his surprise, he was refused at the door. The excuse given was simple: My daughter was required to meet with either myself or my representative once every six months, but six months had not yet elapsed since the previous visit.

"My new solicitor, not particularly familiar with what had happened under his predecessor, did not challenge that refusal. He returned to his office and wrote me. His letter, because it was not marked urgent, was not seen to for at least a week. When at last the matter came before me, I was perplexed. Had my old solicitor in Britain gone to see her on his own, for some reason?

"Then I noticed something. The commune claimed that a visit from my new solicitor wasn't due until May, because one had taken place in November. But my old solicitor died in October. A telegram dispatched to his firm brought back the disconcerting news that he had not instructed anyone there to visit her on his behalf and certainly none of them had gone on their own initiative."

Charlotte poured fresh cups of tea for everyone. A fragrant steam rose. Such an ordinary sight, such an ordinary scent, were it not for the fact that it was Moriarty himself, his brow knitted once again in fatherly concern, who lifted a gold-rimmed teacup and took a sip.

"My daughter's letters, more than half a year's collection, were brought to me," he said. "She has always been an interesting person, my daughter—possibly too interesting. But her letters, at least those addressed to me, did not make for stimulating reading. They were perfunctory recitations of a weekly routine that never varied, and I'd stopped anticipating them long ago.

"And stopped reading each one as it came in. Sometimes I skimmed through a few at a time; sometimes I failed to do even that. Needless to say, this entire batch at last received its due attention. The letters were as monotonous as ever. But one glaring omission stood out. She did not mention any visit by any solicitor—which she had always done before, as it constituted an event.

"I was more than a little alarmed at this point, and then I learned that she had sold the house that had belonged to her grandmother. It was not part of the untouchable principal I had mentioned earlier—that was what I had set up for her. In addition, she had a small inheritance from her grandmother, along with the house, though it must be said that every penny of that inheritance was needed to maintain the old house.

"She loved the house. She used to draw it from memory. In its every nook and cranny there were memories she treasured." His voice softened, as if he, who had never visited his daughter in her childhood, shared those memories with her and treasured them just as deeply. "I cannot believe she would have sold it except under duress."

*I don't believe you. I don't believe you care whether your troublesome daughter lives or dies. Why don't you stop this pretense and tell me exactly why you have darkened my door?*

Charlotte exhaled carefully, set down her pen, and straightened. "Mr. Baxter, does it not strike you as odd that she had lived among them for so long, apparently without any problems, but that things should suddenly change to this extent?"

"No, indeed, Miss Holmes. There is a distinct possibility that those running the commune learned of my incapacity, threw aside all caution, and at last acted with the cupidity they'd long kept hidden."

"You mean, they pressured Miss Baxter to sell the house she inherited from her grandmother and then made up the lawyerly visit last November in the hope that their arrogation of her property would go undetected?"

"Exactly."

That sounded plausible. However— "Mr. Baxter, why not simply remove Miss Baxter from this commune?"

"As I did once before to such great success? No, this time I will not march in to impose my will," said the man who imposed his will with every breath and every deed.

But as he regarded Charlotte, he radiated only the virtuous resolve of a desperately worried father. One who had tolerated enough questions from the lowly consulting detective. "Per my agreement with my daughter, once every four years, I can appoint a neutral party to inspect her living situation, provided she approves of my choice. I have made inquiries. Your clients, Miss Holmes, while in awe of your brother's great deductive abilities, are no less complimentary of your courtesy and good sense. Now that I've met you, I see that they are right. You are well suited to the task at hand, which calls for a subtle yet trenchant approach."

From the first mention of the Hermetists, Charlotte had guessed where this conversation was going. Still, her stomach dropped. "Are you suggesting, sir, that I should enter this commune?"

"I am willing to pay handsomely for your trouble."

He was the supplicant here, the one ostensibly seeking help. Yet Charlotte felt as if she were but a knight who must obey the command of her liege lord. "You mentioned that Miss Baxter must approve of your choice of a neutral inspector—"

Moriarty smiled. "She has already approved of my choice of a representative from Sherlock Holmes—or so I have been informed by those responsible for the running of the Garden of Hermopolis."

His statement felt like a grip tightening around Charlotte's throat.

"That is good to hear, Mr. Baxter. But I know next to nothing about this community where you wish me to take up temporary residence. Moreover, I am an unmarried young woman; to travel respectably, I must have a companion. Not to mention—however much I hate to point it out, sir—that something untoward might have befallen Miss Baxter. While I am distressed about her fate, I would be greatly more distressed about my own safety."

Her disequilibrium seemed to please Moriarty. His smile widened. "Fear not, Miss Holmes. I have brought a dossier—after reading it, you will feel sufficiently well informed. And of course you must do everything you deem necessary for your respectability and your safety. I'll leave the measures entirely up to you."

She could protest more, but it would be useless and she wanted her adversary gone. "In that case, I shall first need to consult all those who will be involved in this endeavor. If you will leave your address, Mr. Baxter, we will deliver our answer tomorrow."

The vainer and stupider Charlotte she had been playing would have wanted this meaningless victory, to be able to say that she didn't give him a response right away.

Moriarty, who seemed to understand the vainer and stupider Charlotte very well, inclined his head, his courtesy edged with a trace of contempt. "Very well, I shall send someone for your reply at nine o'clock tomorrow morning."

Charlotte mustered a weak smile. "That is perfectly agreeable."

"Then we will leave you to your deliberations and look forward to a favorable outcome," said Moriarty, rising.

Mr. Marbleton, who had been as still as a statue for several minutes, scuffed his shoe against the carpet one last time and stood up, too.

Charlotte saw them out and offered her hand to each man to shake. "Good evening, gentlemen. Thank you again for your confidence in Sherlock Holmes—and myself, of course."

## Five

After the door had closed, Charlotte stumbled backward and collapsed onto the staircase. With some difficulty, she turned sideways. Her hands on the balusters, she tried to pull herself up again. But her arms—and every other part of her—seemed to have turned into gelatin. Her breaths echoed; their unsteady cadence didn't sound so much exhausted as frightened.

Strong hands lifted her to her feet. Lord Ingram. He took hold of her hand and wrapped an arm around her middle. Leaning on him, she slowly began to climb the steps.

Livia, too, had rushed down the stairs. She grabbed Charlotte's other hand. "Oh, Charlotte. Are you all right?"

Charlotte both nodded and shook her head, and even she wasn't sure whether this second motion was to tell Livia not to worry or to negate what had been conveyed earlier with the nod.

Back in the parlor, Mrs. Watson pressed two fingers of whisky into Charlotte's hand as soon as Lord Ingram and Livia lowered her into a chair. Charlotte's nerves almost never needed shoring up, and certainly never needed shoring up with anything stronger than a slice of cake. But this time she drained half the whisky in one gulp, set down the glass with a heavy *thunk*, and then grabbed an éclair and devoured it in five seconds flat.

No one told her to eat more slowly. No one cautioned her not to choke on her food. They stood stock-still, watching her wash everything down with a cup of cold tea.

Only then did Lord Ingram grab the kettle. "I'll get more water."

Mrs. Watson, next to the chair, draped an arm around Charlotte's shoulders. Livia sank to her haunches, divested Charlotte of plate and cup, and took her hand with a grip strong enough to pulverize stone.

"Charlotte, did you hear anything I said? Are you all right?"

Clearly Charlotte was not. Were she all right, she would have carried on a conversation with Livia, kept abreast of a dozen other people in her vicinity, *and* given due attention to Lord Ingram's superlative form as he left the room in a hurry.

And she would have noticed far sooner that Livia's hands were ice-cold. "Go sit near the fire."

Her voice sounded raspy, but steady enough.

Livia didn't budge. "You come, too. We'll all sit by the fire."

Charlotte shook her head. "Not me. I might fall asleep if I became much warmer. In fact, I'll go sit on the windowsill."

But she didn't move, neither did she let go of Livia's hand. In fact, with her free hand, she took Mrs. Watson's hand, too. When Moriarty had announced that he'd come for his daughter's sake, she'd known that for the moment, at least, everyone who mattered to her would remain safe. But sometimes knowing did not offer the same solid reassurance as hands held together, palms against palms.

Only after Lord Ingram returned with the kettle did Charlotte at last move to the windowsill. At her request, he helped set chairs closer to the grate for Mrs. Watson and Livia, both of whom continued to hover around Charlotte. Next he went into the bedroom and came out with the large black shawl that had been left on Sherlock Holmes's bed and draped it over Charlotte's shoulders. "You may not want to be heated, but you shouldn't be chilled either."

Charlotte placed her hand over his, too, as he gave the shawl one last adjustment. On a different occasion, the gesture would have made him—and Livia and Mrs. Watson—feel self-conscious. But today he lifted her hand to his lips and the ladies didn't bat an eyelash.

He let go of her hand and turned to Mrs. Watson. "I'm going to take a look outside and check on your household, ma'am. If all is well, would you like me to inform your staff that they can transport Miss Bernadine Holmes back to her room and return to their duties?"

"Yes, please," said Mrs. Watson gratefully. "Thank you, my dear."

He settled his hand briefly on her shoulder, glanced back at Charlotte, and left.

The parlor was silent for several minutes, until steam issued from the kettle and Mrs. Watson went to make tea.

"Ever since I first heard his name, I've always feared him," Livia muttered, sitting down next to Charlotte. "I had no idea I've been afraid of the wrong things."

Charlotte felt as if she were recovering from a high fever, limbs weak, mouth dry, temples faintly throbbing, but at least a conversation was no longer beyond her. "No, we were afraid of the right things all along. It's just that now we have even more to fear."

Livia laughed, a sound like sobbing. "I hope you didn't mean to comfort me with that."

Charlotte exhaled. "I am at least somewhat comforted by the fact that we learned a great deal about him without losing our freedom—or far more—in the bargain."

More silence. Mrs. Watson used the poker rather forcefully on the coal in the grate.

The next moment Charlotte was on her feet, rising so fast, she swayed a little.

Livia leaped up, too. "What's the matter, Charlotte?"

Charlotte rushed to where Mr. Marbleton had been sitting and got down on all fours.

The slender chairs Lord Ingram had placed before the grate for the ladies had come from the bedroom. The two newly reupholstered armchairs had not been budged. One, they were far heavier. Two—and this was the more important reason—they had been carefully set in place so that images of the visitors who sat in them would be captured by the camera obscura set up between the rooms, and so that as clients in the parlor gave the details of their problems, observers in the bedroom would not only hear them, but have a good look at them as well.

The armchairs, after their recent improvement, boasted tasseled fringes on the bottom, a wink from Mrs. Watson to Charlotte, who adored frills and furbelows, and whose sense of fashion had been compared by her favorite great-aunt to a needlepoint footstool. Charlotte, needless to say, had been tickled by these additions.

Mr. Marbleton must have been overjoyed to see them, too.

She swept aside the fringes and—saw nothing. Only then did a biscuit-colored scrap of paper become visible against a stretch of carpet of a similar hue.

She got up, went to the desk, took out a pair of tweezers and a small wooden tray, and returned to the chair. Livia now knelt there, too, looking underneath. "Is that a railway ticket?"

"I believe so."

The ticket on the tray, dirty and crumpled, showed signs of having been stepped on more than once. In that regard, it was a most ordinary stub, the kind that dotted railway platforms, dropped by those who no longer needed them and trampled underfoot by other harried travelers.

About a quarter inch had been torn away from one end of the stub. But otherwise the printed information let them know that it had been issued by the London, Chatham and Dover Railway, for travel between Snowham in Kent and Victoria Station, London, valid for a single second-class journey.

And when Charlotte turned it over with her tweezers, the reverse merely presented the conditions of travel and more boot marks.

After a while, the other two women turned their attention to Charlotte, who shook her head. "I can fathom no particular secrets from looking at this ticket."

Livia frowned. "But is this left behind by Mr. Marbleton and not some previous client? We've traveled with him and more than once during those journeys I saw him tearing a stub to pieces and putting all the shreds into a rubbish bin before we left the station."

"I saw him do that with ferry tickets from crossing the Channel," said Mrs. Watson. "Luggage tags, too—he disposed of them as soon as they'd served their purpose. His habits made sense. At any moment he could have been coming from a place where his parents and sister had been staying. At any moment Moriarty could have found him. So he could never carry anything on his person that might give hints as to the location of the rest of his family."

Charlotte did not dispute their accounts, as she had observed the same with regard to Mr. Marbleton. Instead she asked, "Mrs. Watson, I believe the parlor was cleaned today. Shall we ask the Bannings whether they swept under the chairs?"

Mrs. Watson leaped up. "I will go do that. The two of you catch up."

---

When the door closed behind Mrs. Watson, Charlotte set down the tray containing the possibly precious railway ticket and embraced Livia.

Livia held on hard. Charlotte hugged her back with almost as much ferocity. Livia could barely breathe, but she welcomed it, this wonderful suffocation.

They let go at last, and looked toward the torn ticket. Charlotte gave her head a small shake. "I don't know how he managed to withstand Moriarty day in and day out, but I believe he has indeed managed to do so."

Livia's eyes welled with tears. When she thought of Mr. Marbleton, she always remembered his smiles, his innate kindness, and his irrepressible joie de vivre. But because he and his family had spent decades on the run, she didn't often think of him as brave or strong. How wrong she had been. To have lived the life he had and still be capable of smiles, kindness, and joie de vivre was in and of itself a testament to his strength of character. And then, to have had enough nerve and tenacity to hold on to their secrets, keeping them safe . . .

"There was so much he didn't tell us," she murmured.

Charlotte rubbed her on her back. "Because you made him think of lovelier things. You made him think that perhaps a different life was possible, a normal life."

Livia leaned against Charlotte. "That life is further away now than ever."

"True," said Charlotte. "We are at a greater disadvantage than we have ever been, vis-à-vis Moriarty."

Livia's anguish turned into a bark of bitter laughter—trust Charlotte never to call a spade anything except a spade. Needing something to do, she went to the grate and banked the fire. Heat radiated against her skin, an almost oppressive warmth. Yet even that could not stop the sensation of shadows spreading, of a sinister chill growing in the room. In their lives.

"But do you know who hasn't given up, Livia?" came Charlotte's voice, still a little raspy but growing stronger.

Livia, still on her haunches, turned around.

Charlotte once again held the torn ticket in a pair of tweezers, extending it toward Livia as if it were a torch to be passed. "Mr. Marbleton hasn't. The effort he expended, the risks he ran, *today*, as a captive, as someone Moriarty already considers one of the defeated."

Tears once again rushed into Livia's eyes.

If he of all people hadn't given up, then what reason did she have to despair?

———※———

Lord Ingram returned with the news that Bernadine was about to wake up and that Charlotte and Livia were needed.

Bernadine was not accustomed to sedatives and it was possible that as she regained consciousness, she would become disoriented and distressed. But Bernadine, upon opening her eyes in her own bed, took a look at the crowd in her room, moved to her spinning station in the corner, and set to work on two spools and a wooden cogwheel.

When it became apparent that she needed no special attention, at least not right away, Mrs. Watson shepherded everyone to the dining room, where Mr. Mears had already laid out an early supper.

"It isn't much, only what Madame Gascoigne packed for us to eat on the road," said Mrs. Watson in apology.

But as far as Charlotte could judge, Madame Gascoigne had not forsaken her standards while preparing a meal for potential fugitives. On the table were sliced roast beef, potato croquettes, small ham pies, oyster patties, grilled mushrooms, and for dessert, a fig pudding and a cheesecake.

Lord Ingram studied the railway ticket—he hadn't been at number 18 when Charlotte discovered it under the chair. Mrs. Watson informed them that she had spoken to her maids, the Banning sisters. Polly Banning had been certain she'd swept under the fringed chairs this morning, and Rosie Banning corroborated her account, saying that she remembered teasing Polly about how she'd looked, with her bum up in the air.

The ticket could not have been left by anyone except Mr. Marbleton.

Livia was clearly breathing fast and trying to calm herself down with sips of wine. Lord Ingram studied the ticket again, a crease of concentration across his brow. Charlotte ate three potato croquettes in quick succession. It had been some time since they had been fried and they no longer had a perfectly crispy shell, but still they were delicious.

Lord Ingram put the ticket stub back into the small cloisonné jewelry case that had become its temporary container and closed it with a soft *click*. "It would have been nice if Mr. Marbleton had been able to convey something less cryptic."

Mrs. Watson set down her utensils and turned a cameo ring round and round on her little finger. "On the other hand, Moriarty spoke a great deal. But can we believe a word he uttered?"

Charlotte speared yet another potato croquette and drizzled some of the hollandaise sauce intended for the oyster patties onto it. Let the valiant effort to fend off Maximum Tolerable Chins begin again on the morrow. Tonight she would devour everything.

Ah, the croquette slathered with hollandaise sauce tasted even better.

"I don't believe in Moriarty as a loving father. However, I am inclined to believe at least a portion of the story concerning his daughter," she said. "Remember, at Château Vaudrieu, Livia and Mr. Marbleton witnessed several men with their ears pressed to the floor, trying to hear something. And you, Lord Ingram, heard that something by chance because your path that night took you closest to the château's dungeons. Those sounds you heard—and recorded— turned out to contain the combination to the safe that we eventually opened.

"Moriarty had to have been the one making those sounds. The transmission of the sounds was him fulfilling his end of a bargain, to give the code to those who were coming to rescue him. But he made sure that particular bargain would be completely useless to anyone who, one, wasn't in the exact right place to overhear the sounds, and two, didn't have an experienced cryptographer among their ranks.

"I used to think he had a twisted sense of honor. But having met him, it's more likely he disdains lying as a tactic for the weak. It must make him feel powerful to have his way *while* being truthful."

Like Mrs. Watson, Livia had also put down her fork and knife, giving up all pretenses of eating. "You are saying that the tale he told about his daughter is the truth? But we don't know that she has gone to live with a band of occultists. We don't know that there is something amiss with this community. We don't even have the means to verify that he has a full-grown daughter."

Charlotte cut into a small ham pie, the crust baked to a beautiful golden brown. "Mr. Marbleton once mentioned that the first Mrs. Moriarty died in childbirth. He said nothing about whether the child survived. But it is not impossible, or even unlikely, for Moriarty to have a grown daughter. Whether such a community of Hermetists exists should not be difficult to ascertain, given a specific location, and that should be supplied by the dossier. And once we are standing before a real place, there will be nothing to prevent us from asking the residents whether Miss Baxter has long been one of them.

"That said, the relative ease of verification concerning Moriarty's claims is not the reason I believe he told the truth about his daughter. Rather, it's the nature of his story that convinced me of its veracity—or at least its partial veracity. He is not a kind or tolerant individual—for decades he pursued the wife who dared to leave him. So for him to admit that he had so little control over his own child? I am compelled to conclude that the general outline of his story has not been made up."

"It's for precisely the same reason that I doubt the whole of it," said Lord Ingram. He still had his utensils in hand, but was rotating a piece of roast beef slowly on his fork instead of putting it into his mouth. "I could not in the least believe his claim that he's learned his lesson and will no longer overtly interfere in his daughter's life."

"I can't give that claim any credence either," echoed Mrs. Watson.

"Nor I," said Charlotte. She was beginning to feel conspicuous about her appetite but that did not stop her from eating more of the ham pie. "There was a moment at number 18 when I thought to myself, in overwhelming relief, that of course Moriarty hadn't come to see me, but because he happened to need a female investigator. Now I wonder whether I wasn't too optimistic. What if it is the other way around? That he *happened* to have a situation involving his daughter with which he could approach me?"

Everyone else at the table sat up straighter. Mrs. Watson stopped fidgeting with her ring, Livia's wineglass paused on its way to her lips, Lord Ingram not only put down his knife and fork but pushed away his plate.

Charlotte hadn't thought it that alarming a notion, but perhaps it was. "At the end of the Treadles case, we were careful not to make any connection between the culprit and De Lacey Industries. But were I Moriarty, I would have immediately suspected that we knew more than we let on.

"Also, while it was Lady Ingram and not Sherlock Holmes who pointed an accusatory finger at Moriarty after the events of Stern Hollow, Lady Ingram would not have known the truth had Sherlock Holmes not discovered it.

"So Moriarty has reason to see me as a bigger nuisance than I'd initially supposed. But if that is the case, why doesn't he simply get rid of me, but instead demands my help?"

"Maybe he wants you out of London," said Mrs. Watson. "Maybe there is something he wants to do, and he doesn't want you underfoot."

"Well, let's see how far he wants me from London then." Charlotte wiped her fingertips with her napkin and picked up the dossier, which she had placed on an empty chair next to hers.

She slid a three-quarter-inch stack out of the brown envelope. The papers, of varying sizes, rustled as she removed the strip of rubber that bound them. On the front page was typed THE GARDEN OF HERMOPOLIS. She was about to turn it aside when four smaller words under the title leaped out at her.

"What is it?" asked Lord Ingram.

Charlotte squinted to make sure she hadn't misread and only then looked up. "Do you recall that in December, Inspector Treadles went to various locales around the country, to see the places where Moriarty's preferred main contractor had worked?"

"How can we forget?" said Mrs. Watson. "He had to flee from the last place and was chased all the way back to London."

Where his desperate flight ended with him locked in a room with two dead men.

"Shortly after the New Year, Inspector and Mrs. Treadles paid Mrs. Watson and myself a call," said Charlotte to Livia, who hadn't been there. Lord Ingram hadn't been present either but had been informed of the contents of the meeting by correspondence. "During this visit Inspector Treadles told us everything he'd gleaned in the course of his investigation into the finances of Cousins Manufacturing, including the location of the compound he'd fled that night in December. It was on the south coast of Cornwall, three miles from a village called Porthangan."

She handed around the front sheet. Underneath THE GARDEN OF HERMOPOLIS were the words NEAR PORTHANGAN IN CORNWALL.

Mrs. Watson sucked in a breath.

"I thought that was a Moriarty stronghold," said Lord Ingram.

"So did I. But apparently it's exactly the opposite."

Livia shook her head. "It has to be a ploy. Moriarty is trying to lure you there."

"A distinct possibility." Charlotte did not deny that. "But to do what?"

"That doesn't matter," said Livia vehemently. "We know it must be something nefarious, and that's reason enough for us to stay well away from this Garden of Hermopolis."

"And what do you think would happen when I decline to offer my services to Moriarty, after he already confessed the mortifying story concerning his daughter?"

Silence.

Mrs. Watson drained her glass. "We should have fled as soon as we learned we were under surveillance."

No one said anything because there was nothing to be said. Because Lady Ingram had realized early on the truth behind Sherlock Holmes, Moriarty knew Charlotte's true identity. He knew where to find her family—and presumably Miss Redmayne, too, if he were in the mood for it. That threat alone would have kept Charlotte and Mrs. Watson in place.

"I still don't think the substance of Moriarty's story is false," said Charlotte, breaking the grim silence. "That his preferred main contractor worked on the Garden of Hermopolis does not necessarily imply that Moriarty is, in fact, its master and overlord. Perhaps it was his way of spying on the community. Or perhaps the community chose to obtain new buildings cheaply, knowing that he would charge less for the opportunity to peek at its inner workings."

Mrs. Watson was again rotating her ring. Livia eyed the wine bottle. Lord Ingram set the front sheet on top of the dossier. No one looked remotely convinced.

Charlotte served herself a good dollop of fig pudding—the time had come when something stronger than potato croquettes, even potato croquettes drenched in hollandaise sauce, was needed. "Again, if the substance of Moriarty's story is true, then an antagonistic relationship has long existed between him and the Garden of Hermopolis. If our occultists had done something to Miss Baxter during Moriarty's ouster, then they had every reason to be on high alert against threats of retaliation. And the man who chased Inspector Treadles all the way to London, instead of being a Moriarty loyalist, could be someone who thought he was in pursuit of a Moriarty loyalist."

Livia gaped at her. "How is that an improvement?"

Charlotte dug deeper into the dense, decadent pudding. "I'm not sure I have much of a choice, now that Moriarty's gaze has landed on me. It's simply a matter of unpleasantness now or unpleasantness later."

The room again fell quiet.

Mrs. Watson poured wine for Livia, and then for herself. In the silence, the garnet stream falling into goblets sounded as loud as a sputtering spigot. Mrs. Watson set down the bottle and looked at Charlotte, her eyes clouded with misgivings. "And what will you choose, my dear?"

## Six

It was with a heavy mood that Livia settled into Mrs. Watson's carriage, to be taken back to Claridge's. Charlotte and Lord Ingram, accompanying her for the trip, climbed in after her.

"It's still early," said Charlotte, setting her boots on the foot warmer, "and you barely ate anything. Order yourself a supper when you get back, and no one will have any idea that it's your second meal of the evening."

The inside of the town coach was redolent of leather polish, the scent of which Livia usually found pleasant. But today it assailed her nostrils. "I'll order a supper, but I still won't be able to eat anything."

"Don't torment yourself with hunger. Eat and stay strong, especially if you suspect difficult times ahead."

Livia never tormented herself with hunger. Her appetite simply disappeared under duress. "Are we expecting difficult times ahead?"

Lord Ingram knocked on the top of the carriage with his walking stick. The coach glided into the flow of traffic, and Charlotte took the opportunity not to answer. Instead she said, "If you need to, Livia, you can always lean on Mrs. Newell. I daresay she brought you to London so that you may meet with me."

*"What?"*

Between the streetlamps and the carriage lanterns, there was enough light for Livia to make out Charlotte's smooth, placid face. Across from them, Lord Ingram seemed a little taken aback by her statement, but not to the extent Livia would have expected.

Charlotte adjusted the brim of her hat. "Mrs. Newell has known us since we were children. She knows how my mind works. After the events of Stern Hollow, if she hasn't put two and two together and deduced that Sherlock Holmes is none other than Charlotte Holmes, I would be very surprised. To wit, when you reached your hotel this afternoon, did she tell you that she would be more or less incapacitated for the rest of the day and that you should therefore spend your time as you wish?"

"Y—yes, but I thought—I thought—"

"That she was weary from the journey? That woman has more energy than you and I put together. She knew you'd be off to find me faster than a pointer at a fox hunt. A sovereign says she'll do something similar tomorrow."

"I—I had no idea," Livia sputtered some more.

She had thought she knew Mrs. Newell well. She had thought Mrs. Newell, like everyone else in Society, had remained in the dark about Charlotte's fate. She had thought—oh, never mind what she'd thought, she'd obviously never met an assumption she couldn't carry to her grave.

Lord Ingram chortled. "Did you know that she once planned to broker a mariage blanc for Holmes?"

Livia blinked. A mariage blanc was an unconsummated marriage, unusually unconsummated because the husband did not incline toward women.

"What do you know about Mr. Newell?" asked Charlotte.

Mrs. Newell's late husband? Mr. Newell had passed away long ago, when Livia was still a child. She had a vague recollection of a man with a head of snow-white hair and a booming laughter. A mischievous and impetuous figure. Someone who did as he wished.

"I can't say I remember much about him other than the stories

Mrs. Newell told. There was that time he chased a stamp collector all over the Continent for a rare misprinted stamp. And the time— Wait! You don't mean to imply that Mr. Newell was—"

"I'm not implying anything. Mrs. Newell told me so herself," replied Charlotte, a smile in her voice, clearly savoring Livia's astonishment. "Other than the few occasions necessary for the procreation of heirs, theirs had been a mariage blanc. He had been dogged by certain rumors best dispelled by marriage and children, and she had wished to be an independent spinster but lacked an inheritance to finance it. Theirs was a harmonious union and she thought the same might prove the solution for me."

"When was this?"

"Last spring, before the start of the Season. I gave it serious consideration."

Her answer earned her a look from Lord Ingram. "I agree with Holmes," he said. "I believe Mrs. Newell has guessed that Sherlock Holmes is none other than Charlotte Holmes and that she has found both a means of self-support and a source of satisfaction in her work. Nor has Mrs. Newell deemed you, Miss Olivia, at all contemptible for not having cut off all sisterly ties. In fact, she has spoken of you with greater warmth, even admiration, since the events of Stern Hollow."

Livia's cheeks warmed at that. All the same, she had to give her head a shake for everything she'd just been told to settle down a little. Her hat ribbon, tied under her chin, chafed faintly, a reminder that she was not dreaming.

Charlotte smoothed her gloves. "Indeed, you could do far worse for an ally than dear Mrs. Newell."

"You mean that I should speak to her openly about what you are doing these days?"

"Yes, in general terms. No need to burden her with details."

At the mere mention of details not to be discussed, Moriarty's shadow once again fell upon the company. An uneasy silence grew.

Livia placed her gloved hand over Charlotte's and stared out of the window, her mind overstuffed with dire possibilities—and an occasional gleam of hope, quickly dimmed by its own unlikeliness.

As they neared the hotel, Charlotte gave Livia the small cloisonné jewelry case that held the ticket stub from Mr. Marbleton. "Why don't you keep this?"

"Thank you. I'll guard it carefully." Livia's hand closed over the box. In the dark, she caressed it with the skin of her wrist, feeling the smoothness of enamel interspersed with the slight scratchiness of wirework. "I know we've discussed this ad nauseam at supper but are you sure that you can only answer Moriarty in the affirmative?"

"I'm afraid I must," said Charlotte.

Livia looked toward Lord Ingram.

"In life you play with the hand you are given, and this is the hand we've been given," said he with an outward calmness that matched Charlotte's.

After she had alit from the town coach, Livia remained on the curb for some time, watching it drive away. Back in Mrs. Newell's suite, faint sounds emerged from her chaperone's room, possibly the dear lady speaking to her maid. Livia stood in place, feeling both immensely grateful and almost as mortified over her obliviousness.

Should she speak to Mrs. Newell tonight herself, to thank her and to tell her as much as Charlotte permitted—and to perhaps, during that telling, mention that she'd written a novel inspired by Charlotte's exploits, which would be published at Christmas in a popular annual magazine?

She vacillated. And vacillated some more.

Mrs. Newell's maid came out, saw her in the drawing room, and asked whether she needed supper.

Livia had already ordered her own supper. Still, she could ask the maid whether Mrs. Newell was amenable to a short bedside visit. But she only shook her head, wished the maid good night, and headed to her room to change and await her meal.

Later, as she hunched over her tray, picking at her food, she wondered why she had not wanted to hold a frank, lovely conversation with dear Mrs. Newell, whom she had always both admired and adored.

Charlotte must have suspected for months that Mrs. Newell had learned the truth about Sherlock Holmes. During that time, she had not said anything to Livia. But tonight, right after Moriarty's visit, she paved the way for Livia to have a new ally in her life.

With a shiver, Livia understood why she had refused to take that last step toward Mrs. Newell.

She already had the staunchest allies in Charlotte, Mrs. Watson, and Lord Ingram. Had Charlotte foreseen something? Did she believe that soon Livia would not have these allies anymore?

— ❈ —

For most of its life, the Garden of Hermopolis had been a private dwelling, a remote, ramshackle edifice that bore the grand appellation of Cador Manor, but was more of an enlarged farmhouse than anything resembling a stately home.

The last local occupant died in the 1840s. His descendants sold the place to a Plymouth shipbuilder, who, like so many in the Age of Steam, wished to have a place in the country, far away from the coal and soot that had been the foundation of his prosperity.

His family having predeceased him, upon the shipbuilder's death the property went to a reform-minded widow intent on creating a sanctuary for young women in trouble. The widow shed her mortal coil before she could turn her vision into reality. Her son renovated the main house and added on a collection of smaller cottages with the goal of establishing a holiday destination that was readily accessible by railway, but as of yet unspoiled by hordes of unrefined tourists.

Alas, his commercial paradise failed to attract tourists, refined or otherwise. The resort was sold to a noted eccentric who aimed to construct his own castle on the spot. But as the eccentric dismissed one architect after another, only the castle's walls were ever built.

After his death, the property proved difficult to sell. No one else wanted the trouble of constructing a castle, and those who would have been tempted by the promise of a resort stayed away because its views had become obstructed by the walls. Which was how Miss Fairchild, the founder of the Garden of Hermopolis, managed to acquire the compound for very little outlay.

Miss Fairchild, born to the owner of a mercantile fleet, was independently wealthy. As a younger woman, she had sailed the seven seas and written a dozen travelogues set in Russia, Australia, and the Yoruba country, among other far-flung destinations. According to her own writings, it was during her travels that she encountered the teachings of Hermes Trismegistus and was sufficiently enamored to decide, when she settled down again in Britain, to form a community of like-minded thinkers.

This summary was given in Moriarty's dossier. But Charlotte wished to consult someone who had personal experience with the Garden of Hermopolis. When she and Lord Ingram arrived at the location of the rendezvous, a house near Portman Square that had been used for more than its share of clandestine discussions, the officer of the law was already nursing a glass of whisky, seated in a spectacularly gaudy drawing room. Golden fringes and tassels bedecked every perimeter, tiger skins proved as abundant as antimacassars in an ordinary parlor, and the most garish hues of every color strove mightily for the gaze of the overpowered beholder.

Charlotte once again regretted that she had on only the same very staid jacket-and-skirt set and could not add to the splendid chaos.

In an earlier era, such a gathering might have been trickier to accomplish without alerting Moriarty to the fact that immediately after meeting him, Charlotte wanted to see Inspector Treadles. But with Mrs. Watson and the Treadleses having both recently installed residential telephones, and with certain code words they'd agreed to ahead of time in anticipation of just such a moment of need, Lord

Ingram had been able to ring Inspector Treadles from Mrs. Watson's house before supper and arrange a meeting for the same evening.

The men greeted each other warmly, then Inspector Treadles bowed to Charlotte.

She inclined her head.

There was a time when Inspector Treadles had regarded her with both mistrust and distaste. Even now, in his otherwise respectful gaze, there was still a hint of wariness, but it was the wariness of a traveler on the savanna coming across, say, a rhinoceros, rather than that of one facing a pack of hyenas.

They'd barely sat down when Inspector Treadles said, "I was almost certain I'd misheard Lord Ingram on the apparatus. Did you really say Glasgow? What happened?"

Glasgow was the term they'd designated as the level of highest alarm, with regard to Moriarty.

At Charlotte's indication, Lord Ingram gave a brief account of Moriarty's visit. He was seated in a red velvet chair with a thick beard of fringes and a tiger skin draped over the back, but his inner gravitas was such that the chair, by being in his vicinity, appeared close to majestic. Briefly she imagined him fainting into such a chair, her slightly indecent story crumpled in his hands—and cursed Moriarty for not giving her more time to enjoy her dear Ash's glorious letter.

Inspector Treadles listened, his hands clenched around the armrests of his chair, with an attention that was no doubt much less questionable than her own. He sucked in a breath when Lord Ingram explained that they'd wished to see him right away because Miss Baxter's commune appeared to be none other than the Cornwall compound he'd attempted to reconnoiter in December.

He looked from Lord Ingram to Charlotte. "You are sure?"

Charlotte again indicated for Lord Ingram to answer the question— if she did the answering, she would need to look at Inspector Treadles. And she preferred to ogle Lord Ingram instead.

He gave her an odd look, but complied. "Yes, we are sure, unless in that specific area of Cornwall there are two sizable walled compounds."

"No, there aren't." Inspector Treadles shook his head. He stilled abruptly. "Does this mean that the place was *not* under Moriarty's control at the time of my visit?"

Lord Ingram raised a hand and slid the back of it along the tiger skin above his shoulder in what appeared to be an absentminded gesture. "That was certainly the gist of Moriarty's narrative."

Inspector Treadles's brows shot up. "The occupants have nothing to do with Moriarty, except for hosting his daughter in their midst?"

"So it would seem," said Lord Ingram. He dropped his hand, removed a blue-and-orange cushion from his chair, and placed it on an occasion table to his left.

"And one such peaceable occupant chased me all the way to London and wounded me with a knife?"

"If you believe Moriarty."

"Do you?"

"Not I, but Miss Holmes does to a certain extent."

Now Charlotte had no choice but to clarify her position. "It's true that I do not believe Moriarty to be altogether lying. However, I feel that I have been put in a lightless room, only able to see out through a peephole with smeared lenses. Am I looking at a festively decorated village, with hausfraus hurrying to and fro—or merely the façade of an elaborate clock?"

"You fear that it is a trap?"

"I don't fear so; I know it is one. What I cannot fathom is the purpose of this trap."

Inspector Treadles exhaled unsteadily. "Is there anything I can do? Any assistance I can render?"

"Yes," said Charlotte. "Inspector, when you called on Mrs. Watson and myself in January, I asked you about what you saw in Cornwall. At the time you said you didn't have much to share, and I don't doubt that. But today we are in need of any and all details you can recall."

"I'll try," said the inspector. He took a sip of whisky and held on to the glass. "I do remember how high the walls were. There are old castles in the area and they have high walls. But in a fortified structure, the castle itself is more prominent. In this compound, however, the walls dominated. Even standing on the highest point in the surrounding area, I could not see inside."

Charlotte explained about the eccentric who could never agree with his architects and how only the walls were ever built, not the castle itself. "I'm curious, Inspector. How did you scale those walls then?"

"I had a blacksmith make me a grappling hook."

"A commendable idea," said Lord Ingram. His hand settled on the blue-and-orange cushion that he had a minute ago placed on the occasion table next to his chair.

"At the time I thought of it, I certainly congratulated myself," said Inspector Treadles wryly. "The climate in Cornwall is relatively mild, so I couldn't count on deafening gales to obscure the thud of a grappling hook landing against stone. But it was December, the wind was high, and there was a drizzle. I wrapped the prongs in cloth, except for their very tips, and thought that between the wind, the rain, and the muffling effect of the cloth, I wouldn't be overheard."

He gave a rueful sigh. "I couldn't have been more wrong. Well, in terms of the thud, I felt it was acceptably muted. Yet I was barely one third of the way up the wall before someone at the top shone an extremely bright lantern into my face and demanded to know who was there. I heard a firearm cocking, too. I got down and ran, leaving my shiny new grappling hook behind."

"So you didn't get a look at the inside of the compound?" asked Lord Ingram.

"Not at all."

The round cushion under Lord Ingram's hand had elaborate blue ruffles along the circumference, which reminded Charlotte of the neckline of a few ballgowns she'd worn in her time. The cushion was tufted, one deep indentation at the very center, which made the rest of the cushion bulge up. And since the ruffles already reminded Charlotte of a neckline, she couldn't help but view the bulge as what a neckline on a dress tried to contain.

Lord Ingram dragged a knuckle where the ruffles met the bulge.

Charlotte was well aware that with the occasion table lower than the rolled arm of his chair, Inspector Treadles couldn't see the cushion, nor what Lord Ingram was doing. Still, she glanced at Inspector Treadles, who frowned up at the overgrown chandelier on the ceiling and said, "I think the person who caught me mid-ascent was a woman. Now, the one with whom I fought was definitely a man, but the one who shouted 'Who's there?' had a woman's voice."

"Were you pursued?" asked Lord Ingram.

This time he rubbed a thumb along the top of the ruffles. Charlotte's throat went dry.

Inspector Treadles—the innocent, incognizant man—placed a hand under his chin. "At the time I didn't hear anyone running behind me. But looking back, I think they must have fanned out to railway stations up and down the branch line. I had enough presence of mind not to go to the nearest one, but the next nearest still wasn't good enough."

Lord Ingram leaned forward in his chair, removing his hand from the cushion, much to Charlotte's relief—and disappointment. "The man who followed you to London—and who eventually assailed you there—do you remember anything about him?"

"He grabbed me by the sleeve and asked, 'Who are you and what do you want?' A fog was rolling in. So even though we weren't that far from a streetlamp, I couldn't see his face very well, except that he had a cut to his upper lip. And he was a ferocious knife fighter—I'm fairly certain the only reason I managed to run to 33 Cold Street and take shelter there was because he was wary of following me into an enclosed garden."

Inspector Treadles looked in Charlotte's direction. "And Moriarty says the place in Cornwall is, in fact, a site of learning and contemplation?"

"In that regard your doubt matches Moriarty's."

Inspector Treadles scratched at his jaw. "To be sure, ferocious knife-fighting skills and an interest in Hermetism are not mutually exclusive. But what disconcerts me more, now that I think about it, is the speed with which I was discovered. At the time I thought perhaps it was tightly patrolled because Moriarty's secrets were kept there. But if it's a religious community, even an occult one—well, we don't hear of churches or cloisters being so ready to repel all comers, do we?"

---

"You mean to tell me that the Garden of Hermopolis has sentinels stationed atop its high walls to drive off any would-be trespassers?" exclaimed Mrs. Watson.

Charlotte and Lord Ingram were back in Mrs. Watson's afternoon parlor. Livia adored this space, deeming it an admirable mélange of comfort and elegance. Charlotte, on the other hand, had always found the blue-and-white décor a little too muted for her taste. But after the cacophony of colors and textures of the house near Portman Square, Mrs. Watson's choice of interior was now rather . . . restful.

"Inspector Treadles certainly thought the place carefully guarded," answered Lord Ingram. "Though, to be fair, he is only one eyewitness on one reconnaissance sortie."

The sight of this man, on the other hand, was the opposite of restful.

Mrs. Watson had offered him a "dram" of Mr. Mears's homemade whisky liqueur. He had accepted it, placed the cordial glass on the small table beside his chair, and sat with his hand curled loosely around the stem. Occasionally, as he listened to Charlotte repeat for Mrs. Watson's benefit what they had learned from Inspector Treadles, he turned the glass a few degrees.

Other than that, he barely moved, let alone performed any gestures that could be construed as suggestive.

Still, she felt restless—and overheated.

At least she had recovered from the lingering effects of Moriarty's visit and a little restlessness—and overheating—did not interfere with her ability to pay attention to the discussion at hand.

"Is it possible that the woman on the wall who saw the inspector was simply enjoying a winter stroll?" asked Mrs. Watson hesitantly.

"At night, in the rain?" murmured Lord Ingram.

He traced an index finger around the foot of the cordial glass. Such a minor motion, that of a man deep in thought. Yet Charlotte felt his touch, as if he had caressed her bare skin.

"Livia might do something like that," she said. "But the lantern negates the idea of someone out for a leisurely stroll."

Mrs. Watson pinched the spot between her brows. "The lantern?"

Lord Ingram, too, glanced at Charlotte, his expression serious, yet his direct gaze made her stomach skid.

"Inspector Treadles wrapped his grappling hook in cloth," she said, "so I must assume he also made sure that there was no lantern-swinging patrol atop the ramparts before he made his attempt. Yet not long after he started his climb, the light of a lantern shone into his face. Outdoors on a rainy night, with a high wind blowing—the condition was not ideal for lighting a lantern. It's much more likely that the lantern was lit earlier, and that it had a shutter to prevent its lights from being seen. Such is not the illumination of choice for a casual nocturnal ambler, but of someone lying in wait."

Lord Ingram's thumb grazed the bowl of the cordial glass, a light, upward flick. Charlotte swallowed.

"This place sounds more perilous by the hour," he said. He

shook his glass a little by the stem. The butterscotch-colored liquid inside eddied and swirled. "I'm beginning to believe that they have indeed done something to Moriarty's daughter. Why else would they be so nervously looking out for anyone approaching, and in the middle of the night?"

Mrs. Watson turned pale. "I was reading the dossier while you two were out. It's mentioned in there that for such a small community, members sometimes die at a rapid pace. What if Miss Baxter is not the only person to have been afflicted by the Garden of Hermopolis? How—how dangerous do you think this place will be for us?"

"Deaths in clusters is hardly a remarkable occurrence—there could have been a communicable disease," answered Charlotte. "And as for how dangerous this place will be, it need not be dangerous for *us*. I can go alone, posing as a widow."

Mrs. Watson stared at her a moment. "Nonsense, my child. I cannot possibly allow you to venture in there by yourself."

Charlotte had not expected anything other than great gallantry from Mrs. Watson. Yet every time Mrs. Watson's gallantry manifested itself, she became only more amazed that such valiant generosity had not been lessened or exhausted in the giving of itself, but was always renewed and replenished.

"From the very beginning, ma'am, I have relied on your wisdom and your lionheartedness. I pride myself in being your junior partner. But this is not simply another case entrusted to Sherlock Holmes. I would have refused it for myself if I could. Allow me to at least refuse it for you."

Mrs. Watson's countenance took on a carven determination, like a bright-eyed Athena ready to cast her spear. "My dear, how can you turn down a chance for me to meet a woman who managed six fiancés in the span of a mere fifteen months?"

Charlotte rose from her seat. "Ma'am—"

Mrs. Watson not only got to her feet, but came forward and took Charlotte's hands in her own. "It would be much too unkind of you, my dear, to leave me behind. You know I will work myself into a froth of agitation. I will be unable to eat or sleep. I will drift in a veritable sea of worst-case scenarios. *And* I will never forgive you. All of which will be detrimental to my health and terrible for my beauty.

"You might be too young to care about your health, but you understand very well how difficult it is to undo damage to one's beauty." She smiled ruefully. "So I must go, for my health and my beauty—my beauty above all, of course."

Mrs. Watson's absurd, seemingly lighthearted pleas struck Charlotte hard. It was not her wont to catalogue the dangers they faced over and over again, yet she found herself inventorying all the risks, as if by doing so she could find a new one that would convince Mrs. Watson to stay behind.

Such a thing did not exist. Mrs. Watson, by her greater imagination and sensitivity, had already inundated herself with thoughts of every possible danger. In spite of that, and in spite of not being naturally inclined to hazardous undertakings, she would make sure that Charlotte did not proceed alone.

Charlotte could not say no, but she also couldn't bring herself to say yes.

The silence grew louder.

Mrs. Watson's lips parted slightly, as if she were about to persuade Charlotte some more. At the same time, her grip on Charlotte's hands loosened—was she losing hope?

Her grip became firmer again. And she did not say anything else, but only gazed into Charlotte's eyes with an infinitely patient entreaty.

"It shall be as you wish, ma'am," Charlotte heard herself say.

Mrs. Watson took her by the shoulders and kissed her on the forehead. Then she returned to her chair and said, "You haven't said how dangerous you expect this place to be yet, my dear."

Charlotte slowly sat down. "Inspector Treadles was a nighttime

trespasser—a man, no less—and the residents of the Garden of Hermopolis did not shoot him on sight. We are two harmless women
who are going to walk through the front door in plain daylight and
be gracious guests. We are therefore even less likely to be shot."

Not immediately, in any case.

Mrs. Watson and Lord Ingram exchanged a glance, as if to confirm that they both heard what Charlotte did not say aloud.

Mrs. Watson sighed. "I find myself wondering, as Moriarty
must, what exactly Miss Baxter saw in this place."

Lord Ingram set his thumb against the fob of his watch. "I am
most struck by the six engagements Miss Baxter engineered to force
her father to relent. However she began, by the time her father made
her leave the commune, she was so determined to get back that she
overawed Moriarty himself."

Such had been Miss Baxter's devotion to the Garden of Hermopolis and to her fellow acolytes. And yet, if Moriarty was to be
believed, they had betrayed her.

Charlotte blinked. Since the arrival of de Lacey's letter, their
greatest preoccupation had been Moriarty and the stark danger he
presented. It was not until this moment that Charlotte thought of
Miss Baxter not as a pawn in the games Moriarty played, but as a
flesh-and-blood woman, one who yearned for both freedom and
belonging, and who might have paid too great a price for what little
she'd received of either.

Mrs. Watson went to kiss Lord Ingram on his cheek. "It's getting late, my dear. I will retire now. Miss Charlotte, will you continue to make his lordship feel welcome?"

Charlotte's heart beat a little faster. "It would be my pleasure."

And he would like it, too.

She had not, however, anticipated that as Mrs. Watson departed,
he would pick up the dossier again. His forehead furrowed as he
turned a page, then another, then yet another.

They had already spent their time alone in the carriage solemnly discussing what they had learned from Inspector Treadles and how to help Livia look into the ticket stub. Surely a man who had recently sent her a pair of pink stockings—and even more recently consumed her moderately indecent story—could not have only Moriarty on his mind?

He dropped the dossier and ran his hand through his hair. "What a day."

*Shall we go to bed while we are still alive?*

But given the gravity of the situation, even she couldn't be that flippant. "Yes," she murmured halfheartedly. "What a day indeed."

He rubbed his right temple and sighed, a sound full of distress and exhaustion. At last he glanced at her. "Well, Holmes, there is nothing else we can do now. Shall we go to bed?"

# Seven

The question hung in the air, full of shimmering, delicious implications. They could sneak up the stairs, tiptoeing so as not to alert Mrs. Watson to the clandestine goings-on. Or they might resort to the service staircase, which, being dark and narrow, would lead to fevered kisses and embraces between flights.

Charlotte might find herself with her back against a wall. Lord Ingram might find himself pushed down onto the steps . . .

"I have my things at number 18," he said, his tone perfectly unexceptional. "I'll stay there tonight."

He only stood there. But with his physicality, remaining still was all he ever needed to do for her to be aware of every detail of his frame, from the gleam of lamplight on his dark hair, to his even, open shoulders, to the slight turn in his body that gave the impression of contrapposto—dynamic poise.

She rose. "I'll walk with you. Moriarty left a volume of Hermetic teachings, and it's still in the parlor at number 18."

He opened the parlor door. "After you, Holmes."

*Don't you wish to go up with me via the service stairs? Make a few preposterously libidinous stops along the way and then see me in those pink stockings afterward?*

But no, he allowed her no pause on the way down, helped her

into her coat with unnecessary efficiency, and then they were out the back door, wending around the mews toward Upper Baker Street.

It was a bit difficult to bring up those licentious stockings when she felt as if she were being rushed after a departing train.

"Miss Lucinda and Master Carlisle aren't in London," she said in the end.

He had not gone to his town house to see them at bedtime, which meant he hadn't brought them. But she also didn't think he had left them behind in Derbyshire.

He looked ahead. "No. I've taken them somewhere out of the way."

Upper Baker Street was deserted at this hour. A slight drizzle fell. Rust-colored light from streetlamps pooled in faintly glistening circles on the pavement. Her gaze flicked to the flat that housed Moriarty's minions. Its windows were as dark as all the others, no curtains fluttered, no shadows slithered.

But this did not mean that no one was observing.

"Miss Potter is with the children?" she continued with her questions.

"Yes."

Miss Potter had been his governess, once upon a time, and had agreed to come out of retirement to look after Miss Lucinda and Master Carlisle.

"And Miss Yarmouth?"

Miss Yarmouth, the children's previous governess, had, much to Charlotte's amusement, proposed a marriage of convenience to her employer.

"Miss Yarmouth left for Australia weeks ago," he said rather archly, "to join her cousin for a delightful future filled with wealthy suitors."

"Let us wish her good hunting," she murmured.

He hadn't said where his children were, but now she wondered . . . "Lord Bancroft had a few properties here and there, didn't he?"

Lord Bancroft was Lord Ingram's disgraced brother, but his disgrace was known only to a few. For fear of alerting the general populace that something was amiss with Lord Bancroft's retirement from public life, the Crown had not confiscated his properties.

"Correct. Bancroft's holdings were entrusted to Remington, and with his permission, I've put the children up at one of them."

Lord Remington, another one of Lord Ingram's elder brothers, was abroad most of the time, in charge of the queen's clandestine services on the Subcontinent.

"Are you sure Moriarty doesn't know about the place?"

Lady Ingram had spied for Moriarty.

Charlotte opened the door of number 18, and turned a little to look at her not-quite-lover.

Light from the nearest streetlamp threw his profile into sharp relief. He snorted. "Bancroft kept his own secrets better than he kept the Crown's secrets. Lady Ingram didn't know about this place, I didn't, and not even Bancroft's solicitors did."

At number 18, on the floor above the parlor and "Sherlock" Holmes's bedroom, there was another bedroom. Mrs. Watson had outfitted it in silks and florals, befitting Sherlock Holmes's sister who had done so much for him. Charlotte had never stayed there but Mr. Marbleton had, on occasion. And it would be where Lord Ingram would spend the night.

He did not, however, head there directly, but came with her to the parlor. "I need to disassemble the Maxim gun. It wouldn't be much use here."

"Show me first how to load the cartridge belt."

The Maxim gun had become almost unrecognizable. Not only had a large canister—the cooling jacket—been fitted to the barrel, but steel plates—shields—had been fastened to the top and the sides of the assembly, giving it an oddly leonine appearance.

The long cartridge belt came neatly folded in a box. He fed the first round into the barrel, made sure it was held firmly in place, and said, "That's it. The rest will load by recoil."

He demonstrated the process one more time, then stepped aside for her to try.

Shouldn't he remain right behind her, his hands over hers, so that the two of them were practically in an embrace? Years ago, she had seen a gentleman instruct a lady in archery in such a manner. They had married other people but subsequently came together in a torrid affair.

Alas the operation was simple enough that she managed on the first try and was able to perform the feat three consecutive times without any mistakes, obviating any need for him to give hands-on demonstrations.

"Go ahead and take the gun apart," he said, handing her a spanner. "Then you'll be able to put it together next time."

Charlotte had been raised in the country and had done her share of shooting. She knew how to take apart ordinary firearms for cleaning and maintenance. The Maxim gun was different, but not so different as to render her experience useless.

The joints had been properly oiled and separated with only moderate effort. She handed each component to Lord Ingram. The trunk the disassembled Maxim gun had come in had been specially built with padded trays to accommodate all the parts. She kept track of how the parts fit together, and also where everything went in the trays.

They worked largely without speaking. Having been correspondents for almost as long as they'd known each other, their exchanges were easier and more relaxed in writing. But in person, especially after a lengthy absence, they tended to revert back to silence.

Some silences felt like a cool shade under summer foliage, others like dark, foggy nights. This silence made her think of reading in the branches of a tree and lifting her head because a breeze had brought with it the scent of a rich yeast dough rising nearby.

A silence filled with anticipation.

But was the anticipation mutual, or only on her part?

She calculated the weight of everything, the Maxim gun itself, the shields, the ammunition, and the water required in the cooling jacket to keep the barrel from overheating. "Would you have been able to move this thing, fully assembled, to where you could provide a burst of fire for me to escape out the back into Mrs. Watson's town coach?"

Or had he really prepared for the bleakest outcome, a last stand right here in Sherlock Holmes's bedroom?

"Of course," he said lightly, packing the box of cartridges into a different case. "You can go wash your hands now, Holmes. I'll do the rest."

She regarded him a moment, sitting cross-legged on the carpet, the alignment of his torso at once perfectly straight and perfectly loose, before she rose to leave. When she came back from the basement, Sherlock Holmes's bedroom was spotless and he was no longer there.

She returned to the parlor. She had just picked up the book on Hermetic teachings from Moriarty—she had not lied about that—when he entered with a black umbrella and held it out toward her.

She was about to tell him that she already had a weighted umbrella that doubled as a rapier when she took this umbrella in hand. The bulbous handle felt different. She turned it around and spotted a hidden firing mechanism. She opened the umbrella. Aha, halfway up the stalk was a chamber that—she peered inside—looked like . . .

"It takes two rounds?"

"Two rounds. However, sometimes the fabric of the umbrella catches on fire," said he, his eyes crinkling a little. "I assume you won't care too much about that if you choose to use it as a firearm."

"Oh, rest assured I will care. It would be mortifying to carry a burnt umbrella afterward," she said airily, even as her stomach tightened.

Between the hiding place for his children, the umbrella, and the

Maxim gun, he had prepared for cascading catastrophes—and she could not deem him to be overreacting.

"Well, with this umbrella, you'll be safe enough walking back home by yourself." He wrapped an arm around her shoulder and kissed her on the cheek, as if he were her affectionate but not terribly amorous husband. Or, God forbid, her fond brother. "I'm off to bed. Enjoy your studies of Hermetism."

He was gone the next second, closing the parlor door behind himself and mounting the steps.

Charlotte played with the umbrella some more. Then she sat down and picked up the book again. From upstairs came the soft sounds of someone moving about, opening and shutting a drawer. In the grate, a piece of coal in the fire that had been banked hours ago popped softly. The spine of the book creaked as she flipped the pages from beginning to end.

She returned to the first page, reading more carefully. Six pages in she snapped shut the book, left the parlor, climbed up the steps, and knocked.

He opened the door without too much delay, a quizzical expression on his face. "Yes?"

She walked past him. The room was about the same size as Sherlock Holmes's and furnished simply, but with extravagant-looking orange-and-gold wallpaper, the gaudiness of which was tempered somewhat by a pair of landscape paintings that consisted largely of sky and meadows.

Her quarry moved to the grate and smoothed the banked coals with a fireplace rake. He had removed his jacket and necktie. His shirt, open at the collar, revealed a lovely triangle of skin.

She licked the back of her teeth. "I forgot to tell you. We had some work done on the house and now there is a properly plumbed commode on this floor. But it's a little temperamental; you must remember to prime the water tank with two quick pulls. Wait ten seconds or so, and then pull slowly and firmly."

Alas, her preamble, full of useful information, inspired in him not lust, but a richly layered doubt. His reply was guarded. "I see. Thank you."

Silence.

And to think she'd left both her tea gown and her new stockings at Mrs. Watson's, a stone's throw and half a world away.

"I also have something else to tell you."

"Yes?"

He didn't look impatient, merely a little puzzled, as if he absolutely couldn't fathom what else she could possibly have to tell him. And she, who had cackled with glee as she had penned her faintly smutty scene, and who had propositioned him time after time over the years, almost couldn't go on.

She pulled a little at her collar. "I've decided that you're right. It's time for us to go to bed."

"Ah," he said.

What did this *ah* mean?

He set down the fireplace rake, moved the brass candlestick on the mantel a fraction of an inch to the left, glanced back at her, who stood stock-still in the same spot, and said, "Well, aren't you going to take off your clothes?"

※

Charlotte had the urge to throw something at him. A bag of feathers, perhaps. Or maybe a freshly baked bun. The rascal! She'd been about to doubt herself.

At the same time, she felt a bubble of mirth rise up, threatening to erupt into an unusually wide smile. So he was paying her back for the provocation of her little story, was he? She flattened her lips so she wouldn't actually smile and said rather severely, "Well, aren't you going to protest more?"

He raised a brow. "I can hardly protest when you haven't done anything."

True. Compared to sending him a mildly—all right, highly—

erotic story via the Royal Mail, standing fully dressed in the middle of his room didn't seem much of a transgression. Still, Ash, whose stick-in-the-mud-ness she had bemoaned for years, beckoning her toward *greater* transgressions?

True, the tea gown and the stockings had been explicit encouragements. But those had been *very* recent developments, and without quite realizing it, she was still expecting him to restrain her, rather than tempt her to do her worst.

His new attitude was novel, heartening, *and* a little unnerving.

She unbuttoned and shrugged out of her jacket.

"I've seen you quite a few times in a blouse and a skirt," he said.

His tone remained unmoved, but his gaze slid down the length of her body—and then back up. When their eyes met again, his pupils had become darker.

Her heart beat faster. She discarded her blouse and corset cover. "How about now?"

The column of his throat moved. "I'm beginning to feel my . . . outrage rising."

Outrage. Hmm, was that what rose on a man these days? She hooked a finger at him. "Don't just stand there, young man. Come help me with my corset."

His fingers closed around the candelabra on the mantel. "That is an unspeakable request, young lady. Is there a fainting couch in readiness for me?"

Decorously she tucked a strand of hair behind her ear and patted the bed behind her. "Will this do?"

He left the mantel, his gait slow yet predatory, a panther prowling the jungle at midnight. She held her breath. She loved him in motion, all fluid, kinetic agility. But he stopped halfway across the room. "What if I don't help you with your corset? Will you stop with this debauchery?"

"Hardly. I don't need any help to remove my skirt. See?"

She wriggled out of her grey mohair skirt, stepped on the bed stool, and sat down on the edge of the bed. Many yards of fabric remained on her—corset and chemise, two layers of petticoats, *and* a pair of merino wool pantalets—but her reflection in the mirror appeared distinctly disreputable.

He tilted his head up a fraction of an inch. He'd always had dark, Byronic eyes. But in all their years of acquaintance, he had never considered her like this, a slight smile on his lips, and a heavy-lidded regard that was frankly . . . sexual.

"Looks like I may not escape fleshly corruption tonight," he murmured.

Without meaning to, she licked her lips. "I've only fleshly subli-mation here. It's good for you."

He traced a finger just above the lace top of her corset, much the same way he had traced the ruffles on that blue-and-orange cushion earlier in the evening. "Fleshly sublimation? I like the sound of it."

Even though her chemise separated his skin from hers, the pres-sure of his caress still sent a jolt of heat to her abdomen. His atten-tion had been on the bountiful curvature he was touching, but now he lifted his gaze. Their eyes met and Charlotte felt another jolt of heat, this one singeing her all the way to the soles of her feet.

"But do you know, Holmes?" He spread open his fingers, his eyes never leaving hers. "Between the two of us, I have far superior self-control. And unless I agree to it, there will be no fleshly subli-mation tonight. Or fleshly corruption."

She exhaled and gripped him by the collar. "What can I do to make you agree to something fleshly?"

He spoke directly into her ear, his breath warm against her skin. "You can take me to the Garden of Hermopolis with you."

Her fingers on his collar loosened. "Why must you always put so many obstacles in my way?" she whispered.

"A walled compound near Porthangan in Cornwall, how diffi-cult do you think it will be, Holmes, for me to find it?"

She cupped his face with her hands. "Think of your children."

"I *am* thinking of them. Moriarty is a danger to them as well." He kissed her, a kiss of only their lips. "Now think of yourself. Think of how long you have schemed to have me. If you refuse my request, not only will you be unsatisfied tonight, but I will still turn up at the Garden of Hermopolis tomorrow."

If she were a better woman, she wouldn't accede to his demands. "You want too much."

"I've always wanted a great deal. Now do you want me to sin or not?"

His words were accompanied by little drop kisses to her neck, light, gentle, very slightly moist, followed by a bite that didn't hurt at all, but made her toes curl and her eyelashes flutter.

Of course she wanted him to come with her to Cornwall. She had never been that better woman, and the thought of the Garden of Hermopolis and Moriarty's murky aims chilled her to the spleen.

But to have him tie his fate to hers, even knowing that he would have never chosen any other course . . . She sighed, pulled him closer, and kissed him hard.

"Let us sin then. Let us show Sodom and Gomorrah how it's done."

# Eight

Livia didn't sleep much that night. In the morning she joined Mrs. Newell in the older woman's bedroom for breakfast.

"I was thinking of inviting you to come with me today—I've a long visit with an old friend planned. But I know how much you dislike having to smile at strangers and pretend to take an interest, my dear," said Mrs. Newell with a wink. "So what say you to spending the day away from us old fuddy-duddies and doing only what you wish?"

Livia remembered what Charlotte had said. Mrs. Newell was setting her free again, exactly as Charlotte had predicted.

Her heart thrummed with gratitude. "That would be wonderful. I mean, I'm sure your friend is wonderful, too, but I do yearn to take a nice long walk in the park and then spend some time at the British Museum, especially the Reading Room."

"Then it shall be so," declared Mrs. Newell as she adjusted the lapels of her rose brocade dressing gown. "I am fully settled in for a luxurious breakfast with two newspapers and a magazine and will not leave this table until half past nine. Do things at your own pace, my impatient girl, and don't wait for me to move these old bones."

Her lively kindness made Livia's spirits rise. She, whose appetite was usually anemic, consumed a decent amount of bacon and eggs—and even made all the appropriate responses as Mrs. Newell read aloud passages from a breathless article about the upcoming Jubilee.

When Livia, ready to leave, poked in her head to say her good-byes, Mrs. Newell was indeed still at table, her maid hovering nearby.

"I shall have both luncheon and tea with my friend. So if you come back and I have not returned yet, don't wait for me. Order your own tea," said Mrs. Newell between instructions to her maid on which dresses to lay out.

In town Mrs. Newell took her tea at five and liked to linger a good while for conversation. Livia, therefore, didn't need to return to the hotel before dark. She left with a smile. Her good mood lasted until she turned the first street corner. And then all the doubts and misgivings Mrs. Newell's fortifying company had kept at bay came crashing back.

The last time someone had called on Charlotte on Moriarty's orders, the goal had been to ferret out the whereabouts of their illegitimate half brother, Mr. Myron Finch, who had defected from Moriarty's service. Livia had been awake in the middle of the night wondering what new diabolical schemes required the participation of Moriarty himself, when she'd abruptly asked herself whether Mr. Finch didn't factor into this new charade.

The idea had struck with the force of one of her mother's open-handed slaps, and in its wake, the anxiety pumping through her veins had made her bolt up in bed, breathing hard.

When she thought of Mr. Finch's peril, she usually understood it in terms of Moriarty's vindictiveness—minions were allowed to gather under his banner but never to leave on their own terms. But from time to time she remembered that, according to Charlotte, who had heard it from Mr. Marbleton, Mr. Finch might have absconded with something of Moriarty's, something of vital importance.

So important that Moriarty had risked a valuable and well-placed spy for a chance at its recovery.

That particular ploy, staged the previous summer, had failed. Mr. Finch had disappeared into the ether, not to be seen again. Soon even coded messages from him no longer appeared in the papers. Charlotte and Livia did not speak much of this brother, but Livia knew that Charlotte, too, had become increasingly uneasy about his prolonged silence.

Before Livia had met Mr. Finch, she had never wished to speak of him—the disgust she had felt toward her father for having sired a child out of wedlock had spread to Mr. Finch himself. But he had turned out to be one of the few people she could trust, and his well-being was often on her mind.

Two streets away, Lord Ingram was already waiting in a hackney. Livia could not go to the Garden of Hermopolis, but this morning she and Lord Ingram were headed for Snowham, the country station named on Mr. Marbleton's ticket stub.

After they had exchanged greetings, Livia told him of the misgivings that had plagued her last night. "I have no concrete evidence that this is the case. But if Moriarty still hasn't recovered what he sought from Mr. Finch, then we cannot eliminate that possibility."

"A valid line of thinking," said Lord Ingram.

Livia, habitually starved of approbation, felt the usual nervous fluttering in her stomach, from both pleasure at being praised and fear that ultimately she might not live up to that praise. "Thank you, my lord."

"If it makes you more at ease, there was a message from Mr. Finch in the papers, at the beginning of the year," said Lord Ingram. "I learned of this recently myself, from Holmes."

Livia's hand came to her lips. "So he was all right—at least as of then!"

Charlotte would probably have told her that in person as soon as they'd met, if yesterday hadn't been what it was.

"And if it's as you suspect, that Moriarty is still seeking Mr. Finch with all his might, then that, too, is good news of a sort. It would imply that, as of this moment, Mr. Finch remains at large."

The relief Livia felt, however, proved fleeting—Moriarty's shadow loomed not only large but cold. "I hope he can continue to remain safe," she murmured. "Do you not feel chilled every time you think about what Moriarty might be doing?"

"I do," said Lord Ingram. "At times I feel dizzy."

But he did not look light-headed with fear. In fact, as he knocked on the top of the hackney to signal the cabbie to stop, and then walked a short distance and handed her up into a different vehicle—maneuvers meant to confound anyone who might be following them—he appeared, for all that they were at a difficult, dangerous, and likely futile endeavor, to be . . . well, chirpy.

Not that he babbled or grinned or anything of the sort, but it was hard not to notice the spring in his step and the smile he occasionally wore as he glanced about.

At first she was wholly baffled, until insight landed with a thud: He was happy about Charlotte.

Livia dared not think too deeply on what exactly they had done to delight him so. Perhaps it was simply the fact that they had been apart for months and were now together again.

She wondered whether Charlotte was as happy—she couldn't quite imagine Charlotte being over the moon. Livia didn't want Lord Ingram to be alone in his happiness, as he had been when he fell in love with his wife. But she could scarcely ask the man whether he wasn't too giddy.

He secured a railway compartment for them. When the train left the station, he asked for the ticket stub Mr. Marbleton had left them. Livia produced the ticket. He spent a silent quarter hour scrutinizing it, holding it in a pair of tweezers with padded tips, turning it this way and that. She had done the same both the night before and this morning, staring at the once light brown scrap of paper until she was cross-eyed, but the ticket yielded no clues.

"Do you have any idea what we might find in Snowham?" she wondered aloud.

He put the ticket back in its box and handed the box back to her. "My first thought was that it might be another Moriarty holding, but the area around Snowham is not industrial. We are far more likely to come across rolling countryside and a modest manor or two than premises that would produce great wealth."

"Maybe it's not a mill or a factory but something like Château Vaudrieu?" she ventured.

Château Vaudrieu, outside Paris, was a Moriarty stronghold. It was also where he had been imprisoned for a while by his erstwhile lieutenants. Who was to say that he wouldn't have a similar place in Britain? And who was to say that—

Her heart pounded. She turned the cloisonné jewelry box in her hands, faster and faster, the peach and pink flowers on the lid blurring into the cobalt enamel setting.

Lord Ingram looked at her. "You think Snowham might be where Mr. Marbleton is being kept?"

Her thoughts had indeed sprinted in that direction.

The next moment they shook their heads together.

Livia set down the jewelry box and rubbed her temples. "No. What was I thinking? He would not tell us such a thing even if he could."

Because that would place the onus to free him on them and he would never put them in such danger.

Then what? What could he possibly hope to convey with a torn railway ticket that didn't even have any handwriting on it?

She rubbed her temples some more. "Do you really believe we'll find anything in Snowham?"

It seemed almost too obvious a clue.

"After Mr. Marbleton left London, it was more than possible that he went through Snowham," mused Lord Ingram, "if he crossed the Channel from Dover. But I'm not optimistic about unearthing anything significant today. I can only hope that what he wishes to tell us isn't hidden beneath a puzzle too byzantine for our aptitude."

Livia was about to voice her agreement when a knock came at the door of their compartment.

"Your tickets, please," said the conductor.

They produced their tickets to be punched. The conductor nodded and left, closing the door behind him. Livia put her punched ticket away. Lord Ingram, however, stared at his as if he'd never seen it before.

"What is it, my lord?"

"Mr. Marbleton's ticket, please."

The suppressed excitement in his voice made Livia's pulse accelerate again. With unsteady fingers, she opened the jewelry box. Inside, the ticket stub lay nestled on a bed of black velvet. Lord Ingram placed his own ticket on the table next to the box. Livia did likewise.

Mr. Marbleton's ticket was beige and the tickets they'd purchased today a muted green. But all three were issued by the same company and nearly identical in format, except that theirs was London to Snowham, and Mr. Marbleton's Snowham to London.

"Do you see now?" asked Lord Ingram, his voice kept deliberately low.

Livia nodded hard. The part of Mr. Marbleton's ticket that had been torn away was the portion where the date valid for travel had been stamped and also where the ticket would have been punched by a conductor.

"I can see why he wouldn't want the date to be known," she said. "A ticket stuck on the bottom of one's boot is one thing. A ticket from two months ago stuck on the bottom of one's boot is something else altogether."

The former was a minor annoyance that could happen to anyone who had walked through a railway station of late. The latter could be explained only if the same boots had not been worn for an entire season. After all, railway platforms were swept and washed and there was no reason for a stub from Christmas still to be lying in wait.

"And it would also mean that it might be this ticket, rather than Snowham the locale, that is the most important." But the light that had come into Lord Ingram's eyes quickly dimmed. "We have looked over this ticket in excruciating detail and I don't know what else can be gleaned by more examination."

"Can we put it under a microscope?"

"We can, but the paper is opaque. For a microscope to work properly, light must be able to pass through the specimen. Otherwise all the details of the magnification would be lost."

Livia grunted her frustration.

Lord Ingram examined the ticket some more, closed the box, and gave it back to her. "Patience, Miss Olivia, patience," he said with a sunny smile. "We haven't even started yet."

—❖—

At precisely five seconds past nine o'clock, the doorbell rang at 18 Upper Baker Street.

Charlotte adjusted the turban on her head. Late the year before, she'd shorn off most of her hair to better wear wigs and pass herself off as a gentleman. Since then, her hair had grown back some, but was not yet long enough for her to go bareheaded before callers.

Her dress was a blue-and-green plaid trimmed in yellow, and the turban a matching yellow with dark blue silk roses on the crown. She would have preferred the flowers to be purple or pink, but then the entire ensemble might be too much for dear Mrs. Watson, who shared Livia's taste for elegant simplicity but, unlike Livia, was too reticent to point out that the surfeit of colors in Charlotte's outfit constituted an assault on the eyes.

Although, to be sure, Mrs. Watson hadn't paid any attention to Charlotte's toilette today. She had been pacing, jaw clenched, for the past quarter hour, wearing a path in their lovely new carpet, which allowed Charlotte's sporadic smiles, both uncharacteristic and unsuitable to the occasion, to go unnoticed.

It had been a marvelous night. Her lover had refused to do anything that could get her in the family way. But he'd been both naughty and creative and she'd been happy to explore the many ways two people could derive pleasure together while bypassing the elementary piston-and-cylinder route.

Yes, so very naughty.

She suppressed her smile just in time for Mrs. Watson to jump at the sound of the bell.

"I doubt it is Moriarty himself," said Charlotte.

After all, the man had stated plainly that he would send someone. But she, too, tensed, flexing her fingers and expelling a long breath.

Mrs. Watson left and returned a minute later with a man in his early forties, average in height, unremarkable in features, yet wearing very well-made clothes—black frock coat and striped city trousers, boring but of excellent material and impeccably cut. He seemed to aspire to looking like a lawyer and might have made a passable facsimile were it not for the scar on his face—not obvious at first glance but it caused a gash in his beard that took a fair amount of pomatum to conceal.

"Mr. de Lacey to see you, Miss Holmes," said Mrs. Watson.

Charlotte rose with a becoming smile. "How do you do, Mr. de Lacey? Were you the one who wrote me in the first place?"

*And how long have you been at your current appointment?*

Moriarty's chief lieutenant in Britain was referred to as de Lacey, but she had her suspicions that the man who had held the position the previous summer had not survived the year.

De Lacey bowed. "That is correct, Miss Holmes. I wrote on Mr. Baxter's behalf—I look after his interests in the British Isles."

He had a clear, careful enunciation. Mrs. Watson would be able to pin down his exact origins. Charlotte, without as expert an ear, could still tell that much effort had gone into the taming of his vowels, turning them round and polished.

She offered him a seat. A round of obligatory small talk ensued as their tea steeped in the teapot. Mrs. Watson had gone into Sherlock Holmes's room on the pretext of looking after the invalid sage, so it was only Charlotte and de Lacey in the parlor.

She poured a cup of tea and gave it to him along with her answer. "After much consideration, we have decided to accept Mr. Baxter as a client."

"Mr. Baxter will be pleased to hear that. Will you be departing today?"

Charlotte and Mrs. Watson were prepared for an imminent departure—everything they had packed for the purpose of fleeing Moriarty would come in handy for a forced excursion to Cornwall. But de Lacey's bald question still gave her pause.

She took a sip of her very hot tea. "Before I go, I have some questions."

"I would be glad to answer them for you, Miss Holmes," said de Lacey earnestly.

His helpfulness seemed genuine. For a moment Charlotte didn't know which was worse, a Moriarty, whose ruthlessness had ambition and megalomania at its root, or someone like de Lacey, content to be a henchman to the Moriartys of the world.

"My questions are of a sensitive nature, best posed to a family member. If Mr. James Baxter himself is not available, perhaps Mr. Stephen Baxter can step in for him—assuming, that is, the younger Mr. Baxter is also related to Miss Baxter."

"Mr. Baxter is indeed otherwise occupied. Mr. Stephen Baxter is gallivanting about London, not expected back until the afternoon. Every moment counts and I assure you, Miss Holmes, that I have been authorized to dispense all necessary information."

Mr. Marbleton, gallivanting about London?

If de Lacey—or Moriarty, by extension—didn't want Charlotte to speak to Mr. Marbleton, he could have come up with a number of excuses other than that Mr. Marbleton was out enjoying himself. A good liar always lied as little as possible. Did this mean de Lacey was telling the truth?

"Very well, then, Mr. de Lacey. I would like to know what Mr. Baxter believes to be the reason for Miss Baxter's initial interest in and commitment to the Garden of Hermopolis. In particular—my apologies in advance—I would like to know whether there were any romantic attachments on her part."

"That is possible, of course, but we do not believe so."

People had a tendency to perform certain actions when they had trouble stating the truth. De Lacey's gaze, however, did not shift to some corner of the room. He did not fidget. Nor did he make the sort of shoulder-rounding movement that would cave in his chest. Instead, he smoothed a hand down his lapel, but that seemed more a gesture of enjoyment than one of nerve, as if he still couldn't believe that he was wearing garments of fine cashmere.

"What makes you think that wasn't the case?"

"For one thing, in its most embryonic stage, the Garden had only female residents."

"That there were only other women did not preclude the possibility of a romantic attachment on Miss Baxter's part."

De Lacey didn't so much as twitch an eyelid. "We have no reason to believe that Miss Baxter possessed sapphic leanings."

"I see," said Charlotte, though all she saw was that this line of inquiry would yield her little. "Mr. Baxter made the point that Miss Baxter, despite her decision to join the commune, is an otherwise intelligent and discerning woman. Does he not have any theories about why she still opted for the Garden of Hermopolis?"

"He does, though it pains him to admit it. On the whole, he believes that Miss Baxter, as a child, was deeply unhappy to be removed from her grandmother's care. That unhappiness never dissipated and transformed itself into a resentment against her father."

"But however pointed a resentment, once she won his permission to return to her grandmother's house and live on her own, would that not be enough distance between father and daughter?"

De Lacey coughed rather delicately. "Her late grandmother was some years departed by that time. And the house's former staff had also dispersed to other places of employment. The new staff put into place had been selected by Mr. Baxter."

"Ah," said Charlotte.

"You must also see, then, how it was the proper thing to do, on Mr. Baxter's part, to make sure that his daughter was surrounded by personnel he trusted?"

"I can certainly understand a father's anxiety. So you believe that Miss Baxter felt her old home still did not afford her enough autonomy, and therefore she had to decamp even farther."

"I do."

Charlotte tapped her fingers against the side of her teacup. "The staff would have realized that she'd left and immediately reported it to Mr. Baxter?"

"Yes."

"And yet, according to Mr. Baxter himself, he did not learn that she had absconded from her grandmother's house until some months later."

Moriarty's precise words had been, *When she was twenty-one, she did just that, moving to England and taking up residence in the old house. But she did not stay there for long. Some months later, I learned that she'd packed up her worldly goods and joined a group of Hermetists who had formed their own community in Cornwall.*

That *some months later* could be interpreted to mean that Miss Baxter had stayed some months in her grandmother's house before leaving or that Moriarty did not learn of her flight until after some months.

De Lacey blinked a few times before saying, "Perhaps you mis-understood, Miss Holmes. I'm sure Mr. Baxter meant something else."

"Oh?"

De Lacey considered the fireplace to Charlotte's left, then looked back at her. "I'm sure he meant that he met with Miss Baxter months later, not that he only learned of her departure then."

*Interesting.*

Charlotte nodded, letting this particular detail go—for the moment. "To go back to our point, I can imagine Miss Baxter heading into the commune in a state of rebellion. But at some point, one must think of one's welfare and not just the satisfaction of chopping off one's nose to spite one's face, no matter how irritating said nose must seem at first. Does Mr. Baxter believe that Miss Baxter re-mained in the Garden of Hermopolis, to her own eventual detri-ment, solely because of her continued resentment of him?"

De Lacey stroked his neatly groomed beard. There were scars on his hand, but otherwise the hand appeared well cared for, at least in recent years, with soft-looking skin and beautifully clean nails. "If her circumstances worsened dramatically, she might have been jolted out of that false sense of security. But I have observed that people can become accustomed to almost anything. When changes are subtle and gradual, they adjust to the new state of affairs and carry on until the moment it becomes too late for them to do any-thing."

Charlotte only looked at him.

De Lacey scuffed one elbow against an armrest and added rather reluctantly, "I suppose it behooves me to mention that part of the compromise between father and daughter was Miss Baxter's agree-ment that if she left the commune, she would return to Mr. Baxter's care."

As Charlotte had thought. "Would you be more specific as to what this 'care' entails?"

"It would be similar to what she'd known at her grandmother's place. She would have a choice as to where she lived and he would appoint the staff that would look after her."

A gilded cage.

"So in the end, you—and Mr. Baxter—believe that she chose to remain in deteriorating conditions at the Garden of Hermopolis rather than live under Mr. Baxter's surveillance."

This sounded better than, *She would rather die than have anything to do with her father ever again*, but still de Lacey winced. "Miss Baxter was— Miss Baxter has always been very proud, and yes, Mr. Baxter does believe that, in this case, she unwisely opted to place her pride above her well-being and is paying a price for it."

Charlotte pounced. "At the beginning of your reply, you spoke of Miss Baxter in the past tense, Mr. de Lacey. Do you or Mr. Baxter believe that Miss Baxter is no more?"

De Lacey's expression turned grave. "It is a possibility that we have considered but not yet one that dominates our thinking. We would be acting very differently if we indeed believed that Miss Baxter had met with an untimely demise."

*Would you?*

The day before, Charlotte's suspicion that Moriarty had given her a highly incomplete picture had been largely based on an analysis of the man's character and his position vis-à-vis Charlotte. De Lacey, not as gifted a liar as Moriarty, had in fact let something slip: that Moriarty had not removed his daughter from the Garden of Hermopolis as soon as he'd learned of her new allegiance but only sometime later.

Was it an important detail? She didn't know enough to judge. But it buttressed her hypothesis that she had been kept as much in the dark as possible about Miss Baxter, the Garden of Hermopolis, and Moriarty's ultimate aims.

She wondered whether de Lacey knew of Moriarty's true plans. "Have you ever met Miss Baxter, Mr. de Lacey?"

"I have not had the pleasure of being presented to her, but I've served Mr. Baxter long enough that I know the general outline of her story. Not to mention, one of my duties has been to keep an eye on her safety."

Charlotte adjusted the lace of her cuff. "Did Mr. Baxter discuss her with you either yesterday or today?"

It was a simple question, yet de Lacey again scuffed an elbow on the armrest. "We did not have a discussion per se. I received a note last night informing me that I was to call on you this morning and facilitate your investigation by answering any questions you may have and furnishing you with Miss Baxter's photographs."

As if to prove his sincerity, he handed Charlotte an envelope. Charlotte glanced at the three pictures inside. Miss Baxter, perhaps a year or two senior to Charlotte in age, did not resemble Moriarty as Mr. Marbleton did. Hers were haughty and angular features, those of a woman who suddenly found herself a beautiful adult without having ever been a pretty child.

She looked back at de Lacey. He was warier than he had been earlier—he'd pulled his feet in and crossed his ankles, and his hands were on his lap now, instead of the armrests. Because of what he'd unwittingly told her?

"I still find it astonishing that Mr. Baxter left the discussion of such private matters to someone else."

De Lacey swallowed. "Mr. Baxter is a very busy man."

"Does he have other children?"

De Lacey again blinked a few times. "I'm afraid I'm not at liberty to discuss that."

Charlotte was only trying to gauge how important Miss Baxter might be to Moriarty. De Lacey's answer, however, reinforced how little he was allowed to discuss with regard to father and daughter.

"Very well, then," she said. "In that case, Mr. de Lacey, I would like to know how you have kept an eye on her safety over the years."

---

The station at Snowham was about an hour east-southeast of London. Detrained passengers exited quickly, leaving Livia and Lord Ingram to tour the place at leisure. There wasn't much to see, only a single half-covered platform next to a small building, indistinguishable from any other minor country stop. A few travelers awaited the next train headed for London, a bored stationmaster spoke to the ticket agent, and an occasional express train rumbled through, not deigning to slow down.

"Do you remark anything at all?" Livia asked her companion, after they had been at the station for a while.

"No, nothing, I'm afraid," said Lord Ingram. "Shall we take a look beyond the station?"

They found a hackney and asked to be driven around, pretending to be a pair of siblings looking to settle down nearby. The cabbie, not surprised by the purpose of their journey, informed them that the village had more than doubled in size since the railway came through in the sixties.

"Much cheaper and nicer compared to London, innit?" he opined.

The village was indeed composed of a core of older buildings around High Street, their red roofs darkened with age, and some other streets with newer but more uniform-looking houses. After a quick detour into the surrounding countryside, Lord Ingram asked to see any mills, factories, or other such sites that one might conceivably invest in.

They were taken to a brick kiln, a tannery sitting idle, and lastly, the only inn in the village, freshly painted and put up for sale because its owner wished to retire. Lord Ingram whispered to Livia that none of these establishments remotely approached the scale and sophistication of the De Lacey Industries premises he and Charlotte had seen.

But they alit at the inn anyway, as Mr. Marbleton almost certainly would have patronized the place, if he had spent more than a day in Snowham.

It was early for luncheon and they were the only diners in the dining room, the windows of which looked onto green countryside and a willow-lined riverbank in the distance. Their steaming shepherd's pies came with a white-haired innkeeper, who was happy to inform them that two parties were already interested in his establishment. "Very well kept this place has been, if I do say so myself. And I'm not asking too much, just its fair value."

They chatted a little more on the history of the inn, its current operations, and the innkeeper's plans after retirement, before Lord Ingram said, "If you don't mind, Mr. . . ."

"Upton is the name, sir."

"Right, Mr. Upton. My sister and I are on a possibly fruitless quest in search of a friend. He departed from our midst several months ago and hasn't been heard from since. Recently we learned that he'd passed through Snowham. Yours is the only inn in town, from what I understand?"

"The publican does have two rooms above the taproom, but those rooms aren't listed in any travel guides. So if your friend came from elsewhere and stayed here overnight, he would have stayed with me," said Mr. Upton proudly. He then sighed. "But I no longer have as good a memory for names and faces as I did when I was younger, just so you know."

Lord Ingram held out his hand. "Be as it may, this is a photograph of our friend."

Livia stilled. *She* did not have a picture of Mr. Marbleton, but Lord Ingram did?

In the photograph, Mr. Marbleton stood in an open field, his arms wide, his face tilted up to the sky.

The innkeeper excused himself and went to fetch his reading

glasses. Livia leaned closer to Lord Ingram and whispered, "My lord, where did you obtain this?"

"Long story," he whispered back. "The picture was developed last summer from one of the negatives I borrowed from the Marbletons, during the Sackville investigation."

*"Borrowed?"*

"Yes." He grinned. "Though when I attempted to return the plates, the Marbletons did not take it too kindly."

The innkeeper returned with glasses on, and with one look at the photograph said, "Why, yes, I remember him. That's Mr. Openshaw. A more amiable young man I've rarely met, and I've seen the whole world pass by."

Something cracked inside Livia. Having seen Mr. Marbleton with her own eyes, she knew that fewer than twenty-four hours ago he was still alive and in one piece. Yet this unexpected confirmation of his itinerary last December made her feel . . . as if he'd been gone a decade and this was the first time she'd had his news.

Yes, something had been fractured—the protective restraint she'd put into place so that she did not obsess over his fate every hour of the day. Through this damaged dam streamed all the questions she'd had no one to ask. How had he looked? What had he said? Had he eaten properly? Had he given any hints about his past or his future?

She bit the inside of her cheek. Best let Lord Ingram do the talking. If she opened her mouth, her emotions wouldn't just spill all over the table, they would submerge the inn, possibly the entire village.

Lord Ingram looked at her before he turned to the innkeeper again. "That is excellent news indeed, Mr. Upton. Do you recall when he stayed with you?"

"Toward the end of last year. But I can fetch the exact dates for you from the register."

The innkeeper departed yet again, this time to consult his books.

"Are you all right, Miss Olivia?" asked Lord Ingram quietly.

"Yes, I think so," she said, even as she shook her head.

She had not cried once after Mr. Marbleton's departure, but now tears welled in her eyes, stinging her corneas. She had the wild urge to leave the table and run through the inn, as if Mr. Marbleton might be waiting for her atop the staircase or at the end of a corridor.

The innkeeper came back with a satisfied rub of his hands. "Mr. Openshaw stayed for two nights shortly before Christmas. The twentieth and twenty-first of December, in fact."

Livia's stomach rolled over. December twentieth was the day Mr. Marbleton had left London. So when he'd stayed in this little inn, under the care of Mr. Upton, he had indeed been on his way to Moriarty.

"Two nights, you said?" Lord Ingram's voice came as if from a great distance. "Do you remember anything else about his stay?"

"And did he tell you where he was headed?" asked Livia, despite her desire not to betray herself.

She knew—they all knew—where Mr. Marbleton had ended up, but she was still hungry for the details. Ravenous.

Lord Ingram pulled out the chair nearest him and indicated for the innkeeper to take a seat, but Mr. Upton only braced his hands on top of the chair. "Mr. Openshaw said he planned to cross the Channel soon, that I remember. Said he might not return to England for a while—and that he'd miss it.

"As for what else I remember about him—he was mostly in his room during the time he was here. Came down for an hour or so in the evenings to have his supper and a drink. Didn't mind listening to me rambling on about my day—I was used to talking to the missus, but she went to her rest three years ago and it's been hard to find anyone else who's half as patient."

"He was always the kindest listener," said Livia, her impulse again overwhelming her desire to appear only moderately interested.

"Aye, that he was. Quite sorry I am, to hear that he's been missing."

They were silent for a moment, then Lord Ingram said, "May we see the room he took, Mr. Upton? We'll be happy to compensate you for your troubles, of course."

The innkeeper smoothed his hand over his head twice, as if weighing his choices. "Come along then. It said on the register that he stayed in room 5, which doesn't have anyone at the moment."

Room 5 was on the next floor. As they followed the innkeeper up the stairs, Livia whispered to Lord Ingram, "Do you think he left anything in that room?"

Lord Ingram shook his head. "I wouldn't have. It has guests coming and going, not to mention maids cleaning and the innkeeper inspecting everything."

But Livia's hope persisted until she saw the immaculate floor and the gleaming furniture inside room 5. From fluffed white pillows to trimmed lamp wicks, everything spoke of attention to detail. She bit the inside of her lower lip. No, indeed, Mr. Marbleton couldn't have hoped to hide anything here, unless . . .

"He didn't leave anything behind, Mr. Openshaw," said Mr. Upton, as if hearing her unspoken question, even as he opened armoire doors and pulled out nightstand drawers for them to inspect. "I keep careful track of forgotten belongings, as some will write to inquire. If they enclose the correct amount of postage, I send their things via the post. And Mr. Openshaw didn't leave anything behind, not even a scrap of paper. Very tidy he was."

"Do you remember anything else about him?" said Livia, no longer capable of any pretense of sangfroid. "Anything else he might have said or done?"

Mr. Upton gave her a sympathetic look. "Well, you know how it is, miss. Sometimes you get very amiable guests, but it's only after they leave that you realize they haven't told you much about themselves. And I thought . . ."

He hesitated a moment. "He was quick to smile, our young Mr. Openshaw. Had a nice smile to him, too. But even though he smiled, I was sure that he was sad on the inside. Full of sorrows."

*You already know this. You knew, from the moment you realized that he'd left under duress, that he must have felt wretched.*

Still, the innkeeper's words fell like an avalanche upon her chest.

Lord Ingram placed an arm around her shoulder. Livia allowed herself to lean into him. They asked more questions, but soon it became apparent that the innkeeper had told them all he could remember. Lord Ingram thanked him and wanted to know whether he could speak to the maid who cleaned Mr. Marbleton's room.

"That would be Ellen Bailey. But she no longer works here. I'll give you her new employer's address."

Ellen Bailey's new employer lived in a house on the outskirts of the village, with large gardens both in front and in the back. After much knocking, they learned from the caretaker that the family and most of the staff, including Ellen Bailey, had returned to town. And no, he could not give out their London address without first consulting the mistress herself by post.

Lord Ingram wrote a note and gave it to the caretaker, along with a sizable tip to send the note to Ellen Bailey.

Livia observed the proceedings, but her mind remained fixated on Mr. Marbleton. The fear he must have felt in his final days of freedom, the isolation, the horror of being at last towed under by those malevolent forces he'd been fleeing his entire life.

Lord Ingram had to hold her by the arm for them to return to the carriage.

Instead of taking the backward-facing seat, as he always did, he sat down beside her and allowed her, once again, to lean on him. This time she even buried her face in his sleeve.

"It's all right," he said again and again. "It will be all right."

It might not be. They could all meet a horrible end, and Fate would laugh at those who had the audacity to assume otherwise.

And yet, somehow, his patient, kind voice, the soothing iterations of his reassurance, and even the soft, starch-scented wool of his greatcoat comforted her.

*It's all right,* she began to repeat silently after him. *It will be all right.*

# Nine

Excerpts from reports by Theresa Felton,
as dictated to [Redacted]
(Part of the Garden of Hermopolis dossier)

August 1883

I think I've been here long enough—four months—to say
these are some peculiar people. Not eccentric, just awfully
quiet-like. No one says anything to me about themselves.
Not about their days, not about their aches and pains, not
about how so-and-so is wonderfully good-looking or downright annoying.

Now there are hoity-toity ladies and gentlemen who won't
speak to the likes of me, a mere charwoman. But even the
servants in this commune here aren't any friendlier. They
never ask about pubs in the area, which ones have good ales
or make a proper Sunday roast. Surely, out of sheer boredom
some of them should make conversation, shouldn't they?
What's there to do out on these headlands, and them servants
not even the ones interested in this foreign religion here?

And I rarely see them with one another either. When I
clean I look out of the windows a lot—keeping an eye on

those around Miss Baxter is part of watching out for her, innit? I hardly ever see more than two people walk together. And even those who do walk together—well, I don't want to say they don't enjoy one another's company, but they always look so serious and no one ever just bursts out laughing.

Still, all in all, they seem to be decent people. And not any odder, if you ask me, than any other collection of folks who don't need to work for a living. No one gives me a hard time. No one, that is, except Miss Baxter.

Nothing I do is ever good enough for her. If I clean thoroughly, she says I take too long. If I work fast, then I'm sloppy. To tell you the truth, I'm beginning to dread going into her place.

May 1884

Miss Baxter is the same. I see her about once every other week. She still finds my work awfully lacking and I still dread working for her.

This probably isn't my place to say but I really don't see how anyone can take advantage of Miss Baxter. I haven't met everyone at the Garden and maybe Miss Fairchild will be a fair old battle-ax if she ever recovers her voice. But I've worked for rich folks and wellborn folks and folks that are both and I can't say I've ever met anyone who makes me feel half so useless.

Miss Baxter is the sort that if she doesn't find faults with you, you're on your knees thanking the Almighty. I don't know who's grand enough or stupid enough to try to get the better of her.

I still haven't been allowed into the library or the sanctuary. Once I asked Mr. Kaplan's valet whether he'd seen them from the inside and he very huffily told me that he hadn't and had no plans to!

I've also asked Miss Ellery a second time whether those places need to be thoroughly cleaned once in a while and she said again that the members would do that and I didn't need to concern myself.

If it's all right with Mr. de Lacey I don't think I'll ask anymore. Every place I've worked, I've left with glowing letters of character. I should hate to be thought of as being too nosy.

August 1886

I saw Miss Baxter only once this month—usually I'd see her twice—and when I saw her, she was feeling unwell.

Of course everyone is under the weather sometimes, but Miss Baxter has always been so imposing that I couldn't imagine her ever suffering from ill health. But here she was, looking almost green in the face.

Mrs. Crosby was with her that day—it was the first time I'd seen someone else in her lodge. Later, when I saw Mrs. Crosby again, I asked about Miss Baxter. She assured me that Miss Baxter was better, that she'd simply eaten something that disagreed with her.

And I suppose that's that.

September 1886

Again, I saw Miss Baxter only once this month. And again, she was taken to her bed. Miss Fairchild was with her this time. Since Miss Fairchild doesn't speak, I asked Dr. Robinson—I mentioned him in spring, when he first joined the Garden—about Miss Baxter.

Dr. Robinson wasn't any more concerned about Miss Baxter's health than Mrs. Crosby was earlier. He said that she was recovering from a bout of mild pneumonia and required only time and good beef tea to be back on her feet.

But I'm bothered. Maybe I shouldn't be, but I am.

October 1886

Last time I said that I was bothered. This time I'm really
bothered. That's three months in a row now I've seen Miss
Baxter laid up. My heart trembled a bit when I saw her on
the settee by the fire, buried under a pile of blankets.

Mrs. Crosby was with her again. Later, I asked her about
Miss Baxter, telling her that these past three months I'd only
seen Miss Baxter laid up. Mrs. Crosby said that I just
stumbled on the few days Miss Baxter was feeling poorly.
And that Miss Baxter wasn't even ill this time, but merely
suffering from an unusually uncomfortable monthly.

I don't know that I believe her. But I also have no way of
proving her wrong. I just don't feel right about it. Goodness
knows Miss Baxter has never been nice to me. But she's
grand—scary-grand, like a tiger stalking through the forest.
If you saw a tiger lying on the ground, being badly off, even
if you were scared of tigers, you'd still feel bad for it,
wouldn't you?

### THE FOLLOWING REPORT WAS WRITTEN IN ITS ENTIRETY BY THERESA FELTON

It's been ages since Mr. [Redacted] came and took down my
report. I hope he's all right. Please send him or someone else.

I won't write much as writing is hard for me, but I'm
more worried than ever about Miss Baxter. I last saw her at
the beginning of October. At the end of that month, I last
spoke with Mr. [Redacted]. Since then, all of November and
December and most of January have gone by. That makes it
at least three whole months I've only heard but not seen
Miss Baxter.

I can explain what I mean but it would be too much
trouble to write down. Please send someone. Mind you, I
can't prove that anything is wrong, but I feel downright
uneasy.

---

"At least it's good weather," shouted Mrs. Watson. "Why, the sun
feels almost warm!"

Charlotte, too, had her face tilted back to feel the hardly dis-
cernible prickles of heat on her skin.

London remained cold and wet, but here in the very southwest
of Britain, winter seemed to have quietly departed. The sky was a
clear blue dome, the breeze cool but not biting. The sea undulated
gently, and the small boat they had hired cut through the waves
with the flair of an experienced footman gliding across the floor of
a ballroom.

The coast was high, but not forbiddingly so, the sheer cliffs
largely bare, with patches of moss green here and there. They sailed
past inlets and stony coves, mostly empty except for an occasional
scavenger, hunched over among the rocks.

Mrs. Watson had the rudder in hand, Mr. Mears sat by the
mast, and Charlotte, not much use on a sailboat, occupied the bow
to stay out of the way. From time to time, the coastline lowered to
near sea level, and a village would appear, a few dozen red-roofed
houses nestled against the slopes. And then another expanse of unclaimed nature, white foam caps crashing into the base of the crags,
while above, green moorland stretched into the distance.

Delightful day, delightful scenery, yet other than Mrs. Watson's
comment on the weather, the company had been almost entirely
silent, their attention on the coastline not so much enjoyment as
watchfulness.

The inclusion of Mr. Mears, Charlotte had half anticipated. The
dossier concerned itself almost exclusively with what took place in-

side the Garden of Hermopolis; they needed someone in the village
of Porthangan to gather more context. Just as importantly, given all
the known and unknown dangers, they didn't want their nearest ally
hundreds of miles away.

Mr. Mears had already proved his usefulness by being a good
sailor, a skill he and Mrs. Watson had acquired together, she as the
late duke of Wycliffe's mistress, he as His Grace's then new valet,
upon her recommendation. He read the wind, adjusted the sails, and
scanned the coastline with an unhurried competence, as if he were
at home in the domestic offices, polishing the silver while waiting
for the water to boil for Mrs. Watson's afternoon tea.

"I see it," he cried.

At first sight, the Garden of Hermopolis reminded Charlotte of
nothing so much as a private asylum she'd once visited, a seemingly
idyllic country dwelling made subtly sinister by the presence of unusually high walls.

On the map, the south coast of Cornwall extended roughly east
to west-southwest. But this particular stretch was oriented north to
south; the high bluff on which the Garden sat overlooked the sea to
the east. The bluff dropped nearly vertically to an inlet to the north,
but on the seaward side it dipped like the side of a bowl toward a
promontory, flattening out in a shallow depression that resembled
the palm of a slightly cupped hand, then rising again on the other
side to two thirds the height of the bluff, before plunging into the
waves.

"I think there's someone on the little promontory," said Mrs.
Watson. "Actually, I see two people."

The wind was rising. Mrs. Watson not only raised her voice, but
stood up and leaned forward, and still her words barely reached
Charlotte.

Charlotte looked through her binoculars. "It's a woman and
a man."

The woman was elderly—Miss Fairchild, perhaps? The man

appeared young. He spoke intently to the older woman, who listened with a grave expression.

Charlotte and company had meant to pass by close to the cliffs beneath the Garden of Hermopolis, but if those were indeed residents of the compound, then that would verge too much on trespassing. Mrs. Watson was already steering the boat seaward. Charlotte handed the binoculars to Mr. Mears, who looked through them for a moment before offering them to Mrs. Watson.

"There's someone on the wall also," she reported. "I hope it's because the day is glorious and not because they are on the lookout all the time."

The day had become less glorious—clouds gathered on the horizon. Charlotte was no old seaman able to predict storms with a look at the sky, but she would not be surprised if the weather took a hard, tempestuous turn.

When the binoculars came back to Charlotte, she saw that the person on the wall was a woman, also holding a pair of binoculars. She waved, but the woman did not wave back.

Their coastal voyage ended three miles farther south, at the village of Porthangan. There Mrs. Watson and Charlotte disembarked with their valises.

They were met by Mrs. Felton, a large-boned, ruddy-faced woman who was the source of much of the intelligence in Moriarty's dossier. According to the file on *her* in the dossier, she was a native of Porthangan, but had spent nearly twenty years in domestic service in Exeter, before returning to her natal village to take up cleaning at the Garden of Hermopolis.

"Oh, but I'm glad you've come, ladies. I've been feeling so uneasy that I didn't want to go into the Garden no more. Mr. Baxter's man said I must carry on as usual. But how do I do that when I'm worried sick about Miss Baxter?"

These words were whispered to Charlotte and Mrs. Watson as Mrs. Felton led them to a shiny, lacquered dogcart trimmed in green.

"Nice conveyance," said Mrs. Watson, taking the hand Mrs. Felton held out to help her up to the driver's box. "Is it the Garden's?"

"No, it's me own," said Mrs. Felton proudly. She handed a carriage blanket to Charlotte, who had taken the rear-facing seat, then got up on the driver's box herself and sat down next to Mrs. Watson. "The horse is me own. And I've me own house, too."

As women who cleaned for a living didn't usually receive much compensation, it stood to reason that de Lacey paid generously.

The road climbed up and out of the inlet. Fields and pasture rolled away before them, their grassy scent mingled with that of the tang of saltwater. The sun dipped near the horizon, its pale yellow light elongating the carriage's shadow toward the now-choppier sea.

The dogcart was the only vehicle on a lane that was merely two parallel lines of shorter grass, worn down by regular but sparse traffic. Mrs. Watson cleared her throat. "Now that we are at last away from potential eavesdroppers, Mrs. Felton, will you give us a full account of everything?"

<hr />

Lord Ingram and Miss Olivia returned to London early in the afternoon. They visited two newspaper archives, and Snowham was barely mentioned in any indexes as a locale, let alone as anything else. Afterward, Miss Olivia expressed a desire to consult another archive and Lord Ingram took his leave of her: He had someone to see before he left London, his second-eldest brother, Lord Bancroft Ashburton.

Bancroft had once looked after the Crown's more clandestine concerns. But he had betrayed both the Crown and Lord Ingram and was now under confinement, though in surroundings that most prisoners would consider luxurious: two rooms to himself in a house with mahogany wainscoting and cream-and-rose toile wallpaper, books and newspapers at his disposal, and a view of a garden outside his—albeit barred—windows.

Lord Ingram had not visited him since the previous autumn,

when Bancroft was first stripped of his office and his freedom. A betrayer had this power: He had held the trust of the betrayed, while never extending the same. To see Bancroft again was to feel the same vulnerability, the same anger against both Bancroft and himself.

"What brings you here, Ash?" asked Bancroft, a trace of suspicion to his otherwise colorless tone. "And how goes the divorce?"

"It will be granted soon, thank you."

"A good thing. One should keep one's friends close and enemies closer—but not under the same roof, if at all possible."

Bancroft, of course, knew all his soft spots. Lord Ingram made no answer.

After a while, Bancroft said, "And thank you for the wine and pastry at Christmas. Alas, they were finished far too soon."

Lord Ingram smiled slightly. Good. He had sent the wine and pastry not out of the goodness of his heart but because they'd be finished far too soon—and remind Bancroft of everything he now had to do without.

He wasn't sure whether himself of yesteryear would have done such a thing, but some of Holmes's ruthlessness was rubbing off on him. And when he'd written to her about his malicious gift, she'd responded with full-fledged approval. *Well done, Ash. That is the only way to treat a man who framed you for murder.*

"I've brought you more. A bottle of Sauternes and a pear tart."

Bancroft sniffed. "For a pear tart, I would have preferred Riesling, but Sauternes would do."

The wine had been decanted into an old-fashioned wine bag, and the pear tart, in its pasteboard box, had already been cut into small pieces to eliminate the need for knife or fork.

With an eagerness that his former self would have scorned, Bancroft tucked into the pear tart, only to look up a few seconds later. "This isn't made by the woman on your estate."

"No, it's from the Reform Club."

Bancroft sniffed again. "Lesser, but still acceptable."

He luxuriated in a few more morsels of the pear tart. "You still haven't said why you've come. I assume you didn't simply wish to see me dine well."

"No, indeed. I've come to ask you about a certain someone."

"Who?"

"We first spoke of him last summer. And you told me then, in no uncertain terms, never to be personally embroiled with him."

Moriarty.

Bancroft frowned. "I believe I know of whom you speak. What happened? Did you go against my advice?"

"One could easily contend that I have been personally and inextricably enmeshed with that particular character ever since he subverted Lady Ingram against the Crown's interests, but no, I have refrained from putting myself into his orbit. However, it often turns out that his reach is far greater than we anticipated. Perhaps you've read in the papers of my friend's investigation last December?"

"I have indeed."

Something dark and hostile gleamed in Bancroft's eyes—it had been the same investigator, Charlotte Holmes, whose work had resulted in his apprehension.

Lord Ingram felt another surge of satisfaction. "What you did not learn in the papers was that the true culprit was in league with the person you warned me away from. The stolen funds at the heart of the case had been funneled to build factories for him, from which he could henceforth derive legitimate gains."

Bancroft's brow rose a fraction of an inch. He wiped his hand with a handkerchief, took a wrapped crayon out of his pocket, and wrote *De Lacey Industries?* on a scrap of paper.

"You knew?"

Bancroft threw the scrap of paper into the fireplace. "No, not about how the construction of the enterprise's factories was funded. But last summer, once we learned the name of this person's lieutenant in Britain, I had someone look into entities associated with that name. His minions must have stolen a fortune."

"It seems likely that he did not use the gambit only on one firm. But in any case, although my investigator friend hadn't the least intention of provoking this person, this person saw it differently."

"Oh, he would most certainly see it differently." Bancroft laughed softly. "In fact, he would be highly displeased with said investigator."

His voice was sharp with pleasure. Bancroft, who probably did not believe that he himself had been responsible for his downfall, must feel that Charlotte Holmes, the proximate cause, bore the greater part of the blame.

"The person whom we haven't named called yesterday upon the investigator and engaged the investigator to find out the fate of his daughter at a certain Hermetic religious community," said Lord Ingram.

And Holmes, his Holmes, was at this very moment on her way to meet mortal danger.

A gleam came into Bancroft's eyes. "What is this community called?"

Lord Ingram's fingers dug into the armrests of his chair. "Why do you ask?"

"Your investigator's work this past summer gave us keys to the ciphers that man's minion used over a long period of time. My people went back and combed through everything in the archives that had been intercepted and was thought of as either unimportant or undecipherable. We then applied those keys, and some of the messages that newly made sense concerned what was referred to as the Garden."

"What did those messages say?"

"'All's well at the Garden' and the sort."

Disappointment tasted acrid. Lord Ingram hadn't come merely to learn that the Crown had got hold of some messages in which de

Lacey passed on news of Miss Baxter's well-being to her father. "Anything else you can tell me?"

*Something worth the revulsion and heartbreak of a visit with you.*

Bancroft did not answer.

After a while, Lord Ingram said, "I'd be glad, of course, to send a bottle of claret from my late godfather's vineyard in Bordeaux, to go with a chocolate tart."

Bancroft remained silent but poured some Sauternes into a tin cup and swirled it around, conveying, with every gesture, the insufficiency of Lord Ingram's offer.

"Or I could spare myself the trouble," said Lord Ingram, "since, unfortunately, I already know more about this man than you do."

Bancroft set down the cup abruptly. After a moment, he said, "The claret must be at least twenty years old, and the chocolate tart has to be made by the woman who works for you."

"What vintage you receive and who makes the chocolate tart will depend on what I learn today," said Lord Ingram coolly. He didn't care to play games, but he had served for years under Bancroft and learned from the best.

Bancroft's eyes narrowed. Lord Ingram met his cold gaze. Bancroft thought he still had some hold over his little brother, and perhaps he wasn't entirely wrong about that. But Holmes's safety was at stake here, and for Holmes he would crush ten of Bancroft without a second thought.

Bancroft looked away first. He took a large gulp of the Sauternes, frowned, and pushed the tin cup away. "A woman came to see me last night. Strictly speaking, we are not allowed conjugal visits. But when palms are sufficiently greased, eyes look elsewhere. I had not anticipated this caller and was—very briefly—pleasantly surprised. I didn't think either you or Remington loved me enough to send such a consort, and she looked very agreeable indeed.

"Alas, she only wished to speak to me. And the message she conveyed was not intended for me, but for you. She said that she had kept the mother of your children safe. And that she hoped you would return a favor in time."

This Lord Ingram had not expected. The only woman who could have protected Lady Ingram would have been Madame Desrosiers, Moriarty's former mistress who had staged a coup and dethroned him—for a while—and with whom Lady Ingram had thrown in her lot.

Was that why Moriarty was in England, to catch Madame Desrosiers?

"You said she came last night?"

"Odd, is it not? She had a message for you, who never visits, and here you are the next day."

Lord Ingram leaned back and gave Bancroft a look as long and cold as any Bancroft ever meted out. "And when were you going to tell me this, brother dear?"

Bancroft shifted in his chair. "She didn't leave any means of contact, so why would I rush to tell you anything?"

Lord Ingram wondered whether Madame Desrosiers took a look at Bancroft, decided he was going to be a most unreliable messenger, and therefore left no means of contact. But why had she approached Bancroft, rather than him? Was it because she thought that Bancroft was less likely to be under Moriarty's surveillance?

He rose to leave. At the door Bancroft's voice came, his tone almost conciliatory. "I wouldn't worry too much about your investigator, if I were you. To you she might not be an agent of the Crown, and to herself even less, but she has worked with our other brother and you know how he is."

Lord Ingram's hand, raised to knock at the door to be let out, stilled. Remington was a better man than Bancroft, but Remington would indeed consider Holmes a spare agent of the Crown, one currently on furlough, perhaps, to be summoned when the need presented itself.

"Therefore," continued Bancroft, "for this person to harm her would be the same as for him to pit himself against our other brother. Would he take on that sort of trouble for your investigator? I think not. Not yet, in any case. So rest easy, little brother."

———※———

Mrs. Watson had been wary of Mrs. Felton—after all, she worked for Moriarty. But Mrs. Felton was a chatty woman who enjoyed talking about herself and who seemed to have no idea of the sinister web at the center of which sat her clandestine employer.

To her, Miss Baxter was simply an heiress. And heiresses, especially heiresses who chose to live in communes that practiced dubious foreign religions, absolutely needed an extra pair of eyes on them. She felt fortunate to have been chosen for this task—"Miss Fairchild wanted someone from Porthangan and Mr. de Lacey's man found me in Exeter"—and was grateful for the income and the prestige that it brought—"It sure feels nice, oh, it does, to drive into the village for church on Sunday morning in this here fine cart and with a proper hat with feathers."

Mrs. Watson nearly gasped at her proud indiscretion—was this any way to be an agent of Moriarty's? But since Mrs. Felton did not bother to conceal her income from De Lacey Industries, then her true function must be known to everyone at the Garden of Hermopolis, or at least to Miss Baxter herself. Which would also explain, in part, why Miss Baxter could never be pleased with her work.

"And Miss Baxter, she does make my knees knock when she stares at me," continued Mrs. Felton blithely, giving the reins a shake, her butter-colored driving gloves looking as smooth and supple as the pair on Mrs. Watson's own hands. "She can kill with a glance, that one. But when I tell folks in the village about her, they are right curious and right envious, too."

The idea of Miss Baxter being openly bandied about as a topic of conversation came as an even bigger shock to Mrs. Watson, who was accustomed to speaking as little as possible of Moriarty—and everyone and everything associated with him. "What do you tell the villagers about her?"

"Everything," said Mrs. Felton with a grand wave of her hand. "Her parlor is like nothing I've ever seen in Exeter. Her clothes—oh my, but everyone's seen her fine clothes when she came into the village. It's what she puts on at home what's got me all dazzled. They don't look that different from what other ladies wear, but they just look better on her, for some reason. Even when she cleans, she looks like she ought to be in a picture—an oil painting."

"She cleans?" marveled Mrs. Watson.

"Light cleaning," Mrs. Felton clarified. "Not everyone in the Garden wants their house cleaned every other day, the way the Steeles do. Some don't want my help at all, as they've already got servants of their own. Miss Fairchild and Miss Ellery has me over twice a week. Miss Baxter needs me only once a week.

"I'm paid to do the heavier cleaning. So most often, if she is there when I clean her place, she'll dust the ornaments, wipe down the wardrobe, and polish the looking glass."

Mrs. Felton fell silent. Ahead of them, her docile mare plodded on good-naturedly, its mane tossing in a gust of wind. "But it's been a while since I saw her do any of these things."

Her sadness felt genuine.

*If you saw a tiger lying on the ground, being badly off, even if you were scared of tigers, you'd still feel bad for it, wouldn't you?*

"You did mention in your reports that the last few times you saw her, she was always unwell."

Mrs. Felton nodded heavily. "There are ladies like that. I once worked for two sisters and one of them had lost so many husbands and children, it was frightful how many hair ornaments she had lying about, all made from the locks of the departed. And she herself, God grant her strength, was exhausted by grief and I never saw her except huddled in a rocking chair. But Miss Baxter wasn't like that at all. She was . . ."

She looked up, as if seeking the right words. A pair of seabirds, their black-tipped wingspans three feet across, wheeled overhead.

"A force of nature?" supplied Miss Charlotte from the back. She'd chosen the spot because Mrs. Watson was better at putting people at ease and drawing out confessions. But that might not have made any difference today, given how keen Mrs. Felton was to tell them everything she knew.

"Yes, that's it!" cried Mrs. Felton. "She was a force of nature, before she took to her bed."

"If I understand your reports correctly," said Miss Charlotte, "you saw her once a month for three months, with her incapacitated each time, and then you never saw her again but only *heard* her?"

"That's right."

They crested a small rise. In the distance, the stone walls of the Garden of Hermopolis came into view, tall and golden in the light of the setting sun. A rather unsettling sight, such high walls in the middle of nowhere. Yet Mrs. Watson could not deny that there was also something spectacular about this remote bridgehead of Hermetism.

Miss Charlotte continued with her questioning. "Can you describe for me what transpired when you heard but didn't see her?"

"Yes, miss," said Mrs. Felton with alacrity. "The first time it happened, she asked, 'Is that you, Felton?' when I entered the lodge. I was relieved to hear her voice after all that time. She hadn't spoken to me at all the previous three times, when she was unwell—might not have even known I was there. So this time, even though she sounded weak and a little hoarse, I still thought that was an improvement.

"I said it was me and she said, 'The grates need attention. I don't think you've done them properly of late. Make sure they are bright and spotless before you leave today.'"

"She wasn't wrong about the grates. Since she hadn't admonished me for a while, I'd been a bit lax. So I set to rub and shine the grates something fierce. And when I was done, I called her so she could see that I'd heeded her. But nobody answered. I walked through her lodge twice, calling her, but the place was empty.

"At the Garden, there are cabins and there are lodges. A lodge is larger than a cabin but it isn't enormous. On the ground floor there be a parlor, a dining room, and a study. Upstairs are Miss Baxter's bedroom and a sitting room. There are two house doors, one in the front, one in the back, but the back door is always bolted shut, and the entire time I was polishing the grates, I didn't hear either door open or close. I didn't hear anyone moving about at all. And I certainly didn't see her going out."

Mrs. Felton looked expectantly at Mrs. Watson. Obligingly, Mrs. Watson said, "Very odd, that is."

"I thought so myself!" Mrs. Felton exclaimed, vindicated. "The next month, she spoke to me again when I entered her lodge. This time, she asked me to go to Miss Fairchild's place and retrieve a book for her. I'm usually not asked to go on these kinds of errands, but I said I'd go. And she said to leave the book on the mantel when I had it.

"When I came back with the book, I remembered that I was going to pay more attention to her whereabouts. I called her, but there was no answer. I walked through the lodge and she was no longer there. This time, I couldn't say that there was anything odd about her disappearance—obviously she left after I left. But I felt strange about it. I felt she arranged it so that I'd be out of her house as soon as I'd heard her voice."

Mrs. Watson wished she could see Miss Charlotte's reaction, even if her countenance would be, as usual, sweetly bland, giving nothing away. She glanced over her shoulder at the girl, who was looking down at a piece of plum cake in her lap.

"And the third time?" asked Mrs. Watson, willing the girl to turn her face to the front of the dogcart, but she only picked out a raisin from the cake and put it in her mouth.

"The third time was even more . . . normal, I suppose," said Mrs. Felton. Yet her expression, full of puzzlement, suggested otherwise. "I was in Mrs. Crosby's house. Someone knocked at the front door. Mrs. Crosby went to answer it and I heard Miss Baxter's voice, saying that she had some pastry from Miss Fairchild to give her. Mrs. Crosby invited Miss Baxter in for tea but Miss Baxter declined and said maybe another time."

Mrs. Watson again glanced out of the corner of her eye at Miss Charlotte. She was now looking in the direction of the setting sun, the horizon ablaze.

"But?" said Mrs. Watson to Mrs. Felton.

Mrs. Felton, as if she'd been waiting for just that question, lifted one hand off the reins and gestured triumphantly skyward. "But Miss Baxter said, 'Miss Fairchild asked me to give these to you.' Now I'm not saying Miss Fairchild won't ever do anything for anyone else; I'm sure when the spirit moves her, she does whatever she pleases, and I'm sure from time to time it pleases her to lend a hand.

"But she is grand, Miss Baxter. And not the kind of grand you'd call *putting on airs*. She doesn't have to put on airs; she came with airs. If she offered to carry your pastry to your friend, you wouldn't dare not let her. But if she didn't offer, you'd never think to trouble her for it. You see what I mean?"

"I do. But is it not a bit extreme to suggest that Miss Baxter would never say that someone asked her to do something?" This time Mrs. Watson did not look back at Miss Charlotte. She'd become accustomed to the young woman's extraordinary perspicacity, but she herself was no slouch at reading people and making inferences. "What *really* made you uneasy, Mrs. Felton?"

Mrs. Felton moved closer to Mrs. Watson and lowered her voice, even though there was no one else on the open headland, and the walls of the Garden, though much closer than they had been earlier, were still half a mile in the distance. "Well, it's Mrs. Crosby, you see. She's quite the mimic. Once, in summer, I realized that I'd left behind my new tippet in her cottage. The front window was open, and as I came up the walkway I heard a conversation between her and several other women, planning a picnic on the beach in a nearby cove. I heard Miss Ellery, Mrs. Steele, and even Miss Baxter. I remember being mighty surprised that Miss Baxter was there. Because I was so surprised, I even remembered what she said. 'You'll just get dozens of sand fleas in your nice lobster salad. And you'll be clearing sand out of your clothes for weeks to come.'

"But when I got close enough to look into the window, the parlor was empty except for Mrs. Crosby and Mr. Peters. He was chuckling as she said, in Miss Ellery's voice, 'Sand fleas, my goodness. How I detest sand fleas.'"

"So you think on that occasion it wasn't Miss Baxter speaking but Mrs. Crosby playing a role?"

"I don't know. I really don't know." Mrs. Felton's face scrunched up. "It makes me feel strange—like having ants crawl all over my feet—to talk about it. To even think about it."

"But you do suspect that perhaps Miss Baxter has disappeared and Mrs. Crosby is helping to cover it up?" came Miss Charlotte's inexorable question.

A gust blew. Mrs. Watson shivered and slapped a hand over her hat.

Mrs. Felton, too, shuddered. "I suppose that must be it. Isn't that why her family wanted me to keep an eye on her in the first place? Because they worried that someone in the Garden might do away with her?

"And then I ask myself if I've gone completely mad. I cleaned Miss Baxter's lodge this week. The hairs I sweep up, I'm sure they belong to Miss Baxter. Her hair is auburn. No one else here has hair that exact same color. And since I've been wondering whether she's still there, I've been paying attention.

"Her pillow looks like it's been slept on. There is more hair around her vanity chair than elsewhere in the house. There are long strands and some little strands—you know, exactly how it is with hair."

At this contradictory evidence, Mrs. Watson's head throbbed. A hand settled on her shoulder. She looked back. It was Miss Charlotte, who had at last shifted in her seat so that she faced the front—and the approaching Garden of Hermopolis, whose high walls, painted by sunset, had become redder and more ominous-looking.

"You are stating, Mrs. Felton, that the distribution of Miss Baxter's hair very much accords with the natural patterns you've noticed over the years," said she.

"Yes, that's what I'm saying." Mrs. Felton turned toward them, her brows knit together. "I'm all confused as to what's going on. It's awfully strange that I've only heard her voice but not seen her for so long. But if I look at some other evidence, it seems like she's right there, living as safely and as peaceably as she's done for as long as I've been working at the Garden!"

# Ten

When Mrs. Watson first saw the inside of the Garden of Hermopolis, she thought of a fortified medieval village, the kind one might come across in the French countryside, with dwellings packed together in the shadow of high walls and residents who peered warily at tourists from behind drawn curtains.

But now that she and Miss Charlotte had spent some time settling in at their assigned cottage and were once again walking across the Garden, the impression of a medieval village had receded—the dwellings here were nowhere near crowded enough. Rather, the Garden appeared as what it was, a collection of buildings and architectural elements that had been accumulated pell-mell over the years, intended for vastly different purposes by vastly different people.

At the approximate center of the enclosed space was a largish building, likely the original farmhouse, which now served as both the Garden's sanctuary and its library. Behind it—to the west—was the kitchen building and not far to the north stood a smaller edifice with a peaked roof, the Garden's meditation cabin.

Around these communal buildings were scattered fifteen or so freestanding houses in three rough clusters—mostly small cottages, and a few larger ones referred to as lodges. The cluster that included Miss Baxter's lodge occupied the northwest quadrant of the compound. The moorland in these parts tilted toward the sea. In the days before the walls had been built, houses in that cluster would have enjoyed the most commanding panoramic views.

Mrs. Watson and Miss Charlotte's cottage, in a different cluster, was situated almost diagonally across the compound at its southeast corner, with the communal buildings, alas, blocking much of the direct line of sight toward Miss Baxter's lodge.

Mrs. Watson did not consider that a coincidence.

But from their cottage they *were* able to see the third cluster of dwellings, where Miss Fairchild lived, toward which they were now headed on smooth stone paths, their cloaks whipping in the dusk.

Overhead clouds covered half the sky; where it remained clear, pinpricks of cold starlight shimmered. It was dark enough that Mrs. Watson would have had trouble seeing the sea and the moorland even without the walls blocking her sight. But the walls were there, a greater darkness in all directions, and they made the place, with its increasingly fierce crosscurrents of wind, feel airless.

Earlier, as they'd unloaded their luggage and entered their cottage, the weight of attention from the Garden's unseen residents had stifled. But now, with at least half the houses lit and no one at the windows watching the two newcomers wending across the grounds, lanterns swinging, the lack of attention was just as disconcerting.

"I don't know whether I'm feeling Moriarty's long shadow, the machinations of the residents of the Garden, or merely the changing weather," she brooded. "Which one makes your heart palpitate, your spine tingle, and your joints ache?"

"But leaves your sense of humor intact?" murmured Miss Charlotte, pulling her cloak tighter about herself. "You can handle it, ma'am, whatever it is."

Mrs. Watson hoped so, although by the time she shook hands with their hostesses, she also had icy fingers, to go along with all the other symptoms of nervousness.

Miss Fairchild was a tiny bird of a woman, with hair that was more salt than pepper, and a direct gaze that revealed little. Miss Ellery, much taller and rounder, hovered around Miss Fairchild with great solicitude, adjusting the latter's shawl as she offered words of welcome.

"Miss Fairchild regrets that she cannot speak to you as she wishes," she added. "She suffers from a painful condition of the voice cord and has been advised by her physician to be on silence rest."

The dossier from Moriarty included a section on the residents of the Garden, which mentioned that Miss Fairchild was rarely heard from and that Miss Ellery, her companion, served as her deputy in the day-to-day operations.

Their parlor certainly did not make one think that the two women who lived here either founded or ran a pagan religious community. Were it not for Miss Fairchild's travel souvenirs—a large silver samovar on its own plinth, a pair of boomerangs with incised patterns—the place would be just watercolors, framed embroidery, and bouquets of silk flowers, pretty but too ordinary for a second glance.

"We are sorry to hear of your affliction, Miss Fairchild," said Mrs. Watson. "We hope your recovery will be quick and complete."

"That is very much our hope, too," said Miss Ellery. "Did you have a smooth trip, ladies? Is your cottage to your liking? And did Mr. Hudson not come with you?"

The number of visitors had been reported to de Lacey, who would have passed on the information to the Garden.

"We did have a pleasant trip. We find our cottage very soothing. And my nephew had a few other matters to see to, but should be joining us later tonight." Mrs. Watson inclined her head. "We are very thankful that you have graciously permitted us to experience the peace and enchantment of the Garden."

Thanks to her years on the stage, she managed to maintain an even tone and an amiable smile. The smiles she received from their hostesses were a little stiff, but Miss Ellery said gamely, "We hope you will enjoy your stay. And that you will find the peace and enchantment you seek."

Seats were offered and glasses of sherry passed around. Miss Charlotte raised her glass and said, "We look forward to meeting everyone in the community."

Her statement was uttered brightly, but Mrs. Watson winced on the inside. Moriarty had placed them in an impossible position: Unless they put a firearm to Miss Fairchild's head and demanded that she produce Miss Baxter, whatever they said would always ring false.

And in this particular instance, even sound a tad threatening.

Miss Ellery cleared her throat. "The community, at the moment, is a bit thin. Some of our members are visiting friends and family, others are making scholarly inquiries at universities here and abroad."

*Why? Have they already fled ahead of anticipated trouble? Or were they "indisposed," like Miss Baxter?*

Miss Charlotte set aside her sherry glass. "Did the previous occupant of our cottage undertake such a trip?"

"Mr. Craddock?" said Miss Ellery. "No, the Angelino brothers went to the University of Palermo and Mr. Craddock took their cottage. It has a view of the fruit trees espaliered against the inside of the wall."

With such a spectacular panorama outside, inside the compound the residents were reduced to looking at fruit trees? Mrs. Watson almost asked whether Mr. Craddock had faced competition for the view, but she was preempted by Miss Holmes, who said, "May I ask how many are present as we speak?"

"Fourteen, Miss Fairchild and myself included. Mrs. Crosby, Mr. and Mrs. Steele, Dr. Robinson, and Mr. Peters you will meet tonight. There's also Miss Stoppard, Mr. Craddock, Mr. McEwan— and Miss Baxter, of course. Besides them, we also have Mrs. Brown, our cook; Abby Hurley, her kitchen maid; and John Spackett, who looks after the horses and the carriage and the grounds, too."

Fourteen was also the number given in the dossier. And the names Miss Ellery listed accorded with those provided by Mrs. Felton, who worked at the Garden but lived in her own house in Porthangan.

"Did you say that several of the other residents will be coming here, too?" asked Mrs. Watson. "Oh, but I'm happy to hear that. I adore a good getting-acquainted dinner."

She might as well sail full speed ahead on winds of hypocritical agreeableness.

"I want to be clear that this dinner will be an exception, rather than the rule. We do not socialize much, even among ourselves," said Miss Ellery apologetically. "Our community is one for quiet contemplation, rather than vigorous interaction."

Miss Fairchild, beside her, nodded slowly.

Mrs. Watson put on a crestfallen expression. "Oh, are we not to expect regular communal dinners then?"

Miss Ellery rose and crossed to the other side of the parlor. "Our door is always open to anyone in the mood for a cup of tea, but no one else at the Garden is obliged to entertain."

"No, no, I didn't mean that. I simply thought that members of the Garden would dine together, much as the faculty and students of a college would in their refectory."

"I see." Miss Ellery returned with a dark blue shawl and smoothed it over Miss Fairchild's lap. "It might be more helpful to think of us as a monastic order devoted to study and contemplation. And as such, the atmosphere is ruminative, rather than boisterous. Silence is greatly valued."

Mrs. Watson already knew, from the dossier, that the residents did not partake of luncheon together. As luncheon had always been the afterthought among meals, it made sense to inquire about dinner. But how truthful was Miss Ellery's answer? Was the tradition of dining separately long established or solely for the benefit of intruders sent by Moriarty?

She glanced at Miss Charlotte, but the young woman's thoughts had gone in a different direction.

"Would it not aid in the members' peaceful contemplation," she asked, "to have views of the headland and the sea from their windows? I hear that a sweeping panorama of natural beauty is of the utmost benefit to those living a meditative life."

"You mean, demolish the walls?" Miss Ellery's eyes widened. She hadn't returned to her own seat, but stood beside Miss Fairchild's. "But all anyone needs to do for panoramic views is to climb to the top of the walls, or to walk out of the Garden."

Miss Fairchild raised her hand toward Miss Ellery, as if beckoning her to say more.

Miss Ellery bit her lower lip. "Not to mention, the walls sometimes do what walls are supposed to do and keep us safe from intruders."

Mrs. Watson felt her fingers tighten around her sherry glass. "Oh?"

"It was this past December. Miss Stoppard, while taking a stroll inside the Garden one evening, heard a thud upon the wall. As she was near one of the access ladders, she climbed up for a look, only to see a grappling hook, of all things, and below it, a gentleman climbing up with all his might."

As she spoke, Miss Ellery gazed at Miss Charlotte and Mrs. Watson by turn. As did Miss Fairchild, her eyes piercing. Mrs. Watson's pulse raced. She could only hope her expression gave away nothing besides polite concern.

"A local youth?" asked Miss Charlotte, thoroughly unbothered by those searching looks.

She wore a lilac dinner gown with a matching lilac turban and would have looked like a porcelain doll come to life, almost unspeakably darling, but for that imperturbableness, a non-reaction that, under the circumstances, felt as aggressive as a bared blade.

"Oddly enough, we do not think so." Miss Ellery's voice took on an edge. "One of our residents followed the intruder and saw the latter jump onto an express train that had slowed down, but not stopped, near a railway station. The train was headed to Plymouth. Doesn't seem like something a local youth would do, does it? There are plenty of places to hide around here. We cannot peer into every nook and cranny. A local youth merely needs to secrete himself in a small cave or behind a crag until we weary of our search."

"Hmm," said Miss Charlotte. "If not a curious thief, who do you think that might have been then?"

Miss Ellery glanced at Miss Fairchild. When the latter nodded, she said, "The consensus in the Garden is that our would-be intruder was an emissary of Miss Baxter's father."

Mrs. Watson's heart thudded. Moriarty had entered the conversation.

"Miss Baxter?" said Miss Charlotte, as if she'd never heard the name before.

"Yes, our member Miss Baxter. We value her greatly. Alas, her father is the overbearing, interfering sort. She is a grown woman who joined our community after she came of age. We are a collection of seekers who have no quarrels with the world or with one another. But judging by Mr. Baxter's conduct, you would think we'd abducted Miss Baxter into a den of iniquity."

Miss Ellery stepped away from Miss Fairchild's chair, as if her agitation had become too great for her to remain in the same place. "The first time she joined our community, he forcefully extricated her, threatening all sorts of dire nonsense if we didn't let her leave— as if we would ever keep anyone here against their will. When she returned, it was under ridiculous conditions, the most onerous being that we must admit his solicitor into the Garden, so that this man could speak to Miss Baxter and ascertain for himself that she was in tolerable shape. Not to mention, Miss Baxter's annual contribution to the Garden was capped, never to increase, as if we'd ever increased the amount wantonly for anyone else."

Her grievances sounded very real. And very trivial, in light of what could be happening behind the scenes. But to Miss Ellery they seemed to be of world-shaking importance. Her face had grown red, her eyes overbright, a tiny strand of hair had even escaped her neat coiffure, to add to the general picture of righteous indignation.

"To have imposed all those conditions upon us, which no one else has ever had the gall to do," Miss Ellery was still ranting, her index finger jabbing in the air, "and then to turn around and try to spy on us? What is the matter with that man?"

A bravura performance. Were she venting to anyone else, Mrs. Watson would not have doubted her sentiments. But she railed against the very man who had sent Mrs. Watson and Miss Charlotte, and therefore Mrs. Watson must consider it a performance. Animated by real sentiments, possibly, but a show put on for their benefit nevertheless.

*We cannot stop you two from coming into the Garden. But by God we will not take this lying down, and we will denounce your paymaster to your face most vigorously and at every turn.*

Miss Charlotte smoothed her skirts. "Miss Ellery, did you personally witness Miss Baxter's father forcibly extricating her from the Garden?"

Miss Ellery blinked. "Ah, at the time I had not joined the Garden yet. But what I related just now was told to me by none other than Miss Baxter herself."

"I see. And what *do* you suppose was Mr. Baxter's reason for sending an intruder all of a sudden?"

Miss Ellery gave her a wary look, as if suspecting a trap. "We asked ourselves the very same question. Someone came to see Miss Baxter on his behalf only the month before. Granted, it was a different gentleman who came that time. But he had the correct letter of introduction and he followed all the usual procedures. It made no sense that Mr. Baxter should have been satisfied in November but sent someone to commit espionage in December.

"Mrs. Crosby said Miss Baxter was as baffled as anyone else. And we were all most disconcerted when yet another gentleman showed up some weeks later, claiming that he, and not the person who came in November, truly represented Mr. Baxter."

"Did Miss Baxter not know either of them?" asked Miss Charlotte. Her expression betrayed no disbelief, yet every syllable radiated skepticism.

Miss Ellery, in response, went to fetch a cushion to place behind Miss Fairchild's back—she seemed to perform these services not because Miss Fairchild needed them, but as an outlet for her own nerves. "Miss Baxter did not know either man. She did not, in fact, meet with this second caller. But when he was received by Mrs. Crosby, Miss Baxter was in the next room. And when he was gone, she was highly upset. Later Mrs. Crosby told us that Miss Baxter feared something was terribly wrong."

Miss Charlotte raised a brow. "Because two different men she didn't know had been sent to see her?"

"That, and they both carried letters of introduction written by her father, yet the second 'solicitor' claimed that the first one must be counterfeit."

Mrs. Watson was confused. She raised her glass to her lips. "In such situations, shouldn't she have met the second 'solicitor,' too?"

Miss Ellery, now once again standing beside Miss Fairchild's chair, lifted her chin a fraction of an inch, looking triumphant. "According to Mrs. Crosby, who heard all this from Miss Baxter, the last time a different person was 'sent' by her father, Miss Baxter was kidnapped."

Mrs. Watson stopped sipping her sherry. "Goodness gracious! How terrifying that must have been!"

But also, what a wonderful explanation for Miss Baxter's refusal to meet with anyone sent by her father, if her fellow acolytes had indeed done away with her. Had Miss Ellery or Miss Fairchild come up with this fanciful tale?

"Kidnapping . . ." murmured Miss Charlotte, sounding even more unconvinced.

Miss Ellery went to her own chair and braced her hands on top, as if that would lend her words greater authority. "Miss Baxter was a child then. Her grandmother had just passed away and she was waiting for her father's people to come and take her to him on the Continent. A woman who wasn't the one who had visited her regularly on her father's behalf showed up and said that the other was unfortunately unwell, so she had been sent in her stead. Like the one before her, she presented proper credentials and took charge of Miss Baxter. They traveled to London, then crossed the Channel. But there was a telegram waiting for them at their hotel in Paris, saying that Mr. Baxter had some business in Greece and would they please join him there instead? So from Paris, they went to Marseille and got on a boat for Athens.

"In Athens they disembarked and toured the sites of antiquity. But after a week or two they left again, this time in a smaller vessel that made a leisurely tour of the Aegean Sea, then up the Dardanelles to the Sea of Marmara, then ultimately Constantinople. Her third day in Constantinople, Miss Baxter woke up alone in her hotel room. The woman who had been looking after her was gone. She waited and waited. She was a young woman of great fortitude. So instead of telling anyone that something was wrong, she simply ordered food to be brought up and left outside the door.

"Two days passed and on the third morning her father arrived, took her in his arms, and informed her that he and his men had been seeking her with all their might. Because the woman who had taken her from her grandmother's had not been sent by him at all but was a kidnapper who had made a huge ransom demand.

"He had paid the ransom by wire immediately, but it was only weeks later that he was told to come to Constantinople to retrieve her. Needless to say, all this was tremendously confusing and disturbing for young Miss Baxter. Many years have passed since the incident, and she stopped fearing for her safety, but when that second man came, she was forced to relive that entire episode and she could not help but be distressed."

Two seconds after Miss Ellery had finished, Mrs. Watson realized that her jaw hung slack. She closed her mouth and glanced at Miss Charlotte, who folded her hands together in her lap in a gesture of great primness.

Mrs. Watson had previously considered herself an expert at gauging truthfulness. After Lady Ingram had come to them with a sorrowful tale that had later proved entirely false, she'd become a little more mistrustful of her judgment, knowing that she could be carried away by her own sympathetic nature.

But this thirdhand account, even refracted via the prism of her newfound cynicism, had a ring of truth to it. Perhaps it was Constantinople as the apogee of the flight, perhaps it was the detailed itinerary, but Mrs. Watson found herself close to believing that Miss Baxter had truly been whisked away as a child and taken on a memorable, if sinister, grand tour.

"Does Miss Baxter believe that the same people who kidnapped her years ago are back to make more trouble?" mused Miss Charlotte.

"According to Mrs. Crosby, Miss Baxter does not know. All she would say to Mrs. Crosby was that her father is a powerful man, but has dangerous and equally powerful enemies. And that she once again fears for her own safety."

Miss Charlotte's gaze swept over their hostesses. "Do you suppose that her father might also be worried for her safety, especially if the second solicitor that came was the real one and she refused to see him?"

Miss Ellery puffed her chest out. "Mrs. Crosby asked her the same, and she said that she must concentrate on her own safety above all and that if her father was alive and well and in charge of his own movement, he would come to see her himself and she would learn everything from his own lips. Until then, she must view with suspicion anyone who claims to have been dispatched by her father."

❖

Since Mrs. Watson and Miss Charlotte were very much Moriarty's emissaries, at Miss Ellery's righteous declaration, the conversation came to a dead halt.

Fortunately, at that moment, a knock came at the front door.

Miss Ellery, who answered the door, brought back four people, introduced as Mr. and Mrs. Steele, Dr. Robinson, and Mr. Peters.

Mrs. Watson took a deep breath. Upon meeting Mrs. Felton, it had become clear that despite de Lacey's assertions otherwise, the rather naïve Mrs. Felton couldn't possibly be Moriarty's only eyes and ears inside the Garden. Who else worked for Moriarty? Was it one of these four new arrivals?

Dr. Robinson, a tall, dignified man of around sixty, laughed easily. Mr. Steele had wire-rimmed glasses and a scholarly air; Mrs. Steele's ornate coiffure, twisted, braided, and studded with pearls, made Mrs. Watson wonder if the woman badly missed ordinary society. Mr. Peters, probably a year or two younger than Miss Charlotte, had a mop of brown curls and charming features. Had he appeared at a London function during the Season, young ladies would have flocked to him.

They greeted Charlotte and Mrs. Watson with a mixture of curiosity and caution, and inquired after the absent "Mr. Hudson," not very different from how anyone would react, in a small isolated community, to a sudden influx of new people.

The rattan-and-leather baskets they'd carried in, on the other hand . . .

At Mrs. Watson's quizzical look, Mrs. Steele said, in an eager-to-please tone, "Oh, has no one explained to you about the baskets yet, ladies? You see, since we do not practice communal dining, the kitchen instead prepares baskets. They are to be picked up for luncheon or dinner at the kitchen, or Mrs. Brown's assistant can deliver them—and collect them again later—for a small fee."

Another knock came at the door. "Ah, that must be baskets for this lodge," said Miss Ellery to Mrs. Watson.

She brought back with her not only baskets but also a tall, stately woman of about thirty. The woman wore a lovely dinner gown of copper velvet and strode forward with a commanding demeanor.

Mrs. Watson's breath caught.

Miss Baxter, in the flesh?

But the resemblance was only in the general shape of her face. The woman was introduced as Mrs. Crosby. Mrs. Watson noticed the wedding ring she wore on a chain around her neck. Mrs. Watson, too, carried her old wedding ring as a pendant, though hers was hidden beneath layers of clothes, close to her heart.

True to their claims of insularity, Miss Fairchild and Miss Ellery's dining table, even after its leaf had been inserted, seated only six. Dr. Robinson and Mrs. Crosby joined the hostesses and the visitors at the table, while the Steeles pulled up a pair of chairs to the sideboard, and Mr. Peters simply set his basket on his lap.

At the table the baskets were opened. The hearty aroma of a meaty stew filled the air. Mrs. Watson had to admire the baskets, which had been made with the precision of good luggage, with pockets for utensils and condiments, and belts and buckles holding down various containers, preventing their lids from sliding off during transport.

Miss Ellery took out an urn-shaped container from one of the baskets and placed it before Mrs. Watson and Charlotte. She turned the dome-shaped lid over and said, "In households with two people, the lid serves as the bowl for one resident and the crock for the other."

The flatware, curiously enough, was of wood. And only wood spoons, which turned out to be all that was needed for the beef and mushroom ragout, and the carrots and peas besides. Miss Charlotte, who wanted a slice of bread, found a wooden spreader for the butter.

"I like these utensils," she said. "They are simple but elegant."

"Thank you," answered Mr. Peters immediately. "I made them."

"Indeed," said Mrs. Crosby, looking at him fondly. "Mr. Peters has the most dexterous and skillful hands."

Mr. Peters received her compliment with a gleeful, dimpled smile. "Thank you, lovely lady. I find that woodwork aids in contemplation, which is what most of us are here for."

His words were spoken to Mrs. Crosby, but their intended recipients were no doubt Miss Charlotte and Mrs. Watson—who else needed the reminder that this was a quasi-religious community?

Miss Charlotte helped herself to a spoonful of carrots. "Speaking of contemplation, I am terribly curious about how the disciples of Hermes Trismegistus present tonight found their way to his teachings. Will you tell us a little of your journeys?"

The residents of the Garden all looked toward Miss Fairchild. Miss Ellery, at her nod, said, "Miss Fairchild had a travel companion for many years, a bosom friend who was the first to come across the teachings of Hermes Trismegistus. Her devotion eventually influenced Miss Fairchild to also take an interest. The friend passed away in the course of their final voyage, and the Garden of Hermopolis is as much dedicated to her as it is to other learners on the same path.

"As for myself, I am only Miss Fairchild's companion and assistant—Christmas and Easter you might even find me at the nearest church. I cannot speak with any authority on Hermetic teachings, but I believe that Miss Fairchild is the best person I know, and the teachings that she espouses must therefore also be good and admirable."

"Hear, hear," said Mr. Peters and Dr. Robinson together.

Dr. Robinson smoothed his neckcloth and confessed that he was also not interested in Hermetism, but the community wished to have a physician on hand and he was happy to live among such agreeable folks in his old age, being irreligious enough to have no quarrels with their pagan beliefs.

The Steeles came to Hermetism because Mrs. Steele's father had been a minister interested in pre-Christian thoughts. Mr. Peters had studied the history of medieval alchemy and found that mentions of Hermes Trismegitus peppered almost all the important alchemical writings.

"My late husband was a man of many and varied interests and collected books accordingly," said Mrs. Crosby, her fingers on the wedding ring she wore as a pendant. "But I didn't attempt to familiarize myself with his books until after he'd passed away. Perhaps it was my new widowhood, but when I read 'All upon Earth is alterable,' that single sentence took my breath away."

Her fellow acolytes nodded solemnly. Miss Ellery, seated beside her, even gave her a gentle pat on the arm. Mrs. Watson, who had lost a husband in a sudden and devastating blow, felt her eyes mist and had to remind herself that everyone in the compound was a potential murderer and poisoner, including this elegant young widow.

Miss Charlotte concentrated on her stew and let the moment pass, before returning to her informal interrogation. "Can anyone here tell me how Miss Baxter came to the Hermetic teachings?"

At the mention of Miss Baxter's name, there seemed to be a collective pause of . . . *embarrassment?* Mr. Steele turned his spoon over, Mrs. Steele cleared her throat, Miss Ellery scratched herself just under the ear.

But there was also Mrs. Crosby, her cool gaze aimed squarely at Miss Charlotte, and Mr. Peters, whose appealing face took on a hard edge far more swiftly than Mrs. Watson would have thought possible.

"Miss Baxter isn't one for chitchats, you see," said Mrs. Steele apologetically. "At least I have never been able to wrangle her into a proper conversation."

"Nor I," said Miss Ellery with an air of regret. "I have asked Miss Fairchild the same question, but Miss Fairchild also doesn't know the origin of Miss Baxter's devotion."

Miss Fairchild shook her head slowly, as if to underscore Miss Ellery's answer.

Mrs. Crosby sat back in her chair. "I don't know how Miss Baxter came to the teachings, but she once gave me a handkerchief embroidered with *That which is sown is not always begotten; but that which is begotten always is sown.* When I asked her why she had chosen that quote in particular, she said that it reminded her of her grandmother, who was a great believer in justice."

She spoke not with pride at her greater knowledge of the enigmatic Miss Baxter, but with the straightforwardness of someone giving directions to a lost traveler.

Miss Charlotte took a leisurely sip of water. "When did anyone here last see Miss Baxter?"

Another awkward pause.

"Not for months," said Miss Ellery. "I daresay I haven't seen her since September."

"Probably about the same time for us," said Mr. Steele. Then, at his wife: "Would you not say, my dear?"

Mrs. Steele nodded. "That's correct, my dear."

"Miss Fairchild," asked Miss Charlotte, "have you seen her since September, when you stayed with her on a day she wasn't feeling well?"

Miss Fairchild shook her head.

"I saw her this past week," said Mr. Peters breezily. "I was out for a stroll in the small hours of the night and she happened to be out and about, too. She was headed back inside, or I'd have escorted her on the rest of her walk."

Mrs. Watson stared at him, unable to conceal her astonishment.

Miss Charlotte cocked her head. "How did she look?"

"It was dark, but she looked fine to me."

"Funny you should mention her late-night stroll. I also saw her this week," said Dr. Robinson with an easy demeanor, "to consult on her insomnia, of all things. She has a strong disdain for laudanum and wanted to know whether I had anything else that could help her. But she also rejected cannabis, chloral, and potassium bromide. In the end I recommended greater activity. In my experience there is no one who doesn't sleep soundly after a ten-mile walk. But I most certainly didn't advise her to do so at night."

Mrs. Watson had not expected this corroboration. *Robinson.* Robinson was a most English name, yet she thought she heard a trace of a Continental accent in his speech.

"I saw her today itself," said Mrs. Crosby.

Mrs. Watson had to suppress an urge to bang her hand on the table and shout, *Now this is going too far!*

"Is her insomnia better?" inquired Dr. Robinson immediately.

Mrs. Crosby shrugged. "She detests questions concerning her health, especially when something about it displeases her, so I didn't ask. But she was cross about her father sending outsiders to the Garden."

"Most understandable," said Miss Charlotte amiably, as if she weren't one of those loathsome outsiders. "Is there pudding, by the way?"

It took everyone in the room, including Mrs. Watson, a moment to understand that the topic had moved on from Miss Baxter.

"Yes," said Miss Ellery, "there should be a nice suet pudding. Mrs. Brown has a way with boiled puddings."

"Oh, I adore a good boiled pudding," said Miss Charlotte.

Miss Ellery showed Miss Charlotte how to retrieve the pudding container from a basket. Of the others in the room, only Mrs. Crosby and Mr. Peters also dug into their puddings. Mr. Peters had the air of someone who simply needed more food, but Mrs. Crosby seemed to enjoy her pudding as much as Miss Charlotte did, issuing a small sigh after her first spoonful.

For some time, the three ate, and the rest, drinking tea and coffee brought around by Miss Ellery, watched them with varying degrees of uncertainty.

Mrs. Crosby set down her spoon with another sigh. "Mrs. Watson, Miss Holmes, Mr. Peters and I plan to visit the sanctuary after dinner. It's a tradition at the Garden to offer one's gratitude there after a safe return from a trip outside. The sanctuary doesn't open for many other occasions. But since we are going, would you care to join us? I would hate for you to leave without having seen its lovely interior."

"Why, thank you!" said Mrs. Watson, her surprise genuine. Was this the sanctuary the inside of which Mrs. Felton had never seen, despite her years of service? "We did not expect this privilege, but I assure you we are most appreciative of the opportunity."

"Do be forewarned that the sanctuary is hardly mysterious. It was once the mess hall, when these cottages and lodges were intended as part of a seaside resort. We've made it prettier on the inside, but there are no arcane objects or phenomena to be had."

"I enjoy a séance as an entertaining way to pass an evening, but please rest assured that I did not come to the Garden expecting the occult," Miss Charlotte answered gravely.

Mrs. Crosby smiled. "Indeed, we have none of that here, only good people gathered together in search of the inner light."

# Eleven

The inside of the former mess hall had been painted blue. The color began as an aquamarine that reminded Mrs. Watson of the clear beach-lapping waters of the Mediterranean, and gradually darkened as the eye traveled upward. Aquamarine, sky blue, twilight blue, and at last, overhead, midnight blue, with constellations and their associated astrological signs depicted in gold.

The hall was oriented so that its long side faced the sea. Without the walls it would have offered a good panoramic view. But now all the windows were covered with thick curtains, a dark blue outer one and an inner one that was gold-flecked gauze.

The place felt romantic to Mrs. Watson. True, she was a romantic soul. But skies and stars and candlelight, who could object? Why, if one of these days, Miss Olivia married her dear Mr. Marbleton, Mrs. Watson could make her a wedding bower like this. Maybe not blue and gold but blue and silver. How lovely it would be, a ceiling full of silver stars overhanging a bed covered in blue silk and strewn with blush-colored petals. And—

"The eye is interesting," murmured Miss Charlotte.

Mrs. Watson came out of her reverie. What eye? Miss Charlotte had her head craned back, looking directly overhead. Mrs. Watson, who was a little older, heard her neck creak like an insufficiently lubricated hinge as she, too, tilted up her chin so that the back of her head nearly paralleled the floor.

She almost fell in a heap.

What she'd earlier taken to be perhaps the sun at its zenith was in fact the pupil of an enormous eye.

The eye stared down at her. At first it appeared expressionless, as blank as those of stone statues. Yet the more she stared at it, the more coldly and malevolently it seemed to stare back, until she wrenched her gaze away, her heart thudding.

"An all-seeing eye," said Miss Charlotte, with a tone someone else might use to say *Another overcast day*, in the middle of an English winter.

Mrs. Watson, still unnerved, looked about for something less objectionable on which to rest her attention.

Directly beneath the eye stood a large altar shaped like a gourd, potbellied at the bottom, cinching in roughly three-fifths of the way up, and then bulging out a little again. After a moment she realized that it was meant to be a representation of the cucurbit, the lower portion of an alembic.

A canopy had been erected above the top of the cucurbit. Mrs. Watson stepped a little closer and asked with some hope, "Is the altar, by chance, shielded from the all-seeing eye?"

"Indeed not," answered Mr. Peters who, alongside Mrs. Crosby, was lighting fat candles set on columns that rose four and a half feet from the floor. The columns were arranged in two concentric circles, two dozen in all, with the cucurbit altar at their center. "There is another iteration of the eye on the bottom of the canopy."

Nothing occult, eh? Nothing occult, her foot. Mrs. Watson was beginning to yearn for a heavy cross to wave about.

When Mr. Peters and Mrs. Crosby finished illuminating the sanctuary, they bowed to each other and then to the altar.

"Now this next bit might seem a bit . . . unnecessary," said Mrs. Crosby, "but it is simply part of the homecoming ceremony, during which those who have returned and those who have kept the fires of transformation burning in their absence unite to reaffirm their allegiance to the cause and to one another."

Mrs. Watson forced a smile. "Please do not be hindered by our presence."

A low table had been set before the altar with cushions to either side. Mr. Peters placed a large chalice on the table and poured what looked to be wine into it. Mrs. Crosby set an oil lamp beside the chalice. Now the two knelt down on cushions on opposite sides of the table and bowed to each other again.

Mr. Peters handed Mrs. Crosby a slender instrument. Mrs. Crosby passed the tip of the implement several times through the flame of the oil lamp and then jabbed it into the palm of her other hand.

Mrs. Watson's gasp echoed in the sanctuary.

She gripped Miss Charlotte's arm as Mrs. Crosby held her hand above the chalice. A drop of dark liquid fell inside. Mrs. Crosby passed the instrument back to Mr. Peters, who heated it in the lamp flame for two seconds and did the same to his own hand, squeezing out a drop of blood for the chalice.

*Surely* . . . the thought bounced wildly in Mrs. Watson's head, *surely they aren't going to* . . .

But they did. They shared the wine, emptying the chalice with three draughts each.

It wasn't until Miss Charlotte caught her hand that Mrs. Watson realized that she was rubbing her stomach in an agitated manner, trying to calm her nausea.

Mrs. Crosby and Mr. Peters wrapped their injured hands with handkerchiefs and bowed to each other one last time. Mr. Peters rose and carried away the empty chalice, the oil lamp, and the pick. Mrs. Crosby got up more slowly and smiled at the interlopers.

"As I said, ladies, a simple little ceremony."

---

"A simple little ceremony?" fumed Mrs. Watson. "They were only this far from human sacrifice."

She held her thumb and index finger a bare inch apart.

She and Miss Charlotte were walking the yarrow-lined path that surrounded the former dining hall. Mr. Peters had—maliciously, in Mrs. Watson's opinion—inquired whether they wished to see the library and the meditation cabin and Miss Charlotte had leaped at the chance. But out of consideration for Mrs. Watson, she had said that they would wait outside while Mr. Peters and Mrs. Crosby finished cleaning up inside the sanctuary.

In fact, she'd told Mrs. Watson that she needn't come with them, but Mrs. Watson, as much as she wanted to be gone, refused to leave the girl alone with two unpredictable occultists.

"Were I anticipating human sacrifice, I'd have been sorely disappointed," said Miss Charlotte with her customary sangfroid. "There wasn't even a beheaded chicken in the mix."

"They drank their own—and each other's—blood." Mrs. Watson shuddered. The sight made her not want to have wine ever again and she loved a glass of good claret.

Miss Charlotte remained unexcited. "Conceptually it isn't that different from the Eucharist."

"But the Eucharist isn't done with the collected vital fluids of the congregation!"

Mrs. Watson managed to keep her voice down to a whisper, but she couldn't help the movement of her arms. The light from her lantern, a circle of weak coppery glimmer, jerked to and fro as she gesticulated wildly.

"At least we've now seen the inside of the sanctuary. I no longer need to find a way to break into it without getting caught."

Mrs. Watson sighed. Miss Charlotte had mentioned, once upon a time, that Miss Olivia did not find her a very satisfying partner in the airing of grievances: She frequently failed to vindicate Miss Olivia's passionate feelings of dissatisfaction.

Mrs. Watson tried to explain herself better. "I don't think it's the blood and whatnot that I mind the most—although I do mind it greatly—it's more that I'm now afraid these people might be fanatics under their seemingly rational and civilized veneers. What if they are? And what if Miss Baxter realized it much too late, wished to leave, but couldn't?

"A simple rite of homecoming is already so . . . unconventional. What if there are other rituals that *do* feature the sacrifice of chickens, goats, and such? If word got out, what do you think would happen? I'm not saying that the residents of the Garden would be tarred and feathered, but do you think they'd still be allowed to have their heathen community and their little homecoming ceremonies in peace?"

Before Miss Charlotte could reply, a cheerful voice called out, "Mrs. Watson, Miss Holmes!"

Mr. Peters, coming to them with a sweet smile on his face.

With a similar smile, Miss Charlotte greeted him, "Why, good sir, how do you do? And will Mrs. Crosby not be joining us?"

"Mrs. Crosby wants a minute alone in the sanctuary and then she will be off to call on Miss Baxter, who, I'm sure, will be most interested in hearing her impression of you ladies."

Mrs. Watson had not believed Mrs. Crosby's claim that she saw Miss Baxter this very day. But with Mr. Peters's fluent assertion that she would shortly see Miss Baxter again, Mrs. Watson began to wonder whether her judgment had been too premature—or whether she was somehow responding to the authority with which these lies were being repeated.

"Miss Baxter can take our measure herself," answered Miss Charlotte. "We'll be happy to meet with her anytime."

"All in good time, I'm sure," said Mr. Peters, still smiling. "All in good time."

He indicated the side of the building. "Shall we?"

The former farmhouse had been a larger house and a smaller house divided by a shared wall. The bigger part had been turned into a mess hall and later, the sanctuary. The lesser part, when the place had been intended as a holiday village, had already been a reading room, a place for the guests to sit down with a book or to write letters and postcards to friends and relatives back home. Therefore, when Miss Fairchild took over the property, it had seemed natural to convert the space to a library to house the collection of Hermetic writings that the community intended to acquire.

This, Mr. Peters told them while they walked up to the door. As he put key to lock, Miss Charlotte said, "I'm looking forward to seeing the library—I enjoyed the sanctuary."

*Oh, this girl*, grumbled Mrs. Watson silently. It would be just like her to have sincerely reveled in the spectacle, too.

Once inside, Mr. Peters lit a pair of sconces in quick succession, and Mrs. Watson very nearly stumbled at the sight of an enormous skull with a serpent emerging from one empty eye socket and a nearly naked young woman held between the grinning teeth.

It was a large painting, six feet wide and eight feet high at the very least, so eerie and macabre that after Mrs. Watson closed her eyes and reopened them, she still had to suppress a gasp: This time she noticed the blood dripping from the skull's other eye socket, which eventually fell into the young woman's long loose golden hair, dying it scarlet, before dripping off again from its tips.

"Fascinating," said Miss Charlotte.

She walked forward. Mrs. Watson, unwilling to go any closer to the painting, but even more unwilling to be left alone, followed closely in her wake. She averted her gaze from the awful image, only to see, on the shelves that lined the walls, between books, manuscripts, and alembics, a great many more skulls, both animal and human.

And now that they stood immediately before the painting, Mrs.

Watson had no choice but to witness the hundreds of tiny skulls that had been set into the large, ornate frame. She recoiled, her stomach feeling rammed through.

Miss Charlotte reached out one gloved finger and caressed the frame. "Are these rat skulls?"

"Indeed they are," answered Mr. Peters, his easy smile remaining in place. Mrs. Watson had the sense that he was mocking her chagrin. "The painting was done by Miss Baxter, by the way, a masterpiece on the human condition and what we must overcome to achieve any measure of transcendence. She was very particular about how it was to be framed, and I had to go into Exeter and find a ratcatcher to obtain the number of skulls needed to cover the frame. But what effect, do you not think?"

"I think so indeed," agreed Miss Charlotte readily. "But surely the other animal skulls did not come from an Exeter ratcatcher."

There was a whole zoo's worth of additional animal skulls, a big cat, a shark, a crocodile, all with their maws open and their sharp teeth pointing out. But these predators Mrs. Watson found less disconcerting than the score or so smaller skulls that must have belonged to cats and dogs.

"Most of those we inherited from Mr. Kaplan, who was an amateur naturalist," answered Mr. Peters.

The name sounded familiar to Mrs. Watson—she had come across it in the dossier. Mr. Kaplan was one of the three who had died in rapid succession several years ago. She'd mentioned the deaths to Miss Charlotte and Lord Ingram, but Miss Charlotte had not thought them necessarily ominous. "The late Mr. Kaplan who passed away from pneumonia?"

"Yes, that estimable gentleman."

"Did he bequeath to you the human skulls, too?"

There were a good dozen, grinning from everywhere. Miss Charlotte, as she asked her question, ran her finger directly over the incomplete teeth of one.

"Most of the human skulls are plaster replicas and will shatter if you drop them," said Mr. Peters. "We only have one that is real—the one you are studying, in fact."

Miss Charlotte lowered her head for a closer look.

"Someone gave it to Dr. Robinson long ago," continued Mr. Peters, "and once he saw the interior of the library, he decided to deposit it here."

Mrs. Watson had been married to a doctor who had boasted not only a plaster skull in his possession but an entire plaster skeleton. When they'd lived in India, her dear John had even kept an excised tumor in a jar of formaldehyde and they had clinked glasses and shared meals in its vicinity. Her niece, too, was a medical student and did not shy away from discussing what she witnessed during her coursework.

Human anatomy, on its own, did not disconcert Mrs. Watson. But here the human skulls did not exist so innocently. She didn't believe Mr. Peters's claim that most were plaster replicas. And if they weren't, whose skulls were they?

She shuddered.

Miss Charlotte at last turned away from the "only" real human skull and swept a hand around the room. "Are skulls particularly important to the study of Hermetism?"

Mr. Peters shook his head. "We had the ambitious plan to fill this place with books and manuscripts, but despite our best efforts, there simply aren't that many works to be acquired. To make the shelves look less empty we began to decorate them with alembic sets. And then, once Miss Baxter's painting was installed, with its abundance of rat skulls, it became natural to add other skulls."

He looked about. "I still wish we had more books, but since we don't, this current collection looks very nice, too. I love spending time here."

This last was said with a happy little sigh that made Mrs. Watson's face feel as stiff as dried glue when she tried to smile.

The meditation cabin was once the chapel for the former holiday compound. Like the sanctuary, it, too, had a painted interior, except the hues were gradients of red, ending in a color on the ceiling that felt uncomfortably like clotted blood. Another eye looked down from the very zenith. Mrs. Watson quickly dropped her gaze, only to see a set of implements reminiscent of what Mrs. Crosby and Mr. Peters had used for their "simple little" homecoming ceremony.

She was, therefore, more than ready to depart from Mr. Peters's company once Miss Charlotte had her fill of the meditation cabin. Mr. Peters, however, issued an invitation. "Would you ladies care to join me for a little promenade on the wall?"

"Oh, could we?" replied Miss Charlotte brightly. "I thought we'd need a special dispensation."

"Of course not. Everyone here is welcome to go up and take in the view." Mr. Peters smiled at her. "The stars can be breathtaking on a clear night. Sometimes the sea shimmers with starlight and I feel as if I am looking upon the very youth of the world, unpolluted by the passage of time or the advance of industry."

Mrs. Watson blinked. Was she mistaken about Mr. Peters's intentions? Was he taking them around not because he wanted to unnerve them but because he wanted to spend time impressing Miss Charlotte?

If Miss Charlotte thought the same, she gave no hint, but only looked up at the clouds that had rolled in since nightfall. "What a shame that there are no stars left tonight. Still, the air will be fresh and bracing up there."

"I shall be delighted by the company, if nothing else," said Mr. Peters, half bowing. "This way, please."

❈

The night had grown sharp. The wind almost whipped off Mrs. Watson's hat.

Mr. Peters led them toward the west. "That's my favorite building, the kitchen. I always go and get my own basket—it's nice to anticipate one's meals. I'm not sure whether you can see it when it's so dark but there's our kitchen garden, of which the gardeners among us are very proud. I'm not a gardener—not yet in any case. But Dr. Robinson is adamant that horticulture will sink its tendrils into every man at some point. Are either of you ladies interested in spring planting?"

Did they plant hemlock here? Or belladonna?

Miss Charlotte shook her head. "Is it already time for spring planting?"

"Not quite, but Dr. Robinson and Miss Ellery have some carrot seeds growing under cloches. And they've already loosened the soil."

They walked all the way to the front gate, to either side of which was a wrought iron ladder sunk into the monstrously high wall. Mrs. Watson, who did not normally fear heights, had to grit her teeth to make herself set foot on the first rung. Two thirds of the way up, when a strong gust blew, she whimpered but kept going.

The top of the parapeted wall was just wide enough for one person. Dresses these days had a narrow profile from the front, so there was a bit of clearance to either side. But if Mrs. Watson were to turn around, the bouffant folds to the rear of her skirt would scrape against the masonry and possibly sustain damage.

So she walked forward in Miss Charlotte's footsteps, one hand on the parapet.

The wind had become fierce; clouds tumbled across the sky like blown fleece—barely visible blown fleece. Inside the compound, half a dozen windows were lit. Little else could be seen. Even on the eastern ramparts, closest to the edge of the cliff, the sea remained a specter that could only be heard, the headlands a dark, silent solidity.

"Lovely," said Miss Charlotte. "It's all lovely. I like how the air smells brinier at night, as if the sea has come closer."

They were back near the front gate, on the western wall. Miss Charlotte had her hand on the side rail of a ladder.

"Indeed," said Mr. Peters. "We are all most fortunate to be here. I have never felt as safe and at peace as I have since I arrived in the Garden. And I am determined to do everything in my power to keep things as they are."

*And not let two women from London muck everything up?*

His gaze flicked over Miss Charlotte, who leaned forward, looking down the length of the ladder. "You should be careful, Miss Holmes. That is a fatal drop."

Mrs. Watson looked sharply at him. Was that a threat?

"My falling over would make no difference in the larger scheme of things," said Miss Charlotte, responding directly to the threat. "Mr. Baxter would simply send someone else."

"No matter how many people he sends, Miss Baxter will outlast them all."

His tone sounded almost childlike in its unshakable faith.

"That is certainly our sincere hope as well," replied Miss Charlotte, her voice cool and calm. "We have no quarrels with either Miss Baxter or the Garden of Hermopolis. We only wish to see that she is safe and sound."

"Well, there she is," said Mr. Peters.

As if on cue, down in the Garden, a dark window glowed from within.

"That's Miss Baxter's bedroom," said Mr. Peters. "And this is the time of the day she usually goes to bed."

Miss Baxter's bedroom window was separated from the interior by only a layer of translucent fabric. A woman's silhouette, clad in a dressing gown, appeared. She shut the heavier outer curtains and they could see no more of her.

# Twelve

Mrs. Watson would have liked to part ways from Mr. Peters as soon as possible. As it turned out, however, they had to spend some more time with him, because at that moment, Miss Charlotte looked to the southwest and said, "Is that a vehicle approaching?"

It was indeed a carriage, the light from its lanterns shining on none other than Lord Ingram, driving himself.

They descended the ladder, Mrs. Watson so fortified by her dear boy's arrival that she barely noticed how far down she had to go or the winds that would peel a gecko from a wall. Mr. Peters opened the solid metal gate. The carriage pulled up and Lord Ingram leaped down from the driver's perch.

Mr. Peters, who must not have a proper sense of Miss Holmes yet, displayed a much greater wariness upon meeting the formidable-looking "Mr. Hudson." Lord Ingram was his usual courteous self, his demeanor one of gentlemanly ease. Of the two, one would have guessed that he was the gracious host, and Mr. Peters, the awkward guest.

The introduction was performed quickly and the small talk took only two minutes, before a sleepy-looking man—the Garden's groom, presumably—came to take charge of horse and carriage. Mr. Peters bowed and walked away.

Lord Ingram, luggage in hand, regarded his departing back. A few seconds later his eyes met Miss Charlotte's, then Mrs. Watson's. He smiled.

A weight lifted from Mrs. Watson. She linked her arm with his and sighed in relief.

He leaned down and kissed her atop her hat. "It's good to see you, ma'am."

And then, after a moment, "You, too, Holmes."

"Let's speak inside," murmured Miss Charlotte.

Mrs. Watson could not see her face, but she heard a smile in the young woman's words.

Ah, but they were not being very secretive, were they? The night before, Mrs. Watson, unable to sleep, had gone to discuss matters with Mr. Mears. Afterward she'd knocked on Miss Charlotte's door to tell her that Mr. Mears had volunteered to come with them to Cornwall—and she'd found the girl's room empty.

It had been just as empty this morning, when she'd checked it again.

The development did not greatly surprise Mrs. Watson. From the moment Lady Ingram had been revealed as an agent of Moriarty's, it had been more or less a foregone conclusion that these two young people would find their way to each other.

Mrs. Watson loved a romance. She loved an engagement announcement in the papers. She loved a summer wedding, with flowers in the bridesmaids' hair. But she was also old enough to know all that was only Act I and the play could turn out to be a tragedy.

Lord Ingram and Miss Charlotte suited each other both very well and not at all. She wanted to picture a lovely future for them, but she could just as easily imagine a slow, soul-crushing disaster.

Mrs. Watson buried her face in Lord Ingram's sleeve. Whatever the future held, they needed to first live to see it.

Earlier, when they'd first settled into their cottage, Miss Charlotte had inspected it for such things as spyholes and listening ports. Now that Lord Ingram had arrived, she asked him to perform a similar scrutiny.

The cottage was not big, a parlor and a bedroom on the ground floor, and another bed on a parapeted loft. Lord Ingram took his time. While he worked, Mrs. Watson asked him about his journey, and whether their temporary dwelling, with its exposed rafters, brick fireplace, and simple rustic furnishing, bore any resemblance to his own seaside cottage on the Devon coast.

Only when he was satisfied that they wouldn't be overheard did they exchange what they'd learned during the course of the day. Mrs. Watson marveled that the torn railway ticket had led him and Miss Olivia directly to a place where Mr. Marbleton had stayed. And Lord Ingram was satisfyingly scandalized by her account of the "homecoming ritual" in the sanctuary.

But after she detailed Mr. Peters's threat atop the wall, he didn't say anything, only glanced toward Miss Charlotte, who stood at the window, looking out. She likewise said nothing.

Their silence unnerved Mrs. Watson. "Perhaps—perhaps Mr. Peters wouldn't have made those threats against us if you'd been there, my lord."

Lord Ingram leaned his shoulder against the mantel, a rough-hewn beam of wood. "I doubt that it would have made a difference, since he—and this Mrs. Crosby, too—seem determined to make an impression upon us."

Mrs. Watson snorted. They had indeed made quite an impression, forcing her to witness apparently normal people drink wine polluted with their own blood, and then, face threats made by a pipsqueak less than half her age!

A few seconds passed before the implication of Lord Ingram's words sank in. Surely . . . She massaged her temples and looked about the room. "Do you mean to say that everything I've been railing against has been calculated moves intended to unsettle us, or at least me?"

"You would not have remained disconcerted for long," said Lord Ingram.

Miss Charlotte, at the window, turned halfway around. "Indeed, you wouldn't have."

Their clear eyes and sincere words made Mrs. Watson feel only more sheepish. "I don't know about that. I was going out of my mind thinking that we—and Miss Baxter—had somehow become involved with a satanic cult, in which anyone who dared deviate even slightly from the demonic orthodoxy would pay with their lives.

"But now that you've pointed out the possibility that we've been given a spectacle . . ." The dinner invitation still lay on the trestle table where Mrs. Watson had last set it down. She flicked it. Obviously, Mrs. Crosby and Mr. Peters had lead roles in the performance. But everyone else at dinner, had they also played parts? And what of those residents who hadn't attended the dinner?

She looked again toward her companions. "Had we been stranded travelers overstaying our welcome, these tactics would have been perfectly deployed to get rid of us. But we are Moriarty's agents, however temporarily. They must know that we can't be so easily shooed away. Or do they sincerely *want* us to report to Moriarty that they are a community of religious fanatics with a murderous bent?"

Lord Ingram rubbed his chin. "It certainly appears that way, doesn't it?"

"If that's the impression they *wish* to give . . ." Miss Charlotte dropped the curtain she'd been holding up. "Makes you wonder, doesn't it, what they cannot possibly allow us to know."

❊

Mrs. Watson retired shortly afterward, saying that she had slept poorly the two nights before and needed to catch up on her rest. As soon as she had disappeared into the ground floor bedroom, Charlotte raised a brow at Lord Ingram.

He shook his head exaggeratedly, as if to say, *No, I am not going to do anything with you in that bed.*

He had been assigned the loft, the half wall of which offered only enough privacy for slumbering on the small cot behind it.

She advanced toward him, her hands stretched out.

He caught her hands. "Not to mention you are loud," he said in a whisper.

Charlotte winked.

"Holmes!"

She batted her eyelashes. "It's all right, Ash. I don't want to do anything—I just wanted to see that scandalized look on your face again."

"Oh, you do, huh?"

He poked her lightly under her rib cage. She leaped away. As a child she had not cared to be petted or touched, except for her hand to be held by Livia or her father. Once she'd grown older, she was very much left alone in that respect. Not until last night had they accidentally discovered that she was ticklish.

And of course he would not settle for one single tickle. She retreated, going backward. He advanced, a predatory smile about his lips. All of a sudden he lunged forward, caught her right shoulder, and made to poke her under the rib cage again. Charlotte emitted a muted yelp and lifted her hands in resistance. He picked her up bodily, set her on the bench by the trestle table, and sat down next to her.

So this was what becoming lovers entailed, that they would sit so closely even when they had no intention of disrobing. She gave herself a minute to become accustomed to the idea—then she lifted her hand and stroked his hair.

"I should go to bed soon," he said, sighing. "I was planning to get up at one or two and go out and take a look. See whether anyone's on the walls and whatnot."

"I brought hot water bottles in case we needed to do some surveillance at night."

"Oh?" He turned toward her and grinned. "Did you make any new hot water bottle cozies?"

Her Christmas present to him had been a pair of rather spectacular hot water bottle cozies that she'd knitted herself. "Yes, I was so taken with the idea of sending you smut in the post that I knitted two cozies to look like stamped envelopes."

He bent over laughing. She, too, emitted a smile.

The silence that followed was lovely, the silence of flowers blooming.

He sighed when he broke the silence. "I saw Bancroft today."

"Oh?"

He gave an account of what he'd learned from his brother. "You wondered earlier whether Moriarty might have come to England for some other purpose and sought you only incidentally. I think he would have crossed the Channel to hunt Madame Desrosiers."

Charlotte played with his collar, enjoying the slight scratchiness of the wool. "What do you think of Lord Bancroft's claim that I am in no danger from Moriarty because Lord Remington considers me an asset to the Crown?"

His lips thinned. "I doubt Bancroft feels much goodwill toward you. If he'd warned me in the starkest terms about your perils, then he might have been exaggerating to make me worry. But for him to all but dismiss the danger outright? I am not assured."

Neither was she.

She leaned in and kissed him on his jaw. "Go to bed. It will be a long night for you."

❖

*Paris. Spring. Birds sang, children laughed, sunlight danced on the clear water of the fountain. In the background, the Palais du Louvre soared, all slate roofs and glistening windows.*

*The broad walking path teemed with gleaming black top hats and pastel parasols. Mrs. Watson and Penelope walked arm in arm, trailing behind Miss Charlotte and Lord Ingram, also walking arm in arm. The sight reminded Mrs. Watson that*

*Penelope didn't yet know of the latest development between these two. She turned toward her niece, planning to surprise the girl.*

*But romance appeared to be the furthest thing from Penelope's mind. "A real human skull in the library?" she said, her face alive with interest. "I should like that. It would make for an excellent addition to my bookshelf."*

*Mrs. Watson, thwarted, called out to the new lovers. "My dears, what are you talking about?"*

*Surely, those two must be discoursing on their passionate desire for each other, long denied and now, at last, consummated.*

*Miss Charlotte and Lord Ingram turned around, both looking grave.*

*"It's the Battle of Paris," declared he. "I can hear the artillery in the suburbs. The Coalition army has begun their attack."*

*Miss Charlotte shook her head. "No, we are in the Paris Commune. The bombardment is in the city itself; cannons have been moved to Montmartre."*

*They looked to Penelope and said in unison, "What do you think, Miss Redmayne?"*

*Penelope bowed her head and listened. Mrs. Watson, too, was beginning to hear something. A crack. A boom. The placid water of the fountain shuddered. People ran, shouting to one another.*

*"It is the Paris Commune," said Penelope. "But it's not the cannons on Montmartre we are hearing. The fighting is close by, right outside the Louvre. They are defending the barricade on the Rue de Rivoli!"*

*As if to punctuate her statement, another loud crack.*

Mrs. Watson opened her eyes, groggy and confused. She was in a small bedroom. A taper had been lit. Miss Charlotte, standing by the side of the bed, her pantalets and petticoats already on, was stepping into her skirt.

"Fireworks are going off outside," she said. "I'm going to take a look."

"Fireworks?" croaked Mrs. Watson.

So she hadn't been dreaming—at least not about the noises. "I'll come, too."

Miss Charlotte lit another taper and said, "I'll have a lantern ready for you."

Mrs. Watson dressed quickly. When she stepped into the empty parlor, there was indeed a lit lantern waiting for her. She picked it up and opened the front door.

A gale nearly shoved her backward. Candles in the parlor sputtered to nothing, plunging it into darkness. She shouldered her way out. A few steps away, Lord Ingram, clad in a mackintosh even though it wasn't raining yet, ran back and helped her pull the door shut again.

"Miss Charlotte is further ahead," he told her.

Theirs was the eastmost dwelling in this cluster of four cottages, closest to the sea—and the eastern wall. The path on which they walked led in a west-northwest direction and went past the nearest cottage.

Something made Mrs. Watson look up. The windows of the cottage were dark, but she had the uncomfortable sense that someone was looking at her.

"When I was waiting for you, I saw a curtain move slightly in that cottage," murmured Lord Ingram.

On the tail of his words, a firework shot up with a boom and a whistle, exploding almost directly overhead in a shower of green-and-gold sparks.

They ran forward. At the center of the compound, an open space ran east to west—the central carriage path dating from the pre-wall years, when the front entrance was to the east. After the construction of the walls, with the new gate in the west wall, and the stable and carriage house immediately in the southwest corner, there was no more carriage traffic on the former path, and it grew into a grassy tract.

Miss Charlotte stood on the grass, her head slightly raised, her person still. Before Mrs. Watson could speak to her, another firework burst, letting loose a cascade of bright red trails.

"The fireworks are being released beyond the north wall. Will you go take a look, my lord?" she asked.

Mrs. Watson's stomach tightened. They needed to know what was going on, but what if this was a plot to isolate Miss Charlotte and herself?

Lord Ingram looked at them. "You have your weapons, ladies?"

Miss Charlotte nodded. Mrs. Watson's hand went to the pocket of her skirt, where she had a derringer. She also shifted her left foot, feeling the outline of the pistol stuck into her boot.

"Yes," she said hoarsely.

"Then be careful."

"You, too," said Miss Charlotte.

Their knight ran off, the light from his lantern skidding fast across the ground. Mrs. Watson worried for a moment over how he was going to get out—Mr. Peters had used keys to open padlocks that kept several heavy bolts in place. But as he reached the gate, one more firework shot skyward, its golden combustion illuminating two people coming down the wall from ladders to either side of the entrance.

It was too far for Mrs. Watson to make out their faces, but they seemed to be a man and a woman. The woman let the man and Lord Ingram out from the gate, closed it, and then again climbed up to the ramparts.

Miss Charlotte was already walking. "That might be the same woman we saw on the wall in the afternoon, when we were on the boat," she murmured.

Mrs. Watson caught up to her and looked behind herself. To one side, the cottage nearest their own was still pitch-dark. To the other side, across a dormant garden bed—a flower garden, not a vegetable garden—figures emerged from dwellings in Miss Fairfield's cluster.

Miss Charlotte crossed the old carriage path. Mrs. Watson had thought they would follow that path to the gate in Lord Ingram's wake, but they were now north of it, skirting the edge of the kitchen garden. Were they headed for the north wall instead?

"Miss Stoppard, Miss Stoppard!"

Mrs. Watson whipped around. The out-of-breath voice belonged to Miss Ellery, who was some twenty feet behind them and shouting with her face upturned. "What's happening, Miss Stoppard?"

"I don't know yet!" The answer came from the ramparts. "Mr. Peters and one of the visitors have gone for a look."

"What time is it?" asked Mrs. Watson, realizing that she hadn't given that any thought.

"I left our cottage at five past midnight," said Miss Charlotte. "So it should be about ten after now."

"What a strange occurrence," said a man's voice just ahead, startling Mrs. Watson. "Lovely, to be sure, but strange."

Dr. Robinson. How long had he been standing there in the shadows?

"I take it this isn't something that happens frequently then?" asked Miss Charlotte, her tone placid, as if they were conversing around a dining table.

"I saw fireworks once in Falmouth, for Guy Fawkes, but never in these parts. I can't fathom what hidden significance this day holds that would mandate fireworks."

Mrs. Watson was about to agree when Miss Charlotte veered off. "My dear, where are you going?"

The girl didn't answer, but not far away loomed the cluster of six dwellings that contained Miss Baxter's lodge. Mrs. Watson's heart beat faster. She picked up her pace.

At least four of the houses in the cluster had their windows lit. Miss Charlotte skirted the first cottage. She was about to go around a larger, unlit house when a woman said sharply, "Where do you think you are going, Miss Holmes?"

Mrs. Crosby, a heavy coat over her dressing gown, stood on the veranda of this lodge.

Miss Baxter's lodge.

Miss Charlotte's lips parted. A fusillade of sharp cracks came. Everyone jumped. Mrs. Crosby whipped a pistol out of her coat. But it was only half a dozen fireworks rocketing skyward at the same time, leaving behind a brilliant and gaudy display of golden sparks, red streaks, and violet glimmers.

What happened? Did the mischief-maker, about to be pinned down by a ferocious Mr. Peters, set off all the remaining fireworks at once?

Miss Charlotte waved a hand in front of her face, as if she could fan away the sulfurous odors. "I thought I saw firelight coming from this direction—and I was correct."

A look of clear disdain crossed Mrs. Crosby's face. "Really, Miss Holmes—"

"Goodness gracious, she's right," cried Dr. Robinson.

He ran around to the back of the house. There came an explosive imprecation. "The woodpile has caught on fire. Quick, quick, we need to put it out!"

Mrs. Crosby bounded down the steps from the veranda and half lifted her firearm toward Miss Charlotte, as if *she* were somehow responsible for the fire.

With a cry Mrs. Watson sprang forward and stood in front of Miss Charlotte. But the girl walked out from behind her, pushed Mrs. Crosby's arm down, and asked, without any inflection to her voice, "Are there buckets in this house?"

"There are in ours," said Mrs. Steele, who had arrived on the scene with her husband. She sounded breathless and afraid but she immediately ran off. "I'll get them."

Dr. Robinson, just back to the front of the house, hurried after her. "And I'll go get mine."

"Is Miss Baxter still inside? Miss Baxter? Miss Baxter?" shouted Mr. Steele. "She needs to come outside right now. It's not safe."

"She's not going to wake up," said Mrs. Crosby sharply. "She took something Dr. Robinson prescribed. Go get water to pour on the woodpile. She'll sleep through it."

Mr. Steele stared at her as if she'd told him to pour kerosene on the woodpile instead. Mrs. Watson felt so jittery, she had to clench her hand *and* her jaw. She still hadn't recovered from Mrs. Crosby having nearly pointed her pistol at Miss Charlotte, and now the woman was prepared to let someone she claimed to be close to simply sleep while a fire burned against the back wall of her house?

"I don't know how anyone can sleep through this racket," cried Mr. Steele, his voice rising with frustration. "But even if she does, it's all right. I can carry her out. It'll be no trouble at all."

Mrs. Crosby's voice grew colder. "You'll be better off getting water. Miss Ellery is here. She has keys to the kitchen, which has many buckets. Quickly, go, everyone!"

"But I didn't bring my ring of keys when I rushed out of the house," fretted Miss Ellery. "Why, I'm still in my house slippers. I don't know why we are arguing over this, but we have enough people both to move Miss Baxter to a safer location and to put out the fire at the same—"

She was interrupted by a vigorous jangling of metals: Miss Fairchild, arriving with the ring of keys.

Miss Fairchild waved an imperious hand in the direction of the kitchen and led the way. Everyone followed, including Mr. Steele, who shook his head as he ran after her. "I know Miss Baxter hates to be disturbed, but surely one has to make an exception when one's house is on fire?"

Apparently not.

Or at least Mrs. Crosby was not willing to make that exception for her.

"This is madness!" Mrs. Watson whispered to Miss Charlotte. "How can Mrs. Crosby let Miss Baxter remain in place? And to turn down help, too!"

"It's always possible that Miss Baxter's lodge is empty," answered

Miss Charlotte, walking faster to keep up with the herd, "and that's what Mrs. Crosby doesn't want anyone to find out."

Mrs. Watson picked up her skirts to lengthen her strides, her mind in an uproar.

At the kitchen, Miss Ellery took the ring of keys from Miss Fairchild, opened the door, and lit a lamp. By this time Mrs. Brown, the cook, and her assistant, Abigail Hurley, had also joined the throng. Miss Ellery distributed buckets and divided everyone into two groups, one group to use the pump in the kitchen and another to go out to the south cistern. "One person should remain at the pump unless there's no one else waiting with a bucket; that way it will go faster!"

Mrs. Watson and Miss Charlotte's bucket, once filled, was heavier than Mrs. Watson had anticipated. She had forgotten her gloves on her way out of the cottage. The handle of the bucket was cold as ice. Yet she barely felt the burn of the cold or the weight of the bucket digging into her palm.

Was Miss Baxter in her lodge or not? Was Mrs. Crosby helping her or the opposite?

Mrs. Steele reached the burning woodpile first. She heaved her water onto the roaring, wind-whipped fire. Mrs. Watson and Miss Charlotte did likewise. The woodpile began to smoke.

"A few more buckets ought to do," said Mrs. Steele, panting, "but I think we should all go back and get some more water just to be on the safe side."

Mrs. Watson panted, too, from both exertion and relief. She was about to do as Mrs. Steele suggested but Miss Charlotte said, "Ma'am, your health will not permit more labor than this. I'll go bring more water."

Mrs. Watson had the constitution of a horse and would not have been undone by another trip with the bucket. But Miss Charlotte seemed to want her to stay in place.

"Won't the bucket be too heavy for you, my dear?"

Miss Charlotte wiped at her brow with her sleeve. "You're right, ma'am, I haven't thought of that. Oh, I hope we're not in your way, Mrs. Steele."

"Hardly, hardly," said Mrs. Steele, without moving. "Oh, I can hear lots of footsteps approaching. I guess no one needs to make another trip now."

Soon Mr. Steele arrived with his bucket, followed by the kitchen maid. When her load had been emptied, the combustion came to a near-complete stop. More steam than smoke rose from the drenched woodpile, and a scarce spark or two was quickly put out by Miss Ellery and Miss Fairchild, who administered the coup de grâce.

"Has the fire been put out?" asked Dr. Robinson, limping into view. "I'm afraid in my eagerness to be useful I tripped over a rock and fell. Fortunately I'm only suffering from bruised pride and a skinned knee."

He walked gingerly toward the front of the lodge, calling, "Is Miss Baxter all right, Mrs. Crosby?"

"She must have slept through it all," came Mrs. Crosby's voice. "Doctor, would you mind coming in and having a look?"

Mrs. Watson scowled. She still hadn't forgiven the woman.

The physician turned around. "Is everyone else all right? In need of medical attention before I look in on Miss Baxter?"

Everyone shook their heads.

Miss Ellery said, "What about your knee? Would you like me to bandage that for you first?"

"Most kind of you, Miss Ellery," said Dr. Robinson, already trudging away. "But that can wait a bit."

The crowd followed him to the front of the house, but by then he and Mrs. Crosby had disappeared inside. All Mrs. Watson saw was the door closing.

Yet another gust blew. She shivered. The water in the bucket had sloshed and her right sleeve was sodden. The damp cold pierced to the bone.

To her surprise, Mrs. Crosby emerged again from Miss Baxter's lodge, holding a bright lantern. But before she could say anything, Miss Stoppard on the wall shouted, "We caught them. We caught the troublemakers."

# Thirteen

The troublemakers turned out to be a mortified-looking man in his late twenties and a trembling boy of about nine. The man had his hand over the boy's shoulders, even as his other hand opened and closed compulsively.

Mr. Peters did not bring them inside the compound, but rather dragged them near the still-locked front gate. Lord Ingram stood a few steps away. The residents who had put out the fire, plus Mrs. Watson and Miss Charlotte, looked down from the top of the wall.

Mrs. Watson wondered whether from far below on the ground those who crowded the ramparts resembled saints and sages on a trompe-l'oeil ceiling, embodying an august judgment—when several of them were in dressing gowns, Miss Ellery had on mismatched slippers, and almost everyone was shivering. It was colder on the wall, the wind fiercer, and her arm in that wet sleeve felt as if it had been encased in ice.

"This man claims that he is Sam Young, a boatbuilder from Porthangan," said Mr. Peters, his voice carrying up clearly, "and that this is his orphaned nephew, who lives with him. He says Mrs. Crosby and Miss Ellery can both attest to his identity."

Miss Ellery squinted. "Yes, that's them. What in the world were you thinking, Mr. Young, lugging young Master Timothy about in the middle of the night and creating a racket? One of your fireworks nearly set Miss Baxter's lodge on fire, and we are all cold and wet from hauling water to put it out."

"I'm sorry, Miss Ellery," said Sam Young, his voice quaking. "I'm mighty sorry. I didn't mean to do any harm. Is there anything that needs replacing? I'll do all the repairs."

"That will not be necessary," said Mrs. Crosby coldly. "And you have not answered Miss Ellery's question."

The man lowered his face and did not speak. He was bare-headed. The boy had a cap on, but he had no headgear. Had he lost it trying to run away from Mr. Peters or Lord Ingram?

After a few seconds, Mr. Peters said, "He told me earlier that he'd heard today is the feast day of your namesake saint, Mrs. Crosby, and that it is considered a romantic gesture, in Catholic countries, to set off fireworks at midnight on the feast day of a beloved."

There was a collective intake of breath. Mrs. Watson, who usually loved a juicy bit of gossip, was horrified by how the poor villager must be feeling.

"Who told him such a thing?" Mrs. Crosby sounded as if she spoke through gritted teeth.

"He said it was a gentleman who sailed into the village today by the name of Brothers. This Mr. Brothers visited him because he'd heard that Mr. Young here makes a fast sloop. He later asked why a nice young man like him hadn't married yet, and Mr. Young answered that he was in love with you, who never looked twice at him. Mr. Brothers was very sympathetic and asked whether he knew your given name. When he heard that it was Isabel, he said how interesting it was that St. Isabel's feast day was on the morrow."

Mrs. Crosby spun around to face Mrs. Watson and Miss Charlotte. "Did you arrange for this? You brought a man with you, didn't you?"

The force of her wrath was so great that Mrs. Watson, whose teeth were beginning to chatter, nearly took a step backward. She scowled at herself and immediately advanced a step. Mrs. Crosby was not the only one who could whip out a firearm at a moment's notice, if it came to that.

"We were accompanied to Porthangan by a member of our domestic staff," said Miss Charlotte coolly. "But he was not involved in any mischief."

Mrs. Crosby sneered. "You can answer so conclusively for him?"

"Indeed, since we brought no fireworks with us, not a single one," said Miss Charlotte. She turned to face the two men below. "Mr. Young, upon informing you that the feast day would begin at midnight, did this Mr. Brothers immediately remember that he happened to be carrying with him a supply of fireworks in his boat?"

Sam Young raised his head and nodded hard. "Yes, yes, he did."

"Did he sail away from the harbor after he gave you the fireworks?"

"Yes, Timmy and I watched him go."

"At what time?"

"Before sunset."

Miss Charlotte turned back to Mrs. Crosby. "Our hired boat is called *A Tide of Hope*—you can send someone to check but it should still be in the harbor. And our man is staying above the pub, if you want to verify that, too."

"Mrs. Crosby," shouted her admirer all of a sudden, "please let me apologize. I'm sorry to have made a hash of things. I had no idea it would cause so much trouble."

"Oh, you didn't?" retorted Mrs. Crosby. "You thought that by setting off fireworks at an ungodly hour outside the dwelling of a woman who barely knows you, you would instead bring her honor and glory?"

Mr. Young fell mute.

Mrs. Crosby turned to Miss Fairchild. "I had better leave before I shoot this fool in full view of a child."

Miss Fairchild, looking very tired, waved a hand, indicating that Mrs. Crosby should go. She repeated the exact same gesture to Mr. Peters.

"Mr. Hudson," said Mr. Peters to Lord Ingram, "if you'll keep an eye on these gentlemen, I'm going to fetch myself a mackintosh and escort them back to the village."

The company took some time to safely get down from the wall. By the time Mrs. Watson had set foot on the ground, her fingers felt as if they would lose all sensation from gripping the ladder's piercingly cold side rails.

Lord Ingram was waiting for her at the bottom; Mr. Peters had departed with the mischief-makers.

"Let's disperse," said Miss Ellery. "It's going to rain."

Mrs. Steele, whose shoes had been drenched earlier, held on to her husband with both hands for warmth. "Well, when—when it rains," she said, stuttering from the cold, "at least nothing else will catch on fire."

—❧—

Back at their cottage, Charlotte put water to boil and changed out of her wet clothes. Most of the water went into the hot water bottles, but Mrs. Watson also made tea. She gave Charlotte a cup as Charlotte pulled on her gloves.

"Should I come with you?" asked Mrs. Watson a third time. "I won't be able to sleep anyway."

Charlotte had the opposite problem. She *would* have been able to sleep soundly, but the events of the night were such that she could not permit herself to go back to bed yet. "I don't have an extra hot water bottle for you, ma'am, and it's too cold a night to remain out for long without any heat source. Rest if you can. If not, keep an eye on what you can see of the Garden."

She took a sip of the tea and gave Mrs. Watson a quick hug. "And thank you for shielding me from Mrs. Crosby."

How fortunate she was, to have come into this remarkable woman's orbit.

At least the cold air outside, cutting across her face, made her feel more awake and alert. She found Lord Ingram near the meditation cabin, where he'd been watching Miss Baxter's lodge.

She handed him a hot water bottle, a canteen of hot tea, and a flask of whisky. "Has Dr. Robinson left?"

"I don't believe so. Careful."

A ray of light shone down from the eastern wall and zigzagged along the carriage path. Then it swept toward Miss Baxter's lodge and missed them by only a few feet.

Charlotte would have preferred to take another look at the woodpile, but even without the light beaming down from the wall, it would have been no easy feat for her to approach Miss Baxter's lodge. But she'd prepared an alternative: She could try to get into the homes of Mrs. Crosby, Mr. Peters, and Dr. Robinson.

Of those three, Dr. Robinson's cottage was her first choice: Mrs. Crosby and Mr. Peters both lived near Miss Baxter, but the physician's place was in a different corner of the Garden, in the same huddle as Miss Fairchild and Miss Ellery's lodge. For that reason she had asked Lord Ingram to keep an eye on Dr. Robinson's whereabouts.

"The light coming down from the walls is passing too close to this spot. I need to move," said Lord Ingram.

Theoretically they were free to stroll through the Garden, but still, as nighttime observers, it was better to remain unseen. And Charlotte had come up with a barely plausible excuse if they were caught by a Mr. Peters or a Miss Stoppard: They would claim to be looking for other spent firework shells, to eliminate the fire hazard they posed.

"Be careful, Holmes," continued her lover. "And go back inside soon. Both of us don't need to be out here."

"You be careful, too," she said.

He pulled her close, kissed her on the lips, and disappeared into the night.

She set out in the opposite direction, toward Dr. Robinson's accommodations. Earlier, in the middle of the fireworks fiasco, houses had been lit and lanterns had swung about freely. But now the Garden was almost entirely dark.

It hid her, but also made her progress slow. The carriage path would have made for a far smoother walk, but another beam of light swept down its length just now, before streaking away toward Miss Baxter's lodge again. She stole forward carefully. Two minutes later she barely avoided pitching face-first into a sharp dip in the ground, and almost rolled her ankle on the very next step.

But even as she sat down to scoot on her bottom, she wished for greater darkness. Miss Fairchild and Miss Ellery's lodge still had a lamp in a window. Its light was too far away to illuminate the terrain underfoot, but just might prove bright enough, up close, to let her be seen by the observer in the cottage next to her own, should she set herself before Dr. Robinson's front door.

The lamp kept burning. She got up, stumbled again, and went on. The lamp kept burning. She stopped—she'd come as close as she dared to Dr. Robinson's place. The lamp kept burning. She rubbed her gloved hands together. Despite the hot water bottle tucked into her shirt, her extremities were losing their warmth.

Hoofbeats. Wheels bumping and cutting. A carriage approached. Instantly two lanterns came to light, one on the north wall, the other on the south wall. The one on the south wall extinguished quickly. The other, however, remained lit, traveled to the western wall, and descended the ladder.

Its light illuminated the gate swinging open. Mr. Peters had returned. Three miles to the village and three miles back, he must have driven at a breakneck speed, kicked Mr. Young and the boy off the vehicle, and turned around with the same urgency.

In daylight, the carriage lane on the headlands was not treacherous. But at night, with a storm brewing, she would not have operated a vehicle at such speeds, not even if she had one lit like a Christmas tree. And what was his rush? Had he no interest in verifying her claim that *A Tide of Hope*, the boat Mrs. Watson had hired, was still in port?

Also, with his return, would Dr. Robinson head back home before Charlotte could have a look inside his cottage?

Her fingers dug deeper into the pockets of her mackintosh. She expelled a long breath, then another. The air still smelled faintly of minor explosions, underpinned by the tang of the sea. The waves, whipped by a turbulent air, walloped into the cliffs—crash, rumble, a sharp retreat like an indrawn breath before the next assault.

Darkness. Utter darkness. Someone had at last snuffed out that lamp.

Another beam of light shone down from the walls. When it dissipated, Charlotte moved.

Dr. Robinson's cottage had been unlit this entire time—the tapers inside had likely been extinguished when he'd first stepped out to see what was going on. Mrs. Watson had left their cottage in enough of a hurry that she hadn't locked the door. If Dr. Robinson had been in as much of a rush . . .

Gently, she turned the door handle. It gave. She slipped in, then closed the door just as gently—or at least as gently as she could with the wind threatening to blow it wide open again.

She took out her pocket lantern, let out a smidgen of light, and looked about. This cottage seemed to be of the same design as the one she was currently occupying, but with a change to the orientation. In her cottage, the fireplace was to the right of the door, here it was to the left. Beyond the fireplace, curtains that hung on curved rods obscured an entire corner—an examination area, most likely.

On the same side as the fireplace but nearer to the door stood a large glass-front cabinet. She walked closer and set the pocket lantern almost directly against the panes to read the labels affixed to the items inside. On the shelf most convenient for a man of Dr. Robinson's height were arrayed supplies such as carbolic acid, chloroform, and other antiseptics and anesthetics necessary for surgical procedures. Other shelves held tablets for reducing fever, tonics for the stomach, strychnine for those with heart problems, tinctures for pain and sleeplessness such as laudanum and morphine, and even a stimulant like cocaine.

This was Dr. Robinson's dispensary, with the usual remedies necessary for common ailments, all the jars and bottles grouped by usage and clearly labeled.

She tried to open the doors of the cabinet and found them locked.

His bag sat on a low stool beside the locked cabinet and did not appear to be secured. She crouched down and reached out a hand.

Footsteps. Running footsteps. Coming toward the cottage.

She blew out her pocket lantern, headed for the curtained-off examination area, lifted a handful of curtain from the floor, and ducked under. Before she could straighten, a large cloth came over her head and a hand, on the other side of the cloth, covered her mouth with surprising force.

Her heart thudded. She cocked her derringer and poked it hard into the man's side—a man, judging by the strength with which she was held. He seemed not to care that he was in greater danger from her than vice versa and pulled her deeper into the examination area. She twisted, lifting her hand to smack him on the head with her derringer. The cottage door burst open, bringing with it a rush of cold, salty air that still carried a whiff of black powder and phosphorus.

Charlotte and the man both stilled. Even with the cloth over her head, she could tell that the room brightened considerably. The person who entered must be Dr. Robinson then—an intruder wouldn't be so reckless with light.

A key turned. A cabinet door opened. Bottles clinked against one another. A few seconds later, the front door opened and closed one more time and the wind that rushed in once again extinguished the light. But this time, Dr. Robinson did not neglect to lock his door.

Time passed, second by second. Charlotte counted, her arm raised, the barrel of her derringer resting directly against the man's head. He remained motionless. When she had counted to one hundred and fifteen the man pushed her out of the curtained area and only then withdrew the cloth that covered her head.

Charlotte relit her pocket lantern. She supposed she could ambush the man and find out his identity but he had been relatively civil and it seemed only decent to leave his identity alone for the moment. She went to the glass cabinet instead.

The doctor's bag next to it was gone. She examined the contents of the glass cabinet and saw that both the carbolic acid and the chloroform had been taken.

A cough came from the examination area.

Very well.

She left via a sash window, closing it only partially on her way out. If her fellow intruder wished to depart from the same window, he could do so with her blessings. If not, then he could close it for her since she'd caused him no trouble at all.

Outside her cottage, Charlotte stood with her hands on her hot water bottle.

A man and a woman patrolled the walls, beaming the light of their lanterns into the Garden at irregular intervals. They also shone their light outward, but less frequently. The woman was the indefatigable Miss Stoppard, the one who had likely caught Inspector Treadles climbing up the wall. As for the man . . .

Mr. Peters didn't match the description Inspector Treadles gave of the man who had chased him to London. Could this be him?

Charlotte let herself back into the cottage, took off her mackintosh, and lit a taper. Mrs. Watson, clad in a thick dressing gown of scarlet wool, had fallen asleep in a chair by the window. Charlotte brought a counterpane and covered her.

Mrs. Watson opened her eyes. "Oh, you are back. Goodness, I was dreaming about Miss Baxter. It must be what you said about her lodge possibly being empty. In my dream she escaped the Garden with Mrs. Crosby's and Mr. Peters's help, and Mr. Peters wasn't even all that detestable."

She yawned and Charlotte could not help yawning with her. "It's as good a hypothesis as any."

"I've lost count of how many good hypotheses there are." Mrs. Watson pushed out of her chair and stretched, a grimace on her face. "Miss Baxter gone, Miss Baxter dead, Miss Baxter still alive but in bad shape. This entire Garden a charade put on by Moriarty. Miss Fairchild and Miss Ellery working for Moriarty but deciding to abandon him while he was deposed. And that's only what I can remember right now, in the middle of the night."

They had indeed generated a number of propositions and corollaries during their railway journey to Cornwall—though it must be said, Mrs. Watson had done most of the speculating.

Charlotte brought Mrs. Watson's chair nearer to the fire. She doubted the older woman would consent to go to bed, knowing that Lord Ingram was still out. "All those explanations made sense at the time."

Mrs. Watson shuffled to the new location of her chair and stood with her arms braced against its top, again stretching out her back. "But?"

Charlotte pulled up another padded chair to the fire. "But tonight Miss Baxter remained unseen while her house burned, so to speak. Something has to change. Hypotheses will be collapsing soon."

With a groan, Mrs. Watson sat down. "Are you planning to report it to Moriarty? Or to wait for this to reach Mrs. Felton's ear and for her to report it?"

"The fire behind Miss Baxter's house was arson, most likely. And whoever set off the fire will inform Moriarty that Miss Baxter remains unaccounted for."

Mrs. Watson's hands rose to her throat. "Why then does Moriarty need us to be here, if he can verify that Miss Baxter is no longer at the Garden without our help?"

Charlotte yawned again. "Let's speak of this in the morning. My brain suffers from the same condition as Cinderella's carriage—it turns into a pumpkin after midnight. And what can a pumpkin possibly say of Moriarty's purposes?"

—⁎—

The previous December, while reconnoitering at night, Lord Ingram had leaped into a nearly frozen lake to avoid detection by guard dogs. The memory of the bone-biting agony—and the even more frightening lethargy that followed—had stayed with him a long time.

Compared to that, this night was both less cold and less dangerous. At times the squalls seemed strong enough to lift him off his feet, and temperatures had fallen sharply, but still it was the chill of early spring and not the rawness of deep winter.

Not to mention he had a hot water bottle in a knitted envelope cozy.

Alas, the night was long. At first he had moved about more, familiarized himself with the disposition of the buildings and other features inside the Garden. But after Mr. Peters's harried return, he had taken up position under the shade hut next to the kitchen garden, from which to keep an eye on Miss Baxter's cluster of dwellings.

Not that he could see much, the night being lightless. He could not even hear much over the shriek of the wind and the pounding of the waves. But the spot still seemed optimal—among a dearth of choices—not easy to detect by the sentinels on the walls, open in several directions so that he could evade Mr. Peters, who was on patrol, and still remain close enough to Miss Baxter's house.

To his surprise, Mr. Peters's patrol was less than thorough.

The lanterns of those on the wall must have been fitted with specially made reflective lenses. They generated a bright and concentrated beam of light whenever their shutters opened. The light lingered on Miss Baxter's lodge more frequently than anywhere else. And often, when the lodge was illuminated, Mr. Peters's form could be seen, pacing either the front veranda or the periphery of the lodge.

About twenty minutes after Lord Ingram had taken up his position—he could not check his watch when there was no light—someone holding a lit lantern and exhibiting a small limp ran out of the lodge. The Garden's physician, who, according to Holmes, had taken a fall earlier in the night? He hoped Holmes, who had wanted to look inside Dr. Robinson's cottage, had finished with her inspection. A few minutes later, the physician returned with a doctor's bag and a few other items in hand. Lord Ingram let out a breath: It seemed that Dr. Robinson's expedition had gone off without any incidents.

After Dr. Robinson went back inside Miss Baxter's lodge, the door of the lodge opened and shut another few times. Lord Ingram could not tell who darted about in the dark, though he did occasionally make out harried footsteps, those of a single person running.

In the middle of these rushed entrances and exits, a lantern shone down from the south wall.

"Not now, Mr. McEwan," growled Mr. Peters.

The light went out immediately. And didn't shine again until whoever was running in and out of the house appeared to be done with their task.

Lord Ingram imagined a dying Miss Baxter being kept alive by strange and terrible means, just so that she could last through one interview with Holmes and exculpate the other members of the community.

Since Mr. Peters seemed committed to remaining in the vicinity of Miss Baxter's lodge, Lord Ingram crept closer. At around half past one, he had just set himself under the eaves of a nearby cottage when Mr. Peters's lantern suddenly came on. "Who's there?"

Lord Ingram's heart pounded. Had he been seen?

"Craddock," answered a gruff voice from the other side of the cottage, closer to the lodge.

Lord Ingram clenched his teeth and tried not to breathe too loudly in relief.

"Go back inside, Mr. Craddock," said Mr. Peters. "There's nothing for you to do or see here."

Craddock. Lord Ingram remembered the name from the dossier. But also from Mrs. Watson's incredulity that anyone would move across the Garden of Hermopolis for a view of fruit trees espaliered against a wall.

There was no more answer from Mr. Craddock, presumably he did as Mr. Peters asked—or at least appeared to do so.

Probably another hour passed before Mr. Peters again called out sharply, "Who's there?"

"The Steeles," said a woman, her tone ingratiating. "We were about to go to bed when we saw Dr. Robinson running to his cottage, and then run back here with his bag. Since then we've been waiting for him to go back to his cottage again but that still hasn't happened. Is everything all right? Is Miss Baxter all right? We're worried."

"I haven't the slightest idea about Miss Baxter," said Mr. Peters. "I'm just here because Mrs. Crosby told me to stand here. But I'm sure Miss Baxter must be fine or Mrs. Crosby would have said something to me."

"So Mrs. Crosby is inside, too?" came a man's somewhat reedy voice, likely that of Mr. Steele.

"Yes. And if you think Mrs. Crosby will let you in, feel free to knock."

Apparently the would-be callers didn't think so. The woman sighed. "All right. We'll go back for now. But don't you think all this is awfully strange?"

"Not particularly," said Mr. Peters. "When I last saw Miss Baxter, she was perfectly fine. Mrs. Crosby has seen her more than once in the past twenty-four hours and hasn't mentioned anything being amiss."

"All right, then, if you trust Mrs. Crosby," said Mr. Steele, sounding petulant.

"I trust her with my life, and so does Miss Baxter," said Mr. Peters coldly. "Good night, Mr. Steele. Good night, Mrs. Steele."

Approximately another quarter hour afterward, Mr. Peters's lantern came on again. "Miss Ellery, can I help you?"

The brusqueness in his tone had become pointed. The young man was running out of patience.

"Y—yes. Neither Miss Fairchild nor I can sleep. I thought I'd come and see whether everything is all right with Miss Baxter."

She sounded sincere and—embarrassed.

"Miss Baxter isn't seeing anyone now, and I don't think Mrs. Crosby has the time either."

"Oh well, then, do you mind if I have a look at the woodpile? Seems strange that it simply caught fire like that."

"It's already been looked at: Someone poured a small amount of kerosene on the pile and added a few matches."

"What?" cried Miss Ellery, her dismay stark.

"Yes, I know," said Mr. Peters wearily. "But there's nothing we can do now, so why don't you go back inside and take some rest. I would, too, but Mrs. Crosby has stationed me here."

Lord Ingram felt very much the same, except he didn't even have anyone to blame. He'd stationed himself there.

He threw himself to the ground. A beam of light passed by with barely two feet to spare.

The patrols had been shining their lanterns from the north, eastern, and south walls—the reason he dared to put himself to the west of this particular cottage. But now they performed their inspection from the western wall again.

He slipped back under the shade hut.

His hot water bottle still emitted some warmth, but his feet were cold and he could barely feel his cheeks. He squatted down and stood up, stretched his legs to the side, and walked in place. Earlier he'd avoided detection; now he half hoped that Mr. Peters would patrol properly, notice him, and tell him to get back inside, too.

But no one discovered him. Or at least no one cared. Light flooded down from the walls from time to time. When Mr. Peters was illuminated, he paced either on the veranda of or around Miss Baxter's lodge. Same as before.

No one else came to see how Miss Baxter fared. The door of the house did not open or close again. Lord Ingram's eyelids grew heavy. He swayed. If he sat down, he'd still be able to see the front of Miss Baxter's house.

Silently he yawned. And yawned again.

His children must be sleeping soundly. Holmes, with her propensity for a good night's rest, was likely also sleeping soundly. He would like to sleep soundly, too—he was too old to stay up all night.

Even Mr. Peters yawned loudly enough for him to hear. Fatigue surrounded him like the night. He could sit down, draw his knees up, and set his chin between his knees.

He started—he'd almost fallen asleep on his feet and lost his balance. He rubbed his eyes, opened them again, and was nearly blinded by a flash of lightning that threw the entire compound into sharp relief.

Thunder cracked with ground-shaking force. He covered his ears. On the southeastern corner of the walls, a man did the same.

A more brilliant bolt of lightning sizzled, followed by an even more deafening boom. Rain poured, striking the top of the shade hut with such force that he barely heard Mr. Peters scream, "Get off the walls, you two," at the top of his lungs.

The two people on the walls obeyed. Lanterns swinging, they ran and climbed down the ladders, then headed for Miss Baxter's veranda.

Lord Ingram was no longer on the verge of falling asleep, but his head was filled with glue. He remained where he was not because it made sense, but because he couldn't arrive at a new decision.

He did, however, dig out his pocket watch. Another streak of lightning lit the sky; he looked at the time. Quarter past four. Almost morning. He could endure until sunrise.

The rain let up briefly, only to come down harder. Thunder roared. He glanced at his watch every time lightning flashed. Time crawled. He felt like a tree in winter, all bare trunk and peeling bark. For a while after the rain started, it had not been difficult to keep awake. But now hibernation beckoned, the idea of being unconscious for an entire season the most appealing idea he'd ever encountered.

By the time he awoke again, Holmes would have sorted out matters with Moriarty, somebody would have informed his children about the divorce, and he would begin anew, well rested, if nothing else.

He was jerked out of his lethargy by the sight of Mr. Peters, a lantern in hand, running onto the central carriage path. Was he headed for the gate? No, he veered off to the southwest, where the stable and the carriage house were located. Ten minutes later, a coach came down the carriage path.

Lord Ingram blinked. But the carriage path going east ended in a wall.

Mr. Peters did not drive the coach into a wall but went around a circular flower bed and stopped, the vehicle now pointing west. A man with a lantern sprinted for the gate. At the same time, a woman rushed toward the waiting coach, a satchel in one hand, a lantern in the other. Lord Ingram recognized her from when she'd stood on the wall and glared down at Mr. Young—Mrs. Crosby.

As soon as Mrs. Crosby was inside, Mr. Peters cracked his whip and the coach shot forward, bolting out of the compound just as the man at the gate opened it fully.

Lord Ingram hesitated. Lanterns had been freely deployed while all this running and driving took place, but now it was pitch-black again, rain coming down loud enough to drown out his thoughts.

He swore, lit his pocket lantern, and left the protection of the shade hut. The ground squelched underfoot as he made his way to the western wall. The gate had been locked again. He fought his way up a wet, slippery ladder, the pocket lantern's grip clenched between his teeth. From the ramparts, the coach was still visible, by virtue of its two exterior lanterns. It was headed not toward the village but northwest across the moorland.

A noise made him look back. A flash of weak lightning illuminated a man coming up the other set of ladders, in a mackintosh similar to his. A muffler covered most of his face. Sensing Lord Ingram's attention as the man reached the top of the wall, he headed in the opposite direction.

For some reason, though their eyes had met for only a second, Lord Ingram thought he'd seen this man before. He tried to rack his exhausted brain, but couldn't think of when or where such a meeting had happened, let alone who the man might be.

In the distance, the coach disappeared.

He waited for some time before deciding he was no good to anyone anymore, descended the ladder with as much care as he could muster, and headed back to Holmes.

## Fourteen

Mrs. Watson had been startled awake when it sounded as if the sky was tearing in two. But once the rain began, though the thundering continued, she drifted back to sleep and didn't open her eyes again until morning.

A dull grey light hovered in the parlor. Rain drummed steadily on the roof. Miss Charlotte slept next to her, her chin on her chest, her plump lips in a slight pout. She looked younger when she slept, young and adorable. Mrs. Watson had the urge to pet the girl on the head.

She refrained. But as she worked to revive the banked fire, from behind her, Miss Charlotte yawned and murmured a sleepy "Good morning."

They found bread and butter in the larder and made toast. Over this simple breakfast, Miss Charlotte told Mrs. Watson of what had happened during Lord Ingram's watch, her voice low so as not to disturb his slumber in the loft.

An engrossing and puzzling account. It was only later, after Mrs. Watson had brushed her teeth, that she remembered to ask, "Lord Ingram told you all this and I just slept?"

"I woke up at six and went out to take a look," answered Miss

Charlotte. She stood before a mirror in the parlor, ran her fingers through her still-short hair, and shoved that hair under a blue-and-white turban. "He came back then. We spoke outside."

"Oh, the poor boy, out all night in that horrendous weather."

"He had a hot water bottle. But yes, the poor fellow." Satisfied with her appearance, Miss Charlotte went to the window and lifted the curtain. "Oh, there comes a mackintosh-clad figure. I think it's Mrs. Felton. Let's go meet her."

Not knowing what else might happen, they had gone to sleep fully clad, with dressing gowns on top. Hours in a chair had wrinkled their clothes, but that hardly mattered now, especially when they took off their dressing gowns and threw on their even more enveloping mackintoshes.

Mrs. Felton had dressed for work. Her boots were ancient, the hem that peeked out from under her mackintosh coarse and dingy. Her bare hand, large-knuckled and roughened with labor, held the handle of a bucket. "Ladies, you are headed somewhere?"

"Yes," said Miss Charlotte, walking toward the central path, Mrs. Watson beside her. "Will you accompany us to the carriage house, Mrs. Felton? I have some questions I need to ask you."

Mrs. Felton's eyes brightened. She fell in step next to them. "Did you find out anything about Miss Baxter, miss?"

As the question left her lips, she looked about. The Garden was rain-shrouded. Smoke rose from a few chimneys. But all the houses had their curtains drawn and no one else was abroad.

"We've made some progress," said Miss Charlotte, "but not as much as I'd like. Now Mrs. Felton, do you know a man in Porthangan named Sam Young?"

Mrs. Felton blinked. "Mr. Young, the boat maker? I do know him. Why?"

"Mr. Young came around at midnight last night and set off a dozen or so fireworks and greatly disturbed the peace."

"I had no idea." Mrs. Felton stopped walking for a moment in her surprise. "But whatever for?"

"He claimed to have done it for the woman he loved."

Mrs. Felton's mouth became a perfectly rounded O. "And was Mrs. Crosby properly furious? She was, wasn't she? Oh, Mrs. Crosby would not have liked that."

Mrs. Watson and Miss Charlotte exchanged a look. "Is it common knowledge in the village then, Mr. Young's interest in Mrs. Crosby?" asked Mrs. Watson.

"I should hope not," said Mrs. Felton, her tone vehement. "Gossip like this can damage a lady's reputation. I knew because Mr. Young asked me a few times about the goings-on in the Garden, but his questions always went around to Mrs. Crosby eventually. It was easy to see. But I didn't say anything to anyone."

Rain slanted onto Mrs. Watson's cheek. She flicked away the moisture. "You didn't include it in your monthly reports?"

"Of course not. That's no business of Miss Baxter's father's."

But if the party that had arranged for last night's debacle hadn't learned of Mr. Young's infatuation from Mrs. Felton, then who had been the source?

"Does Mr. Young know anyone else in the Garden?" asked Miss Charlotte. "Do members of the Garden socialize with the villagers?"

"No, they don't, not really. But Mr. Young is a good boat maker, and Miss Baxter bought a boat from him several years ago, so did Miss Fairchild more recently. And the Steeles were talking about commissioning one, too. There isn't much to do around here, and sailing is as good a way to pass time as any."

Miss Charlotte thanked Mrs. Felton and said that they would not keep her from her work. The women parted ways not far from the vegetable patch, Mrs. Felton with a frown on her face. Half a minute later she caught up to Miss Charlotte and Mrs. Watson again.

"Ladies, ladies, I forgot to ask you, did Miss Baxter come out to see the fireworks?"

They all stopped. "No, she didn't," said Miss Charlotte slowly.

"Not even for fireworks? But she loves fireworks."

"Does she?"

Mrs. Felton scratched the side of her red-tipped nose. "Come to think of it, she's never told me anything of the sort. It's just that on her bedroom mantel she has postcards with fireworks on them. So I always thought she liked them."

Mrs. Felton was silent for a moment. "Maybe she was watching from inside. I do hope so."

—————※—————

There were four vehicles in the carriage house: Mrs. Felton's dog-cart, the remise driven in by Lord Ingram, a Victoria, and a large and ancient-looking charabanc that could seat fifteen and probably came with the property when Miss Fairchild had acquired it.

Mr. Peters had used the charabanc to transport Mr. Young and his nephew the night before. In the early hours of the morning, when he'd disappeared with Mrs. Crosby, he'd taken a coach, which remained conspicuously absent.

"Do you think the coach might have come back and gone out again?" asked Mrs. Watson.

Miss Charlotte shook her head. "I see the muddy marks left by Mrs. Felton's carriage coming in, but not a set of muddy marks coming in and going out again."

The remise readied, Miss Charlotte took the reins, Mrs. Watson rode inside. They first went to the village to speak to Mr. Mears, then drove to the nearest railway station.

Mrs. Watson had her eyes peeled. She had no idea what the coach Mr. Peters drove away looked like, but Miss Charlotte said that the other two Garden carriages bore crests with stylized alembics and this one would, too.

Few vehicles stood before the small rural station where they rolled to a stop. Mrs. Watson alit and circled the carriages one by one. She encountered only one rudimentary crest, and it did not feature an alembic.

Miss Charlotte, waiting by the remise, was not surprised or discouraged by their lack of success. They traveled north to a second station, where their search was equally unfruitful. Mrs. Watson took the next turn driving. The remise bounced along narrow country lanes and splashed through puddles. She prayed that the wheels wouldn't get stuck in a rut.

At least the rain was lifting. Sunlight spilled from seams in the clouds, bright slanted rays that haloed the sheep that grazed on the headlands. The air smelled of freshly washed grass. There was even a faint rainbow to the west, a beautiful mirage astride the firmament.

But would their case clear up like the sky after a thunderstorm? Or would it—she looked east at the increasingly foggy coastline—shroud itself in a great maritime brume?

At the third and fourth station along the only railway line in this part of the world, their quest remained futile.

"Is it possible that they didn't board a train but simply drove where they wanted to go?" asked Mrs. Watson, plodding back to the remise.

"They would only do that if they were leaving on a boat. We'll have to look into that possibility if we don't find their coach soon."

Stations weren't that far apart on the branch line. And they'd started south of where Mr. Peters and Mrs. Crosby were apparently headed—in case those two had turned around once they could no longer be seen by watchers on the Garden's walls. So it was within the realm of possibility that the fugitives had driven a little farther.

What were Mr. Peters and Mrs. Crosby fleeing? Mrs. Watson recalled the various cases her late husband had attended. Had it been an appendectomy gone wrong? Did Miss Baxter suffer an aneurysm of the brain? Did her organs, deteriorating over years of slow poisoning, at last fail catastrophically?

Miss Charlotte had predicted that hypotheses would collapse soon. Mrs. Watson hadn't been too sure then, but now she agreed with Miss Charlotte—something significant had happened overnight. If only she knew what it was that caused Mrs. Crosby, who had been glued to the phantom Miss Baxter, to run out with only a satchel and no longer care whether Miss Baxter's house was sufficiently guarded.

The fifth station was larger, with more carriages outside. Still, Mrs. Watson immediately spied the gleaming coach with a golden alembic crest—and the child next to it.

She exclaimed and thumped the top of the carriage with her umbrella. Miss Charlotte, already slowing the carriage, stopped. Mrs. Watson leaped off.

"Oh, look at this. It's my friend's coach," she said brightly as she approached the child standing guard. "Did he pay you to look after it, young man?"

"You ain't be getting it from me, lady," said the urchin. "The guv'nor tole me not to give it to nobody 'cept 'im."

"Goodness gracious, what would I do with his carriage when I've already got my own? But I'm surprised he isn't back yet. I didn't know he was going to take so long when he left this morning. When did he say he'd come back for the carriage?"

"Afore teatime."

"Billy Simmons, who you talking to?" An older urchin with an obvious family resemblance to Billy Simmons came running.

"Nobody."

"And what did you tell her?"

"Nothing."

The older urchin looked at Mrs. Watson warily. "We've nothing else to tell you, lady. Best you be on your way."

"I was just asking the young man here whether he would be interested in joining the Salvation Army's Prodigal Sons Society," said Mrs. Watson smoothly, "but perhaps another time."

Inside the station, the ticket agent was not terribly helpful, though he was apologetic about it. The early morning had been busy and he had looked only at the amount of money handed in, not at the faces of the travelers.

They yielded their place when others queued up at the window. Mrs. Watson paced in frustration. At last they'd found the carriage, but where had Mr. Peters and Mrs. Crosby gone?

When the ticket-buyers had left, Miss Charlotte went up to the window again and asked the clerk if by any chance one of the urchins that hung about the station had bought any tickets this day. The man blinked but said no, he did not believe so.

On the drive back, Mrs. Watson joined Miss Charlotte on the driver's perch. The scenery would have been beautiful but for the fog that already obscured the sea and crept steadily inland.

At one point, a gust dispersed some of the vapors, only to reveal three sinister-looking tombstones on a desolate headland, one of which tilted drunkenly.

By the time they arrived at the Garden of Hermopolis, Mrs. Watson's mood had become as overcast as the day. But Miss Charlotte leaped down from the driver's seat, stretched, and said cheerfully, "It's time for lunch. I hope they have a good pudding."

❖

The previous afternoon, Livia had spent futile hours scouring newspaper archives, seeking information on Snowham. Today, her venue was the Reading Room at the British Museum, but her work was no more productive: She called for books, flipped through them, and found little of note.

She closed her eyes and rubbed her face. The last time she had been in the Reading Room, it had been summer and she'd arranged a clandestine meeting with Charlotte. The occasion had been hopeful, very nearly giddy. Charlotte had just found her footing as Sherlock Holmes, Livia had decided that she would write a story based on Charlotte's exploits, and the future had seemed bright and appealing.

The name *Moriarty* had not yet entered their lexicon. And she had yet to meet Mr. Marbleton—though undoubtedly he already knew of her. And was probably following her about town, waiting for an opportunity to introduce himself.

Her hand settled atop a hidden pocket in her skirt and felt the outline of the cloisonné box. *Please. What are you trying to tell us?*

Agitated, she rose and returned a stack of books to the clerks at the catalogue tables. She still had a few more books to go through, but what should she do after that? Ask for the even more marginally related tomes? What other avenue of inquiry was left?

She turned around to go back to her seat. Three men marched in her direction. A jolt shot up her vertebrae.

The man in the middle looked like Mr. Marbleton.

No, it *was* him.

The moment seemed caught in tree sap, barely flowing. The light washing down from the oculus of the dome overhead gleamed upon his top hat. The flaps of his long coat fluttered sinuously around his knees, like water plants in a pond. He pulled off his gloves and took all of eternity to gently tuck them into a pocket of his coat.

Alarm surged in her veins. No, no, she must not stare at him. The men beside him were Moriarty's minions. It would not do to attract their attention. Not only would she put herself in harm's way, but she would make his already-trying situation that much more difficult.

She looked straight ahead and marched on limbs that felt like wet clay. Her hands tight around her reticule, her face pinched, she hoped she presented the very image of a bluestocking, even though she wasn't learned enough to be one. As she passed the trio, however, she couldn't help but glance in his direction, a look toward his chest rather than his face.

Only to see him raise a hand and touch something on the lapel of his greatcoat.

As slow as the earlier moment had been, everything now happened in acceleration. Whatever he'd touched was a blur of color and texture. And then he and his escorts were behind her.

Her heart pounding, she didn't dare turn around, but headed directly for her seat and sat down. She shook. Even her teeth chattered.

What was he doing at the Reading Room? Had Moriarty let him out? Perhaps he was permitted to go about London, or whichever city he and Moriarty happened to be in, as long as he was properly "escorted."

But why the Reading Room?

In all their exchanges—too few, alas, always too few—he had never given her the impression that he was a scholar. To be sure, Charlotte, a frequent visitor to the Reading Room, wasn't one either, but she was encyclopedic in her reading habits. Mr. Marbleton, like Livia, preferred fiction, not exactly what the Reading Room was best known for in its collection.

Had he come for her, by some chance?

She pressed a hand over her heart, trying to slow its thunderous beat.

Hadn't she just been thinking about the previous summer, when he had followed her in secret around London? Had he observed her trip here to meet with Charlotte?

Present-day Mr. Marbleton, if he wished to see her or give a message to her, could not possibly drop by Mrs. Watson's place. Nor could he approach her hotel, even if he knew where she was staying, for the same reason that a minute ago they hadn't looked at each other.

Was the Reading Room his educated guess then?

If—if his presence here was intentional, then he must have a purpose. Did he want to convey something that would help her understand the message embedded in that lowly, dirtied, precious ticket stub?

But how could he, when he was being watched?

She gripped the edge of the table, needing to hold on to something solid and heavy.

Under the Reading Room's 140-foot-diameter dome—the information was printed directly on the back of her reader's ticket, a proud boast on the part of the institution—the large, circular space was anchored by the superintendent's table at the very center. Catalogue tables formed a close ring around the superintendent's table. From there, reading tables, measuring around thirty feet in length, radiated like spokes on a wheel.

Livia, being herself, had chosen an empty table and a seat far away from the center of the room. Each reading table had a high partition running down its center, to give those on one side privacy from those on the opposite side. Normally, Livia was grateful for such man-made hedges to hide behind. But the partitions on her own very long table and the adjacent one, while shielding her from the attention of Moriarty's men, also blocked her view of Mr. Marbleton.

She could crane her head all she wanted but see only a narrow alley. And if she stood up, which she dared not do, she still wouldn't be able to peer over the partition, not without stepping on the crossbar of a chair, at the very least.

She loosened a button at her collar—she was breathing fast and perspiring. Not knowing what to do next, she flipped her notebook to an empty page, scribbled down the date and her location, and stared at the words until they swam.

How much time had passed? How long would he be allowed to stay? And could he relay anything to her when she couldn't see him?

Tears of frustration stung the backs of her eyes. She hoped—she prayed hard—that he had given this some thought before he arrived. That even though the chance of him running into her was small, he'd prepared for this lucky encounter.

202 · *Sherry Thomas*

Another ten minutes elapsed, the passage of time as swift as a flood *and* as slow as a retreating glacier. She was still shaking, still waiting, still not sure what she could do, when Mr. Marbleton appeared at one end of her alley, toward the center of the Reading Room.

Some reading tables had a bookshelf appended—hers was one such. He stood before the bookshelf. Or rather, he and his two minders stood shoulder to shoulder, and she almost couldn't see him at all.

"It's time to go," one of them said to him.

In German.

"So soon?" he replied in the same language. "I haven't been here since summer. How about a little more time?"

*No, please, not so soon.* She hadn't even had a good look at him.

"We are sorry. It's time to leave," repeated the other escort.

The escort suddenly turned in her direction. She averted her gaze to her still-open notebook, not daring to look up even with her peripheral vision.

The floor of the Reading Room had been covered with a special material to reduce the sound of footsteps. Livia barely heard their departure.

She dropped her head into her hands. She wanted to whimper. She wanted to scream. Had he tried to tell her something? And had she already failed him?

# *Fifteen*

Only after a quarter of an hour had passed did Livia get up, tiptoe to the very rim of the Reading Room, and slowly walk its circumference, pretending to be interested in the books that encircled the room while casting furtive glances into the alleys created by the high partitions. And when she had completed the circle, she walked the smaller round between the catalogue tables and the reading tables, surreptitiously checking the alleys again from their inner ends.

"Miss, are you searching for something?"

She nearly jumped.

An attendant stationed at a catalogue table, a man with what seemed to be a perennially suspicious expression on his face, had asked the question. Faced with disapproval, Livia usually found it difficult to retain her composure. But today her nerves were too frayed for her to care.

"My friend was going to join me here today. She is about this tall"—she gestured with her hand held up to her ear—"and has dark hair and green eyes. Have you seen her, by any chance?"

"I'm afraid I haven't."

She turned her back to him and went to the bookshelf at the end of her reading table, where Mr. Marbleton had stopped briefly. It held volumes of *Encyclopaedia Britannica*. Could he have done anything here? Left her something, the way he'd left a ticket stub at 18 Upper Baker Street?

She crouched low. But the bottom shelf rested directly on the floor, with no space underneath.

Had he picked up a volume while he'd stood here, and slipped a note inside?

She took the encyclopedias one by one to her desk. At first she flipped each page religiously. When that proved too slow, she examined a volume sideways at eye level and searched for any tiny gap in the pages. And then, when her patience wore too thin for even that, with her back to the catalogue tables and with many apologies to the encyclopedias themselves, she held the volumes by their spines and shook.

A card fell out of the third volume she shook. Her heart thudded violently. But it was only a card the publisher had put in.

As she returned once again to the bookshelf, the attendant who had earlier asked whether she was looking for something looked at her oddly. Her disappointment cut so much, she barely heard his sniff of disfavor. With a wooden resolve, she checked until she ran out of volumes.

Back at her desk, she pressed her palms against her eyes.

She didn't want to move, but she also couldn't stay where she was. Even if the Reading Room were open twenty-four hours a day, she still needed to go back to her hotel. Soon.

With hands that didn't seem to be her own, she put her pencil and notebook back into her reticule and checked that she still had Mrs. Watson's reader's ticket. Officially tickets were not transferable but she hadn't brought her own, as she hadn't expected to be in London in the first place.

On the front of the ticket was written Mrs. Watson's name and the period of time for which the ticket had been granted. Tickets were rarely issued for more than six months at a time. Mrs. Watson's had been renewed in September and would be usable until the beginning of next month.

Renewal . . .

Livia sat up straighter. Mr. Marbleton had said himself, didn't he, that he hadn't been to the Reading Room since summer? That being the case, had he needed to renew his ticket?

She was afraid to try. What looked like an avenue of hope would most likely turn out to be another blind alley, another wall for her to smash into.

But she also couldn't not try. She swallowed, gathered the rest of her things, marched to the catalogue tables, and approached one of the attendants—not the one who had spoken to her, but a kindlier-looking man who hadn't been there earlier. "Good day, sir. I do believe I need to renew my ticket."

"Very well, miss," he replied. "Here is the register for you to sign."

The register was a thick bound book, open to a page marked with the date. Underneath, the space was divided into ten rubrics, each identical except for the printed number to the left. Above the number, either a large R was written, indicating a renewal, or two numbers were written, separated by a slash, to show that the reader was new to the Reading Room.

Inside each rubric were printed the words *I have read the directions respecting the Reading Room and I declare that I am not under twenty-one years of age.* And under that, a space reserved for the reader's signature and address.

A quick scan showed no names that she recognized—nor any handwriting that she could be sure belonged to Mr. Marbleton. She would not be surprised if he wrote in several scripts. It was a useful skill to have, especially for a man in his circumstances. But at the moment it worked against *her.*

"Your ticket, please, miss," said the attendant.

She was beginning to perspire again. "A moment, please. Let me find it. Oh, there's a gentleman waiting there. Perhaps you can help him first?"

Since it was so easy to renew tickets, the Reading Room rarely renewed them before they expired. If she were to present her ticket right away, she would be gently but firmly turned away.

The attendant went to assist the other reader. Livia opened her reticule and stuck a hand inside, giving the appearance that she was conducting a search. With her other hand she flipped the register back a page.

This spread of two pages also contained registrations and renewals from today. Again, she encountered no names that she recognized. What if he used an alias with which she was unfamiliar? How would she know that it was his?

The Reading Room was not a bustling place, precisely, but hundreds of readers did come through daily. How many renewals and new ticket issuances would there be on a given day?

Eight signatures there had been on the next page, and on these two pages, twenty. Twenty-eight altogether. He had come less than two hours ago. Even if these twenty-eight did not represent the whole day's count, they had to exceed the number that had taken place since his arrival.

So if he had written anything in here, it must be either on these two facing pages or the next.

She read over the lines, her heartbeat thudding in the back of her head. So many names. So many bewilderingly different styles of handwriting. But still she didn't see anything she associated with him. Nor was the word *Snowham* visible anywhere.

"Miss, have you found your ticket yet?" asked the attendant.

Her heart thumped even faster. Could she say she'd misplaced her ticket? No, then she'd need to leave her spot to find it. Could she pretend that she was having trouble locating it in her handbag? Well, under the attendant's gaze, she'd probably need to remove her eyes from the register and actually look into the handbag.

There was no point doing either. She bit the inside of her cheek, pulled out Mrs. Watson's ticket, and handed it to him.

The moment he took it to look, she flipped the register ahead to the latest page, where she was supposed to sign and put down her place of residence.

"Mrs. Watson."

He meant her, the imposter. Was he about to take away the register? She gripped it tight, her eyes glued to the page.

*Charles Edmonds, 36 Piccadilly W*
*John Dore, 37 Chalcot Crescent, Primrose Hill*
*Elliot Hartford, 23 Hanley Street*
*Clarissa Cockerill, Marble Hill House*
*Alfred Barr, 41 Eden Grove*
*Charles Bird, 8 St. Marys Road*
*Victoria Rowland, 15 Park Lane*
*William Korley, 13 College Place, Camden*

No, she did not know *any* of these people, and she did not know anyone who lived at these addresses.

Except . . . something skittered across the surface of her mind. What was it?

"You don't need to renew your ticket yet, Mrs. Watson," continued the attendant, interrupting her train of thought. "You've still two weeks left."

She nearly tore off the page in her frustration.

But wait, it was the name *Elliot Hartford* that had plucked at the edges of her memory.

*Elliot Hartford.*

She sucked in a breath and looked into the attendant's baffled face.

She remembered now. Last summer Miss Marbleton, Mr. Marbleton's sister, had gone by the name *Ellie Hartford*. It might be a coincidence. Or it might not be.

She stared down at the address again, imprinting it on her memory.

And then she said to the attendant, her heart still pounding, "Oh, I don't need to renew my ticket now? Very well, then, thank you and good day."

—✣—

Lord Ingram awakened a little past ten, groggy and hungry. He found the note the ladies had left, as well as slices of buttered toast they had made for him.

Those were good, but not enough. He visited the kitchen and asked for some more bread and butter, which Mrs. Brown, the cook, readily dispensed, alongside a jar of raspberry jam, a jar of potted chicken, half a dozen boiled eggs, and two sausages. When she heard that he planned to heat water for the ladies' bath, she even sent the kitchen maid to bring him a few extra buckets.

When Mrs. Watson and Holmes returned, he'd already placed a pan of hot coals in the bath and heated enough water for two people. The ladies both expressed great gratitude and great interest in a wash, but Holmes had, as he'd thought, a more pressing need for food.

After Mrs. Watson left for her ablutions, Holmes, spreading butter and potted chicken on her toast, glanced up and said, "So you have found favor with Mrs. Brown."

"Have I?" he murmured, his face heating a little.

She took a bite. "I approve. You should make it your mission to find favor with every cook we come across."

His face heated more. "I could have bought all these for you at the village, without finding favor with anyone."

She took another bite. "But I prefer that she gave this feast to you because she likes the way you look. God took His time to make you striking, Ash. Don't let His effort go to waste."

"And I will have squandered His effort if I don't charm every cook for your sake?"

She smiled very slightly. "Yes, indeed."

He poured tea for her. "Very well, you continue to write your erotic tale and I will inveigle unsuspecting cooks into offering me additional breakfast dainties."

She stopped eating—he'd managed to astound her. "You *want* more epistolary prurience?"

"I've come to enjoy the feeling of . . . outrage."

She resumed chewing, looking him up and down. Then she took two sips of tea, looked him over some more, and licked her lips in a gesture of provocation.

One second passed. Two seconds. Three seconds.

He licked his lips in the exact same manner. Or, perhaps, more blatantly.

She stared at him. "That is . . . shameless."

"You wouldn't have kept after me all these years if you didn't always believe me to be shameless, deep down."

She perused him again, her gaze passing over him like a flame. "Others have esteemed my judgment for years. For the very first time I, too, am filled with admiration for my insight."

He laughed—and put his head down on the table because he couldn't stop laughing.

Sounds came from the bath—not sounds of water, but of Mrs. Watson gathering up her things. He rose. "I'll go fetch our luncheon from the kitchen."

In case he couldn't stop laughing even in front of Mrs. Watson.

The sea fog that had rolled in earlier in the day still persisted, not as bad as a pea-souper but dense enough that visibility was reduced to fewer than twenty feet. He checked the carriage house first—the coach taken by Mr. Peters hadn't returned. Then he walked by Miss Baxter's lodge—walked three times around it, in fact. The house had its doors and windows tightly secured, but not a single person came to demand what he was doing.

At last he headed for the kitchen, skirting around it so it would appear that he'd come from the direction of his own cottage, rather than the cluster of houses that contained Miss Baxter's lodge. As he approached, voices rose from the large portico in front of the kitchen. By habit he concealed himself along a side wall.

"Miss Stoppard, Miss Stoppard, did I hear you say that you are picking up Miss Baxter's luncheon today?"

He recognized the voice less by its timbre than by its marked tone of ingratiation. Mrs. Steele.

Miss Stoppard's reply was curt. "Yes."

"Is Mrs. Crosby unwell? She's usually the one who does that for Miss Baxter, isn't she?"

"And I do it in her absence. Mrs. Crosby has gone to visit a friend in Brighton."

"All of a sudden?" This voice belonged to Miss Ellery. "And how is Miss Baxter?"

"She is well."

"When can we call on her?" Mrs. Steele again. "We are anxious to see her."

"Shortly, I'm sure. Shortly," said Miss Stoppard, sounding as impatient as Mr. Peters had in the small hours of the morning. "Good day, ladies. Miss Baxter is waiting for her meal."

She departed, her footsteps light but brisk.

"Shortly. Shortly," mumbled Mrs. Steele, her words resigned. "How many times have we been told we'd see Miss Baxter shortly?"

Miss Ellery only sighed.

❖

Lord Ingram spent some time every year at his seaside cottage in north Devon and understood the variability of maritime weather. But after a long inland winter of similarly grey days, the rapidly changing atmospheric conditions of the Cornish coast still managed to startle him. It was as if he'd been living with a companion of a dour but steady temperament and was now thrust into the presence of someone who bawled his eyes out one minute and keeled over with laughter the next.

The fog, so dense and omnipresent before luncheon, had completely disappeared an hour later, when he, Holmes, and Mrs. Watson left on their afternoon excursion. The sky was a bright, transparent blue; the sea gleamed silver with reflected sunlight. The storm of the night before was evident only on rooftops that still glistened damply, and the mud stuck to carriage wheels and soles of boots.

They collected Mr. Mears from Porthangan and drove up the headlands. Several brown goats scrambled away when they alit from the remise. At Mrs. Watson's suggestion, they climbed up an outcrop. At the top, standing in a knot, they listened to Mr. Mears, who had been making inquiries concerning the Garden of Hermopolis and Miss Baxter, give a summary of his findings.

To be sure, there were those who did not care for a heathen outpost here in the heart of Christendom. But by and large, the residents of the Garden were not thought of as heretics. Rather, they were considered peaceful neighbors and, often, generous patrons. Much of their foodstuff was supplied by village fishermen and nearby farmers. They bought local crafts and contributed to local charity efforts. Miss Baxter, in particular, had even served as judge in a village boat race.

Mrs. Felton, the only villager in direct and regular contact with the Garden, inspired mixed feelings. Some thought her too self-satisfied, but even those who believed so had to admit that she had a good heart and was altogether harmless. Mr. Mears had spoken to her brother, who defended her good fortune in *having been remembered in her late employer's will*—the excuse she gave for being able to afford her own house, carriage, and horse—as a natural consequence of her caring nature and capacity for hard work.

With regard to Mr. Young, the disturber of the peace the night before, his skills as a boat maker were universally praised. As a man, he was judged a good uncle to his orphaned nephew, though *a little less steady than he ought to be at his age* was also a recurring refrain.

Mr. Mears confirmed that Mr. Young was seen walking with a visitor to the harbor the previous afternoon. Mindful of Mrs. Crosby's reputation, Mr. Mears had refrained from any questions that directly connected her to Mr. Young, as news of the unwanted fireworks had not yet spread, and the villagers were blissfully unaware that one of their own had been the cause of so much chaos three miles away at the Garden.

"For all that the Garden is a religious oddity," he concluded, "the community seems to enjoy a fine reputation. Miss Fairchild is thought of as a very respectable lady. Miss Baxter, furthermore, is considered grand. More than one person recalled how majestic she had appeared the time she served as the boat race's judge, how she stood on the seawall of the harbor looking like the queen of the sea herself."

From where they stood, the seawall was almost directly below, a ribbon of defense against the ceaseless waves. Lord Ingram tried to imagine a crowd of awestruck villagers surrounding a regal Miss Baxter, her face proudly upturned, her skirts billowing in the breeze. But his gaze kept shifting to Holmes, a few steps to the side, slowly twirling her parasol, observing everything with her usual expression of impenetrable blandness.

"Mr. Mears, do you think that perhaps among the villagers Miss Baxter's prestige outstrips Miss Fairchild's?" piped up Mrs. Watson, kicking away a pebble with the tip of her boot. It fell down the side of the outcrop and landed with a small thud on the grass below.

Mr. Mears scratched his chin. "I never asked that question directly, but judging by everything I've been told . . . Yes, I do believe that to be the case."

Mrs. Watson's meaning was not lost on Lord Ingram. Power struggles among ladies were as real as those among men—albeit since women had access to less power, and frequently only power of a less tangible sort, their jockeying for position was not taken as seriously. But to anyone who must live within a pecking order, the influence and dominance exerted by those at the top was all too real.

If Miss Fairchild, the founder of the community, felt herself playing second fiddle to Miss Baxter . . .

——❈——

They returned Mr. Mears to the village and drove back to the Garden. Mrs. Felton, who opened the gate for them, asked whether Holmes had gone to post her report of the night's events.

"I suppose I can write one now," said Holmes, unconcerned.

Mrs. Felton's hands rose to midair in her shock. "You haven't written one yet, miss? You must hurry or you'll miss the post."

"Do your work, Holmes," said Lord Ingram, smiling. He offered his arm to Mrs. Watson. "Shall we take a walk in the surrounding area, ma'am?"

The day remained incandescently lovely. The headlands were a fresh, primeval green. In the distance herds of sheep grazed, fluffy with a year's worth of wool. Seagulls drifted on the breeze, their caws made musical by the rhythm of the waves.

"Oh, look at that. There's a hole in that rock face," exclaimed Mrs. Watson.

They were walking down the steep slope that led to the small promontory below the Garden. The descent led to a shallow, flat area. But beyond that, the promontory reared up, stony and precipitous. And there was indeed a hole, too small for anything larger than a cat to pass through, but too deep and dark for them to see where or whether it ended.

"There are many caves on the Cornish coast," he said. "Perhaps this is an entrance to a cave."

"Perhaps it has a larger opening somewhere else," mused Mrs. Watson. "Do you suppose it might have been used for smuggling back in the day?"

They did find a larger opening on the seaward side of the promontory. But it narrowed quickly, and four feet in, Lord Ingram not only could no longer move an inch forward but found himself wedged in place. In extricating himself, he tore a button off the front of his greatcoat.

"Are you all right, my dear?" said Mrs. Watson, standing outside the cave.

"Yes, although my coat cannot claim to be equally unscathed."

She fussed over his clothes for a minute. They turned around and faced the sea. The slope here was sharp but not dangerous, and it was not a bad vantage point from which to enjoy a view of the horizon.

"I have been wondering . . ." murmured Mrs. Watson.

Ah, at last. He knew she had questions for him. "Yes, ma'am?"

She'd collapsed her parasol, so that it wouldn't be blown away by an unpredictable gust. Holding its handle, she tapped the tip of the parasol on the ground. "I've been wondering, my dear—too late, of course—but I've been wondering . . . In always creating opportunities for you and Miss Charlotte to be alone, have I been thoughtless?"

He half smiled, half grimaced to himself. Mrs. Watson did sometimes have a certain look on her face, as if she were scheming to physically shove Holmes and him together.

"There have been occasions when I thought you would clap, ma'am, if Holmes and I . . . made certain progress."

"There have been occasions when I had my hands ready and waiting." She emitted an embarrassed laugh. "But now that I can clap for you, I feel . . ."

He had noticed. That look had been absent on this trip.

She gazed at the sea. Under the sunlight it was turquoise with streaks of dark, somber blue. "It's like attending a childbirth. In theory it's a wonderful event. But in fact, no one knows whether the mother will survive, or the baby. If the child survives the womb, it can be felled by pneumonia when it's three, or scarlet fever two years later. And even if the child is strong as an ox, it can still die in a shipwreck or a carriage accident."

"After a hopeful beginning, there is no end to the mishaps and obstacles," he said.

She sighed. "And I've always fretted about all the potential pitfalls."

His heart constricted. "And what potential pitfalls. She loves freedom, but I cannot give her more freedom. I love security, but she cannot give me greater security."

And sometimes, in the midst of his happiness, he felt . . . not dissatisfaction per se but a hollow sensation, an urgent need polluted with a few drops of fear.

The forlornness of someone who wanted to hold on with both hands forced to keep his hands at his side.

A flock of seagulls, which had been floating on the waves, spread their wings and took to the sky. He offered his arm to Mrs. Watson again. "Don't be sad, ma'am. I am far happier today than I was a year ago, far happier even than I was three months ago. I simply do not know what will happen in the future, that's all. None of us do."

She leaned her head on his shoulder. "I suppose you are right."

He was. He was a bit melancholy, too, so he resolved to ask Holmes to make her erotic tale twice as salacious. That wouldn't resolve the fundamental problem—not in the least—but it would be great fun, wouldn't it?

They climbed back up to the top of the bluffs. Near the Garden's gate, Mrs. Felton drove out and waved at them—she'd finished her work for the day and was leaving with Holmes's letter to post. They detoured by the carriage house—the Garden's coach still hadn't returned.

Halfway down the somewhat muddy central path, a woman in a grey jacket and a matching pair of bloomers came around a dormant garden bed.

"Miss Stoppard?" As she neared, Lord Ingram asked with some hesitation. He'd never seen her in good light.

"That's right," said Miss Stoppard.

And walked past them without another word, headed for their cottage. Lord Ingram and Mrs. Watson exchanged a look.

In front of their cottage, Miss Stoppard knocked. Lord Ingram and Mrs. Watson stopped a few paces away. The woman didn't seem to want any hospitality, best let her get on with what she had come to do.

Holmes opened the door.

Without any preamble, Miss Stoppard handed over an envelope. "Good afternoon, Miss Holmes. I have something for you from Miss Baxter."

Mrs. Watson's hand tightened around Lord Ingram's forearm.

"Thank you," said Holmes.

Miss Stoppard nodded, pivoted, and left.

By the time Lord Ingram and Mrs. Watson entered the cottage, Holmes had already broken the seal on the envelope.

She pulled out a card, glanced at it, then glanced up at Lord Ingram and Mrs. Watson. "The card says, 'Miss Baxter will be pleased to receive Miss Holmes and company this evening at six.'"

## Sixteen

Oxford Street ranked among London's—and therefore perhaps the world's—busiest thoroughfares. So it should come as no surprise that Hanley Street, an offshoot of Oxford Street, had plenty of commercial establishments and that 23 Hanley Street was a shop front.

Yet Livia, standing across the street, was so dismayed she could barely understand the words on the display window.

FINE PATRIOTIC SOUVENIRS FOR HER MAJESTY'S GOLDEN JUBILEE.

Carriages rumbled past without cease in both directions. Customers ran with parcels to their carriages. Pedestrians darted between clarences and hansom cabs, then shouted and swore as they were splashed by churning carriage wheels.

With all the commotion, Livia still saw those words much too clearly.

She had made a terrible mistake. This couldn't be the address toward which Mr. Marbleton had tried so hard to point her. Which one should it have been? She tried to recall the other addresses, but numbers and letters ran amok in her head.

Maybe he hadn't touched the register at all. Maybe he'd meant to signal her some other way and she'd missed it entirely. Or maybe he hadn't been able to do anything at all, but was as helpless as she herself and—

She took a deep breath. She must calm down. She must not despair. And she must not have so little faith in herself. For now, she was going to assume that she was correct, that this was the place.

She crossed the street, stopped directly before the display window, and squinted at the rows of neatly arranged merchandise inside. There were yellow-and-purple hats that would have made Charlotte's magpie soul trill in joy; ribbons featuring the queen's pudgy, unsmiling face; and teacups painted with the dates of her fifty years on the throne. There were also stacks of Jubilee playing cards and Jubilee fans, interspersed with cockades and what looked like rather fat Jubilee fountain pens.

*The cockades!*

She blinked and leaned down for a closer look. But there was no question, the glimpse of color and texture she'd seen on his coat—he had worn such a cockade as a brooch.

All at once she could envision him, standing before the register in the Reading Room, looking at his guards and asking softly in German, *What should I put down for my address?*

The guards would respond along the lines of *Anything, as long as it's wrong.*

And he would have shrugged, pulled a card out of his pocket, and jotted down 23 Hanley Street.

*What's that?*

*At the place where I bought my cockade, they gave me a card. Said I should bring the ladies of the family the next time.*

But was it a coincidence or had he planned it?

She had spoken very little with Mr. Marbleton about his upbringing—a subject that made her uneasy. He and his family had never lived anywhere permanently because of Moriarty's long arm and even longer shadow. But she knew that he possessed no particular patriotic fervor for either queen or country. She also knew, from Charlotte's words and her own observations, that his family was adept at disguises and other sorts of subterranean communications.

He had planned it. He might not have expected any chances of success, but he *had* planned it.

But what could Livia possibly learn from a shop full of Jubilee goods?

❊

After the initial burst of chatter over the invitation, Miss Charlotte recommended that everyone should get ready.

By getting ready, Mrs. Watson thought she meant to discuss strategy. Instead, the girl started packing. Lord Ingram took a look at her and did the same. Mrs. Watson hesitated a little longer before joining in. It couldn't hurt, she supposed. After all, if they indeed saw Miss Baxter tonight, then the thing to do would be to catch the next train back to London and disclose their findings to Moriarty.

*If* they indeed saw Miss Baxter tonight, that is.

Lord Ingram, the first to be finished, went out to the walls again. He came back within minutes and reported that Mr. Peters had returned with the coach, but Mrs. Crosby had not come back with him.

Miss Charlotte nodded and went back to buckling her satchel.

"Miss Charlotte, you don't seem surprised about it," said Mrs. Watson, unnerved. "You weren't even surprised about the invitation to Miss Baxter's."

"I don't know enough to judge the significance of Mr. Peters's and Mrs. Crosby's comings and goings," said Miss Charlotte. She rose to her feet, walked to the door, and donned her mantle. "As for the invitation to Miss Baxter's, you are right about that—I wasn't surprised. The events last night were always meant to force somebody's hand."

They walked to Miss Baxter's lodge under a purple dusk, a few rays of light still glowing in the western sky. In front of the lodge, they met Miss Fairchild, Miss Ellery, and the Steeles, also brandishing invitations. Mrs. Watson, already astounded, was now staggered. Were she trying to pass off someone as Miss Baxter at this point, she would not have invited anyone who had actually known her.

As Lord Ingram hadn't formally met the Garden's residents, introductions were performed. Mr. Steele rang the doorbell. Miss Stoppard answered the door and greeted the callers with a nod.

In the vestibule, the company shed coats and stashed walking sticks and umbrellas. They proceeded to a small entry hall, where Miss Stoppard said to them, "I'll let Miss Baxter know that you are here."

She opened the parlor door a crack and disappeared inside; the residents of the Garden followed her with their eyes. The Steeles appeared nonplussed; Miss Ellery, restless and excited. Miss Fairchild, on the other hand, seemed a little troubled.

Miss Charlotte walked about the entry hall, looking at the décor. Mrs. Watson remembered the disturbing painting in the library that was attributed to Miss Baxter. Fortunately, in the entry at least, the pictures were seascapes and still lifes, with little to excite the imagination.

"Miss Baxter is ready to see you," said Miss Stoppard.

And with that, she opened the parlor door all the way.

Mrs. Watson groaned inwardly. A large canvas hung opposite the door. A woman in white, her red hair streaming in the wind, pushed a long gleaming sword into the eye socket of a skull, pinning it to the ground. Blood seeped out from the skull. As if that weren't disconcerting enough, a blood-speckled serpent climbed up one of the woman's bare, shapely limbs, its forked tongue already past her knee.

Mrs. Watson was sure the image would haunt her the entire time she remained in the lodge, but the moment she walked into the parlor, she forgot about the painting.

On any other occasion, she would have marveled at the existence of such a drawing room at the very edge of a Cornish cliff. Between the huge, gilded mirrors, the Watteau-esque murals of brightly dressed revelers against a sylvan background, and the slender-legged furniture upholstered in a creamy silk with just a whisper of green, this parlor would not have felt out of place in the stateliest *hôtels particuliers* in Paris.

But tonight, Mrs. Watson's gaze fell on the woman half inclined on a settee. Her face was very pale, almost translucent, that of an already-fair person who hadn't seen the sun in long months, the auburn hair that Mrs. Felton had mentioned gathered back in a sleek chignon. She wore an evening gown in dark green velvet, with a square décolletage showing off smooth skin and a pair of very pretty collarbones. The sleeves ended at the elbow. On one bare forearm she sported an emerald-studded bangle, on the other, a snake bracelet in shiny gold.

As the crowd entered, she turned her face. Her eyes were long and deep set, the irises a hazel made much darker by her midnight-forest gown. Not the most beautiful woman Mrs. Watson had ever seen, but these were stunning eyes and the effect of their direct sweep . . .

Mrs. Watson had to wrestle with an urge to lower her head and curtsy.

If anything, Mrs. Felton had understated the grandness of Miss Baxter.

"Please sit down," she said.

Her voice was a little hoarse, yet that served only to add to the power of her presence.

"Thank you, Miss Baxter," said the Steeles and Miss Ellery in unison.

The room was not lit like Versailles on the night of a ball, but it was not dim by any means. If anyone was trying to pass off a counterfeit Miss Baxter, they were confident enough to do so not only before people who had known her for years but under full illumination.

The bustle of seven people sitting down and Miss Stoppard making tea to the side further emphasized Miss Baxter's stillness. She moved not at all, except for her transfixing gaze, which traveled from caller to caller, and came to rest on Miss Charlotte, who was at her usual wholehearted inspection of the refreshments on offer.

Miss Stoppard poured tea and handed around plates of pastry. Despite her bloomers, which did her figure no favors—a woman might as well wear narrow trousers if she was going to wear trousers—Miss Stoppard was in fact a woman of refined beauty. Had Miss Baxter not been in the room, Miss Stoppard would have made for a commanding hostess. But with Miss Baxter present, no one could mistake Miss Stoppard for anything other than a dedicated handmaiden.

"I would have risen to greet you all," said Miss Baxter, "but I'm afraid I twisted my ankle badly last night, leaving my bed in a hurry amid cries of fire and ruin."

Mrs. Watson noticed for the first time that Miss Baxter was covered with a thickish black blanket, leaving only the most dramatic part of her evening gown visible. As for the ankle, it was not a bad excuse for someone who had failed to run outside when flames licked the walls.

"But that's terrible," said Miss Ellery. "I hope you weren't too afraid."

"No, indeed, I was not afraid. I heard everyone's voices and knew that if I called for aid, you would all storm the house."

Until this moment, Mrs. Watson had swung between amazement and mistrust. If Miss Baxter had been perfectly fine all this time, why had she let things escalate until her father sent in Sherlock Holmes? Was it really as Miss Ellery had said, that having been kidnapped once, she feared for her safety and refused to meet with outsiders? For what reason then had she changed her mind and was now happy to receive all and sundry?

Therefore, although the woman on the settee looked just like Miss Baxter had in the photographs, Mrs. Watson had been inclined to believe that she was an actress smuggled in from London, and the resemblance a matter of advanced stagecraft. But the unmistakable—and casual—sarcasm in her voice at last convinced Mrs. Watson that she *might* be looking at the genuine article. That and the overwhelmed expression on Miss Ellery's face: She was delighted and flustered that Miss Baxter had deigned to speak to her, even if it had been in reprimand.

Which echoed Mrs. Felton's urgent concern for Miss Baxter, despite the fact that Miss Baxter had rarely been satisfied with her work.

"It's been so long since we last saw you. We thought you'd become ill," said Mrs. Steele.

"I was not ill," said Miss Baxter, resting the side of her head languidly against the back of the settee. "I simply wished for solitude, which we members of the Garden all came for—the ability to be alone, without needing to remove ourselves completely from human company."

Another reprimand, delivered without hesitation. Yet to judge by Mrs. Steele's reaction, it had fallen as a benediction upon her shoulders, the words welcome and cherished.

"But I'm grateful for your concern, which is why I have asked you to join me this evening." Miss Baxter turned her head and for the first time addressed Miss Charlotte directly. "I do apologize for your trouble, Miss Holmes. How and where I conduct my life is a matter of contention between my father and myself. It's really too bad that he refuses to believe regular assurances of my well-being."

Miss Charlotte inclined her head. "It has been no trouble at all. At worst, this has been a pleasant excursion from London, with Mr. Baxter footing all the expenses."

Unlike Mrs. Watson, who still felt at a loss, doubting her eyes one moment, her judgment the next, Miss Charlotte seemed to view everything taking place this evening as a most natural development. Even Miss Stoppard, glancing at the callers once in a while from her position behind Miss Baxter, evinced a more skeptical attitude.

"And my apologies to you, too, Miss Fairchild," said Miss Baxter, lifting her wrist a few inches as if in acknowledgment.

What did she need to apologize to Miss Fairchild for? The presence of three strangers at the Garden?

Miss Fairchild inclined her head, the graveness of her countenance softening a little as she regarded Miss Baxter.

An audience, thought Mrs. Watson. They had all been summoned to an audience—and would be dismissed in time.

Indeed, as everyone drank their tea, Miss Baxter asked about Miss Ellery's plan for the kitchen garden, and whether Mrs. Steele planned to host another picnic in summer. Miss Ellery and Mrs. Steele both gave detailed, breathless answers, which only served to underscore the awkwardness to the chitchat.

After a quarter hour of this, Miss Baxter said decisively, "How lovely it has been to see you all tonight, my friends."

Miss Fairchild immediately rose and inclined her head at their hostess. Miss Ellery stood up much more reluctantly. "Do please come by for tea. Anytime."

"Yes, do please," said Miss Ellery. She stood up much more reluctantly.

"And we can talk more of picnic plans and other plans at Miss Fairchild's," said Mrs. Steele, coming to her feet alongside her husband.

Miss Charlotte, however, remained firmly in her seat. Mrs. Watson and Lord Ingram followed her example. The others, promptly escorted out by Miss Stoppard, regarded them with a mix of curiosity and consternation as they left.

"More biscuits, Miss Holmes?" said Miss Baxter.

"Yes, thank you," said Miss Charlotte, picking up a ratafia. "These are very good biscuits."

Miss Baxter looked her over again, seemingly amused. "You would have a more fashionable figure, Miss Holmes, if you enjoyed biscuits a bit less."

Mrs. Watson might have bristled at her comment, had it been snider. But it was a straightforward observation, offered as such.

"Yes, I know," said Miss Charlotte. "I think about it sometimes, that more fashionable figure, before I eat another biscuit."

Miss Baxter chortled, but her expression soon became sober. "My condolences to you for having caught my father's attention."

"In which case I must thank you, Miss Baxter, for making my task easier. I do have a few questions, if you don't mind."

"Please proceed."

The permission was granted regally, albeit with a slight air of ennui. Or was it fatigue?

Miss Baxter's presence remained powerful, but now that Mrs. Watson was more accustomed to it, she began to notice the heaviness of her shoulders and the droop of her neck—all this while she'd been leaning against the back of the settee, taking advantage of the fact that the settee had been placed at an angle to the rest of the chairs, so that she could see all her callers while remaining in a position of repose.

Mrs. Felton's worried descriptions returned to mind. Of an otherwise vibrant Miss Baxter buried under piles of blankets, dozing, always dozing.

"Mr. Baxter was concerned about the sale of your grandmother's house," said Miss Charlotte. "He did not feel that it was in character for you to have sold the place where you had been so happy."

Miss Baxter smiled coldly. "My father, as always, knows me not at all. It was not the house that made me happy, but my grandmother. Without her, the house was but a pile of wood and stone full of inanimate objects. Why should I not sell it when I felt that it would fetch me a good price?"

"Were you in particular financial need?"

This question made Miss Baxter laugh. "My father has closed his pocketbook to me and I have no other means of obtaining an income. Of course I was and am in particular financial need."

"Very well, then. The man who came last November, and who

claimed to be your father's solicitor—why did you not mention him in your weekly letter?"

Miss Baxter waved an impatient hand. "Please, Miss Holmes, my father knows as well as I do that I write those letters ten or twelve at a time and simply put on different dates. Why should I bother changing them if he doesn't bother reading them?"

Like her father, Miss Baxter was a terrific liar. Mrs. Watson was sure she was lying, yet could not discern where the falsehoods lay.

Miss Charlotte did not appear concerned. "Thank you, Miss Baxter. These are all the answers I need for your father. But if you would indulge me, I do have one more question for my own personal curiosity."

"Oh?"

Miss Charlotte's face appeared especially sweet and innocent, her eyes preternaturally clear. A chill went down Mrs. Watson's back.

"Mr. Baxter told us a rather extraordinary tale," began the young woman. "He said that after he initially retrieved you from the Garden, you were so determined to leave that you managed to become engaged to six different gentlemen over the course of fifteen months. Being of a practical bent of mind, I wonder how you accomplished that. I can't imagine you would have been in a position to meet that many gentlemen, let alone woo or be wooed by them."

Mrs. Watson gripped her skirt. This was a very, very forward question. She knew by now that Miss Charlotte did not waste her words, especially not in the middle of an investigation. But try as she did, she couldn't see why it mattered how Miss Baxter had managed all those engagements.

Miss Baxter only raised a brow. "Ah, but I cannot divulge my secret. I might need to repeat my great achievement someday. But let me ask you a question, Miss Holmes. What are your plans, now that you've been assured of my well-being?"

"I shall, of course, return to London to make my report to Mr. Baxter. We should have enough time to catch the last train out."

Miss Baxter's eyes glittered. "Is this farewell then?"

"Let us hope. And before I go, Miss Baxter, do you mind if I take a photograph of you? Mr. Baxter does not strike me as someone for whom my word alone would suffice. He might be better predisposed to a photograph. And if I may implore you to hold up this newspaper?"

The paper was a local gazette that they had purchased in the village in the afternoon.

Miss Baxter complied, with a contemptuous look at the newspaper. "Have you read this publication, Miss Holmes?"

"No."

On the railway journey to Cornwall, Miss Charlotte had read a West Country newspaper published out of Exeter and a Cornish paper based in Falmouth, but not this one.

"Are you taking it to my father to prove to him that my photograph is of a very recent vintage?"

"Correct."

"Then you might as well read it on your journey back, should you have nothing else to do. But really, would it not better prove you saw me if you were in the photographs yourself?"

The validity of the idea could not be denied. Miss Charlotte gave her detective camera to Miss Stoppard, along with a brief explanation on how to operate it. Miss Stoppard raised the camera, but Miss Baxter said, "Jane dear, don't tax yourself so. Please bring a stool and the stack of papers from my room."

"From . . . your room?" asked Miss Stoppard hesitantly.

"Yes, my room. Thank you, my dear."

"Of course," said Miss Stoppard.

She left, but not without looking back at Mrs. Watson and Miss Charlotte with surprised suspicion.

The room fell silent.

Miss Baxter glanced at Lord Ingram. "You, sir, you haven't said a thing since you came into this room. Have you no questions?"

Lord Ingram had indeed been quiet, his expression carefully neutral as he listened and observed. Now he inclined his head. "I am only here to look after Miss Holmes and Mrs. Watson. But since you asked, Miss Baxter, I would like to know why you approved of Sherlock Holmes as the neutral party."

"I commend you for knowing your place, sir. As for your question, Sherlock Holmes's reputation precedes him. And in this day and age, being on the coast of Cornwall is no excuse not to have heard of the most prominent consulting detective in the nation."

Her attention shifted to Mrs. Watson. "And you, madam, have you also no questions for me?"

Mrs. Watson had dozens of questions but none that she felt would gain her a useful answer. "Mr. Peters said you painted the large canvas in the library. Did you also paint the picture opposite the door? They are both striking."

"Yes, I did," said Miss Baxter with a leisurely look in the direction of woman, skull, and snake. Again, was it languor or weariness? "Someone once said that I am not necessarily a good painter, but at least an expressive one."

"Would you mind telling us what the elements in the image stand for?" asked Miss Charlotte.

"The struggle to achieve even a small measure of transcendence, when evil is all around," said Miss Baxter, echoing what Mr. Peters had said in the library.

Mrs. Watson couldn't help herself. "I could understand that theme very well in the painting in the library, in which the woman, who presumably stands for some measure of truth and innocence, is under great attack from evil. But here she seems to be defeating evil, yet the serpent climbing up her limb suggests that her victory is incomplete."

"Of course it is. The legacy of evil is insidious. Even the ones who seek to overthrow evil must be vigilant of its taint, of carrying evil in their own footsteps."

"Then what is the point of the struggle against evil, if it can never be eradicated?"

"Weeds can never be eradicated either, Mrs. Watson, but gardeners must still uproot them. It is the same with evil. It will always exist, and it will multiply and encroach if it is not constantly pared back."

Miss Stoppard returned then with a low stool in one hand and a stack of newspapers under her other arm. Miss Baxter directed Miss Charlotte to stand behind her settee. Miss Stoppard, after placing the newspapers on the stool and then the detective camera on top of the newspapers, looked into the viewfinder, pulled the stool back a few feet, and counseled everyone to hold still.

When Miss Stoppard declared herself satisfied, Miss Charlotte went to take charge of the detective camera. Casually, she looked through the stack of papers. "I had no idea there were so many local gazettes."

"Yes, our presses are kept busy," replied Miss Baxter.

"May I take some of these to read on my journey back?"

"Alas, those are my personal collection. But you can easily find them at any newsagent's in the area."

"I will look for them, then. Thank you, Miss Baxter, for consenting to the photographs. But since there is no telling how the photographs might or might not turn out, given the relative paucity of light, may I ask that you give me something that proves conclusively that I spoke to you and not to someone else?"

Miss Baxter regarded Miss Charlotte for a while, as if she needed to make a decision. "Very well. I have an annual appointment with my father in London. But what my father didn't know for a number of years was that on those outings to London, I also rendezvoused with another person."

"Oh?" murmured Miss Charlotte.

"Years ago, I had a young man with whom I was very much in love. My father absolutely refused to let me marry him and ruthlessly tore us apart. For his own safety, my young man could not approach me, lest his life be endangered."

The soles of Mrs. Watson's feet tingled—she had not expected a confession of such a nature. Yet Miss Baxter's love story did not make her feel breathless with anticipation. Instead, her whole body clenched, as if bracing for a carriage accident.

"What we resolved to do was to see each other once a year. He was to stand at the foot of the statue of Achilles, at Hyde Park Corner, and I would walk past. For years he kept the appointment. But last year he was not there."

Mrs. Watson had just put a piece of biscuit into her mouth— and very nearly choked on it.

"Do excuse me," she said, swallowing some tea and trying to recover a bit of her dignity. "The biscuit was not terribly cooperative."

"Yes, wayward biscuits, I've known my share of those," said Miss Baxter smoothly.

Mrs. Watson coughed some more and said, "I apologize. Please go on."

"Where were we?"

"You and your beau saw each other once a year at the statue of Achilles for years, but not this last time," said Miss Charlotte.

Mrs. Watson held her teacup in front of her face. She wanted desperately to look in Lord Ingram's direction but also felt she ought to do no such thing. She recognized this story—how could she not—it was nearly the exact same story with which Lady Ingram had come to Sherlock Holmes, supposedly seeking help to find her girlhood sweetheart whom she'd had to give up to make an advantageous match.

"Right, he was not there this last time," said Miss Baxter. "I was very cross with my father. I was sure that he or those acting under him had done away with my beloved. My father, of course, denied it and said that although he would have been happy to remove my beau from my life, as he had no idea who this man was, he could not have so pleased himself.

"Needless to say, we did not part on the best of terms. No one else was present for this disagreement except the two of us—and perhaps a loyal underling or two of his who overheard because I marched in without closing the door and they happened to be nearby."

"Thank you, Miss Baxter," said Miss Charlotte, rising, her expression as serene as ever.

Mrs. Watson stood up, too. "I'm most terribly sorry about your young man, Miss Baxter," she heard herself say. "Were you ever able to ascertain whether he is all right?"

For the first time something approaching a genuine expression appeared on Miss Baxter's face, a mélange of tenderness and regret underscored by something dark and ruthless. "No, to this day I don't know what happened to him. I hope he is all right, and I hope he does not regret everything he has had to endure for me."

## Seventeen

Mrs. Watson drifted about the cottage in a daze. She ought to check for any personal items that had been overlooked when she'd packed earlier, but she only managed to consult her watch repeatedly, and then to forget what time it was in the next instant. Miss Charlotte, on the other hand, not only found a handkerchief and several hairpins that belonged to Mrs. Watson, but set down from memory the names of all the Cornish papers in the stack Miss Stoppard had brought from Miss Baxter's bedroom, as well as the issues' dates.

She then left a note for Miss Fairchild, stating that they would be taking a trip to London.

She was no less busy on the drive to the village. With Lord Ingram outside at the reins, she lit her pocket lantern and used the light to scan the local gazette that she had asked Miss Baxter to hold and which Miss Baxter said that she should read.

Upon reaching the village of Porthangan, Mrs. Watson at last began to recover from her stupefaction. She took a sip from her canteen, rubbed a spot behind her ear, and asked Miss Charlotte, "Anything useful in the gazette?"

The young woman pointed to a small notice that read *I'm glad to see you well. And that you are carrying on as usual.* "I don't know that it's useful, per se, but it caught my attention."

From his room above the pub, Mr. Mears must have seen their carriage arriving. When they rolled to a stop, he was already at the curb, waiting. At Mrs. Watson's beckoning, he entered the carriage.

"We saw Miss Baxter tonight and are headed for London to give Moriarty our report," said Miss Charlotte. She entrusted the piece of paper on which she'd written down the names and dates of Cornish publications in Miss Baxter's private collection to the butler. "Would you visit the archives of these papers and survey the issues I've listed here?"

Mr. Mears blinked at the news concerning Miss Baxter. He then glanced down at the list. "Should I be on the lookout for anything in particular, miss?"

"I'm not sure. If an article makes you think it might be relevant, make a note of that. If there are any small notices that strike you as odd, or indecipherable, copy them down for me to look at. Particularly if you see something that echoes what you find in these other issues."

Mr. Mears asked if there was an order in which he ought to visit the newspaper archives—any order that was convenient to him, deemed Miss Charlotte—and whether he should speak to those running the papers while he was there. That he could decide for himself, answered Miss Charlotte.

He nodded, wished the ladies good luck in London, and bade them good night. With his hand on the carriage door, however, he turned around. "Ladies, should I head for London once I'm finished with my tour of newspaper archives? Or . . ."

Silence. After a while, Mrs. Watson realized that Miss Charlotte had ceded the question to her. "Well," she said, her voice heavier than she'd intended, "one would think Moriarty would be happy to learn that his daughter is alive. But we cannot predict how he will react . . ."

"I see," said Mr. Mears. "I'll come back here and keep an eye on the Garden until you have further instructions for me."

He placed his hand over Mrs. Watson's. It was a fraction of a second, and then he was outside, on the pavement, watching their carriage roll away. Mrs. Watson waved—and understood all at once that in her unexceptional answer he had heard what she herself was only beginning to understand.

The situation was as uncertain as it had ever been.

More so, if anything.

———— ❊ ————

At the railway station, Miss Charlotte read the gazette again, at a slower speed, paying attention to every word.

"Still nothing?" asked Mrs. Watson.

While the girl read, Mrs. Watson had thought over the evening. For some reason, her mind kept returning to what Miss Charlotte had said, shortly before they met Miss Baxter. *The events of last night were always meant to force somebody's hand.*

Did that mean Miss Baxter's hand had been forced?

Miss Charlotte shoved the gazette into her satchel. "I'm beginning to believe that Miss Baxter asked me to read this one only so that I'd be curious about the others, the ones that she considers her private collection."

Their train came. Lord Ingram, who had gone to stow away remise and horse, returned at the same time. Once they were on their way, in a compartment to themselves, he distributed savory pies that he'd acquired at a pub near the railway station. Miss Charlotte nibbled at one. Mrs. Watson was both hungry and in no mood for food. The compartment was silent except for the rustling sounds she made, shifting the pie around in its paper bag.

Lord Ingram rose, went out to the corridor, and came back two minutes later. "There's no one nearby," he said in a low voice.

Miss Charlotte nodded.

With another look at the door, Lord Ingram said, "Surely I'm not the only person who noticed the similarities between the story Miss Baxter gave about her beau and the one Lady Ingram had used to engage Sherlock Holmes to look for her purported lost beloved."

Mrs. Watson exhaled audibly, relieved that he had brought up the subject. "I, too, was struck by the similarities. Do you suppose, Miss Charlotte, that when Moriarty sent Lady Ingram to you, he borrowed his daughter's story instead of coming up with a different one?"

"Possibly," said Miss Charlotte. "It's a memorable story."

"Do you think it's real, though?" asked Lord Ingram.

"It can't be, can it?" said Mrs. Watson instantly.

When Lady Ingram had come to them with her version of that story, which featured her and Mr. Finch, Miss Charlotte's half brother, as star-crossed lovers who walked past each other once a year before the Albert Memorial, Mrs. Watson had been moved in spite of herself—and had felt a fool afterward, for having been so easily deceived.

She did not dare take Miss Baxter's too-similar story at face value.

Miss Charlotte took a bite of her pie and chewed meditatively. "I wouldn't bet on Miss Baxter's story to be accurate in the details. But in the general spirit . . ."

She took a sip of water from her travel canteen. "Mrs. Watson, do you remember my opinion of Lady Ingram's story?"

Mrs. Watson nodded. "That there was something not quite right about it."

And she, completely witless at the time, had thought Miss Charlotte's skepticism heartless.

"Lady Ingram's story did not fit with the reality of her. For all that Lady Ingram was animated by a great deal of antagonism against the world and everyone in it, she was also brittle. In contradiction, the devotion described in her story requires not only a deep initial attachment, but faith and resilience to maintain it, season after season, year after year."

Mrs. Watson chanced a glance at Lord Ingram. Like Miss Charlotte, he, too, held a hand pie that peeked out from a paper bag. But unlike her, he had yet to take a bite. He only looked at her, his interest—or so it felt to Mrs. Watson—entirely on the woman speaking and not the woman being spoken of, his soon-to-be-former wife.

"That Miss Baxter managed to carve out a little haven for herself at the Garden, against all odds, demonstrates a remarkable resilience, to say the least," continued Miss Charlotte. "While her tale might not be any truer than the facsimile related by Lady Ingram, I'm more inclined to believe that she is capable of the patient, sustained effort demanded by such unforgiving circumstances, like that of a seed that finds itself in the cracks of a wall, yet nevertheless manages to grow into a sky-scraping tree."

Mrs. Watson recalled the dazzling woman in that high baroque parlor. Her thoughts had revolved around the woman since, but not in any direction that concerned her character. To her, Miss Baxter had seemed more like a glittering diamond—or a glittering sword. Did such beautiful and dangerous things have character?

"But why has she told us this tale?" asked Lord Ingram, taking out another paper bag from the pocket of his greatcoat. "Granted, you asked for proof that she is who she says she is, and she gave you an anecdote that only she and Moriarty would know. But they are father and daughter; surely she must have other examples she can use."

Mrs. Watson had been wondering the same. "Perhaps it is her intention to counter what her father said about her six fiancés. Imagine if, after all, there was no truth to that fable. Wouldn't you wish to clear up the misconceptions that might have been caused by his lies?"

Lord Ingram handed this other paper bag to Miss Charlotte. "I would, certainly. But were I in her place, I'd have said more about what I was doing these past few months. I find it odd that she spent

more time on a story of woebegone love than on a proper explanation that would make her father leave her alone."

The paper bag turned out to contain jam tarts. "Thank you, my
lord. I'll have them with tea tomorrow," said Miss Charlotte with a
small smile. "And as for why Miss Baxter didn't bother with any
explanations—perhaps she doesn't believe her father will leave her
alone.

Mrs. Watson's scalp tightened. "Perhaps Moriarty wouldn't
leave her alone, but he will leave us alone at least, won't he?"

Ever since they'd said goodbye to Mr. Mears, she'd wondered
how Moriarty would greet the news they'd bring. On the one hand,
what better report could the man expect than that his daughter, despite her claim of a twisted ankle, was not only well but completely
in charge of her surroundings? On the other hand, his ready acceptance of their report would be . . . too good to be true, wouldn't it?

But what would he dispute? She looked like the woman in the
photographs he'd provided, she conducted herself with the grand
condescension Mrs. Felton had described, she was accepted as Miss
Baxter by those who'd known her for years, and she had furnished
a disturbing love story for the purposes of verifying her identity.
Even if the woman they'd met was counterfeit, her story had to be
one Moriarty would recognize—otherwise not only would all the
orchestrations this evening go to waste, but the person behind those
orchestrations would land in even greater trouble.

Miss Charlotte took another bite of her pie. "Let's disregard
Miss Baxter for a moment. Do you believe that Moriarty sent us to
the Garden of Hermopolis solely for Miss Baxter's sake?"

Lord Ingram shook his head. Mrs. Watson, feeling a chill between her shoulder blades, slowly shook her head, too.

"So we agree that he also has a purpose with regard to us. Do
you suppose he has accomplished his purpose?"

The chill between Mrs. Watson's shoulder blades crept down-
ward, wrapping itself around her spine. "No," she made herself say.

Miss Charlotte took a sip of water from her canteen. "Then no matter what we hope for, and no matter how logical our hopes appear, Moriarty isn't done with us yet."

— ❊ —

The morning after his second night at 18 Upper Baker Street, Lord Ingram woke up with Holmes's hand draped over his chest.

He turned his head.

Their first night in this bedroom, they'd stayed up far too late and in the morning had been jolted upright at the same time by the insistent drilling of the alarm clock. So this would be the first time he saw her asleep.

It was still early, and she had most of her face buried in her pillow. He could just make out the shape of one ear amid her tousled hair, barely long enough to hold a curl.

He placed his hand upon hers. She had him in a very loose hold, her body not quite touching his. But he was happy. When he was younger, he did not know how to love except to hold on tightly, so very, very tightly. But with Holmes, he was beginning to see that perhaps space did not always translate into distance.

That her hand upon his chest might convey as much attachment as someone else with all her limbs wrapped around him.

Of course, this might be wishful thinking on his part. Holmes's heart remained ever mysterious, like those parts of the ocean too fathomless even for the fictional *Nautilus*.

Or the great depths of her heart could simply be filled with longing for cake.

He smiled, kissed her on her exposed ear, and got up, untangling one fuchsia stocking from around himself. He had better not recall the sight of those stockings on her . . .

Reaching down to the nightstand for his watch, he instead picked up a ringlike object. Holmes, better prepared last night, had brought not only the stockings but a small silk bag full of contraceptive devices. As they'd lain panting, about to drift off to sleep, she'd reached into the bag, took out the ring, and said, "Oh, I forgot to have you try this on."

In his drowsiness, it had taken him two seconds to recognize the object for what it was. He might very well have mistaken it for a ring that fell off a harness, were it not for her words and the circumstances under which it had been presented.

"Oh, it's too small," he said.

"Is it?" Her words were slowing, but still conveyed her surprise.

"Probably not," he answered, grinning sleepily. "But I just wanted to say that."

He grinned again at the recollection, put the prurient object back in the small silk bag, finished dressing, and left the room.

They had arrived in London to two notes, one from Miss Olivia, needing to see Holmes, the other a message from Ellen Bailey, the maid who had worked at the Snowham inn where Mr. Marbleton had stayed, and whom they had not been able to speak to earlier because she had followed her new mistress to London. But now Ellen Bailey had returned to Snowham, as her mistress had concluded her business in town.

Holmes would remain in London to meet with Moriarty's representative and Miss Olivia; Lord Ingram would head out once more to Snowham, this time accompanied by Mrs. Watson.

On his way to the domestic offices in the basement of 18 Upper Baker Street, where a darkroom had been set up, he saw that various letters and circulars had come through the mail slot and landed inside the front door. Among them was a letter that did not have a stamp—it had been hand-delivered.

From A. de Lacey.

He checked on the negatives that had developed overnight in the basement darkroom and went back upstairs with de Lacey's missive. With her eyes closed, Holmes opened the envelope, and then, with one eye half open, scanned the note, handed it to him, and burrowed under the blanket again. He read the note and saw that she could indeed sleep some more. With a small laugh, he set the alarm clock for her, placed the note under the alarm clock, kissed her one more time, and left.

Over breakfast at Mrs. Watson's, the dear lady kept winking at him. He could be shameless with Holmes, but he couldn't be as brazen before Mrs. Watson. So he kept his face lowered, his gaze on his plate—and ate with an unusually robust appetite.

It wasn't until they were in the carriage, where servants could not stumble upon private conversation, that she said, "I know we spoke of potential pitfalls, my dear. Still, I must say being in love agrees with you."

"I rather like it myself."

It made him shy to have his emotional state commented upon. But what wouldn't he give for the biggest topic on this day to be his heated affair with Holmes.

Mrs. Watson teased him some more but eventually fell quiet. She watched the streets pass by outside—shops were opening, greengrocers inspected vegetables that had just arrived from the countryside, cooks and kitchen maids darted in and out of bakeries, butchers', and cheesemongers'.

Then she looked at him and sighed, a heavy sound. "I will not lie. Last night I lay in bed and wondered whether Miss Charlotte and I shouldn't have gone directly to Southampton and booked a passage overseas."

Lord Ingram felt himself grow tenser. "The same thought occurred to Holmes, I believe. Last night she asked me what the weather in Andalusia is like this time of the year."

More than once they had talked about a long trip abroad, he and Holmes. But the discussion had always been in vague terms, the voyage more a metaphor for the future than an undertaking for which one sketched out an itinerary and packed one's steamer trunks.

Perhaps the time for that trip had come.

Mrs. Watson wrapped her arms around her reticule. "I believe I would like to see Andalusia, too," she murmured.

"We should prepare," he said. "We may not be able to leave to-day or tomorrow, but we should prepare."

---※---

Charlotte adjusted her turban, which did not match her dusty rose day dress, but nevertheless looked very nice on her head. In fact, all of her seemed to look very nice. So much so that she twirled before the looking glass, nodding with approval.

Excellent lovemaking did put one in an excellent mood, even if she'd forgotten about the ring until it was too late. Not to mention that in the morning, Mrs. Watson, being the kind and wonderful person that she was, had sent Polly Banning over to 18 Upper Baker Street with a basket of proper breakfast—eggs, bacon, and buttered toast.

Charlotte had, with her second cup of tea, snuck in one of the jam tarts Lord Ingram had bought for her the night before, which had further improved her outlook on the day.

All the same, when the doorbell rang, as she was swirling around a second time before the mirror, she stopped abruptly, her entire person tensing so much that her neck ached.

Correspondingly, upon opening the door and seeing that only de Lacey had come, her smile became that much more brilliant.

De Lacey, on the other hand, did not appear as pleased to see her. "Miss Holmes, you are back so soon."

"Indeed, we always work fast," said Charlotte cheerfully. "Please come up."

"I'm not sure I understand what is going on," said de Lacey as he took a seat in the parlor. "Only yesterday did we receive news that Miss Baxter refused to leave her house even though a woodpile next to the house had caught on fire. And yet here you are, hundreds of miles from the Garden of Hermopolis."

Charlotte poured tea that she had set to steep earlier. "All to bring welcome news to Mr. Baxter, of course."

De Lacey, regarding her with suspicion, picked up his teacup. "The welcome news being?"

"That we saw Miss Baxter last night. She was in excellent health. Radiated command and, I must say, quite a bit of contempt for those who had the gall to worry about her."

De Lacey set down the cup he had just picked up. This time he looked at Charlotte as if she had taken leave of her senses. "You are sure, Miss Holmes?"

"Believe me, we were no less taken aback. And for that reason, we paid close attention throughout the meeting. In addition to us, Miss Baxter had summoned four other members of the Garden, all of whom had expressed puzzlement and anxiety on the night of the fireworks. They were surprised and delighted to see her. Awed, in fact, and flattered by the least condescension on her part."

"That . . . does sound rather like Miss Baxter."

"Her parlor was brilliant, her person dressed expensively and in the height of fashion. Good décor and good clothes are not cheap, and she saw nothing wrong with selling her grandmother's house in order to maintain herself in the style she is accustomed to, as it was her grandmother she loved, and not so much the house. As for the lawyer . . . Is it true that Miss Baxter was kidnapped when she was young?"

De Lacey came out of his chair. For a moment Charlotte thought he meant to denounce her thirdhand hearsay as a preposterous rumor, but he only sat down again with a look of pure astonishment. "I'm afraid that's something I do not know."

Charlotte gave him a gracious smile. "I was shocked to learn of the story myself. But in any case, that childhood kidnapping made her deeply suspicious. The woman who took her from her grandmother had appeared properly credentialed. Therefore, when a second lawyer came—the one sent by Mr. Baxter—in spite of his credentials, or perhaps because of them, she refused to receive him for the sake of her own safety.

"Sherlock Holmes, however, is a well-known entity who is furthermore completely uninvolved in the enmities and entanglements surrounding Mr. Baxter. Miss Baxter therefore felt that, at worst, a meeting with us would be harmless. And we, of course, were captivated by her presence."

De Lacey shook his head slightly, as if he had trouble following the gist of the conversation. After a moment, he said, "I'm sure her presence is wholly enchanting, but what explanation did she give for the fact that members of the Garden had not seen her for months?"

"A need for solitude."

De Lacey flattened his lips. "And for not coming out of her house when it was in danger of catching on fire?"

"A twisted ankle."

"Do you believe that, Miss Holmes?"

Charlotte shook out the flounces of her skirt. "I could not assess the veracity of that particular statement: She was reclined on a settee during our interview and her feet, indeed all of her lower half, was obscured by a heavy blanket. But given that she was very much in charge of herself and the residents of the Garden were at least deferential and sometimes obsequious in their conduct toward her, it would be difficult for me to construe that any of them had somehow held her hostage the night before."

"True, I suppose . . ."

"Nevertheless, I was suspicious enough to ask for a photograph. My equipment was primitive and the nighttime lighting less than optimal, but the negatives have been developed and I find these to provide clear enough images of Miss Baxter. What do you think?"

She handed over two negatives. De Lacey held them to the light and looked for close to thirty seconds. "We shall need to make prints from them to better ascertain whether that is truly Miss Baxter."

Charlotte smiled. "Of course, of course. In the same spirit, I asked her to relay something that only the real Miss Baxter could tell me. She mentioned a dispute with her father the last time they saw each other, concerning a gentleman she'd been fond of many years ago but was unable to marry."

De Lacey exhaled and reached for a biscuit. "I've heard of Sherlock Holmes's deductive prowess. If you'll pardon the observation, Miss Holmes, you and your brother could very well have arrived at this conclusion on your own."

"True, given Miss Baxter's less-than-harmonious relationship with her father, I could have guessed as much. But could I have guessed about a yearly rendezvous before the statue of Achilles at Hyde Park Corner?"

De Lacey's expression changed. It changed so much, Charlotte suspected he'd have sunk into a chair if he weren't already in one. For the first time, it seemed as if he believed that Miss Baxter was really alive.

"I see—I see," he said, rising abruptly, the biscuit still in his hand. "Thank you, Miss Holmes, you have indeed brought marvelous news. I'll see myself out."

He was halfway down the steps before he climbed back and said, "And you will hear from me again, of course."

———※———

Ellen Bailey was a small, quiet woman in her mid-twenties. Mrs. Watson had worried initially that they'd arrived during hours when a housemaid had a great deal of work, but it turned out that in Mrs. Donovan's household, Ellen Bailey was employed not as a housemaid but as the lady's maid, and had enough stature to receive Mrs. Watson and Lord Ingram in a domestic office of her own.

She explained that when Mrs. Donovan came to Snowham to look for a place, she'd stayed at Mr. Upton's inn and approved of Ellen Bailey's work. And when she had learned that Ellen Bailey had been trained in all the skills of a lady's maid, she asked Ellen Bailey to come work for her, as her old maid was leaving to be married.

The young woman looked up from the lace shawl she was repairing and glanced about her office, on the shelves of which were trays of still-curing soap, jars of hair pomade and bandolines, and a small forest of essences, toilette waters, and hair tonics in brown and green bottles, all hand-labeled and clearly homemade. "It's so nice to have a place of my own."

Mrs. Watson, who had great interest in smooth skin and shiny hair, spent a few minutes exchanging recipes with her, before guiding the conversation to the topic they had come for.

Ellen Bailey was forthcoming. "Ever since I got your note, I've been thinking about Mr. Openshaw. A lovely man—a real gentleman. I didn't see him much when he stayed at Mr. Upton's, once in the dining room, when I was cleaning tables at supper, and once in the hallway, just after I finished with his room."

She threaded her needle through a section of lace that she had pinned to a repair board. "But I can tell you this: He never seemed to sleep, Mr. Openshaw. I don't always sleep well myself. The servants' quarters at the inn are in the half basement and I had a window that looked out to the street. From there I could see lights from the inn reflected in the windows across the street. I worked at the inn enough years to tell, by looking at those windows, which rooms at Mr. Upton's still had their lights on. And when he stayed there, I got up at least a couple of times each night. Mr. Openshaw's light was always on."

"I don't suppose you asked him what kept him awake?" asked Mrs. Watson.

Ellen Bailey shook her head. "Mr. Upton didn't want us chatting up the guests."

Lord Ingram, who had been silent until now, leaned forward in his chair. "When you saw him in the dining room, did Mr. Openshaw do anything besides eat? Did he have a notebook with him or jot anything down?"

"No, sir, I don't believe so." Ellen Bailey frowned a little and pushed at the lace with her fingers. "I believe he read the paper that night—a London paper, by the looks of it."

It had been a notice in a London paper that had forced Mr. Marbleton's departure from their midst. Mrs. Watson's heart tightened. "Was he reading the small notices?"

"That I wasn't close enough to see, mum."

The needle in Ellen Bailey's hand zigzagged with the speed of an eel across a section of torn lace. And when she pulled the matching thread taut, the tear disappeared.

She nodded with satisfaction and looked up at her visitors, awaiting further questions.

"Did you happen to notice anything unusual about Mr. Openshaw's room?" asked Lord Ingram.

Ellen Bailey lifted the lace and held it toward the light. She set it down and pinned a different section to the board. "He kept his room wonderfully neat. Everything he had was in his luggage. If it weren't for the luggage, you wouldn't have guessed that anyone was staying there at all. He didn't even leave behind a hair on the pillow."

Mrs. Watson ached for the young man who had lived the most peripatetic of lives, all his belongings always packed in case he and his family must flee Moriarty's minions.

And leave no evidence behind that they'd been there at all.

A trace of sadness crossed Lord Ingram's countenance. "He didn't have much luggage, I take it?"

Ellen Bailey started to shake her head, then stopped. She stuck her needle into the repair board and looked up at them. "I'd forgotten about this until now, but oddly enough, I saw three pieces of luggage when I cleaned his room after his first night at Mr. Upton's. But the next day, when he left, he walked to the railway station with a valise in one hand and a satchel in the other."

She nodded. "That's right. When he left, he had only two pieces."

## Eighteen

Livia received Charlotte's note in the morning, but could not leave then. The evening before, she and Mrs. Newell had run into Mrs. Graham, a friend of Lady Holmes's, and Mrs. Graham had insisted that Livia and Mrs. Newell come with her for a morning drive in the park.

At Mrs. Graham's suggestion, the drive was followed by a visit to the modiste's. Livia enjoyed fashion, but not so much that she wanted to spend hours at a mantua-maker's when she couldn't buy anything.

She could afford a new dress now: Between what Charlotte had paid her for her contributions at Moriarty's château in France and what she'd received for her Sherlock Holmes novel, she had a bit of money on hand. But Mrs. Graham would have tattled, and she had no way of explaining to her parents where her funds had come from.

So she gritted her teeth and waited. Thank goodness Mrs. Newell, sensing her impatience, allowed her to rush off as soon as they'd returned to their hotel. At Mrs. Watson's, Livia found Charlotte in the late Dr. Watson's study, flipping through a heavy medical tome.

In her note Charlotte hadn't said anything about the Garden of Hermopolis. She had not even mentioned Cornwall, only that they'd returned to London. Livia's gladness upon receiving the note had been quickly punctured by doubts. They'd come back so fast. Too fast. Was it possible that the problem had been solved that easily? Or had the place been so awful that they'd had no choice but to abandon their post?

But seeing Charlotte peaceably reading, Livia's nerves settled. Her sister looked fine. No, better than fine. Why, Charlotte was practically radiant.

They walked to 18 Upper Baker Street. Once there, Charlotte told Livia that she had seen Miss Baxter with her own eyes and that Miss Baxter was not only alive but looked magnificent and masterful.

Overcome with relief, Livia hugged Charlotte tight. The next thing she knew, she'd launched into a breathless account of her encounter with Mr. Marbleton in the Reading Room and her subsequent discovery of the address he had put down when he'd renewed his reader's ticket.

"Well done," said Charlotte when Livia mentioned how she'd recalled the alias Miss Marbleton had used the previous summer. "I must have brought up the name *Ellie Hartford* in front of you exactly once."

"It was a near thing," said Livia, flushing with pleasure. "And then, when I actually went to the address provided by Elliot Hartford, it turned out to be the last thing I expected, a souvenir shop for the queen's Golden Jubilee."

Charlotte raised a brow, an expression of great surprise on her part that further gratified Livia.

"But just as I was beginning to despair about being completely wrong, I saw a cockade in the display window and realized that it was what he had worn on his lapel!" Livia exclaimed in triumph. "So I went ahead and bought one of everything that was in the display window, in case we couldn't examine them to our satisfaction in the shop."

She hadn't made the purchases solely to bring them before Charlotte's gaze, of course. Mr. Marbleton had been to the shop. He had seen and possibly touched these items. To Livia, they commemorated not Victoria's fifty years on the throne, but the trail of breadcrumbs he'd left—and that she'd understood him well enough to follow it.

From her reticule she pulled out a sheet of paper. She'd drawn a picture of the display window, sketched the placement of all the items, and even penciled in the number of each.

"They were laid out like this," she said, and arranged her purchases on Sherlock Holmes's neatly made bed according to the illustration.

"You were very thorough," said Charlotte, who had followed her into the "convalescent brother's" bedroom.

Livia again warmed at the compliment. "I also spoke to the people in the shop, but they didn't have much to tell me."

Charlotte reached out a hand. "This is the kind of cockade Mr. Marbleton wore when you saw him in the Reading Room?"

"The colors and the materials may not be identical, but they are similar enough."

Livia went to the parlor to bring back a cup of tea—she was thirsty from recounting her tale, and in need of something to do so her excitement wouldn't get the better of her. Her excitement and anxiety. She'd followed the trail of breadcrumbs this far; what if she could proceed no farther? Or what if she could? What did the trail actually lead to?

Charlotte, as composed as ever, picked up the items Livia had laid out one by one. "Nice hat. Decent fan. The ribbon is also serviceable. One can have a game of whist with these Jubilee playing cards while drinking from a Jubilee teacup."

"These were all the items closest to the cockade," added Livia unnecessarily, as she'd already told her sister that the arrangement on the bed duplicated that in the display window. "And the Stanhope, too."

The Stanhope, at first glance, resembled an ivory fountain pen. "What does it show?"

"The queen's homes, I think?" said Livia, setting aside her now empty teacup. "There were others that showed her family. Some even showed famous naval ships, but I preferred the scenery."

Charlotte put the optical device close to her eye. "Yes," she murmured. "I can see photographs of Buckingham Palace, Balmoral Castle, and Osborne House."

"You don't think Mr. Marbleton is trying to hint that Moriarty is planning to sabotage the Jubilee, do you?" asked Livia, choking on her own question.

Charlotte put down the Stanhope. "No. If that were the case, Mr. Marbleton would have been taking his own life far too lightly, writing down the address of a Jubilee souvenir shop right in front of Moriarty's men."

Livia rubbed her throat, breathing easier. "But if he isn't hinting at Jubilee-related schemes, why did he point us to these gewgaws?"

Her fear of being completely wrong came back. "It isn't all coincidental, is it?"

Charlotte had removed her turban to put on the Union Jack—festooned toque Livia had bought, which, like the purple turban, did not go with her dusty rose dress at all. "Everything is possible, but this is Mr. Marbleton we are speaking of. Few people in the entire world are as instinctual about clandestine communication as his family must be."

She snapped open the garish scarlet, gold, and blue ostrich-plume fan dyed to match the royal standard—and which had cost Livia dearly—and preened as if before a crowd of adoring beaus. "I do not believe all this to be a coincidence."

"But if it's not a coincidence, then what does Mr. Marbleton want us to arrive at?"

Before Charlotte could reply, a commotion rose downstairs. The front door to number 18 was thrown open. Footsteps rushed up the stairs, along with Mrs. Watson's excited voice. "Miss Charlotte, Miss Charlotte, are you here? We found something!"

— ❊ —

"My dear, you're here, too!" Mrs. Watson took Livia's hands and gave them an affectionate squeeze. "How perfect! Would you believe it? We retrieved a piece of luggage Mr. Marbleton left behind for us. Or for you, rather."

"For me?" Livia's voice rose. Her heart skipped several beats.

How could it be for her?

Lord Ingram entered with a brass-studded brown leather cabin trunk about three feet long, two feet wide, and fourteen inches in height. Mrs. Watson then rattled off an account as breathless as Livia's own mere minutes ago.

She and Lord Ingram had met the maid who had cleaned for Mr. Marbleton while he stayed at the inn in Snowham. The maid had noticed that he had left with one fewer pieces of luggage than had been in his room the previous day. Lord Ingram, after considering the incongruity, had decided to inquire at the left luggage office at the railway station.

The station was insignificant, its left luggage office correspondingly small. The stationmaster, who was also in charge of that office, knew very well the one item that had sat unclaimed for two entire months. He was happy to release it in exchange for the stowage fee, provided the claimants could furnish both the name it was stored under and a description of its contents, to see whether it agreed with that which had been recorded.

Mrs. Watson gave Livia an excited push on the arm. "And do you know what name Mr. Marbleton used, my dear?"

Livia blinked. "Hartford? Or Elliot?"

Elliot Hartford had been the name he'd listed at the Reading Room.

Mrs. Watson was nonplussed. "No, no! Guess again."

Livia couldn't think of anything else. She looked toward Charlotte. "Surely he didn't just put either Marbleton or Openshaw?"

"Knowing Mr. Marbleton, and judging from how much it delighted Mrs. Watson," said Charlotte, "I would guess . . . Augustus?"

"Yes!" Mrs. Watson's hand landed upon her own heart. "Is that not romantic?"

The four Holmes daughters were Henrietta Octavia, Bernadine Claudia, Olivia Augusta, and Charlotte Juliana. Mr. Marbleton had used the masculine version of Livia's second given name.

Livia's face heated. "That is . . . that is . . . How were you able to guess?"

"Lord Ingram thought of it," Mrs. Watson answered gleefully. "He said that if Mr. Marbleton meant for us to retrieve the luggage, he'd have selected a direction only we would think of. And that the masculine version of your or Miss Charlotte's first given name would still seem too obvious to someone like Mr. Marbleton."

He'd been taught to bury his communications under all these protective layers. Yet with Livia, he'd always been so open and candid. A bittersweet warmth pierced her heart.

So as not to appear too affected, she said, "You also had to guess the contents of the luggage, didn't you? How were you able to do it? Surely that can't possibly have anything to do with the Holmeses or our names."

"That was a matter of pure luck," said Lord Ingram. "The door of the stowage room was open behind the counter. When I saw the cabin trunk sitting there, I thought it looked familiar. And then I remembered that I'd seen it last summer, in the Marbletons' suite at Claridge's, when Holmes and I searched the premises."

"I saw it once," said Charlotte. "You must have seen it three times."

Lord Ingram laughed. "True, I did much breaking and entering that Season. But anyway, that's how I knew that it contained a portable darkroom."

Mrs. Watson, who had yet to sit down since she'd entered the parlor, moved to the cabin trunk and laid it flat on the carpet. "We were debating whether to hire a room at Mr. Upton's inn, so we could open this and search it immediately, in case it led to anything else in the vicinity. But since Snowham is only an hour away from London, we decided to bring it back."

"Also because we didn't have bolt cutters or lock-picking tools," added Lord Ingram. "And it would have attracted too much attention to acquire either locally."

But Charlotte had lock-picking tools, and she and Lord Ingram each took on one of the two padlocks on the cabin trunk. Livia went with Mrs. Watson to fetch dust sheets. When they returned to the parlor, the locks had just been opened.

Her heart pounding, Livia helped Mrs. Watson spread out the dust sheets. The interior of the trunk had been custom-made for its contents. From long, deep padded troughs, Lord Ingram lifted a number of collapsible rods. Charlotte emptied several rolls of heavy black cloths. There was a lantern made with dark red glass panels—a safe light. And squarish enamel basins neatly stacked together.

"Didn't there used to be photographic plates stored inside the top basin?" Charlotte asked Lord Ingram.

"Yes," said Lord Ingram.

But the top basin was empty now.

It did not take long to inventory the contents of the luggage. Together, the company inspected the items that had been set out, circling the dust sheets as if they were opening a ball with a minuet.

After a few minutes of this, Charlotte took a pair of scissors, cut away the cabin trunk's linen lining, and examined the bare wooden surfaces underneath. Everyone took turns checking the interior of the luggage, looking for hidden catches. Mrs. Watson even held the lining up to the light and went over every square inch.

Minutes ticked by. Livia's heart slowed, then raced again in a new agitation, a sharp dread that everything would be in vain.

"I don't think we will find anything here," said Charlotte after some more time.

No one spoke. Frustration choked Livia's windpipe. Mrs. Watson looked crestfallen.

Charlotte put water to boil. Lord Ingram brought whisky for Mrs. Watson and Livia.

"Maybe clues weren't *hidden* in the luggage," he suggested. "Maybe the contents of the luggage itself are a clue. Maybe they imply that what Mr. Marbleton did in Snowham had to do with photography."

Charlotte, who had been checking the amount of tea that remained in the tin, stilled. "You may be right, my lord. Livia, can you give an abbreviated account of how you ended up at the Jubilee shop yesterday?"

Livia managed to sum up in five minutes what had taken her nearly half an hour to tell Charlotte.

Charlotte went to the bedroom and came back to the parlor, holding the Stanhope. "Among the things she brought back is this."

With an indrawn breath, Lord Ingram took the Stanhope from her and peered through the eyehole.

Livia supposed the Stanhope did have something to do with photography. After all, the images inside the optic bijou were photographs that had been shrunk to a very small size, and then magnified by a special lens for the viewer. But why did that matter?

Lord Ingram looked up from the Stanhope, his expression torn between excitement and apprehension. "Are you thinking of the Franco-Prussian War, Holmes?"

What did the Franco-Prussian War, which took place when Livia was still a child, have to do with anything?

Mrs. Watson gasped. "I remember now. During the siege of Paris, the French used pigeons to carry miniaturized dispatches and letters past the German barricade into the city. Why, I paid for one such letter to a friend."

Charlotte took the Stanhope from Lord Ingram and turned it

between her fingers. "The gentleman who took charge of micro-filming those dispatches and letters to be carried in by pigeons was none other than the inventor of the Stanhope. It was said that he achieved such reduction by means of special photography that they were able to fit three thousand messages on a pellicule the size of two postage stamps."

*Special photography. Reduction. Messages.*

Did this mean—was it possible that—

"Livia, let me have the ticket from Mr. Marbleton." Charlotte set the Stanhope aside. "Ma'am, my lord, your ticket stubs from today, please."

Mr. Marbleton's effort to guide Livia to the souvenir shop at last made sense. He wanted her—or someone, at least—to notice the Stanhopes, which allowed one to view microphotographs without the aid of a microscope. This was as strongly as he dared hint that he had embedded a minuscule image on the ticket stub!

Mrs. Watson and Lord Ingram produced four stubs. With unsteady fingers, Livia handed over the small cloisonné jewelry box. The sun had emerged from behind the clouds not long ago. They cleared the desk before the window and pulled back the curtains. Charlotte placed a clean handkerchief on the desk, then laid all five stubs on the handkerchief.

With a magnifying glass, she examined today's stubs first, front and back. She then picked up Mr. Marbleton's with a pair of tweezers and subjected it, too, to a close inspection.

When she was done, she set the four most recent stubs in a row and Mr. Marbleton's ticket a few inches to the side. "The difference is on this side."

All the tickets had been arranged so that their front side faced up. On that side, the issuing railway company's name was printed on top, then the departing and destination stations, the class, and the fare. At the very bottom, the line SEE CONDITIONS ON BACK.

Livia was the first person to step up to the desk. After she'd gone to Snowham with Lord Ingram, she had also searched for differences between the ticket stubs she'd brought back and the one from Mr. Marbleton. But this time, she knew what to look for.

And it was as if she'd been trying to read by the flickering of fireflies earlier, and now she had limelight.

"I could be wrong," she said, her voice cracking a little, "but on Mr. Marbleton's ticket, at the end of SEE CONDITIONS ON BACK—is that an extra full stop under this streak of soot?"

On all four stubs brought back today, the line ended with the letter K, and no punctuation mark. But with sunlight, and the squinting of the eye, Livia could barely make out a tiny dot at the end of the phrase on Mr. Marbleton's ticket.

Charlotte nodded. Livia, on wobbly legs, vacated her spot. When Mrs. Watson and Lord Ingram, too, confirmed that they saw the extra dot, Livia asked, "But how can we view it? Lord Ingram, you told me earlier that only something transparent can be viewed with a microscope."

"In theory we should manage it easily enough," replied Lord Ingram. He was on his haunches next to the desk, so that his eyes were level with the ticket stubs. "The dot at the end of SEE CONDITIONS ON BACK is film. Mr. Marbleton will have glued it on. If we place the ticket in water and let it sit for some time, the dot will come off the ticket and we can then place it on a glass slide."

He looked up at the three women who surrounded him. "But in practice it could be harrowing. The dot is minuscule. There is a good bit of soot on the stub. We could very well lose sight of the film amidst other debris once everything starts coming off the ticket."

But they had to proceed.

Mrs. Watson and Lord Ingram returned to Mrs. Watson's house for a supply of creamware finger bowls that Mrs. Watson had never used at her dinner table. Charlotte brought out her microscope. Livia, perspiring with nerves, snipped out a tiny square of the stub containing the film dot.

When Mrs. Watson and Lord Ingram came back, they brought not only what they had gone for but a basket of sandwiches that Madame Gascoigne had thoughtfully prepared.

The square Livia had clipped, barely one eighth of an inch on each side, was put to soak in lukewarm water inside a finger bowl. As the company waited, they tucked into the sandwiches. Mrs. Watson also filled Livia in on what had happened at the Garden of Hermopolis.

Livia, agape, turned an accusatory look Charlotte's way. "You didn't tell me any of the more interesting events."

Charlotte only said, "Now you know everything."

Though the ticket stub had been reduced in size, the soaking water still grew murky. But they knew where the film dot was and were able to verify that it was still in place before transferring the tiny piece of paper to a finger bowl filled with clean water.

The ticket went through three changes of bowls. At last, the dot of film, now under constant surveillance, detached from the paper.

Even the finest pair of tweezers Charlotte owned were still too large at the tips, so she brought Livia a needle. Livia, her teeth clenched tight, used the blunt end of the needle to chase the much-too-small dot around the finger bowl.

At last she closed in on her quarry.

"Bloody hell, it fell through the eye!"

And she could not even care that she'd sworn not only out loud but in mixed company.

On her third attempt she lifted the dot out but it adhered to the needle. Charlotte patiently applied water with a tiny dropper, in the hope that it could be rinsed off onto the slide below.

The vein at Livia's temple felt as if it had already burst.

"Let me try something different," said Charlotte.

She plucked a strand of hair off her head and slowly skimmed it down the side of the needle. Livia held her breath. Even though the waiting slide was placed on a large plate, the least bit of excess force and the scarcely visible dot could land somewhere on the carpet, never to be found again.

"Is it off the needle?" came Mrs. Watson's muffled voice. She sounded as if she were biting her own knuckles.

"I think so," answered Charlotte, "but it's now stuck on the hair. However, I can place the hair on the slide."

After the addition of a larger drop of water, Charlotte placed a smaller piece of glass—a coverslip—on top of the slide and very gently pressed down. The dot, pressured by the liquid, separated from the hair. Ever so cautiously, she pulled out the strand of hair, leaving the infinitesimal dot in place.

At last she pushed the two pieces of glass together.

Everyone exhaled.

Livia wiped at her damp forehead. "My nerves are shattered."

"But now this can go on the microscope's stage," said Charlotte.

The doorbell rang sharply.

Everyone stood still, listening. Livia prayed that it was only a child's prank and there would not be a repetition.

The doorbell rang again, even more impatiently.

"You aren't expecting any clients, are you, Charlotte?" Livia squeaked.

"The only client I have at the moment is Moriarty," answered Charlotte. "I wonder what he wants."

Mrs. Watson hid the microscope in the back of the wardrobe in Sherlock Holmes's bedroom, locked the wardrobe door, and pocketed the key, her knuckles white, her face grave.

Livia, with shaking hands, set the finger bowls of used water, as well as the remnant of the ticket stub itself, on the shelves that held all the tinctures and cures for the care of the "bedridden detective." They dared not throw anything away, lest they'd made a mistake. It was possible that the dot they had painstakingly centered on the slide was but a round particle of soot and the real piece of film was still among the detritus or somewhere else on the ticket altogether.

Lord Ingram entered with a tray that held teacups and plates that had been scattered around the parlor. He set the tray on the bed, which had been cleared of all the Jubilee items, closed the door, and glanced at Mrs. Watson. Mrs. Watson pointed at the wardrobe, indicating the location of the microscope. He took up position next to the wardrobe, pulled out a revolver, and quietly, but with great concentration, checked its chambers.

Only then did it occur to Livia that they might need to defend Mr. Marbleton's secret message. She shuddered but helped Mrs. Watson draw the curtains and place a rolled-up mat against the bottom of the door to block out all the light.

Gradually, a reversed and upside-down image of the parlor coalesced against the far wall—the entire room had been set up as a camera obscura. Voices came. Charlotte's and—thankfully—a voice that was not Moriarty's.

"We will need you to return to the Garden of Hermopolis as soon as possible, Miss Holmes," said the stranger.

Livia sucked in a breath. Mrs. Watson swallowed audibly.

"Oh?" Charlotte sounded a little puzzled. "But why, Mr. de Lacey? Surely Miss Baxter—"

De Lacey's face, also reversed and upside down, appeared on the wall—a neat, ordinary-looking man in his early forties, with an unhappy air, that of a favored dog who had just been kicked by its master.

"I am not here to pick faults with your evidence as to Miss Baxter's well-being—Mr. Baxter is satisfied with your work in that regard," answered de Lacey, sounding harried. "But he is worried for Mr. Craddock."

There was enough light from the camera obscura for Livia to see that both Lord Ingram and Mrs. Watson frowned at the mention of the name.

"Mr. Craddock was assigned to Miss Baxter for her safety," continued de Lacey. "Mr. Baxter is disturbed that in all the accounts of the night of the fire, Mr. Craddock did not make a single appearance. Nor have we received a report on those events from him."

"Perhaps he was unwell that night."

"Unwell or not, he should have performed his duty—or explained why he couldn't," said de Lacey impatiently. "Mr. Baxter is not terribly lenient with those who fail to do what they are paid to do."

A moment of silence, as if the mere thought of Moriarty's lack of mercy overawed de Lacey.

"Mr. de Lacey, I asked you, during our previous meeting, whether Mr. Baxter had anyone else keeping an eye on Miss Baxter at the Garden. You insisted there was only Mrs. Felton."

Charlotte spoke softly, but her words were pointed.

"Mr. Baxter did not believe any mention of Mr. Craddock to have been relevant then. But now that he is missing, it matters."

"Does Mr. Baxter have anyone else in or around the compound keeping an eye on Miss Baxter?"

De Lacey rose to his feet. "You know enough to begin your work, Miss Holmes."

"I have one more question, Mr. de Lacey," said Charlotte, her face at last coming into view on the wall, her purple turban brushing against the floor. "Did Mr. Baxter or anyone allied with him arrange for the fireworks the other night?"

De Lacey gave her a long look, his impatience condensing into hostility. "I have brought sufficient payment for services rendered and to retain you for one more trip to the Garden of Hermopolis. Find out what happened to Mr. Craddock, Miss Holmes."

## Nineteen

"W ell, that was insolent!" huffed Livia. "A man who wasn't important enough to mention earlier—and now it's incumbent upon Charlotte to find out what happened to him."

They were back in the parlor. Charlotte sat on the window seat, giving a drop of whisky to the narcissus. Mrs. Watson poked agitatedly at the coal in the grate. Lord Ingram, standing between the grandfather clock and the umbrella stand, gazed toward the window—or perhaps toward Charlotte.

And Livia, her hand braced against the desk so that she wouldn't shake, continued to vent. "Who does Moriarty think he is, ordering Charlotte about as if she's at his beck and call?"

If she didn't rail against Moriarty, she might cower.

"I don't like this," said Mrs. Watson, looking up, a sharp furrow between her brows. "Moriarty doesn't mean well, Miss Charlotte, sending you back."

Charlotte, having soused the narcissus to her satisfaction, put aside the whisky bottle. "He didn't mean well sending me there the first time."

Livia felt as if she were falling—without knowing how long she'd keep falling. "But who is this Mr. Craddock, and why does he matter? It's the first I've heard of his name."

"That would be my fault," said Mrs. Watson, who, while they'd waited for the film dot to come off the ticket stub, had filled Livia in on the details of the Cornwall trip that Charlotte had omitted. "His name came up briefly at dinner, but he wasn't there himself. I never saw him anywhere else in the Garden and didn't consider him to be at all significant."

She turned to Charlotte. "In retrospect it makes sense, doesn't it? Miss Ellery said that Mr. Craddock used to live in the cottage we were assigned—and out of all the cottages in the compound, ours had the most obstructed view of Miss Baxter's lodge. Obviously Miss Baxter didn't want his 'protection.'"

Charlotte looked at Lord Ingram. "Sir, I believe you heard Mr. Craddock's voice the night of the fireworks?"

"It was about one thirty in the morning. Mr. Peters was guarding Miss Baxter's lodge from the veranda. He called out 'Who's there?' A man answered 'Craddock.' Mr. Peters told him to go home. It was too dark for me to see whether Mr. Craddock did as he was asked, but nothing more was said between them."

Lord Ingram set a finger on top of a walking stick in the umbrella stand—not his, but one with a carved eagle's-head handle that purportedly belonged to the unseen Sherlock Holmes. He picked up the stick and set it back down gently. "Later, after Mr. Peters and Mrs. Crosby drove out, I climbed up to the ramparts to see the direction they were headed. A man came up after me.

"At some point during the night I'd seen all the other male residents of the Garden: Mr. Peters and the stable boy close up, Mr. Steele, Mr. McEwan, and Dr. Robinson from a distance. But this man, though his face was covered, didn't seem to be any of them. At the time I thought he was Mr. Craddock. Assuming that we've been told the truth about how many men currently reside in the Garden, I still believe that to be correct."

Livia didn't know whether she ought to be reassured or even

more anxious. "If you are right, then he was out and about as of two nights ago."

"*If* I am right. But I may be right about only the most superficial aspects concerning Mr. Craddock."

All the same, this meant that Lord Ingram was certain about the exchange he'd heard between Mr. Peters and Mr. Craddock, and by a process of elimination, he was equally sure that the man who'd been admonished by Mr. Peters to go home had later showed up on the wall.

Livia pushed away from the desk and settled herself next to her sister on the window seat. "Maybe—maybe it will turn out similarly to your search for Miss Baxter, Charlotte. Maybe you'll return to the Garden of Hermopolis and Mr. Craddock will be right there."

Charlotte didn't say anything. After a moment, she proffered an envelope to Lord Ingram. "Here's a picture of Mr. Craddock that de Lacey left for us. Does this look like the man you saw on the wall?"

Lord Ingram came forward, took the envelope, and examined the photograph inside. He frowned. "The man I saw had a muffler drawn across his face, so I'm not able to say with any certainty whether the two are the same. Still, the man in the photograph . . . Put it this way: If I came across this man, I would be wary. I wasn't as alarmed about the man on the wall."

He handed the picture to Livia and she saw what he meant. The subject of the photograph had a sharp, opportunistic look in his eyes that made her feel uncomfortable.

Lord Ingram, ever considerate, took the envelope to Mrs. Watson, too. Mrs. Watson put down the poker in her hand and rubbed the space between her brows. "Are you implying, my lord, that the man you saw was an imposter?"

"I don't know enough to suggest that, especially as I have no idea whom I saw on the wall. But with de Lacey claiming something isn't right with Mr. Craddock, the idea has crossed my mind."

"It is also possible that Mr. Craddock decided to throw in his lot with Miss Baxter. But even if that were the case, he still should have reported about the night of the fireworks," said Charlotte.

"In his place, I would have," said Mrs. Watson. "I would not have done anything to draw Moriarty's attention."

Charlotte rose, went to the sideboard, and retrieved a newspaper. "Livia might not recognize this, but it is the gazette we bought at a local newsagent's. I took it with me to Miss Baxter's place so that she could take a picture with it, to prove the picture's recent vintage.

"When Miss Baxter saw the gazette, she suggested I read it. I went through it twice and the only thing of note was a small notice that said *I'm glad to see you well. And that you are carrying on as usual.*

"We don't know whether that was Mr. Craddock's means of making his reports, but let's suppose that it was. Let's further suppose that Miss Baxter observed the regular occurrence of such a small notice and realized that should she rid herself of Mr. Craddock, she could make it appear as if he were still around, still submitting his reports."

Charlotte gave the gazette to Livia and pointed at the exact spot for the small notice.

Livia bit her lower lip. "But why would Miss Baxter get rid of Mr. Craddock? She didn't get rid of Mrs. Felton."

"Perhaps Mr. Craddock learned something about Miss Baxter that she did not wish her father to know," said Charlotte, sitting down again on the window seat.

Mrs. Watson sucked in a breath, her expression almost comical. "You don't mean Miss Baxter reverted to her habit of collecting unsuitable fiancés?"

Charlotte looked toward Lord Ingram. Livia's and Mrs. Watson's gaze followed.

"You know the answer, my lord?" asked Mrs. Watson uncertainly.

Lord Ingram's face seemed to color. "I have guesses, but I would prefer for Holmes to broach the subject."

Charlotte nodded. "I see our thoughts have progressed in the same general direction. Let me ask you, my lord, on your way to Cornwall, what did you suspect we'd find out?"

"That Miss Baxter was dead—or at best, that she'd left the Garden of Hermopolis of her own will."

"Did you think she was in the lodge that was putatively hers?"

"No."

"When did you change your mind?"

Livia heard a crinkling sound—she was crushing a corner of the gazette in her hand. When Mrs. Watson had told the story, it was clear that even when she called on Miss Baxter, at first she suspected that she might be meeting a substitute, a hired actress. But Lord Ingram—if Livia caught Charlotte's drift, Lord Ingram had shed his original theory well before that.

Charlotte, too.

What had *they* seen?

"I began having second thoughts when it turned out that Miss Baxter's lodge was still tightly guarded after Mr. Young, the fireworks-igniting troublemaker, had been dispatched back to the village," said Lord Ingram, his head bent, his chin between thumb and forefinger. "I became convinced that someone was in it when a person, possibly Mrs. Crosby, began running back and forth between her house and Miss Baxter's."

"All that running would indeed have been unnecessary if they'd been guarding an empty house," said Charlotte. Softly, she pried open Livia's still clenched fingers from the gazette. "Shortly after midnight, when Mrs. Crosby claimed that Miss Baxter was sleeping too soundly to be awakened, and refused to allow anyone to carry her out—while flames licked at the wall of her lodge—it seemed more likely than ever that there was no Miss Baxter inside and that all Mrs. Crosby and her cohorts guarded was the paper-thin fiction of her presence. But . . ."

She inclined her head at Mrs. Watson. "Ma'am, if you'll forgive me, I did not tell you about my visit to Dr. Robinson's cottage the night of the fireworks. This was after everyone in the Garden had been sent home and Lord Ingram and I went out again. While I was inside Dr. Robinson's cottage, he came back."

Mrs. Watson emitted a small cry.

"Don't worry, he didn't know I was there. He was in a hurry—grabbed a few things and left. In addition to his doctor's bag, he also took carbolic acid and chloroform."

With that combination of an antiseptic and an anesthetic . . .

"He had to perform surgery?" asked Livia.

"Not necessarily," said Charlotte. "Our sovereign was administered chloroform on two occasions that were not surgical in nature."

It took Livia a moment to understand what she was talking about. Her chin fell. Across the parlor, Mrs. Watson was similarly slack-jawed.

Livia would not have known what Charlotte was referring to but for their eldest sister, Henrietta, who had insisted on being given chloroform for her confinement, over their mother's objection. Henrietta had prevailed because she'd pointed out that the queen herself had taken advantage of the anesthetic for the births of her two youngest children, therefore the use of chloroform was royally sanctioned for all her female subjects.

Mrs. Watson held her hands together just in front of her chin, almost as if she were fending off something. "Miss Baxter was *with child?*"

She spoke in a barely audible whisper, but the question was no less thunderous. Livia, though she'd been thinking the same, nearly jumped.

"And possibly gave birth the night of the fireworks," said Charlotte. "Childbirth would not have been my first suspicion had she not received us the next evening, looking splendid. There are many medical applications for carbolic acid and chloroform—she could have had an appendectomy.

"She did not, however, strike me as someone recovering from surgery, or a prolonged illness. But if her condition had been a case of advanced pregnancy, then everything made sense, especially with regard to the fact that, out of the blue, she could meet with us. One should not tight-lace with a child in utero. But when the womb is once again empty, with the judicious use of a long corset, who could tell that a woman has recently given birth?"

A hush fell.

"So Mrs. Felton—and some members of the Garden—hadn't seen Miss Baxter for months because she was obviously with child and couldn't be seen," marveled Livia.

"I had a look at Dr. Watson's books earlier. There is a condition called *hyperemesis gravidarum*, when an expectant mother suffers from symptoms far in excess of normal morning sickness. Which might explain why for some months, whenever Mrs. Felton did see her, she looked tired and unwell."

"So perhaps Mr. Peters wasn't lying after all, when he said that he'd seen Miss Baxter out for a walk late at night." Mrs. Watson covered her mouth. "Oh my, do you suppose that despite all of Miss Baxter's precautions, Mr. Craddock saw her in her condition?"

"That would be my guess."

The idea of a splendid-looking Miss Baxter coolly ordering the killing of her father's minion who had become too great an inconvenience . . . Livia shivered. "If that were the case, then Miss Baxter really had reason to want Mr. Craddock gone. But who was the man walking around and calling himself Craddock then? An imposter put in place?"

Charlotte thought for a moment. "Possibly. De Lacey once again did not answer my question as to whether Moriarty still had more people in the compound. Were I Miss Baxter, I would have put an imposter in place, so as not to alert anyone that Mr. Craddock is no more."

Livia frowned. "But if the truth is anything close to our conjecture, then Miss Baxter will be thoroughly displeased to have you look into Mr. Craddock's fate, won't she?"

The next moment blood drained from her face. "My goodness, Charlotte, *that* is why Moriarty keeps sending you into the Garden of Hermopolis. First he thought something untoward happened to Miss Baxter and wanted whoever harmed her to harm you, too—the fireworks and whatnot were his attempt to force their hand, wasn't it? Except Miss Baxter wasn't dead and he didn't succeed. Now that his watchdog is missing, he wants *Miss Baxter* to remove you, because she wouldn't wish for you to look too closely at Mr. Craddock's disappearance!"

Mrs. Watson's right hand opened and clenched, opened and clenched. Lord Ingram picked up a miniature marble bust of Diana of Versailles from the mantel and weighed it in his palm, as if gauging its potential as a weapon. Charlotte, rising from the window seat to open a biscuit jar at the sideboard, seemed scarcely concerned.

"Before he joined us in Cornwall, Lord Ingram went to see Lord Bancroft. Lord Bancroft mentioned that Lord Remington likely considers me a latent agent of the Crown and would pursue Moriarty if he were to harm me. As far as reassurances go, neither Lord Ingram nor I thought much of it.

"However, there might be something to be said about Lord Remington's attitude." Charlotte pointed at Livia with a biscuit. "If you were Moriarty, and found Charlotte Holmes to be a nuisance and wanted to be rid of her before she became a bigger nuisance but had to take into consideration possible reprisals by Lord Remington, what would you do?"

"Find someone else to pull the trigger," said Livia, barely able to hear her own voice.

"Moriarty using those whom he believes to have killed his

daughter to eliminate us—that is one thing," said Mrs. Watson hoarsely. "It would be justice served should Lord Remington retaliate against Miss Baxter's murderers. But by dragooning you back into the Garden, he will be forcing Miss Baxter's hand. And should retribution come, it will fall upon his own child!"

The idea did not shock Livia half as much. If Sir Henry, her father, could gain great advantage by sacrificing her, would he hesitate? Not for long.

Charlotte, breaking off a piece of her biscuit, appeared even less affected. "My lord, what would you do if you suspected that residents of the Garden of Hermopolis had murdered your child?"

His lordship returned the marble bust in his hand to the mantel, arranging it with care. "I would not be so patient or cunning as to use them to get rid of Charlotte Holmes, and then wait for Lord Remington Ashburton to perhaps punish them when he learned of Charlotte Holmes's fate."

"Neither would most parents," said Charlotte, at last taking a bite of her biscuit. "But I think Moriarty is fully capable of using a wayward daughter in this way, especially if he realized, as we did, that she might have borne a child out of wedlock."

"Surely . . ." Livia was stunned; she needed a moment to collect her thoughts. "Moriarty is a lying, cheating, blackmailing, murdering reprobate—and that's just what little we know of him. You think he'd mind that his daughter bore a child out of wedlock?"

"Unfortunately, I agree with Holmes," said Lord Ingram. "The world is full of men who believe that rules for men are only for lesser men, but those for women brook no exceptions. That he broke all rules for men would be a point of pride to Moriarty, but that his daughter broke all rules for women, he would find deeply shameful, a stain on her *and* on him."

No one said anything for a while.

Livia shook her head. What was the point of having Moriarty for a father if a woman had to live as carefully and timidly as anyone else? Then she asked, "Where's the baby now, if Miss Baxter indeed had one?"

"Taken away by Mrs. Crosby, most likely," said Charlotte.

Livia remembered what Mrs. Watson had told her, that in the predawn hours of the dramatic night, Mr. Peters and Mrs. Crosby had driven out of the Garden together, but as far as they knew, only Mr. Peters had later returned.

"To the father?" murmured Mrs. Watson. She gasped. "Remember that story Miss Baxter told, about the lover she saw once a year before the statue of Achilles at Hyde Park Corner? You think it's the same man?"

Charlotte reached for another biscuit. "I have no way of knowing, not at the moment in any case."

Lord Ingram, as if sensing that the other two women in the room required something stronger than biscuits, decanted whisky.

Gratefully, Livia accepted the offered glass and took a sip. "So what do we do now?"

To head back to the Garden of Hermopolis was to enter a storm of knives, but not to go—if Charlotte could have refused, she would not have gone the first time.

Mrs. Watson rubbed her own arm, a disquieted gesture. "We don't need to return to Cornwall this moment, do we?"

"Unless de Lacey is prepared to physically shove me onto a train, I am not leaving London tonight—certainly not before we have a look at what Mr. Marbleton brought us." Charlotte pointed toward Sherlock Holmes's bedroom. "Now shall we?"

---

On the slide, there was nothing.

A scream lodged in Livia's throat. While they'd been in the parlor discussing Miss Baxter's possible pregnancy, had Moriarty's minions slipped into the bedroom and stolen the dot of film from right underneath their—

"For a moment I thought we'd lost it," said Lord Ingram, his voice heavy with relief. "It's just too small to see."

Livia clutched at her bodice. The microscope had been set on the window seat, the brightest spot in the parlor. Lanterns had been placed to either side, to supplement the pallid light of a winter afternoon. Livia, standing beyond the lanterns and craning her head, still could not see anything on the slide.

Charlotte sank to her knees on a footstool placed before the window seat, looked into the eyepiece, adjusted the position of the slide, and then twisted several knobs.

"*Is* it still there?" asked Livia, her fingers gripping her skirts.

"Yes."

*Thank goodness.* "What's on it?"

Charlotte rose and indicated that Livia should take her place. "Take a look."

Livia had never looked into a microscope and had not anticipated the brightly lit spread that filled her entire vision. She blinked and looked again.

The dot had been magnified so much that only a portion could be seen: a sketch of a park bench, with an open book resting on it. The book was blank, but at its bottom right corner was written the number I.

Charlotte placed her hand on a knob. "Turn the knob if you want to see the rest."

Livia turned the knob, but the image moved in the opposite direction of what she'd intended and displayed the dot's edge, so jagged that it looked as if it had been hacked with a poleax. She turned the knob the other way. Underneath the sketch were a block of unintelligible, typewritten letters and a photograph of half a dozen strangers, four men and two women, in what appeared to be a mountainous region.

Since neither meant anything to her, she scrolled back to the sketch.

The very first meeting between Mr. Marbleton and herself had taken place in a park. And she had been reading on a bench. Later he had immortalized the scene, as well as the book she had been reading, with the gift of a hand-painted bookmark showing a woman in white sitting on a park bench.

This sketch was a hint, wasn't it, at the key to deciphering the block of letters?

She stared at the sketch a few more seconds before reluctantly yielding her place to Mrs. Watson. Mrs. Watson donned her glasses to study the contents of the slide, only to rise again with an expression of incomprehension.

Lord Ingram, on the other hand, glanced up in astonishment almost as soon as he peered through the eyepiece. He looked at Charlotte, who said nothing.

"What is it, my dear?" asked Mrs. Watson, with a hand on his shoulder.

"You have a better memory for such things, Holmes, but I believe this photograph was among the images we seized from Moriarty's château last December."

On that night, Charlotte had entered the château disguised as a man with a great big paunch. Unbeknownst to all except a few, the paunch was hollow. Later, when Livia had seen it again, it had become quite heavy, filled with loot from Moriarty's hidden safe.

Neither Livia nor Mrs. Watson had been interested in its contents—they wanted as little to do with Moriarty as possible and felt safer not knowing his secrets. Lord Ingram must have felt differently.

Charlotte, however, raised a brow. "I thought you didn't want to know Moriarty's dark deeds."

"At the time I didn't, but before I put the lot away in Hôtel Papillon's safe, I decided that willful ignorance was not the policy. I had a look at the negatives."

Hôtel Papillon was the name of the private mansion in Paris where they had stayed.

Livia's hand balled into a fist; her thumb rubbed nervously over the side of her index finger. "Did—did Mr. Marbleton also have a look at them?"

It did not *sound* as if he'd been invited to a perusal.

Lord Ingram rose from the footstool but offered no answer.

"It would seem that Mr. Marbleton had a look at the lot of them overnight and—took this one with him when he left," said Charlotte. Her tone turned wistful. "Had I known that he excelled at safe-cracking, I'd have asked for his assistance at Château Vaudrieu."

She patted Livia on the arm. "I'm sure Mr. Marbleton had very good reasons. Besides, it was our oversight. We should have invited him to sift through everything with us—Moriarty's doings concerned him more than they concerned us."

Livia exhaled. Strictly speaking, what Mr. Marbleton had done was theft; she was grateful that Charlotte chose to be understanding.

"Miss Olivia," said Mrs. Watson, also looking at her with an encouraging smile, "you would know the book referred to in the sketch, I believe?"

Livia's face heated. "It is either *The Moonstone* or *The Woman in White*, both by Wilkie Collins."

Mrs. Watson tapped a fingertip against her chin. "We shall need to acquire copies of these books."

"Well, if Mr. Marbleton means the opening sentences of these books, then I have them memorized," said Livia, both proud and embarrassed.

At their first meeting, they had spoken of those two books, and it had been the first conversation Livia ever held with someone who read and enjoyed the same sort of books she did.

"If you are sure you know the opening sentences in their entirety, we will begin deciphering the passage," said Charlotte decisively.

"My lord, will you read aloud the block of letters? We will write them down."

"Certainly," said Lord Ingram. "Although now I do wish we had a megascope, to project the image on the wall."

The microscope and the lanterns were transferred to the desk. Lord Ingram sat down and read the letters row by row. And then he read the same letters column by column, while the ladies checked their copies.

Since Mr. Marbleton had already gone through so much trouble, Charlotte deemed that the cipher must be a Wheatstone, nearly impossible to solve if one didn't already know the key.

But the first opening sentence they tried, from *The Moonstone*, did turn out to be the key.

Deciphered, the text read,

*image is for yr brother*
*to know what it concerns compose small notice to ellie hartford start with the word mycenae make the rest a wheatstone cipher with it is a truth universally acknowledged as the key*
*my regards to yr sister*

Mr. Marbleton had left the ticket stub at a meeting with Charlotte. The cipher needed Livia's input. But no matter to whom the note was addressed, *yr brother* could refer only to Mr. Myron Finch, their illegitimate half brother, who had once worked for Moriarty but escaped the organization the year before.

"Interesting," murmured Charlotte, seated in the chair she always took when receiving clients. "Last summer Mr. Marbleton sought Mr. Finch. But Mr. Finch, when I last saw him, wasn't terribly enamored of the idea of meeting with the Marbletons."

"But they did meet on that very night, when Mr. Marbleton came to warn you and Mr. Finch that Mr. Finch was no longer safe.

Who is to say they didn't manage to meet again later?" said Lord Ingram, still at the desk.

Indeed, the situation had been dire enough that night that Mr. Finch had donned women's clothes to facilitate his escape. Livia hadn't known then that he was her half brother, or the real reason he was fleeing. To her he'd been only the groom hired for the London Season who had been surprisingly considerate and helpful. And she'd fretted for months about what became of him, until Charlotte had told her the truth, after which her worries had only sharpened.

Livia, standing by the mantel, took another swallow of the whisky Lord Ingram had poured for her earlier—and wished that liquid courage, rather than liquid anxiety, flowed through her veins. "Charlotte, Lord Ingram told me that you had news recently from Mr. Finch."

Charlotte tapped her pencil against the notebook on her lap, in which she'd done her portion of the deciphering. "He'd sent me two messages last year, which read exactly the same: 'Dear Caesar, how fares Rome? Here in Italy all is well. 3 N N.'

"The mention of Italy meant that he was in Britain. The number indicated the level of danger he was in: three out of ten was not too terrible for someone pursued by Moriarty. The first N signaled that he was north of London, in relative position. The second N meant that no, the message would not be followed by a more detailed letter to be called for at the General Post Office under an alias.

"The message from this January, however, is shorter. 'Dear Caesar, how fares Rome? 5.' Increased danger. No indication of location. But that he was able to send a message at all was good news."

That was what Lord Ingram had said, too, when he'd told Livia about the most recent message, that any communication from Mr. Finch constituted an assurance of his safety, at least as of the time of its dispatch.

"Do you suppose Mr. Marbleton knew where to find Mr.

Finch?" Livia asked Charlotte, then immediately shook her head. "Of course not. If he did, he wouldn't need to pass the message through us."

"What I'm struck by is that this is the last thing Mr. Marbleton did, before he surrendered himself to Moriarty," said Mrs. Watson from the sideboard, a small quaver to her voice. "I don't know the procedures necessary for reducing an image to such miniature scale, but even with that task done, it could not have been easy to cut out such a tiny dot, affix it to the right spot on the ticket, and apply soot in such a way as to both conceal the dot and make the ticket appear naturally trodden."

Charlotte nodded. "He left that day in tears. Still, afterward, he took the time to do this. One could argue that he didn't want to meet his future yet, but all the same, it had to have been extraordinarily important for him to convey this image to Mr. Finch."

*He left that day in tears.*

Livia had not known this. She had left earlier that day, in shock because he had abruptly announced to her that they ought to never see each other again, or even write. She had realized later that he had done so to protect her and had understood that he must have hurt as much as she had.

But to hear that detail from Charlotte—the tears she had not shed that day rushed to her eyes. She blinked them back.

Mrs. Watson came and took her hand. Livia managed a weak smile. She could not free Mr. Marbleton from Moriarty's grip—not yet—but she would do everything in her power to make sure that the image reached Mr. Finch.

"Shall we begin composing our message to Ellie Hartford?" she asked, a catch to her voice. "If we finish and encrypt it fast enough, I'd like to personally take the message to the papers before I must return to the hotel."

## Twenty

After drafting and encrypting a message to Ellie Hartford, also known as Miss Marbleton, Mr. Marbleton's sister, the company dispersed.

Lord Ingram, who had the most experience in evading followers, took Miss Olivia to the papers to post small notices, the first of his many errands. Miss Charlotte dispatched cables. Mrs. Watson gathered her staff for a meeting—arrangements must be made before anyone could flee from Moriarty.

Everyone who worked for her had lived eventful lives before settling down into domestic service. Mrs. Watson had feared that they, even more than she, would be distressed to lose the stability on which they'd come to depend. Instead, they consoled *her*—and assured her that Moriarty would be but a minor disturbance, and that they looked forward to their small adventures much as those who dined on steak and foie gras daily anticipated an occasional serving of eel pie.

Mrs. Watson left the council with her heart full of both sorrow and gratitude. She found Miss Charlotte in the afternoon parlor, hunched over the writing desk, a notebook spread open before her, a pair of telegrams to the side.

Mrs. Watson picked up the cables. They were from Mr. Mears,

sent today, concerning what he'd found in the archives of various Cornish newspapers. Miss Charlotte had asked him to examine those specific issues Miss Baxter had in her collection, copy down small notices that caught his attention, and take note of relevant articles.

Mr. Mears indeed reported some small notices in code. He also came across two articles that mentioned Sherlock Holmes, one on the detective's first case—investigating an apparent accidental overdose in nearby Devonshire—the other about the recent scandal involving Inspector Treadles.

"Was that how Miss Baxter learned about Sherlock Holmes?" Mrs. Watson wondered aloud.

Miss Holmes stared out the window at Regent's Park across the street. The sun had once again emerged from the clouds, but trees were still denuded, and grass grew in irregular patches of short stubbles.

"I believe Miss Baxter had other means," she said, and returned to her ciphers.

By eight o'clock in the evening two more cables had arrived from Mr. Mears. Dinner consisted of Miss Charlotte eating at the same desk, scribbling in her notebook, and Mrs. Watson in her favorite chair nearby, making one list after another. After their meal, Miss Charlotte asked for help in mounting a search of their own archives— Mrs. Watson kept every letter that had ever come for Sherlock Holmes, those containing legitimate inquiries as well as those written by members of the public with too much idle time on their hands.

Two months ago, such a search had turned up important clues from Inspector Treadles. This time, Miss Charlotte wanted to see whether there were any letters that bore postmarks from the village of Snowham. Much to Mrs. Watson's surprise, they discovered not one but two such letters among the rejected post, and each of those contained a sentence followed by an extra full stop.

Knowing now how much information such a seemingly insignificant dot could contain, Mrs. Watson set to the task of removing the film dots from the letters with a dry mouth and a pounding heart. But the dots turned out to be identical to the one they'd found on Mr. Marbleton's ticket stub.

Mrs. Watson was disappointed. But not Miss Charlotte. "It makes sense that Mr. Marbleton sent the results of his microphotography in duplicates," she pointed out, "exactly as the French did during the Franco-Prussian War."

Mrs. Watson sighed and removed the slide containing the second duplicate from the microscope. "I wish he'd come to us in person. He was only an hour away, wasn't he?"

Miss Charlotte, in the middle of preparing a transparent glue from Canada balsam, said only, "Perhaps he wanted to but couldn't. We have no way of knowing."

All this kept them busy until Lord Ingram returned late in the evening. Mrs. Watson uncorked a bottle of her beloved Château Haut-Brion, '65 vintage. Lord Ingram, at Miss Charlotte's instruction, pried open the Stanhope that Miss Olivia had bought from the Jubilee souvenir shop and substituted the film inside with one of the newly discovered duplicate dots.

Mrs. Watson listened to their conversation and sipped nervously. She flipped through Miss Charlotte's notebook, which contained the deciphered text of the small notices Mr. Mears had sent, and made the girl promise several times that once they were back in the Garden of Hermopolis, she would be very, very, very, very, very careful.

In the morning Mrs. Watson began their journey with a dull headache, and in a strange, grimly anticipatory mood. As London fell farther and farther behind, her mood became less anticipatory and only grim.

The night before, Lord Ingram had brought back a copy of the late edition evening newspaper in which the small notice intended for Miss Marbleton appeared. But what if Miss Marbleton didn't pay attention to the evening papers? Or didn't pay attention to that particular rag?

And who was to say that she was, in fact, in London? Certainly Mr. Marbleton could have no way of knowing, could he?

A burly, hirsute man, scratching the back of his neck, strolled by their compartment. Mrs. Watson's fingers knotted together. "The gentleman who walked past just now—this is the second time I've seen him. He first came around a quarter hour ago."

Miss Charlotte and Lord Ingram, in the middle of examining photographs of the countryside around the Garden of Hermopolis, exchanged a glance. The train decelerated—the next station was in sight. Lord Ingram placed the photographs back in their envelope.

The train stopped with grinding brakes and billowing steam. The corridor outside became congested, first with travelers waiting to leave, then with newly boarded passengers peering into compartments, looking for an empty space.

With a start, Mrs. Watson recognized one of the faces filing past their door. "It's that man again!"

Neither Miss Charlotte nor Lord Ingram said anything.

"I suppose . . . I suppose it's possible he detrained to buy something at the station and then came back," murmured Mrs. Watson, trying to comfort herself with a logical and not-at-all-sinister explanation.

The train resumed its journey. Mrs. Watson glanced at her railway handbook. They were already an hour outside London. If Miss Marbleton hadn't boarded the train yet—

The door of the compartment opened. The same burly, thickly bearded man stuck in his head and asked in a gravelly voice, "May I take a seat here?"

"No!" Mrs. Watson's refusal was swift and instinctive.

"Of course. Come in, please," said Miss Charlotte at the same time.

. Without any hesitation, Lord Ingram moved to give the man room. Mrs. Watson stared at her hospitable young friends, and then at the man as he closed the door and sat down directly opposite her. He seemed to have fallen on hard times. The brim of his bowler hat drooped on one side. His brown overcoat, of a decent enough material, had become frayed at the cuffs and was missing two buttons.

"Should I stand guard outside?" asked Lord Ingram.

The man shook his head. "I already checked every compartment in this car and the two adjacent ones. It will be another hour and ten minutes before the next stop. We should be all right."

His voice changed, losing much of its rougher edges, and became more . . . more . . .

Miss Charlotte extended her gloved hand. "Have you been well, Miss Marbleton?"

Miss Marbleton, of course. Mrs. Watson knew that Miss Marbleton often went about in masculine attire. All the same, she had not expected the young woman to be so convincing.

"What do you think? These have been the worst months of my life," grumbled Miss Marbleton as she shook first Miss Charlotte's hand, then Lord Ingram's. The glove on her right hand had a small hole on the index finger, completing the image of a down-on-his-luck man just scraping by.

Belatedly, Mrs. Watson also offered the young woman her hand. "I'm sorry about your family. I'm glad, though, that you are still at large."

"I'm not. I follow Moriarty around, but I don't know whether I'm trying to rescue Stephen or get myself caught, too. And Moriarty knows it. He parades Stephen around, so that I'll think he's thrown in his lot with Moriarty." Anguish darkened Miss Marbleton's eyes. "And sometimes I believe it."

"He hasn't thrown in his lot with Moriarty," said Miss Charlotte quietly. "I do not believe he would."

Miss Marbleton covered her eyes. With a start Mrs. Watson realized that she was weeping—or trying very hard not to.

"Did you manage to see him?" she asked in a quavering voice. "How did he give you the cipher to contact me?"

"We recently discovered that he had sent us two letters before he left England to turn himself in to Moriarty," answered Miss Charlotte. "And affixed to each letter was an identical bit of microphotography."

Mrs. Watson had been more than a little astonished that Mr. Marbleton wanted them to seek his sister—she had thought the latter to be in Moriarty's custody, too. Miss Charlotte had explained that before he'd surrendered himself to Moriarty, Mr. Marbleton's precise words had been *Moriarty has my parents*.

Nevertheless, Mrs. Watson had argued that they ought to be circumspect about what they told Miss Marbleton. What if some sort of understanding existed between Miss Marbleton and Moriarty? It was better not to mention that Mr. Marbleton managed to leave them a note right under Moriarty's nose.

Miss Charlotte, although she had agreed to Mrs. Watson's advice, had pointed out that they would still be discussing a photograph stolen from Moriarty's collection that Stephen Marbleton intended to pass on to Mr. Finch, someone Moriarty considered a traitor.

In other words, if Miss Marbleton was in league with Moriarty, then their goose was cooked.

Miss Marbleton dragged a sleeve in front of her eyes, sniffled, and cleared her throat. "Right. Microphotography. We do use that to communicate with one another."

Mrs. Watson had her hand on a handkerchief, ready to extend to Miss Marbleton. But Miss Marbleton, though her eyes were red-rimmed, seemed to be done with tears.

Miss Charlotte drew the Stanhope from her reticule. Mrs. Watson gripped the handkerchief. She wanted to trust Miss Marbleton, but she felt as if she were on a tightrope. Or perhaps she had already fallen off the tightrope, and the bottom of the abyss was rising to meet her.

"Last summer Mr. Marbleton told me that the Marbletons were looking for Mr. Finch, because you as a family believed that he had something of vital importance," said Miss Charlotte, seemingly free of the misgivings that buffeted Mrs. Watson. "I remember his exact words. 'We want something on Moriarty. Something that would make him anxious about us instead. Something that would force him to leave us alone, because it would destroy him first.'"

"Ah, those halcyon days." Miss Marbleton laughed softly, the sound full of self-mockery. "I know what Stephen said had all the hallmarks of hyperbole, but we did believe it."

"Moriarty has managed to evade prosecution for his crimes for a long time. How would this something have made a difference?" asked Lord Ingram.

Miss Marbleton picked up her walking stick and thumped it on the floor. "The law cares very little for the powerless. When Moriarty preys on those less powerful than him, he can always find a way to escape justice. But have you ever wondered how he reached his current position?"

Lord Ingram glanced at Miss Charlotte and said, "He has a patron? A paymaster?"

"He always did." A trace of pleasure came into Miss Marbleton's expression. "And we are sure he has double-crossed his paymaster. Now this is a crime from the consequences of which he would not so easily escape, provided, of course, that the paymaster is made aware of it."

Mrs. Watson wiped the back of her hand across her brow. Moriarty had always seemed such a monolith of iniquity, she couldn't fathom that he, too, had to answer to someone.

"How did you deduce that Mr. Finch might have such evidence that would at last condemn Moriarty?" asked Miss Charlotte.

"Because of the vigor with which he has been pursued. We have been running from Moriarty for decades, but that's because my mother was his wife and my father his kin—the betrayal was personal. And the longer we eluded him, the worse he looked for still not having captured us.

"Most other defectors aren't chased with such zeal. Moriarty has minions who are devoted to eliminating defectors, and they are very good at what they do. But in Mr. Finch's case, people and resources have been diverted from other parts of the organization and dedicated to the hunt. And that, as far as we know, has never happened before."

Mrs. Watson's head spun. "Did Mr. Finch ever confirm to you that he had this kind of earthshaking intelligence?"

"No, but he did ask what we were willing to trade for it. We said anything in our power. First we offered him a sanctuary where he would be safer—but he said he already knew about the sanctuary and it was not suitable for him. Then he asked whether we had information on das Phantomschloss."

Mrs. Watson had only the most rudimentary grasp of German. "What's that? The Phantom Castle?"

"It is said to be the headquarters for a part of the organization that is hidden from the rest of the organization."

Then was the organization still one organization? Or two separate ones?

"Do you know why he was interested in das Phantomschloss?" asked Lord Ingram.

"We tried to find out. He said that he could not divulge his reasons. But, as a gesture of good faith, he gave us keys to several ciphers, so we could read some of the documents we'd obtained earlier.

"At the time, only Stephen and I were in Britain. Later, when we met our parents, we asked about das Phantomschloss. They'd heard conflicting reports, some of which claim that it's in the Bavarian

Alps, others point to the outskirts of Vienna, and still others insist that das Phantomschloss doesn't exist and was made up by Moriarty to keep his minions in line."

She looked around at them. "Did Stephen somehow find a picture of das Phantomschloss?"

Miss Charlotte handed the Stanhope to her.

Mrs. Watson held her breath.

Miss Marbleton raised the Stanhope to her eye—and lowered it a few seconds later, her face thoughtful. "Not a single person in the photograph was looking at the camera, which makes me wonder whether the picture wasn't taken in secret, with a detective camera of some sort."

Miss Charlotte must have heard something in her words. "And?"

Miss Marbleton's bearded jaw moved. "And the woman on the left might be someone Mr. Finch is looking for."

Mrs. Watson had studied the image at length. She could see in her mind's eye the pretty young woman on the left, with a voluptuous figure and a face that looked lively even in a photograph.

Miss Holmes must remember her features even better than Mrs. Watson did. Nevertheless, she took the Stanhope from Miss Marbleton and looked through it again. "Is she connected to das Phantomschloss?"

"He didn't say. When we told him we barely knew of the place's existence, he showed us a pencil sketch of this woman and said he was also willing to trade for news of her whereabouts, though it would be a lesser exchange."

The woman obviously mattered to Mr. Finch. But in what sense? Because she might lead him to das Phantomschloss? Or because he cared for her in some way?

Or both?

Miss Charlotte handed the Stanhope to Lord Ingram and said to Miss Marbleton, "Do you know how we may convey a message to Mr. Finch?"

Miss Marbleton shook her head. "That tête-à-tête with him was arranged much like our meeting today. Mr. Finch put a notice in the papers with a cipher that my brother had given him and we managed to talk for a while in a train going north to Edinburgh.

"We asked him for a means to get word to him, should we discover something about das Phantomschloss. He only took another cipher from Stephen and said he would ask us for progress with notice in the papers. But we were abroad at times and might have missed it."

She smiled bitterly. "Certainly I haven't been paying very close attention of late. I only saw your notice because my boots got wet and I was looking for some newspaper to stuff into them so that they'd dry faster."

"You should pay more attention," said Miss Charlotte, softly yet implacably. "Your brother hasn't given up."

Miss Marbleton chewed her lower lip. Her glued-on beard moved with the motion of her lips and teeth. Mrs. Watson wanted to giggle. But more than that, she wanted to hug this girl, who found herself all alone in the world, so that she would have a shoulder to cry on.

Miss Charlotte leaned forward half an inch. Mrs. Watson's heartbeat accelerated: Miss Charlotte had thought of something.

"Miss Marbleton, would Mr. Finch's notice to you have started with the word 'Corinth'?"

Miss Marbleton sat up straighter, her hands on her wide-apart thighs. The masculine posture and her thick beard still made Mrs. Watson feel disoriented, especially contrasted with her feminine voice, which had risen further with surprise. "So he did post a notice to us?"

Miss Charlotte nodded. "I keep track of unusual small notices in the papers. I remember that one because I could not solve the rest of it. In Mr. Marbleton's microphotography, he gave a cipher that began with 'Mycenae.' The similarity struck me, so last night I took another look at 'Corinth.' Of course I still couldn't solve it because it had a different key."

Miss Marbleton immediately furnished the key. Miss Charlotte recited a string of letters. Everyone took out pencils and notebooks to help.

The deciphered text was simple. *If you have anything for me, use the cipher that starts with Phthia.*

"When did this notice appear?" asked Miss Marbleton.

"December thirtieth of last year."

"Oh no," cried Mrs. Watson.

It was a week or so after Mr. Marbleton had left to surrender himself to Moriarty. If that hadn't been necessary—if he had been able to hand over the information to Mr. Finch himself . . .

"I wasn't in the country at the time," said Miss Marbleton, her shoulders hunched as if under a weight.

That would have been the time her adoptive parents were taken from her. And her brother, too.

She took a deep breath. "Mr. Finch hadn't wanted to involve you, Miss Holmes, in his dealings with either Moriarty or with us. Stephen must have seen you as a last resort for reaching Mr. Finch. And he must have seen Mr. Finch as the only person who could perhaps help us now, when we can no longer help ourselves.

"But I'm no longer so sure." She spread open her hands, palms up. As if by reflex, she picked at the hole in her right glove. "If Mr. Finch really possessed such marvelous evidence against Moriarty, why hadn't he helped himself? Why is he, too, still a fugitive?"

———※———

Outside the train the sky was a pale, tentative blue, as if the very air had been sodden for so long it no longer remembered how to be bright and vivid. But the most uncertain of sunny days was still a sunny day. Perhaps on the morrow a cold drizzle would bring back winter for another fortnight. But this moment, with its early-morning light sweeping across fallow fields and small duck ponds, felt like a harbinger of spring.

Charlotte gazed at sunlit pastures and gleaming farmhouse windows and thought of Livia, who sometimes sank into a prolonged melancholy as winter ground on, and who yearned ever for warmth and light.

Livia.

Mr. Marbleton.

Mr. Finch.

*I am a queen upon this board*, Charlotte had once told Lord Ingram, *and I do not play to lose*. That had been a much smaller match, with only a few moving pieces. And even then, she'd known that most of the playing field was hidden from her. Still, at every move, with every revelation, the scale and complexity of the game gave her pause.

By this point, however, the only true surprise left was how deeply she herself was enmeshed in the situation. It was knotty enough with her brother having possibly absconded with Moriarty's dirty linen, and with Livia in love with the man's estranged son, but now . . .

She glanced at Miss Marbleton, whose hands were clamped around her knees. "You mentioned earlier, Miss Marbleton, that your family offered sanctuary to Mr. Finch. Can you tell me where this sanctuary is?"

She herself might be in need of a sanctuary soon.

"It's in Cornwall, an exotic sort of community that worships some pagan prophet."

Mrs. Watson half rose. Lord Ingram turned sharply toward Miss Marbleton. Charlotte did not move, but for a moment she did not feel the seat underneath her.

"Pagan prophet? Hermes Trismegistus, you mean?" she asked.

Miss Marbleton eyed Mrs. Watson, who was slowly sitting down again. "That sounds about right. You know the place?"

"We've been investigating a missing-person case nearby," Charlotte answered, "in the very shadows of the Garden of Hermopolis. It did not occur to us that the Garden would be a haven for someone on the run from Moriarty. How did you know that?"

"For as long as I've known them, my parents have formed alliances with other sworn enemies of Moriarty," said Miss Marbleton, still studying Mrs. Watson's expression, as if fascinated by her capacity for shock. "The lady who founded the community in Cornwall is one such ally."

Mrs. Watson's mouth opened to form an O, but this time Charlotte was not surprised. She glanced at Lord Ingram and saw in his eyes a similar acceptance: Assuming that Miss Marbleton spoke the truth, then someone in a position of power at the Garden must be willing to countenance the perils of hosting those who had defected from Moriarty.

"What caused her enmity with Moriarty?"

Miss Marbleton stroked her luxuriant beard. "Something about the death of her best friend. And also that she herself was garroted by mistake, causing such damage to her vocal cords that she can never speak normally again."

Which explained why Miss Fairchild always had Miss Ellery speak for her.

"She must be a very capable lady," murmured Mrs. Watson.

"According to my mother, her genius lies in having lured Moriarty's daughter to live among them."

This time Mrs. Watson appeared only moderately surprised. "As a hostage?"

"As diversion, so that Moriarty would never think to look there for those he pursues. Granted there are risks involved, as the daughter is under surveillance, too. But there are always risks involved when one opposes Moriarty."

Lord Ingram tented his fingers. "The religious community bears all the hallmarks of an excellent situation for someone fleeing from Moriarty. Why did Mr. Finch not care for it?"

"He didn't give us a reason, only that it wouldn't suit him." Miss Marbleton sighed. "It would have been nice, wouldn't it, if he had agreed to go there. Then you could have given this photograph to him right away."

—◦✷◦—

While London was still trying to edge its way to spring—like a suitor circling the outer peripheries of a ballroom, too timid to approach the belle du jour—the south coast of Cornwall was already on calling terms with the new season.

Charlotte, Mrs. Watson, and Lord Ingram arrived under a brilliant sky, in perfect time to see Mrs. Felton, in a hat laden with pink silk flowers, emerge from the village church after Sunday service. Mrs. Felton was taken aback when she saw them, but did not refuse an invitation to share a meal at the pub, where Mr. Mears also joined them.

As platters of roast and peas were passed around, Mrs. Felton told the company that the day before, she had at last seen Miss Baxter in the flesh—and the latter had promptly berated her for being inattentive to the floor in her overweening excitement.

"Perhaps I shouldn't have been so happy to see her," moaned Mrs. Felton dramatically. "She hasn't forgotten how to dress me down, Miss Baxter."

She laughed. Her exasperation was genuine. But her relief was also immense—with her laughter, her eyes had nearly disappeared.

When Charlotte had been a child, the emotions of others had been, by and large, strange and unpalatable—much like the sip she'd once taken from a wineglass abandoned by her mother. But these days she sometimes appreciated the sentiments radiated by those around her. Perhaps she still had an immature palate, for she enjoyed those potent yet simple feelings best. Livia's delight in summer, Mrs. Watson's warm sympathy, and Mrs. Felton's contentment in Miss Baxter's well-being—the emotional equivalent of pastries and cakes, perhaps.

She turned her face. Her gaze landed on her lover. All his emotions used to be so complicated. But now . . .

He looked up, caught her stare, and smiled, with a slight rise of one brow.

Now he was letting himself be happier—and she relished his happiness.

She looked back at Mrs. Felton. "At least you no longer need to worry about Miss Baxter."

"True, true," Mrs. Felton readily agreed.

Mrs. Watson raised her glass mug of ale. "To Miss Baxter, long may she be grand."

"Hear, hear! And may she grow a little sweeter in temperament someday," said Mrs. Felton, clinking mugs with her.

She took a good gulp of her ale and looked about the table. "But how is it that you are back again? Miss Baxter said she already met you and spoke to you."

"Mr. Baxter sent us back to find out what happened to Mr. Craddock," said Charlotte.

Mrs. Felton's eyes widened. "Mr. Craddock? What's the matter with him? And why does Mr. Baxter care?"

"According to Mr. de Lacey, Mr. Craddock is Mr. Baxter's man, there to keep an eye on Miss Baxter," answered Mrs. Watson. "But he failed to send in a report after the fireworks."

Mrs. Felton sputtered. "How many people does Mr. Baxter need to keep an eye on his daughter?"

And then, after a moment of silence: "No report?"

Mrs. Watson shook her head.

Mrs. Felton looked around the table again, her bafflement turning into dismay. "Come to think of it, I haven't seen him since he moved out of your cottage last December."

"When in December?" asked Lord Ingram.

"Miss Ellery gave me a few days off before Christmas. When I came back, Mrs. Crosby told me that Mr. Craddock had moved.

She also said that he'd started a meditative retreat and wouldn't need me to clean for him for a while."

Charlotte ate a piece of potato from her plate. "Do you know what happens to a body that is cast out to sea around here, Mrs. Felton?"

Mrs. Felton choked on her ale. Mrs. Watson thwacked her on the back. Mrs. Felton coughed, panted, and coughed again. "Surely—" she began, still catching her breath, "surely Mr. Craddock just decided to take a holiday."

"You're most likely right," said Charlotte. "But we must consider all the possibilities."

Mrs. Felton looked about the pub and then whispered, "You can't just cast a body out to sea in these parts, Miss Holmes. The sea washes them right back to Fetlock Cove, two miles southwest."

"I've heard the same," said Mr. Mears. "It's no use weighing bodies down either. The currents are such that not even clothes can stay on, let alone ropes and chains and whatnot."

Mrs. Felton quailed. Mrs. Watson hastened to put her mind at ease. "I wouldn't worry about Mr. Craddock yet. Remember how anxious everyone was for Miss Baxter? She proved right as ninepence, didn't she?"

That reassurance worked. Mrs. Felton, her good humor restored, finished her hearty lunch and shared a heroic serving of rice pudding with Charlotte before bidding the London visitors good day outside the pub. The London visitors, driven by Mr. Mears, headed for the Garden.

The day continued to be beautiful, the air clear and pure, with bright notes of salt and grass. But perhaps because there were more clouds in the sky, or perhaps because the wind had nearly sheared Charlotte's turban off her head as she was about to climb into the remise, it seemed only a matter of time before atmospheric conditions changed.

Charlotte watched the sea for another minute, then turned to

Mrs. Watson. "Ma'am, I didn't give you a complete account of what happened when I went to Dr. Robinson's cottage."

She brought up the man who had been in Dr. Robinson's cottage when she'd stolen inside and who had clamped a hand over her mouth to keep her silent when she'd happened upon his hiding place.

Mrs. Watson worried the drawstring of her reticule. But she only said, after a moment, "I'm glad you escaped unscathed, my dear. Please go on."

"I'm likewise glad to have been unharmed." Charlotte inclined her head toward the dear lady who always wanted to protect and comfort everyone. "Now this man couldn't have been Dr. Robinson, who was in the cottage at the same time. He wasn't Mr. Peters, who, according to Lord Ingram, did not stray from the vicinity of Miss Baxter's lodge.

"The man wasn't Mr. McEwan, who was on the wall with Miss Stoppard. He didn't smell of horses, so he wasn't John Spackett, who had harnessed a horse to a carriage just before that. And he also didn't smell of Mr. Steele's cologne water.

"At the time, I thought he had to be Mr. Craddock and suspected him of being Moriarty's minion. I also thought it likely that he trespassed for the same reason I did: to obtain indirect intelligence on Miss Baxter.

"That in itself was not remarkable—it was already a foregone conclusion by then that Mrs. Felton could not be the only Moriarty spy at the Garden. But if the man was an imposter—*that* is much more interesting. The imposter, chosen to replace the original Mr. Craddock, should number among Miss Baxter's loyalists. Yet he was there spying on Dr. Robinson, who is surely someone she trusts completely."

"Is it possible that . . ." Mrs. Watson's voice trailed off. "What is going on?"

Their remise crested an incline. The Garden of Hermopolis, its castle-like walls gleaming under the sun, came into view, looming in the distance with a vaguely sinister magnificence.

Except now, on the headland to the west, several tents were being erected. Or rather, one was staked in and ready, and half a dozen men were working on two more.

Camping had been a popular pastime along the Upper Thames for years, developed in conjuncture with pleasure boating, as heavy tents were more easily transported by watercraft. But the Garden was not situated along any river, and its surroundings, while beautiful, would not have lured Charlotte to spend a night outdoors in February.

Mrs. Watson must have come to a similar conclusion. Her fingers closed around the handle of her umbrella—also a gift from Lord Ingram, capable of firing two shots. "Did . . . did Moriarty send these men?"

"Probably," said Lord Ingram. His tone suggested that the probability verged on one hundred percent. "But why?"

Why indeed?

--- ❋ ---

The residents of the Garden of Hermopolis had noticed the men and the tents outside their front gate. With her binoculars, Charlotte counted eleven figures atop the wall—everyone except Mrs. Crosby, Miss Baxter, and Mr. Craddock.

As the remise drew near, several people disappeared from the ramparts. Mr. Peters and John Spackett opened the gate. Miss Ellery greeted them. Charlotte had cabled the Garden the day before, soon after she learned they would be forced to return. Their arrival therefore surprised no one, but Miss Ellery's smile was both awkward and uneasy.

Charlotte, leaving Mrs. Watson to speak with Miss Ellery, went in search of Abby Hurley, the kitchen maid. Abby Hurley, who had just climbed down from the wall, was surprised to be accosted, but told Charlotte readily enough that yes, Mr. Craddock used to pick up his meal baskets himself. But around Christmas he moved to another cottage and left to visit some friends. When he came back, he began a meditative retreat. Since then, she had delivered and retrieved his baskets, leaving them outside his door and picking them up again from the same spot.

Charlotte thanked her and proceeded directly to the cottage currently occupied by "Mr. Craddock," in the back of Miss Baxter's cluster, with its noted view of fruit trees espaliered against the wall. A slate tablet hung on the door: Meditative retreat in progress. Pray do not disturb.

By this time, Lord Ingram had caught up with her. So had Mr. Peters.

"Miss Holmes, are you planning to disturb Mr. Craddock?" he asked with a tilt of his head.

Before he'd threatened Mrs. Watson and Charlotte on the wall, their first night at the Garden, Mr. Peters's boyishly good-looking face had appeared convivial and occasionally mischievous—Mrs. Watson would have characterized that mischief as malicious. Now there was no trace of playfulness—malicious or not—left in his countenance, and no round cheeks or mop of hair could soften the iciness of his gaze.

"Mr. Craddock does not observe his retreat strictly." Charlotte made her counterargument. "He was out and about, wasn't he, the night of the fireworks?"

"Therefore?"

"Therefore I am going to inform him of my deep interest in his welfare. I don't believe I will be allowed to return to London unless he proves himself to be in good condition."

She pulled out a folded piece of paper from her reticule and slipped it under Mr. Craddock's door. Then she headed toward Miss Baxter's lodge.

Mr. Peters caught up with her on the lodge's veranda. "Miss Baxter will not receive you."

"Perfect, as I am only leaving a calling card, now that we are back."

She folded a corner of one of Sherlock Holmes's cards and left it under the door.

"Aren't you going to leave one for Miss Fairchild, too?"

Normal rules of card-leaving stipulated the acknowledgment of one's hostess.

Charlotte rose and turned around. "Would that help me depart here sooner?"

Mr. Peters said nothing. He glanced at Lord Ingram, who stood against the handrail of the steps leading up to the veranda, two steps behind him.

"Mrs. Crosby is still not back?" asked Lord Ingram.

A pause. "No," answered Mr. Peters quietly.

"Miss Baxter is lucky to have her," said Charlotte.

Mr. Peters regarded her with narrowed eyes.

Charlotte headed toward the kitchen garden. "Does Miss Baxter know what's happening outside?"

Mr. Peters fell in step beside her. "Yes."

Charlotte took Lord Ingram's arm—he was on her other side—and waited, in case Mr. Peters had anything else to say. But the young man only glanced toward the western wall, his jaw set.

He was afraid. This was the first time she'd sensed fear in him. Did this mean that Miss Baxter was also afraid?

"The campers arrived mid-morning," he said eventually. "And looked around for some time before they erected the first tent."

The "campers" had to have come on the overnight train. De Lacey had given no hint that such a thing was being planned. Had it been decided only after he had called on Charlotte the second time yesterday?

*But why?* Lord Ingram had asked earlier.

Why indeed.

They reached the shade hut, under which Lord Ingram had

stood long hours the night of the fireworks. The hut's two support pillars in the back were in fact two small storage sheds. Charlotte opened the door on the support shed to the north, took out a long, sharp wooden stake meant for building trellises, and marched toward the kitchen garden.

Mrs. Steele, who stood at the edge of the kitchen garden, said from underneath her creamy lace parasol, "Why, hullo, Miss Holmes. Hullo, Mr. Hudson. You came back on a lovely d——"

She leaped back in surprise as Charlotte struck the stake directly into the kitchen garden's tilled, loosened soil. "Miss Holmes, what are you doing?"

"How do you do, Mrs. Steele? And yes, indeed, since we must come back, we've at least come on a lovely day," said Charlotte, pushing the stake farther into the ground. "By the way, Mrs. Steele, have you heard the local wisdom that a body tossed off these cliffs would wash up in due time in Fetlock Cove not too far from here?"

"Ah, no, I'm——I'm sure I've never heard of that."

Mrs. Steele, her eyes bulging a little, stared at Mr. Peters, as if he could furnish an explanation for Charlotte's macabre question.

"I have, from multiple sources." Charlotte pulled up the stake and sank it into a different spot. "Therefore, if one wants to get rid of a body, one cannot shove it into the sea. But a vegetable patch might not be a bad place for it, don't you think? Much easier to dig up a vegetable patch than an unimproved spot of headland."

Mrs. Steele's lips flapped. Once again she stared at Mr. Peters, who glowered at Charlotte but didn't say anything.

Charlotte was about to pull the stake up again when Lord Ingram said, "Allow me, Miss Holmes. I found this in the storage shed."

*This* was a hammer. He struck the stake straighter and deeper into the ground, before pulling it up and repeating the action two feet away. Memories of long-ago summers came to mind, halcyon days when she used to watch him drive small stakes into the ground, and then mark the peripheries of his dig by tying strings to those stakes. The man always knew his way around a hammer.

"Excellent work, Mr. Hudson."

He smiled at her. "I have dealt with a kitchen garden or two in my time."

"Indeed, I am very fond of your kitchen garden. And no disrespect to the Garden of Hermopolis, of course, but truly your fruit trees are vastly superior."

"Do fruit trees mean something different these days?" Mrs. Steele asked her husband, who had just arrived at the vegetable garden and responded to her question with a look of thorough confusion.

She took him by the hand. "Let's go. I'm going to ask the campers why they couldn't set up their tents a mile south or a mile north, rather than exactly in front of our gate."

Mr. Steele didn't look at all eager to accompany his wife but allowed himself to be led toward the gate.

"Before you leave, Mr. Steele, Mrs. Steele," Charlotte called out, "when was the last time you saw Mr. Craddock?"

"Not since he went to see his friends before Christmas," said Mr. Steele. "Why, is anything amiss with him?"

Mrs. Steele, too, turned around.

"No," said Charlotte. "I just realized that I haven't met him, that's all. I've met everyone here except him."

Mr. Peters's countenance grew even darker.

Charlotte was never going to omit him in her questioning. "Mr. Peters, when was the last time you saw Mr. Craddock?"

"Three nights ago."

"It was dark that night. Did you see his face?"

Mr. Peters's voice became ever brusquer. "No."

Dr. Robinson sauntered to the edge of the plot, glanced around, and said, "Oh, have we already started spring planting?"

❦

"I hear you are a sworn enemy of Moriarty, Miss Fairchild," said Mrs. Watson.

With Miss Ellery having gone with Dr. Robinson to see what was happening around the kitchen garden, Mrs. Watson invited Miss Fairchild for a walk. John Spackett, who had just closed the gate after the Steeles went out, opened it for them again.

The two women rounded south of the compound. Mrs. Watson kept her gaze on the uneven ground underfoot—she did not want to add a bad stumble to her list of troubles. Miss Fairchild, however, glanced several times behind them, at the men who were still putting up one last tent, her expression not so much one of fear as one of consternation, as if she faced not agents of Moriarty but an infestation of weevils.

They went down to the promontory. A few miles from the coast clumps of dark cloud hung low, rain falling in their shadows even as the surrounding sea continued to gleam under the sun.

Miss Fairchild's attention had been behind them. A man stood at the edge of the headlands—one of the campers. She had scanned him, her bearing straight, her face severe.

At Mrs. Watson's statement, however, her expression congealed. Her head turned, a fraction of an inch at a time, until she looked Mrs. Watson in the eye.

"I hear that you are a sworn enemy of Moriarty, Miss Fairchild," Mrs. Watson repeated herself. "And that the blame also falls on him for the condition of your vocal cords."

Miss Fairchild said nothing, only continued to look at Mrs. Watson.

Mrs. Watson genuinely liked and loved people, but in return she also liked to be liked and loved to be loved. It was disconcerting to be on the receiving end of Miss Fairchild's flat gaze.

Miss Charlotte had quite a stare, too, powered by her sometimes-overwhelming perceptiveness. It could produce an effect of mortification, of believing that one had turned into glass and that every last closely held secret was now open to scrutiny.

Miss Fairchild's look did not make Mrs. Watson feel as if she'd been put under a microscope. Rather, it was as if she studied Miss Fairchild through the wrong end of a spyglass, with the silent woman appearing much farther away than she actually was.

Mrs. Watson steeled herself. "I also hear, from the same reliable source, that the Garden of Hermopolis has been, over the years, a place for those who oppose Moriarty to find temporary refuge."

Miss Fairchild persisted in her stony silence.

"We have said nothing to Mr. Baxter, of course. We are neutral parties—Miss Baxter, in allowing us to come here, bears testimony to our neutrality.

"It must be a terrifying time for you, with these 'campers' openly staking an observatory post outside your front gate. It is an equally unnerving time for Miss Holmes, Mr. Hudson, and myself. We are only investigators. Mr. Baxter asked us to ascertain Miss Baxter's safety; we came. He asked us to ascertain Mr. Craddock's safety, and we have returned.

"We do not want to be thorns in your side. We only want to know about Mr. Craddock and then leave as soon as possible."

More silence from Miss Fairchild, before she pulled out a stubby pencil and a small notebook and began writing.

*Mr. Craddock is on a meditative retreat. He is not to be disturbed.*

Mrs. Watson felt a stab of disappointment. "Do you really believe that, Miss Fairchild? While I don't know why the men outside the Garden came today, I don't think they came for you. Not yet. But I have the unhappy feeling that given time, they might make you a target, too."

Miss Fairchild scribbled another answer. *I have nothing to tell you about Mr. Craddock, other than that he is doing precisely what he came to the Garden to do.*

"How can you know nothing, Miss Fairchild? For years, this

man occupied a cottage from which one cannot see Miss Baxter's lodge. All at once he was transferred to another one that was a stone's throw from hers. Similarly, he ambled about for years, only to become a hermit at the exact moment he was moved.

"Are we speaking of the same man? Of only one man? Miss Baxter is a highly intelligent woman. Why would she suddenly allow Mr. Craddock into her orbit after keeping him at an arm's length for so long?"

*That you must ask Miss Baxter.*

"But you are also trusted by Miss Baxter, are you not, Miss Fairchild? She could have gone anywhere to get away from her father. She chose to come here."

*She chose to come here because she is devoted to the teaching of the Great One, and there are not that many like-minded communities nearby, or in the entire world.*

"Nevertheless, she sends Mr. Peters, her watchdog, to confer with you. I saw you two speaking right here where we are standing now. Surely you don't mean to tell me that Mr. Peters wanted to consult you on some finer points of *Hermetica*?"

*Mr. Peters spoke to me because he admires Mrs. Crosby and did not know what he ought to do next, not because he wanted to talk to me about Miss Baxter or Mr. Craddock.*

Mrs. Watson blinked. Love bloomed ever, even inside a fortress to which Moriarty had laid siege.

Miss Fairchild pocketed notebook and pencil. "And as for that so-called reliable source of yours, Mrs. Watson, I would not place as much trust in it."

Miss Fairchild had *spoken*. Her voice had the sound of a dull knife scraping over rough stone, and made Mrs. Watson want to wrap a protective hand around her own throat. A full second passed before Mrs. Watson grasped her meaning.

Miss Fairchild had already started back toward the Garden, her thin back held ramrod straight, but she was nevertheless a small woman, insignificant against these endless miles of craggy coastline.

She had at last disputed the enemy-of-Moriarty designation attributed to her—and cast aspersions on Miss Marbleton's reliability as a conduit of information. One could almost consider it an afterthought but for the fact that she had spoken that objection aloud, using her irreparably damaged voice.

A shadow fell upon Mrs. Watson. She looked up. The nearest dark cloud was almost directly overhead.

The weather was changing again.

## Twenty-one

An invitation from Miss Baxter came by teatime, brought by a dark-faced Mr. Peters, who had recently proclaimed the impossibility of such a thing. Charlotte enjoyed his displeasure; she would have enjoyed it more if she didn't need to face Miss Baxter.

The first time Miss Baxter had summoned her, the hour had been set at six in the evening. Charlotte had immediately started packing: Miss Baxter intended for Charlotte and company to depart the same night and had left them plenty of time for that.

This time, Charlotte was invited to call at eight. Clearly, the matter of Mr. Craddock would not be resolved so cleanly or quickly. The invitation was also for her alone, no guests included. Perhaps they would speak more frankly.

It had drizzled for half an hour around sunset and now a fog was rolling in again. As Charlotte stood on the veranda of Miss Baxter's lodge, waiting for her knock to be answered, she could see barely six feet out. Such atmospheric conditions were not uncommon in London, but here the fog, though as obliterating, did not bring with it the odors of urban and industrial discharge. It smelled only of fresh air and cold, briny sea.

Mrs. Watson's talk with Miss Fairchild in the afternoon had not produced confessions of shared enmity toward Moriarty. Nor had the vegetable garden yielded useful corpses—or indeed anything besides soil, pebbles, and an occasional root. Could Charlotte expect a better result from her meeting with Miss Baxter?

The door opened. Miss Stoppard admitted Charlotte, and showed her to the baroque parlor, where Miss Baxter was once again stretched out on the settee. This time her dress was more informal, a white tea gown embroidered with flaxen leaves and golden flowers. The overrobe was made entirely of lace, with a ruched collar and heavily pleated sleeves that greatly gratified Charlotte's love of elaborate sartorial constructions.

"That is a beautiful frock," she said immediately upon sitting down.

"Yes, it is, isn't it?" Teardrop-shaped beads of turquoise were set amid the embroidered botanical motifs. Miss Baxter fondly caressed one bead, then another.

"Although it has been carefully kept, it is not new. Does it have sentimental value? Did you used to wear it for your lover?"

Charlotte's tone was straightforward. She was not here to ridicule Miss Baxter and certainly not to tease her. She wanted only facts.

Miss Baxter raised a brow. Her beauty had less to do with the arrangement of her features, but owed much more to the animating force of her expression. That simple movement encompassed a wealth of meaning, ranging from surprise, to approval, to anticipation of an equal divulgence on Charlotte's part.

"Yes, a good guess. This was his favorite."

"It was not a guess," said Charlotte coolly. "I know fabric. I know cut. I know fashion. I know this tea gown was likely made between six and eight years ago—it must hold some significance for you to still favor it.

"Moreover, a tea gown is for lounging, but it is also what one dons to meet a paramour who has come to call. Since you made a point to bring up a specific gentleman the last time I was here, it would be rude for me not to make the connection."

Miss Baxter laughed. "I see. You are telling me that I have not been very subtle."

"Most things most people do are not subtle—not to Sherlock Holmes, in any case," said Charlotte. "But here is an actual guess, one that isn't supported by logic and evidence every step of the way, about the deal you struck with your father to regain some sort of freedom."

Miss Baxter's eyes narrowed. "Think before you speak, Miss Holmes."

"I always do."

Except in bed. Occasionally.

With regard to Miss Baxter, however, ever since she'd had a good look at the ciphers Mr. Mears had found in those Cornish publications, she'd been thinking of what she would say to the woman when they came face-to-face again.

"How is the baby, by the way? Has there been any news from Mrs. Crosby? And congratulations, of course."

A muscle leaped at Miss Baxter's jaw.

"I met Mr. de Lacey while I was in London. I didn't breathe a word of your condition to him—that is not the purview of my investigation."

Miss Baxter slowly looked toward the ceiling, a prolonged, nearly balletic rolling of her eyes—Charlotte was not much better at reassuring people than she was at offering unconditional support when they needed to vent. A good thing she had not come to put Miss Baxter at ease.

"But I don't believe anyone needed to tell your father anything," continued Charlotte. "His imprisonment last year had robbed him of vital information; the reclamation of his former throne consumed a great deal of his time and energy. When he finally came around and dealt with reports of unusual goings-on in the Garden of Hermopolis, he made the mistake of attributing to Miss Fairchild his own murderous ruthlessness. So the first time he sent me here, he probably did believe your safety compromised—and perhaps your life, too.

"But in light of subsequent events—your notable absence the night of the fireworks and equally notable appearance the next evening—and given the evidence you furnished that it is really you who is alive and well in the Garden, he would be hard-pressed not to realize that his assumptions had been wrong." She paused. "Especially in light of precedent."

With unnerving speed, Miss Baxter sat up from her near full recline. Mrs. Felton had described her as "scary-grand, like a tiger stalking through the forest." But to Charlotte she resembled more a great serpent, her beauty sinuous and full of peril.

"This is not your first child, is it?" Charlotte carried on. "That time your father dragged you home, it was not because he at last found you at the Garden of Hermopolis but because he found you in an advanced state of pregnancy. I'd even wager that you were only pretending to be at the Garden with a 'meditative retreat' sign on your door, and spending your days elsewhere with your lover.

"But you were caught and put in a gilded cage. And you made a bargain with your father. You would give up your child in order to return to the Garden of Hermopolis and, this time, *stay*."

Miss Baxter watched her, her gaze glacial.

Charlotte selected a piece of coconut biscuit from the refreshments on offer. "You need not fret, Miss Baxter. I am a neutral party and I have kept your secret."

Miss Baxter laughed softly. "I still have secrets left? You just told me that my father not only holds my firstborn hostage but has also deduced the arrival of my second child."

"But he doesn't know where the new baby is. I do." Charlotte allowed herself a small smile. "I know from which railway station Mrs. Crosby left, and I have verified her destination."

Miss Baxter's face, already pale, turned paler. "Are you threatening me, Miss Holmes?"

Of course.

"Hardly," Charlotte said modestly. "I am only trying to arrive at a mutually satisfactory arrangement. You want to keep your child's whereabouts safe. I want to leave the Garden of Hermopolis alive and whole. To achieve my goal, I'll need to give an account of what happened to Mr. Craddock."

Miss Baxter scrutinized Charlotte with green, glittering eyes. "You mean that I should take the blame for his death?"

"He saw you heavily pregnant, didn't he? Could you suffer him to live after that?"

Miss Baxter lifted her chin and slowly rolled her head half a circle. "Miss Holmes, I don't think we have much more to say to each other. Let us end our conversation right here."

"Why? Look outside the walls of the Garden, Miss Baxter. You are surrounded. I believe you face a fate far worse than merely being forced back home.

"Shall I make another unsubstantiated guess? There is a chance that your father has caught Madame Desrosiers and that Madame Desrosiers has given you up as the true mastermind behind his ouster last year.

"With so much danger darkening your doorstep, why not help me, at least? You claim responsibility for Mr. Craddock's death; I go on keeping the secret of your child's location. Perhaps I could even help Mrs. Crosby and the baby after I leave."

"Oh, perhaps you could, could you?" said Miss Baxter lightly.

She cracked her neck. "Too much groundless speculation isn't good for you, Miss Holmes. Mr. Craddock is perfectly fine, meditating in his cottage. And I shall be fine, too. But you, my dear foolhardy girl, you should be careful."

It had been a while since Alain de Lacey had conducted outdoor surveillance.

These days, he was more of a bureaucrat.

Others spoke the word with dread, as if their desks would steal their souls. They must not have known a poorhouse upbringing or life in the streets. Well before he'd ever heard the word *bureaucrat*, he'd gazed with wholehearted envy upon the administrators and functionaries of the world, hurrying past him in their striped city trousers to lord over their little fiefdoms, shielded from the elements, warm with authority and respectability.

His tenure at De Lacey Industries had been a dream come true. He was under no illusion about what kind of enterprise it was—an entity that didn't have one foot in crime would not have invested in educating a petty criminal like him. But it gave him that desk and that little fiefdom he'd longed for.

It was all he wanted, to be a middling minion looking after ledgers and documents. To have a case of calling cards with his name embossed. To put a little money aside every day for his retirement.

He never thought he would become de Lacey. But three de Laceys later—all dead for different reasons—the former Timmy Ruston found himself at the head of De Lacey Industries, answerable directly to Mr. Baxter.

He didn't fancy himself a great beast of a man—no one would compare him to a bear or a lion. He was, however, a good, dependable dog, capable of a surprisingly ferocious bite. But in front of Mr. Baxter he wanted only to hide his tail between his legs, sink to the ground, and whimper.

Mr. Baxter was just a man, he would tell himself, a nobody named Moriarty once upon a time.

And then he would perspire, wondering whether Mr. Baxter could hear his thoughts.

That was with Mr. Baxter on the other side of the English Channel. When news came of the man's impending visit, he became a jumble of nerves, anticipating the worst. Which . . . did not immediately come to pass. Mr. Baxter was distant and preoccupied, but he did not seem interested in finding fault with de Lacey's work.

De Lacey let out a breath. Perhaps it wouldn't be so bad. Perhaps he would be able to retire after all.

But after the meeting during which he informed Charlotte Holmes that she needed to discover what happened to Craddock, he returned to De Lacey Industries to find Mr. Baxter in a rage. Someone else might not even have recognized that he was angry. He listened to de Lacey's report with perfect civility and spoke softly when he replied. Yet all the while his wrath had felt like a barbed wire around de Lacey's neck.

When the order came down that the Garden of Hermopolis was now to be watched round the clock, he volunteered to keep an eye on the operations. It was a relief to be two hundred miles from Mr. Baxter, but his freedom cost dearly. On the coast the wind never ceased, the damp penetrated all layers of garments, and it was *February*, albeit the last day of the month. Even when he'd been a petty criminal, he'd never had to spend twenty-four hours a day in the elements.

At least Charlotte Holmes did not waste time. The day of her return culminated in a raging row between her and Miss Baxter. Such details of Miss Baxter's life emerged in the quarrel, relayed to de Lacey by a note wrapped around a rock and dropped from the walls. When he'd accidentally overheard the argument between Miss Baxter and her father the year before, he'd felt a grudging respect for her stubborn love, mistakenly believing it to be pure as the driven snow. But the reality—truly, he'd never be able to show his face in public again if he had a daughter like that.

The next morning, something unexpected happened. Mrs. Watson's manservant came rushing to the Garden. Barely a quarter hour later, "Mr. Hudson" left with him. Charlotte Holmes and Mrs. Watson stood atop the walls and watched them drive away, as if they were knights headed for the Crusades. By luncheon de Lacey learned from Mr. Baxter's spy in the Garden that a telegram had come for Lord Ingram. Both of his children ran high fevers.

Nothing else happened during the remaining daylight hours,

except a gradual exodus of the Garden's residents, including its physician. De Lacey checked all the departing parties. But they were only fleeing the uncertainty of the Garden's besiegement. No one attempted to smuggle out either Miss Baxter or Charlotte Holmes.

Another night arrived, full of rain and squalls. De Lacey feared he was becoming rheumatic, but he feared Mr. Baxter's mood far more. He dared not sleep, but timed his patrols, watched the front gate, and shivered under his mackintosh.

What was Charlotte Holmes waiting for? Mr. Baxter took extra precautions with the woman, but de Lacey suspected that his overlord gave her too much credit. Every hour of delay further confirmed his suspicions. Wasn't it much more likely that Lord Ingram, a well-born, well-educated, and obviously intelligent man, was the true brains behind Sherlock Holmes, rather than a chit smothered in lace and ruffles?

Now, because he was no longer there, she was mired in inaction. And de Lacey could not proceed to the next step until Miss Baxter had acted against Charlotte Holmes.

The next day, too, dragged on. The only event of note was that the Garden's charabanc, with some of its benches taken off, drove out and returned later with two great big metal drums. The spy reported that Miss Baxter took receipt of them.

It rained most of the time. The sky at last cleared around sunset, but a piercing wind picked up. De Lacey, huddled near an Etna stove, cursed under his breath and prayed that Mr. Baxter would not grow too impatient.

Night came cold and swift. He ate from a tin of beans and thought longingly of dinners past in rooms with blazing grates, free-flowing wine, and gleaming silverware.

Hours crawled by. At midnight he shook awake two sleeping men and sent them to replace the patrol team that circled the compound. The two new patrols, one marching clockwise, the other counterclockwise, met by the gate three times before the gate opened a crack. The moon was new, but the clear night was ablaze with stars. Their frosty glow had chilled de Lacey to the bone earlier, but now he was thankful; the starlight limned the cloaked figure of a woman.

Charlotte Holmes, at last on the move.

He woke up two more men, set one to watch the gate, and brought the other with him. They followed Charlotte Holmes. From time to time she opened the shutter on a pocket lantern to see in the dark. Several times she glanced southeast toward the Garden, but never in their direction, southwest of her.

After another few minutes she opened the shutter on her lantern again and swept the light eastward. She walked faster, then broke into a run toward a rise that jutted out to sea. At the top of the rise she stopped, her lantern shining on a row of three tombstones.

De Lacey had seen his share of deaths, and his own hands weren't all that clean. Still, the dark silhouettes of the tombstones, abruptly lit against the night, halted him in his tracks.

It must have made Charlotte Holmes's knees weak: She sank to the ground. De Lacey nudged his man, reminding him to walk more quietly. They approached the rise and hid behind an outcrop. Only then did de Lacey realize that the woman was *eating*. She drank from a canteen and said, "I hate being up in the middle of the night but biscuits do taste marvelous at odd hours."

He tensed. Had she discovered them? But she seemed to have been talking to herself. She ate another piece of something, drank again from the canteen, dusted off her hands, and rose.

An umbrella and a large cloth bag had been set against the center tombstone. From the cloth bag she pulled out a shovel and sank it once into each of the three graves.

"Yes, this one is definitely much looser," she said at the rightmost grave, and began digging in earnest.

Early in his career de Lacey had dug graves to dispose of bodies. It was hard work. But digging up the same soil for the third time must be much easier. Yes, the third time. He remembered from the dossier that several members of the Garden had died of pneumonia and been buried on the headlands. Judging by what Charlotte Holmes had just said, she suspected that one of the graves had been dug up recently. For the purpose of placing another body inside the coffin?

The coffin was not buried deep. She finished digging with only one rest, and then applied the claw of a hammer to nails from the lid of the coffin.

De Lacey's man tapped him on his shoulder and pointed. He squinted. Two figures emerged from the night.

"Miss Holmes, what are you doing?"

Miss Baxter.

Charlotte Holmes, crouched over the coffin, turned around. "Ah, Miss Baxter, Mr. Peters, out for a midnight stroll?"

De Lacey's heart thumped. Oh, this would not end well.

"Indeed, Miss Holmes. We are enjoying this fine night, Mr. Peters and I," said Miss Baxter. "What are you doing?"

"I have an interview with Mr. Craddock," said Miss Holmes.

She knelt at the edge of the grave and lifted the coffin's lid. "Mr. Craddock?"

No one answered.

Miss Holmes rose. "Would you care to identify him, Miss Baxter? Granted, the man's face is somewhat decomposed, but perhaps you remember his clothes?"

"That is Mr. Kaplan's eternal resting place. I doubt he appreciates being disturbed."

"Mr. Kaplan, who contributed all the skulls to the library at the Garden? The one who passed away years ago? I daresay he's accustomed to being disturbed now, after sharing his casket with a newcomer since December."

Miss Baxter's voice, already cold, turned icy. "Don't press your luck, Miss Holmes."

"You are a woman shut in by the walls of the Garden, Miss Baxter. Your father is . . . your father. I would be a fool to ignore his directive simply because it would inconvenience you."

"You are already a fool, Miss Holmes. You might need to worry about my father after you leave the Garden of Hermopolis, but if you never leave, he'll be immaterial to your well-being."

She lifted a pistol.

Charlotte Holmes picked up her umbrella.

Miss Baxter laughed with derision. "Is your rain gear bullet-proof these days?"

"It's better than that. It's—"

A loud bang. A sudden burst of light. De Lacey blinked. Miss Holmes's umbrella had caught on fire.

Miss Baxter and Peters glanced at each other.

Peters cried, "I think the umbrella is a—"

Another bang.

Miss Baxter laughed wildly. "Oh, Miss Holmes, what use is your clever new invention if you have no aim?"

With a cry Charlotte Holmes threw the umbrella aside. It knocked the pocket lantern, which had been standing at the edge of the grave, into the pit. The fire on the umbrella and the light from the lantern went out at nearly the same moment. In their final glow, de Lacey saw Miss Holmes whip out a derringer.

Darkness. Gunshots. A shrill feminine scream. A thud. Then silence, except the wind, the waves, and loud, harsh breaths.

Which emerged from the man by de Lacey's side. He elbowed the man. The man quieted.

Several minutes passed before someone struck a match—Miss Baxter, lying in the grass but up on her elbows. She looked to the figure to her right. Peters rose from a prone position into a crouch. Farther away, the soles of Charlotte Holmes's boots stuck out from the grave.

Darkness again.

"Light your pocket lantern," said Miss Baxter. "Let's go take a look."

Peters complied, but said, "I'll look. You stay where you are. It could be a trick."

The pocket lantern's handle between his teeth, a revolver in his hand, he crawled forward, hid himself behind the mound of earth that had been dug up, and peered over it.

He then threw a clump of dirt into the grave.

"I think she really is dead," he said after a while.

Miss Baxter crawled forward and put a hand inside the grave, presumably to check for a pulse. "I think you're right."

She laughed, a slightly unhinged sound. "Go bring the charabanc, Mr. Peters. We'll take her body back—Craddock's, too—and put them in perchloric acid. It's what we should have done with him in the first place."

"Why don't we go together? I don't want to leave you here by yourself."

"Leave me your revolver and go. Otherwise my father's minions could come along and stumble upon the bodies."

She also ordered him to take the pocket lantern to hasten his progress. Soon the tombstones and the women, one dead, one still alive, fell into darkness.

It took de Lacey a while to be able to see again by starlight, and then it was only to make out the vaguest outline of Miss Baxter's standing figure.

"My apologies, Miss Holmes," she said slowly. "But I cannot allow anyone to bring murder charges against my friends and allies here at the Garden. They are all I have. The Garden is all I have. My father has been looking to destroy it for years and you would have handed him the perfect cudgel."

She began to sing. After two phrases de Lacey recognized it as "The Lost Chord," a song played in almost every parlor he'd stepped into in the past few years.

He had killed, too, but never sang afterward, and certainly not of his longing for a moment of perfection never to be regained, as if this were any other starry night, just right for a bout of melancholy nostalgia.

As her final note fell away, he shivered.

—❖—

Peters came back with the charabanc and another man. They wrapped the bodies in sheets and heaved them onto the open conveyance, swearing copiously at having to deal with the heavily decomposed Craddock.

Then they shoveled back the soil, righted the tombstone, tamped down everything, and left with Miss Baxter humming another song. De Lacey did his best not to hear what it was.

He went to sleep near dawn. When he woke up a few hours later, it was to the sight of Mrs. Watson and her manservant ranging the headlands, in search of Charlotte Holmes. Several times they stood together, Mrs. Watson wiping at the corners of her eyes, her manservant speaking earnestly, probably offering words of comfort and encouragement.

De Lacey massaged his stiff neck. If they only knew.

Of course, when they approached the tents to ask him, he stately flatly that from sunset the evening before until now, the only people who had left the compound, besides Mrs. Watson herself, had been the Garden's cook and her kitchen maid.

The underling he'd sent to the nearest telegraph office to relay news of Charlotte Holmes's demise returned at noon with Mr. Baxter's response: Mr. Baxter would arrive on the morrow.

De Lacey pulled his overcoat tighter around himself. He hoped that Mr. Baxter was pleased—about Charlotte Holmes, that is. He didn't believe Mr. Baxter would ever again be pleased about his daughter. But with Charlotte Holmes gone, at least de Lacey would be safe, wouldn't he? He only needed to make sure that Miss Baxter remained in place until her father came. And then whatever happened after that would be a family matter, none of his concern.

More residents left the Garden, looking bewildered and afraid. News from inside the compound told of a distraught Mrs. Watson begging to search all the dwellings for a sign of Miss Holmes. She was granted that grace, and even "Craddock" decamped to the meditation cabin so that she could see for herself that Charlotte Holmes was not in his home.

Her manservant organized search parties that set out from Porthangan and combed nearby areas. Near sunset he came again. She'd been standing atop the wall, waiting for him. At his appearance, she descended and met him outside the gate. She seemed calm enough, listening to him speak. But when de Lacey looked through a field glass, he saw tears rolling down her face and disappearing into the fur collar of her cloak.

De Lacey avoided thinking too deeply about Mr. Baxter's reasons. But as Mrs. Watson covered her face with her hands, he wondered why Charlotte Holmes had to die. If it was truly as Mr. Baxter said, because she'd learned that much of De Lacey Industries' revenue came of thieving from other enterprises, then shouldn't Mrs. Watson and Lord Ingram also lose their lives? Yet there had been no such orders concerning those two.

He shook his head and told his men not to slack.

—⁂—

Mr. Baxter arrived early afternoon the next day.

De Lacey didn't know how the man managed it, but he always looked like some grand dame's favorite son, freshly returned from six months abroad—a little weary from his long travels, perhaps, but in good cheer, as he looked forward to being fawned over by his loved ones.

That general air of agreeableness had fooled de Lacey, until Mr. Baxter had shot and killed the first de Lacey that he, the former Timmy Ruston, had served under. That man had dared to steal from the organization's coffer, and until the revolver had appeared in Mr. Baxter's hand, they had been enjoying a convivial dinner.

In fact, that precise moment, there had been champagne going around for toasts. After the former de Lacey's body had slumped out of his chair, Mr. Baxter had raised his glass and ordered everyone else to drink to trust and camaraderie.

Since then, de Lacey hadn't had a glass of bubbly. He'd also been terrified of misreading Mr. Baxter, of thinking he was safe only to learn otherwise with a bullet between his eyes.

He could only hope that Miss Baxter hadn't somehow escaped despite his wholehearted effort to contain her within these walls.

When Mr. Baxter's carriage rolled to a stop before the Garden, de Lacey himself pulled down the steps. His overlord descended, the hems of his greatcoat billowing in the wind. He held on to his hat with one hand and regarded the high wall before him.

He looked . . . Well, de Lacey had thought he'd sense in Mr. Baxter either gratification brought on by Charlotte Holmes's death, or grimness because of the imminent confrontation with his daughter. But if anything, Mr. Baxter seemed distracted, as if the former's fate was but an afterthought and the latter a minor inconvenience, albeit one he must handle himself.

Peters opened the gate.

Mr. Baxter brought four men. De Lacey had six. At Mr. Baxter's signal, de Lacey left two of his six men outside. All the others followed them into the Garden. Peters glanced at the phalanx of men. But if he was intimidated, he did not show it.

He brought the visitors not to Miss Baxter's lodge but to the meditation cabin. Mr. Baxter told the other men to stay put and only took de Lacey inside with him.

The meditation cabin had once been a chapel large enough to seat fifteen families. The pews were long gone but the pulpit remained, and upon it Miss Baxter sat, on a throne-like chair, directly beneath the eye painted on the bloodred ceiling. To one side of the chair stood a man with a cut to his upper lip—McEwan, most likely. Peters went to stand on her other side.

She wore a dark red dress, cut simply but with a most unusual collar that rose like a ruff and framed her bright auburn coiffure and sharp-featured face as if she were Queen Elizabeth herself. Her necklace, shaped like a chain of office with alternating squares and fleurs-de-lis of gold filigree, further reinforced the impression of regality.

Facing her, two steps down, a much humbler chair had been placed. De Lacey thought the deliberately insulting arrangement childish. This woman, at the end of her ropes, was still playing useless games.

Mr. Baxter, his hand on the back of the lesser chair, shook his head slowly. His expression was kindly, indulgent, as if he were faced with a five-year-old girl who insisted on wearing her shoes on the wrong feet. But Miss Baxter must have seen something that eluded de Lacey, for she smiled, evidently delighted by her father's reaction.

"Father, how good of you to come and see me. Do take a seat."

A muscle leaped at the corner of Mr. Baxter's eye, a minute movement yet one entirely at odds with the affectionate smile he returned to his daughter. His hand slid along the top rail of the chair and came to rest on his watch fob.

De Lacey froze.

The other de Lacey—what had been his name, Sumner? At that dinner, Sumner had been as arrogant as Miss Baxter was now. He'd made Mr. Baxter stand up to toast the company, hadn't he? And Mr. Baxter had complied, with a smile as mild as a spring breeze.

But a muscle had leaped at the corner of his eye on that evening, too. And he had stood behind his chair, slid his hand across its top rail, patted his watch fob—and pulled out a revolver and shot the still-grinning Sumner.

A chill gripped de Lacey's lungs. Was he about to do the same to his daughter?

Mr. Baxter sat down in the lesser chair.

Miss Baxter, utterly unaware of her peril, smiled more widely. "Some tea? Coffee?"

But inside the chapel there were no accoutrements for the making of hot beverages.

"Enough, Marguerite," said Mr. Baxter gently, with seemingly infinite patience.

Miss Baxter's smile turned frosty. "Have you ever thought that for yourself, Father? Have you ever looked into the mirror and said, 'Enough, James'? No, of course you haven't. For you the entire world will still be too little. It's only others who must learn to settle for less so that you can have more."

"Because I did not let you do every ridiculous thing that came into your head, you conspired with my enemies to bring me down? My child, you went too far."

So Charlotte Holmes had been right in her guess and that truly was the reason he had been furious the other evening. He'd learned that his daughter had been in league with those who mounted a coup against him. No wonder he'd immediately sent men to make sure that she didn't escape.

"No, Father. Regrettably, I did not go far enough. Madame Desrosiers wanted to kill you. I did not want you to die at my hand. Alas, wouldn't it have been better for me now if I had killed you then?"

His head bent, Mr. Baxter placed a hand over his face. He looked as if her heartless words had crushed his spirit. De Lacey pulled at his collar—the barbed-wire-around-his-throat sensation was back.

"To think of everything I have done for you," said Mr. Baxter, his voice muffled.

"I think of it often, everything you've done 'for me.' Do you know what I think of most often? That when you decided you wanted me to live with you after all, my grandmother had to die because she did not want to let me go and I did not want to leave."

De Lacey swallowed. He did not want to know this.

Mr. Baxter raised his head.

"I see from your expression you didn't think I knew." Miss Baxter set an elbow on an armrest, stretched out her legs, and crossed her booted feet at the ankle. "All these years, all these years I've had to tread carefully around my grandmother's murderer. She loved me as if I were a star that had fallen into her hands. Has anyone ever loved you like that, Father? No, of course not. I can tell that you were never loved."

De Lacey's fingertips shook. He yearned to take a step back but dared not draw any attention. He didn't even dare pull at his collar again—and he could barely breathe.

Miss Baxter raised her free hand and inspected her nails. "Let's see, Father, have we come to the portion of the conversation where you tell me I have no choice but to go home with you?"

Mr. Baxter's voice was strained. "I would have thought that this time I wouldn't need to tell you. You killed Charlotte Holmes. There will be consequences for you."

"Consequences?" Miss Baxter laughed contemptuously. "No, there will be no consequences for me."

She turned to her right. "Mr. Peters, kindly fetch Mrs. Watson for me."

Peters left. Silence descended. De Lacey felt as if he stood on nails.

"Mr. de Lacey, how do you do?" Miss Baxter said all of a sudden.

The silence had been damnable, but her attention was even worse. He did not want any questions from her. He wanted even less for Mr. Baxter to be reminded that he was there.

"Ah, very well, Miss Baxter."

"It is an admirable but thankless task, being Mr. de Lacey, do you not find?"

"No, indeed. I mean, of course it is admirable, but not at all thankless. It is a great honor, the greatest honor of my life."

Miss Baxter was all smiles. "There have been others who leaped at that great honor, thinking that reaching the point of de Lacey meant that they were one final step away from becoming Baxter. When in fact, they are much more likely to become a late former de Lacey."

Her honeyed voice—de Lacey felt as if he'd drunk a whole tankard of vinegar. He chuckled. It came out high-pitched. "Professional hazards, what can I say?"

He was never so happy as he was to see Mrs. Watson more or less dragged into the chapel.

The woman seemed to have aged ten years from when he last saw her. Then she'd looked haunted, but still lovely and glamorous. But now her face, swollen from tears, had lost all youth and elasticity. The grooves beside her mouth furrowed deep as trenches. The skin beneath her chin sagged. The bags under her eyes were the size of fists.

She shook loose Peters's hold on her arm and took two steps away from him—even her movements had taken on an elderly ungainliness, a combination of frailty and hesitancy. "Miss Baxter," she said hoarsely, "is it not enough that you refused to lend me anyone to help me search for Miss Holmes? Must I dance attendance on you now?"

"Mrs. Watson, are you sure you really want to know what happened to Miss Holmes?" asked Miss Baxter, a note of malice in her voice.

Her question made the older woman stumble back a step. She looked about the former chapel, her gaze coming to settle on de Lacey. "Mr. de Lacey. What are you doing here?"

"Mr. Baxter wished to see for himself that Miss Baxter is well," answered de Lacey.

Mr. Baxter's name—and presence—seemed to signify nothing to her. Her eyes continued to bore into de Lacey. "I know I've asked you this question before, Mr. de Lacey, but are you sure that you and your men never saw Miss Holmes leave the Garden night before last?"

"Mrs. Watson," said Miss Baxter coolly, "you can ask Mr. de Lacey all you want. But the answer lies with me. Miss Holmes fired at myself and Mr. Peters night before last. Happily for us, she missed. Unfortunately for her, when we returned fire, we did not miss."

Mrs. Watson visibly recoiled, but she did not even look at Miss Baxter. Instead, she spoke to de Lacey with greater urgency. "I went to sleep before she did that night. When I woke up to drink some water around midnight, she was still reading in the parlor of our cottage. But when I woke up again a little past five thirty, she was no longer there. If she'd left the Garden, it must have been during the hours in between. Did you have anyone watch the gate? Did you see anyone leave in that time period?"

"She is dead." Miss Baxter's voice rang out like a funeral toll. "A bullet went through her heart. I always wondered whether a good corset would prevent such a thing. Apparently not—as Miss Holmes's corset was quite first-rate."

Mrs. Watson's mouth opened and closed. Opened and closed. She spun to face Miss Baxter. "I—I don't understand what you are talking about, young lady. How would you know anything about Miss Holmes's corset?"

De Lacey felt a twinge of sympathy for her. She must be on the verge of losing her mind. Had she not heard a thing Miss Baxter said? Why was she asking about a corset, of all things?

"We had to remove her garments to put her body inside a drum of perchloric acid, so of course I had a good look at her corset. It should have dissolved entirely by now—her body, that is, not the corset."

Mrs. Watson stared at her, as if a crow had alit and croaked some words. Then she looked at Mr. Baxter, and again at de Lacey.

He waited for her to scream, and perhaps to drop to the floor in a dead faint. But she only took out a lace handkerchief, patted her brow, put the handkerchief away, and said, with an earnest yet wooden expression, "As I was saying, Mr. de Lacey, from midnight to an hour or so before sunrise. Did you keep a record of what you and your men saw during that time? I'm sure you must h—"

"Mr. Peters, would you help Mrs. Watson to the drums?"

Peters walked toward Mrs. Watson. McEwan went to one side of the chapel, where there stood a high altar, draped in dark blue brocade, with two tall candelabras on top. He removed the candelabras, whisked off the cloth, and underneath was a tabletop sitting above two large drums that reached his chest in height.

De Lacey recognized the drums—he'd watched them being transported into the compound his third afternoon on the coast.

Mrs. Watson resisted, pushing Peters's hands away and kicking at his knees. But he easily caught her hands by the wrists and then, with one hand under her armpit, dragged her unceremoniously to the drums.

"You must not persist in delusions, dear lady," said Miss Baxter. "The truth is right there, in front of you."

McEwan removed the tabletop and then set to work on the lid of one drum.

Miss Baxter continued, her voice soft yet inexorable. "Such was my father's design that Miss Holmes was doomed from the beginning. I tried—I helped her leave the first time. But he forced her to return. It saddens me that she had to die, yet I cannot let myself be blamed for her death. My grandmother would not have wanted that. She wanted me to move beyond my father's shadow and live free. Surely you can understand a grandmother's love, Mrs. Watson?"

She was mad, this woman. She openly admitted that she shot Charlotte Holmes. Why wouldn't Mrs. Watson hold her responsible?

But perhaps she had long been mad. After all, she had two children out of wedlock, and that spoke eloquently to her dementedness.

Mr. Baxter rose and headed for the drums, forcing de Lacey to follow in his steps. "I would not stand too close," called out Miss Baxter. "Perchloric acid won't just dissolve you. It will explode, too."

Mrs. Watson emitted a whimper. McEwan pried open the lid. An indescribable odor invaded de Lacey's nostrils, as if a meat market had been set inside a chemistry laboratory and caused people inside the lab to vomit.

He waved a hand in front of his face and retreated a step; still, he was close enough to see a clump of yellow hair floating atop the equally indescribable liquid that looked as if milk, urine, and blood had failed to intermingle. And, dear God, were those bits of as-of-yet-undissolved flesh? And was that a *toe*?

Mrs. Watson, who was the closest to the drum, slumped in Peters's arms. Miss Baxter ordered the drum closed, walked up to Mrs. Watson, and slapped her in the face. Mrs. Watson's eyelids fluttered. At the sight of Miss Baxter, she emitted a bloodcurdling scream.

Miss Baxter, however, took her by the hands, and in a wonderfully kind tone that made gooseflesh break out all over de Lacey, said, "Remember, my dear Mrs. Watson, that I had no choice. I'm just a woman who wants to hold on to what little freedom she has. It's my father who sent Miss Holmes to her death. He wanted retribution for it to fall upon me, but you must not let that happen. You know that he is the true culprit, don't you?"

Mrs. Watson, lips trembling, tears spilling from her barely focused eyes, nodded slowly.

"Go with my blessings, dear lady. Be well and avenge Miss Holmes. Go now."

With a cry, Mrs. Watson struggled to her feet, banging her shoulder on the door as she stumbled out of the former chapel.

Miss Baxter walked back to the pulpit, her two loyal bodyguards in tow, and resettled herself on her throne. "You were going to tell me, weren't you, Father, that given I've killed Miss Holmes, the wrath of her allies will fall upon me and that my only hope of survival lies with you?"

Her eyes shone with satisfaction. "But now that Mrs. Watson will carry away a very different message, what excuse do you have left?"

Mr. Baxter sighed softly. He looked at de Lacey. "I should like some tea now."

De Lacey swallowed. "Of course, sir."

He traced the same path Mrs. Watson had taken. Outside the chapel, Mrs. Watson, detained by the men, lay on the ground in a heap, her skirts muddy, her face buried in one arm, bawling. De Lacey signaled for one man to keep an eye on her and the other seven to follow him back inside, firearms drawn.

He breathed fast as he reentered the chapel. They had more men, but when bullets flew, things became unpredictable—and that was without two large drums of perchloric acid in the immediate vicinity. He did not intend to wait for Mr. Baxter's orders. The moment Miss Baxter's men reached for their weapons, he would open fire and try to end the confrontation as soon as possible.

But Miss Baxter's men did not whip out their firearms. And Miss Baxter did not even raise a brow at the sight of a small army piling into the chapel. The strangeness of their response made de Lacey's heart smash against his rib cage. He set the men in formation around Mr. Baxter, he himself standing in front, feeling terribly exposed.

"I give you one last chance, Marguerite," said Mr. Baxter. "You can come with me or you can die right here. And you two," he addressed Peters and McEwan, "there is no need to lose your life alongside hers. Walk out of here and you will be free to live as you wish."

Miss Baxter chortled. "My dear father, you swore to my dying mother, didn't you, that you would always look after me? Breaking your promise so soon?"

She rose from her throne. McEwan dragged the elaborate chair aside, revealing a strange-looking device, covered by a dust sheet.

Miss Baxter positioned herself behind the device and whipped off the dust sheet. The machine that came to sight made de Lacey think of a mechanical lion: It was a rather awkward-looking cube on four legs, the cube surmounted by a number of steel plates. Only then did he see the ominous-looking barrel and the belt of rounds, already loaded.

A Maxim gun.

McEwan hid behind the throne. Mr. Peters crouched down behind Miss Baxter.

Miss Baxter disappeared behind the protective plates fastened to the Maxim gun. She laughed. "Shall we start firing now, Father, and see which side lasts longer?"

—※—

Even Mr. Baxter had to bow to the firepower of an armored machine gun.

Like any victorious force, Miss Baxter required that the defeated be stripped of their arms. The men of Mr. Baxter's party not only had to lay down their weapons but had to submit to a search for spare pistols and knives, while Miss Baxter grinned, her finger on the Maxim gun's trigger, the barrel pointed directly at her father.

De Lacey's face burned as he trudged out of the chapel, Miss Baxter's laughter floating behind him.

Her laughter was not the only thing that followed the vanquished. With only a pair of revolvers, Peters and McEwan herded them, as if they were Roman generals parading captives into the Eternal City. Or new conquerors driving peasants off their land.

At last, the gate of the Garden closed behind them with a clang. Mr. Baxter, at the head of the inglorious retreat, turned around. De Lacey's limbs wobbled.

He expected a rage that would asphyxiate him outright. But oddly enough, Mr. Baxter seemed entirely unaffected. De Lacey rubbed his throat, disconcerted by the lack of uncomfortable feelings.

He recalled that long-ago dinner again, at which Mr. Baxter had shot Sumner. Mr. Baxter hadn't been the least bit upset then either.

Earlier this day, he had still considered Miss Baxter as his daughter. But now she was simply another foe who would be eliminated in time.

The thought did not make de Lacey feel easier. He was still a witness to Mr. Baxter's humiliation. His own life might still be forfeit.

At last Mr. Baxter spoke. "There are other matters that require my attention."

That was true. They still hadn't caught Madame Desrosiers, their ranks might still be riddled with traitors, and it was rumored that Myron Finch was throwing every wrench into the works, though it was beyond de Lacey how much damage a mere cryptographer could cause.

"Keep an eye on Mrs. Watson. Keep an eye on the Garden," continued Mr. Baxter.

"Yes, sir!" If Mr. Baxter still had tasks for him, then at least he wasn't about to become a late former de Lacey.

Mr. Baxter was already leaving with the men he brought. De Lacey hurriedly started giving orders. The patrol around the Garden's walls must resume. The gate, too, must be watched. The rest of the men he sent to Porthangan and to the nearest telegraph office.

Mrs. Watson's manservant came to the Garden not long afterward. When he drove out of the Garden again, de Lacey stopped the carriage. Upon his shabby exit from the chapel, he'd seen Mrs. Watson sitting on the ground, her head in her hands, still consumed with grief. This time she huddled in a corner of the carriage, covered by a cloak. Her face bore signs of having been washed recently, and it seemed that someone had made an effort to comb her hair; nevertheless, she looked disheveled.

As he climbed into the carriage, she only continued to stare ahead, her red-rimmed gaze unseeing.

"Mrs. Watson," said de Lacey, raising his voice, "what happened to Miss Holmes?"

Mrs. Watson twitched. "She ... Miss Baxter ... She ... Perchloric acid ..."

With a small scream she bolted upright. "Nothing has happened to Miss Holmes. Miss Baxter is a liar. As soon as I met her, I knew her to be a liar. Lies. All lies!"

He let the carriage go.

One of his men keeping watch in the village returned to report that Mrs. Watson opened the window of a room above the pub and screamed, *She is not dead! She can't be!* before being dragged away by her concerned manservant, who later told others at the pub that she'd had some bad news and he'd had to administer laudanum.

Not long after, a man stationed at the telegraph office came with news that it was the manservant who'd come in, and his cable stated only that Miss H had met grave misfortune at the hands of Miss B. At least *he* hadn't taken leave of his senses.

At sunset Miss Fairchild and Miss Ellery left the Garden. They had been the last two residents remaining, besides Miss Baxter, Peters, and McEwan.

Numbly de Lacey carried on with his tasks. A little past ten he received report from the village that Mrs. Watson's manservant, since his trip to the telegraph office, had been nursing strong drinks in the pub, looking as if he'd lost his own sister. And the sedated Mrs. Watson never left her room.

De Lacey was writing down what he had learned in the light of a kerosene lamp when the sound of hoofbeats made him come out of his tent.

A carriage, its lanterns swinging, cut across the moors. It came to a hard stop in front of the Garden's gate. Two men leaped off and pulled the heavy rope to ring the bell. The lanterns in their hands illuminated the sharp profile of Lord Ingram—and a fellow who looked vaguely familiar. Inspector Treadles?

A deafening explosion knocked them flat.

De Lacey, two hundred feet away, threw himself down. Beneath him, the ground shook.

"What happened?" shouted his confused men.

Darkness prevailed, then matches flared, both around him and at the gate, as men relit lanterns and lamps that had fallen down and extinguished.

At the gate, Lord Ingram, on his feet again, rang the bell with all his might. But a faint tintinnabulation was all that came from inside the Garden.

"Open the gate," shouted Lord Ingram, beating on that very gate.

Two of de Lacey's men came running, one from north of the Garden, the other from the opposite periphery.

"Go back," de Lacey cried. "Go back and keep patrolling."

This was most likely a diversionary maneuver on Miss Baxter's part. Perhaps she, too, had come to the conclusion that she could not trust Mrs. Watson to deflect all guilt over Miss Holmes's death toward Mr. Baxter.

With her failure would come consequences.

"But—but—" began his confused patrols.

"What but? Are the walls in danger of collapsing?"

"No, but—"

"Then back to your tasks!"

Lord Ingram had gone from banging on the gate to kicking it violently. Inspector Treadles came running. "Mr. de Lacey, is it?"

"Yes?" said de Lacey with great reserve. After all these years, coppers still made him nervous.

"Would you have your men help us force the gate open? We heard there was a great deal of perchloric acid inside the compound. I am not a chemist, but I've been told that it is a highly dangerous, explosive chemical."

De Lacey was torn. On the one hand, Miss Baxter had humiliated him today—greatly, even if he hadn't been the primary target of that humiliation. Also, hadn't he come to the realization that Mr. Baxter had stopped thinking of the woman as his daughter?

On the other hand, how would it look to Mr. Baxter if he did nothing? Even if he'd guessed correctly on how Mr. Baxter felt about his daughter, was this something Mr. Baxter would want him to know?

"Very well," he said. "We will help."

He sent a man to cable Mr. Baxter, who would have just reached London, wincing a little at the cost of waking up the postmaster and the telegraph clerk. Adding another man to the patrol, he brought the rest with him to the gate. The dossier had described the gate as two inches of steel, with bolts as thick as a man's wrist, and plates and hinges riveted either to steel or to well-masoned stone.

Even a tentative kick had him hiss in pain. The strongest of his men whimpered after ramming his shoulder into the gate. The poles and stakes they'd brought for the tents proved utterly useless as ramming devices.

Lord Ingram threw himself at the gate several times before Inspector Treadles forcibly restrained him. "There must be another way in."

But how? De Lacey craned his neck backward. From the ground to the top of the parapet, the wall was at least sixty feet high and perfectly perpendicular, with no toeholds for even a goat—and he'd seen goats leaping merrily across cliffs in these parts.

Lord Ingram sat on the ground, his hands around his knees, his face buried in his arms, his posture reminiscent of a grief-stricken Mrs. Watson from earlier in the day. And then he leaped up and ran to his carriage. "Let's go, Inspector. We have to hurry!"

Inspector Treadles, after a moment of hesitation, sprinted to the carriage, too. They left at a speed far too dangerous for an overcast night.

Despite the late hour, by this time the explosion had brought some villagers from Porthangan, as well as residents of the Garden who had been staying nearby. Some villagers thought to lash ladders together, but two ladders lashed together proved unstable, and three would have been far too dangerous, while being nowhere long enough.

Mrs. Felton, in tears, suggested the culvert, a small drain built into the eastern wall. But de Lacey had already inspected the culvert upon his arrival. The culvert not only boasted a thick metal grille that would take hours to saw through but, should it start to rain, would prove perilous for anyone trying such a thing inside.

And of course it began to pour almost immediately. The villagers and the residents of the Garden left to seek shelter, leaving de Lacey and his men to struggle with their tents and patrol through the rain, with the stench of burned flesh in their nostrils.

An hour after sunrise, Mr. Baxter arrived with dynamite. De Lacey and his men were shooing the crowd that had shown up in the morning to a safer distance when Lord Ingram and Inspector Treadles returned, too, with a large grappling hook.

De Lacey had only ever thought of the grappling hook as something used by pirates, to snag onto a ship's rigging so that it could be boarded. But it proved a decent tool here. Lord Ingram needed only three tries to catch the grappling hook on the parapet. But as he was about to begin his ascent, Mr. Baxter confiscated the spot and had one of his own men climb up, a bolt cutter strapped to his back, and open the gate.

Half a dozen men rushed in at once—and stopped dead in front of the meditation cabin, or what remained of it. Rubbles. Scorched earth. Bodies burned beyond recognition. Two overturned drums, looking as if they had been playthings of a careless giant, lay torn and crumpled.

Inspector Treadles grabbed Lord Ingram by the middle as the latter lunged forward. "None of these bodies can be Miss Holmes. They must belong to Miss Baxter and her two men."

De Lacey tiptoed through the wreckage. The reek of charred flesh had dissipated somewhat overnight, which only brought to the fore a nasty chemical smell that made him want to cough. A glint of gold on a blackened body caught his eye. Turning the body over with a stick, he saw the chain of office it still wore, gold filigree squares and fleurs-de-lis.

Someone crouched down next to the body. Mr. Baxter. He touched the chain with infinite tenderness, then ripped it off the body and threw it on the ground.

"What happened here?" he asked, to no one in particular.

"If Sherlock Holmes were here, he'd probably be able to tell you precisely what happened," said Inspector Treadles after a moment. "I can only offer a guess, which is that the three departed were emptying the contents of these drums. I understand there was perchloric acid inside?"

Mr. Baxter nodded.

"Pernicious stuff," said Inspector Treadles. "I've seen industrial accidents that resulted from it. Even with care, carnage like this can happen."

With a cry Lord Ingram stumbled forward and picked up something next to one of the overturned drums. De Lacey could not see what he had gripped in his hands, but on the ground nearby were two spent cartridges. The bullets that had killed Charlotte Holmes? Lodged in her body until it dissolved?

Lord Ingram fell to his knees and emitted an unearthly sound, between a moan and a strangled wail. His shoulders shook. His entire body was racked with sobs.

"What did you find, my lord?" asked Mr. Baxter.

He seemed preternaturally calm. No, not calm. Unaffected. Perhaps de Lacey had been right after all. He really had decided to sever ties with his daughter. And now, with this accident, he was even able to keep his promise to his late wife. After all, he had taken care of her. And Miss Baxter had died not by his orders but as a result of her own machinations.

After half a minute, Lord Ingram opened his palm. On it sat a large silver ring on a thin silver chain. The ring pendant was like none de Lacey had ever seen, an oddly yet fluidly bent circle.

"What is it?" demanded Mr. Baxter.

"It's—it's—" Lord Ingram's voice caught. "It's a topographical oddity, a shape with only one side. Holmes has always liked odd things."

And with that, and with a wipe at his eyes, he rose and staggered away. Inspector Treadles ran to him, placed an arm around his shoulders, and whispered into his ear.

But Lord Ingram flung his arm aside. "She is not dead! She can't be! Everybody can be dead but not Holmes! Not her!"

---

In the wake of their departure, peace and quiet did not ensue. Miss Fairchild and Miss Ellery stomped into the Garden and demanded that they should be the ones to arrange for funerals and burials for all the dead, especially Miss Baxter's, as she had expressed grave doubt as to whether Mr. Baxter would inter her according to her wishes, alongside her mother and grandmother.

Mr. Baxter did not care about the other two bodies but held firm on that of his child. Though he prevailed, de Lacey couldn't help but feel, once again, that his overlord was terribly distracted. He left immediately, leaving de Lacey to deal with the local constabulary, which had at last got wind of the three accidental deaths.

In the end it was de Lacey who escorted Miss Baxter to her final resting place. She proved prescient: Her father interred her not alongside her enate forebears but in a lonely plot in Lucerne, Switzerland.

Her ornate chain was hung around a bust of Medusa in Mr. Baxter's London office.

On the day de Lacey finally sat down again in his own London office, he heard rumors that Mr. Baxter might have returned to the Continent in a hurry because Myron Finch had been seen near Vienna. He didn't know why Mr. Baxter would take such troubles for Finch, but with the man gone, de Lacey had one less thing to worry about in his own fiefdom.

A week after Miss Baxter's funeral, a notice appeared in the London papers, informing the general public that Sherlock Holmes had gone abroad for his health and would not receive inquiries or clients until further notice.

With red, swollen eyes, Charlotte Holmes's sister boarded a train to go home. Mrs. Watson left for Paris to be nearer her niece. Lord Ingram, whose divorce was granted a fortnight later, made arrangements for digs abroad.

Mr. Baxter became busy with other things. So did de Lacey. Men were needed elsewhere. With Mr. Baxter's permission, those who had been stationed in the vicinity of Mrs. Watson's house and 18 Upper Baker Street were assigned to new tasks.

And de Lacey, having kept both his life and his position, was happy to see spring return at last.

Although from time to time he thought of Miss Baxter, and of the blackened chain in her father's office, and he would feel a similar sense of unreality to what Lord Ingram must have experienced.

*Everyone can be dead but not her.*

And then he would come to his senses.

# Twenty-two

The Garden of Hermopolis
Sometime earlier

The light was lambent, a gentle golden glow. Miss Baxter's green eyes seemed to glow, too. She rolled her head with a languid finesse and spoke with an equally languid menace. "Miss Holmes, I don't think we have much more to say to each other. Let us end our conversation right here."

Ah, but no. Charlotte had not come to the point of her visit yet.

"Why? Look outside the walls of the Garden, Miss Baxter. You are surrounded. I believe you face a fate far worse than merely being forced back home.

"Shall I make another unsubstantiated guess? There is a chance that your father has caught Madame Desrosiers and that Madame Desrosiers has given you up as the true mastermind behind his ouster last year."

Miss Baxter's eyelids flickered.

So Charlotte had guessed correctly: She had been involved in the coup.

"With so much danger darkening your doorstep, why not help me, at least? You claim responsibility for Mr. Craddock's death; I go on keeping the secret of your child's location. Perhaps I could even help Mrs. Crosby and the baby after I leave."

"Oh, perhaps you could, could you?" said Miss Baxter lightly, yet with unmistakable animosity.

She cracked her neck, her motion sharp yet lithe, like that of a cobra uncoiling. "Too much groundless speculation isn't good for you, Miss Holmes. Mr. Craddock is perfectly fine, meditating in his cottage. And I shall be fine, too. But you, my dear foolhardy girl, you should be careful."

And now they really didn't have anything else to say to each other.

Charlotte took an extra coconut biscuit and rose. "I'm sorry we must part on such terms, Miss Baxter. You have lovely clothes and just as lovely biscuits, both of which I appreciate very much."

She saw herself out, whistling as she did so. The night fog was even thicker now, a cloud that flowed around her lantern and drifted on the ground. She returned to her own cottage, put some water to boil, and made two hot water bottles.

As she wiped around the stoppers and made sure they were tight, Lord Ingram came back, too. "Mrs. Steele was listening outside Miss Baxter's window. Mrs. Watson has engaged her and her husband."

Charlotte nodded. They climbed out the bedroom window. In this fog, unless someone stood directly outside, they would not be seen.

She had her umbrella in one hand; he took her other hand. After a moment, she pulled free and took his hand instead. As children, she and Livia often held hands, but always with her holding Livia's hand and not the other way around, so that she could decide for herself when to let go.

He did not object—he probably already understood this about her. It felt . . . very nice. As an adult, she'd never walked holding someone's hand. Granted, she could see nothing on this walk, not him, not the ground underfoot, not even the fog that surrounded them, but she did not feel the need to see either the sky or the earth. Or even him.

His hand in hers was enough as they traveled through pitch-blackness.

When they neared her destination, he left to reconnoiter and returned a few minutes later to let her know she could go ahead. They gave each other's hands a squeeze. He would remain outside and she would proceed by herself.

She found the door of Mrs. Crosby's cottage, let herself in, and locked the door.

Inside, darkness pressed against her eyes. She felt her way with the tip of her umbrella.

"You poked me on my foot," someone said.

Miss Baxter.

"Are the curtains secure?" Charlotte asked.

"Yes. And the windows, too," said Miss Baxter.

A tiny bit of light spread. Miss Baxter had brought a pocket lantern, the shutter of which she raised slightly. She looked rather ghostly in this light. Charlotte imagined she herself did not appear very different, a somewhat chubbier ghost.

She took the chair next to Miss Baxter's and handed her a hot water bottle, keeping the other one for herself. With Mrs. Crosby gone, fires hadn't been lit in her cottage. It was cold and damp.

"Thank you," said Miss Baxter. "And we meet again."

Charlotte nodded. She hadn't dropped off only a calling card for Miss Baxter this afternoon. Underneath the calling card had been a carefully folded note. *I may have glimpsed something in the magazines you wished me to read and would like a meeting. But first we must have a different meeting. I noticed last time that your parlor window was open a crack to let in fresh air. Please make sure of the same tonight.*

She wanted theater. And between the two of them they had mounted a veritable spectacle.

"Did you not go a little too far, though, Miss Holmes?" murmured Miss Baxter. "Even knowing what you meant for us to portray, I was still not best pleased with you."

"If it would make you feel better, I don't know where the new baby is and would never have been able to threaten you with that knowledge."

Miss Baxter sighed. "My poor child. But you didn't come to talk about my children."

"No, I am here because you approached me to be your ally."

With immense subtlety, because the risks involved were those of life and death.

"You have accepted then?" Miss Baxter's lips barely moved as she uttered the question.

It became Charlotte's turn to sigh. "I would have liked to decline, but I do need an ally. And, well, once I saw what you wanted me to see, I could no longer refuse you, could I?"

She had first wondered whether Mr. Finch wasn't somehow involved when Miss Baxter had used the same story that Lady Ingram had. Granted the story had been Miss Baxter's first, but the effect was the same: to make Charlotte think of Mr. Finch.

Then, as it turned out, the small notices in the magazines Miss Baxter kept in her private collection, the ones Mr. Mears had copied down and sent Charlotte via cable, had been instantly familiar: They were but a slightly more complicated version of the cipher Mr. Finch had used to inform her, in the most general of terms, of his well-being and whereabouts.

The man for whom this woman had risked so much was none other than her half brother.

Charlotte sighed again. She didn't think what she felt could be called *emotional*, but it was a far stronger sentiment than what she normally experienced. The woman before her had known fear, anguish, and sacrifice on a scale she could scarcely imagine—and remained unbowed.

"Did you meet my brother because he worked for your father?"

Miss Baxter shook her head, her expression softening a little. "We met because of fate. He went to work for my father after my father caught me heavily pregnant, even though I'd left not only my grandmother's house but the Garden, in order to hide. It was by the grace of God that Myron wasn't there the day my father came.

"Before that happened, we had discussed very seriously what we would do if we were snared, together or singly. From the very beginning, I told him that I would not be able to endure captivity, not even for the sake of my own child. And he told me that if I were caught by myself, then I should leave my father however I could, and he would bring our child back to me."

Charlotte remembered her brother at their last meeting, a taciturn man whose calm demeanor revealed little of his experiences in life. She'd believed then that he had joined Moriarty's organizations because of what it promised to a man of illegitimate birth—and had later become disillusioned and left. That would have been difficult enough. But to have chosen his path, knowing that he was entering an abyss of danger . . .

*I hope he is all right, and I hope he does not regret everything he has had to endure for me.*

"Miss Marbleton said Mr. Finch wanted information on das Phantomschloss. Whatever else the place may be, is it also where your child is?"

"Yes." A rueful laughter emerged from Miss Baxter. "We knew, when we realized that my father had double-crossed his paymaster, that we wouldn't be able to use that against him until our son is safely back with us. But in my euphoria, and knowing that the coup I'd helped Madame Desrosiers plan was on the horizon, I got carried away. I wanted another child, a child I wouldn't need to give up, the thought of whom wouldn't always bring with it a stab of pain."

She hugged the hot water bottle Charlotte had given her close to her chest. "Every day I think of our reunion. But with each passing day, I dread it a little more. He has never met Myron, and he would have forgotten me. What would I say to him? I had to leave you so that I could unseat your grandfather, so that we could all live free in the future? Children do not understand the idea of the future. They only understand now. Today. And we haven't been there for any today that he can remember.

"And the coup on which I'd pinned so much of my hope? We had to hasten it because we were in danger of being discovered, which led to it being only partially successful. When Monsieur Plantier, Madame Desrosiers's brother, came to see me last November, under the guise of being the new solicitor from my father, we had some difficult choices to make, and I don't know that we chose altogether correctly."

The light flickered on her barely lit face. She looked translucent, carven. "Perhaps we should have killed him. Perhaps we should have demanded my son in exchange for his freedom. We were all hoping for the ideal solution, for his paymaster to get rid of him. But without the access Myron had given up when he became a fugitive, even though we knew how my father cheated his master, we couldn't obtain evidence."

Charlotte held on tighter to her own hot water bottle. "The Marbletons will be disappointed when they realize that he has no evidence."

"No more disappointed than we are."

She spoke softly, but her words were heavy with long years of striving that had yet to bear fruit.

They fell silent.

Perhaps because of the near complete darkness inside the house, the sounds of the coast were muffled. No rumble of the sea crashing against the cliffs, no howling of night gales tearing into roofs and rattling windowpanes. It was so quiet that she could hear the hissing of the tiny flame inside Miss Baxter's pocket lantern, and the sound of her boots sliding across the carpet.

Except Miss Baxter had not moved.

There was another person in Mrs. Crosby's parlor.

"Is Mr. Finch here tonight?"

"Yes," came a man's voice from an unseen corner of the room, a rather unwilling voice.

"Please don't mind him," said Miss Baxter. "He's still peeved that I never told him I was with child again."

"You said I couldn't be here because Craddock had seen me before. I'd never have known Craddock was dead if Miss Fairchild wasn't desperate for someone the Marbletons had already vouched for to pretend that he was still alive."

He did sound unhappy.

"I told you, Father had already regained his freedom by then and could find out any day that I was involved with the coup. It was not safe for you to be near me. Besides, I didn't know you were the new Mr. Craddock. How was I supposed to tell you?" Miss Baxter took a deep breath. "Anyway, I apologize, Miss Holmes. Your brother and I will argue to death on the matter later, in our own time. What were we discussing?"

"Das Phantomschloss," said Charlotte. "Mr. Marbleton went through great pains to get a photograph to me, for me to give Mr. Finch. Perhaps we can have a little more light."

Miss Baxter rose—then fell back into her chair. "But photography is not allowed at or near das Phantomschloss."

Charlotte opened the shutter more fully on Miss Baxter's pocket lantern. "I'm under the impression that this picture is notable more for its human subjects than for its locale."

Mr. Finch emerged from the shadows. He looked a little worse for wear but was in decent shape for someone who had been living in fear of his life for nearly a year.

He glanced at Miss Baxter. Charlotte was well-acquainted with how men in love gazed upon the objects of their affection. This look was—different. Every instance of bright, fiery young love must be tossed into the crucible of life, but these two had had to endure the unendurable. Did it make them hold on all the more tightly to memories of the past? And did that, in turn, make it more disconcerting to realize how much they had changed during these long years spent away from each other?

Yet she did not sense disillusionment in him, only a sense of resignation: This woman, whose fate was thoroughly intertwined with his, had become something of a stranger.

"By the way, was that you, Mr. Finch, in the cottage next to ours, observing us?" she asked.

He nodded.

She handed to Miss Baxter the Stanhope in which had been affixed Mr. Marbleton's microphotography and lifted the pocket lantern to better illuminate it.

Miss Baxter gasped as soon as she looked. She gave the optical device to Mr. Finch and took the pocket lantern from Charlotte to hold it for him herself. "Look. *Look.*"

After one look, he enfolded her in a hard embrace.

Miss Baxter laughed, sobbing. "Finally. Finally. After all these years!"

"Yes, finally," mumbled Mr. Finch—and made a sound that sounded suspiciously like a sniffle.

Charlotte gave them a minute. "But you can only take advantage of your new knowledge after Miss Baxter and I extricate ourselves from our current morass, being pitted against each other. I have discussed this with my friends, and we all agree that it would be ideal if Moriarty came to believe that he succeeded in getting rid of me permanently."

"That would be ideal indeed," said Miss Baxter.

"But would he believe it?"

"No."

Charlotte had braced herself for an unfavorable answer. Still, her heart sank at Miss Baxter's unequivocal answer.

"For this we have Mrs. Marbleton to blame, partly. If you were already a suspicious man by nature, *and* your wife counterfeited her own death to get away from you, you probably wouldn't believe any death to be real unless you watched it happen with your own eyes."

Charlotte shook her head. *Alas.* "You said Mrs. Marbleton is only partly to blame?"

"The other part of the blame lies with me," answered Miss Baxter with a pulling of her lips. "I don't know whether Madame Desrosiers has been captured, but I believe you are right about my father having discovered my involvement in the coup. Even behind these walls, I will not be safe for long. Therefore, it's not only ideal but also urgent that he should believe I've met an untimely end.

"If we stage only your death, there is a higher probability that my father would believe it—after all, it is his goal that I should get rid of you for him. But if we both end up dead as a result of our contest—that would strike him as too good to be true."

Charlotte sucked in a breath through her teeth.

Miss Baxter's eyes glittered. "However, we do have one or two factors in our favor. First, the current state of my father's organization. It is not in shambles, unfortunately, but the coup did deal a blow. My father's subsequent cleansing of everyone he suspected to have been sympathetic to the coup likely dealt a worse blow."

"I see," said Charlotte slowly. "He is severely shorthanded."

"Correct. Two, as women, we are not *that* important to him. He is pursuing Madame Desrosiers hard not because she is the mastermind behind his ouster but because she was his mistress and her betrayal is personal. I would be surprised if he didn't believe her brother, Monsieur Plantier, to be her puppet master.

"He thinks of me as a willful girl with more arrogance than intelligence; if he had a better idea of my capabilities, he would have groomed me to be his heir. But no, he only wanted me to be the kind of daughter whose appearance and conduct signaled her father's importance.

"He probably considers you a more substantial threat but still a woman, subject to all the frailties of our sex. The way I see it, he wants to be rid of you less because of your deeds and more to eliminate someone who might provide safe harbor to Myron."

"So by counterfeiting our deaths, we will be doing him a favor. We will allow him to better allocate his men and no longer waste his resources on the likes of us," said Charlotte.

Mr. Finch, who had sat down on a footstool next to Miss Baxter's chair, snickered.

Miss Baxter chortled a little, too. "There is a third factor in our favor. You have probably never been on the run before, Miss Holmes. But I am surrounded by people who have. As long as fugitives do not go back to their old haunts or old acquaintances, it is in fact very difficult to find them, once they have disappeared. So what I need, right now, isn't for my father to believe that I've really died, but only enough time in which to disappear.

"For that I have prepared a surprise or two for my father. What do you think he would do if he was to hear that Myron has entered the orbit of his paymaster?"

"Ahhh."

"Exactly. I will quickly become a secondary concern as he intensifies his hunt for Myron, preferably in the wrong part of the world." Miss Baxter allowed herself a small smile. "And with my father preoccupied with his own survival, the person we really need to convince becomes de Lacey—and the men under de Lacey. And here again luck is in our favor—the previous de Lacey was a wily fox. This one, not so much. So should we succeed, we would have bought ourselves some valuable time."

Time for Miss Baxter and Mr. Finch to find their son. Time for Charlotte and her friends to free Mr. Marbleton. Time to formulate a plan to dethrone Moriarty, this time permanently.

"Good enough for me," said Charlotte. "Now we've just had a tremendous row, witnessed by Mrs. Steele, which should make it appear that we have become enemies. Next I should dig up Mr. Craddock's body—is it in one of the graves on the headlands?"

"Yes." Miss Baxter placed her hand on Mr. Finch's shoulder. "Only one of our people died of pneumonia, but two others wished to take that opportunity to 'pass away,' in case Moriarty traced their footsteps here. We put Craddock in one of the empty coffins."

Mr. Finch placed his hand briefly over Miss Baxter's. Charlotte must still be feeling somewhat emotional: The sight made her want to smile—and sigh. "Did Mr. Craddock see you in an advanced state of pregnancy, by the way?"

Miss Baxter rolled her eyes. "Would I be so careless? No, he was the kind of man who would abuse any little power he had. He didn't dare approach me, but he set his sights on Miss Stoppard and cornered her on the walls one night. Little did he know she's handy with a knife.

"She hadn't meant to kill him, but she did. So she had Mr. McEwan and Mr. Peters come up to the wall, and they were just discussing what they ought to do when a *grappling hook*, of all things, came plonking down."

Charlotte briefly explained the story behind the grappling hook, that it had been launched by a friend who was investigating various properties around Britain that had been worked on by De Lacey Industries' preferred main contractor.

"So there *was* a connection. I was both rattled and perplexed—it didn't seem like my father's modus operandi, yet I also couldn't believe it to be a random happenstance." Miss Baxter held out her hot water bottle to her lover with an inquiring glance; he declined it with a small shake of his head. She returned her attention to Charlotte. "Mr. Kaplan, our friend who died of pneumonia, enjoyed exploring caves. There is a cave a mile or so from here that he learned about from the locals. But inside he found a passage that even the locals didn't know about, and the passage led directly underneath the Garden."

"Oh? Mrs. Watson and Lord Ingram saw some cave openings on the promontory. Do they belong to the same system?"

"No, none of the other nearby caves are connected—or at least, none of them are of any use to human-sized creatures. Even the passage Mr. Kaplan found was deep enough underground that at first we had no way of accessing it. Mrs. Crosby came up with the idea of building cisterns, which would give us a legitimate excuse to dig on the grounds of the Garden. Some of our people were working for the main contractor then, and we made sure they were the ones who dug through to the underground passage.

"Three cisterns were dug. That particular one, once we'd pumped out the water inside, the pump 'broke.' Since the two others provided enough water, Miss Fairchild did not 'bother' to repair the pump. We shut off the inflow pipes years ago, so the cistern should be relatively dry inside and usable right away as an entrance to the cave."

"There is a secret way into the Garden, and you never allowed me to visit?" grumbled Mr. Finch. He sounded grievously hurt.

Charlotte didn't so much see Miss Baxter glare at him as heard it. "It is impossible to walk in this passage. You have to crawl. It takes two hours to cover half a mile. And you need Mr. Peters for a guide because otherwise you'd get lost in there."

Silence.

She sighed and caressed his hair. "Are we going to do what my father couldn't and tear ourselves apart?"

There was fear in her voice, deep, stark fear.

Mr. Finch sighed, too, and rested his head on her shoulder. "No, we won't."

"I'm sorry I didn't tell you that I was expecting again," murmured Miss Baxter.

Mr. Finch's voice seemed to thicken. "Apology accepted. And I'm sorry I was angry at you when in your shoes I'd have done the same thing."

Charlotte took out the coconut biscuit she'd taken from Miss Baxter's place earlier. It went well with a scene of dimly lit reconciliation.

She was just about finished with the biscuit when Miss Baxter said, "So you will dig up Mr. Craddock's body on the headlands, Miss Holmes. And since my father is convinced I killed Craddock, I will, of course, need to appear on scene to prevent you from finding out the truth."

Charlotte nodded. "We can get into another quarrel, and you can shoot me. That seems reasonable enough. But how do we account for the absence of my body?"

"We've been uneasy for a while about Craddock's body—interred, but still in the vicinity," answered Miss Baxter. "Mr. McEwan was trained as a chemist and he suggested perchloric acid, which we've been accumulating in small amounts. We have just about enough to dissolve one person's remains. Shall we dissolve Craddock's and claim that they are yours?"

Ah, but it was a pleasure to scheme with this woman.

"And of course in the meanwhile I would have left via the cistern, with Mr. Peters's guidance. De Lacey and his men would only know that my body had been transported back into the Garden and then was never seen again." Charlotte traced her fingers around the slightly raised stamp on her envelope-patterned hot water bottle cozy. "That works for me. But what about you?"

"It will be more complicated for me. I must orchestrate my death in a way that doesn't embroil the other members of the Garden, especially not Miss Fairchild, who has been a stalwart friend all these years." Miss Baxter rubbed one knuckle across her lips. "It's possible I will need to face my father at some point."

Charlotte's innards tightened. "I had a difficult time with him, when he called on me."

"It's never easy," said Miss Baxter quietly. "I do not have his near hypnotic prowess, but I have learned that for him to be effective, he needs a single-minded focus. And I can disrupt that by upsetting or outright angering him."

A veteran of many battles, this woman. "I'll leave the handling of your father to you. But what about your remains? We can't both disappear without bodies."

"I can have Dr. Robinson locate one for me. He has the contacts for cadavers."

"I suppose since you trusted him enough to deliver your baby, we can trust him on this also."

"His credentials go much further than that. He was the one who found a body for Mrs. Marbleton all those years ago, when she needed to leave my father."

This made Charlotte's eyes widen. Such *profound* knowledge of Mrs. Marbleton's past . . .

Miss Baxter chortled at Charlotte's reaction. "Yes, she was the one who 'kidnapped' me when I was a child, shortly after my grandmother passed away. Here at the Garden we trust only those she has personally vouched for."

She caressed Mr. Finch's hair again. "But even to her I dared not breathe a word about Myron."

Mr. Finch rubbed his head against her palm.

The impossible task those two faced, in trying to reunite their family . . .

Charlotte took out a jam tart that Lord Ingram had given her earlier. "You will have your son back. I will help you."

*Think before you speak, Miss Holmes.*

*I always do.*

Perhaps here was another exception. Or perhaps she had been thinking about this very future since the moment she realized her brother's role in Miss Baxter's life—and vice versa.

Her simple statement made Miss Baxter and Mr. Finch come to their feet. They understood the commitment she had made.

Slowly Miss Baxter sat down again. She offered her hand to Charlotte.

Charlotte shook it. "You are welcome, Miss Moriarty."

Briefly, Marguerite Moriarty covered her mouth with her hand, as if still unable to believe that Charlotte had pledged herself to their cause. And then she smiled. "Perhaps my father will have the last laugh—but I don't believe so. We will overthrow him someday. And he will regret that he has underestimated us all along."

# Epilogue

A marriage is an agreement between two people—and two families—to form an alliance, you see. It's a solemn pact and usually lasts until one of the people is no more. But sometimes those who enter into that agreement realize that they have made a mistake. That the marriage itself is the mistake. And instead of living forever in a mistake, they choose to end the marriage.

"The end of a marriage is just as solemn a pact. A petition for divorce has to be filed and then granted by the court. Very soon, that is what will happen to Mamma and Papa's marriage. The court will grant us a divorce and we will no longer be married to each other."

For months, Lord Ingram had been preparing an explanation for his children, one that grew longer and more ornate with each new mental draft, until he estimated that if he began his oration at their bedtime, they would be an hour asleep by the time he finally reached his point.

Lady Ingram's version, on the other hand, wasted no words.

After Christmas, he had put a notice in the papers for her, offering her a safe place to stay. To his surprise, she had responded and accepted his offer—she had escaped Château Vaudrieu alongside Madame Desrosiers a fortnight before, and hadn't wanted to be a burden on the other woman for much longer.

He gave her a range of choices and she opted for the West Berkshire estate that had once belonged to Bancroft. When he'd needed to stow the children somewhere safe, the place became the obvious choice, so that they could spend some time with their mother.

But now, with him away from Cornwall due to his children's "high fevers" and with Holmes soon to "perish," he could not be sure that the next time he left the Cornish coast he wouldn't be followed.

Nor would he want to shake the potential follower loose, when the time came. To the contrary, for a period of time, until Moriarty's minions were withdrawn, those closest to Holmes would make their comings and goings fully visible, to further bolster the impression of her permanent disappearance from their lives.

So it would be better for Lady Ingram to leave this estate now— for a different hiding place he had arranged—before he came to shepherd the children home, in the wake of Holmes's "demise."

He had not expected that she would take it upon herself to explain the imminent dissolution of their marriage to Lucinda and Carlisle, nor that she would do so in front of him. He was grateful. What she said might be brutal, but so was the reality the children needed to understand.

"Why was it a mistake?" asked Carlisle timidly. He would not turn five until later in the year and probably felt the somberness of the occasion more than he understood his mother's exact words.

Lady Ingram, down on one knee, caressed his cheek. "Sometimes some people are not meant to live together. That's all."

"Remember when you secretly brought Bunny inside? You wanted her to live with us, but Bunny tore everything up," added Lucinda, who would soon be six and had been an independent thinker since she was three days old.

"Oh," said Carlisle, understanding dawning.

Bunny was not a bunny but a puppy that had wreaked havoc in the nursery at Stern Hollow, Lord Ingram's country seat. The memories of her destructiveness were still fresh.

The analogy, however . . .

Lady Ingram did not possess the most robust sense of humor. Lord Ingram glanced at her, wondering whether she would take offense.

After a moment of seeming incomprehension, however, she smiled ruefully. "Yes, something like that. But I will still try to come and see you as often as I can. And I will think of you, as always, every minute of every day."

—⊶—

"It could have gone horribly wrong!" complained Holmes. "The umbrella gun you gave me burst into flames. When we got back to safety, Miss Baxter laughed so hard she was in tears."

Lord Ingram had nearly gone into cardiac arrest when he'd retired for the night and found Holmes on his bed, arrayed in the most beautifully appalling pink tea gown in existence and looking absolutely splendid. They were at his brother's ducal estate, where he had brought his children to visit their cousins for Easter, and it was the first time he had laid eyes on her since Cornwall.

As it turned out, she had hired his brother's hunting lodge— Their Graces, like most other owners of large stately homes, were under pressure to generate greater income, and the letting of smaller edifices on the estate was one such means. In masculine attire, she had moved about the estate freely and even explored the nearby countryside.

Once he'd recovered from his shock, Lord Ingram wasted no time in removing his jacket and waistcoat. "You dare grouse about that umbrella bursting into flames, Holmes? After what *you* did to *me*?"

She was already giggling, not a sight one saw every day. "What did I do to you?"

"The thing you left behind in the Garden as a memento for me to recognize you by—" He sputtered. "You—"

"Oh, you mean the circular metallic object intended to go on your unmentionable parts? The one I showed you one time but we were too sleepy to use?"

He climbed into bed and pulled her into his arms. "Yes, that. Once I saw that, how was I supposed to act bereaved? I nearly choked trying not to laugh—I sounded like a hyena with bronchitis."

"I wish I could have seen it!" she said, her eyes shining.

"Huh. I was going to do the manly thing, shake my fist at Moriarty, and threaten all kinds of retribution. Instead, I had to sprint out of the Garden before I gave myself away."

"But you did well. We all did well," she murmured. And pulled him in for a kiss.

And no one thought of Moriarty again, for a while.

# ACKNOWLEDGMENTS

Kerry Donovan, who has been a dream editor.

Jessica Mangicaro, Tara O'Connor, and Mary Baker at Penguin Random House, for their always excellent work.

And to the production team, members of whom I have never met, for putting up with my messy page proofs year after year—you are heroes!

Kristin Nelson, my incomparable agent, who is just superior day in and day out.

Janine Ballard, who gives incredibly detailed and guided critiques. Even if I am the one groaning under the weight of 500 comments, I am still amazed by my good fortune at every turn.

Kate Reading, the perfect narrator for these books.

My family, for being such great people.

My brain, which held up for this book, too—to be sure there were moments when I thought it would implode.

And you, if you are reading this, thank you. Thank you for everything.

Photo by Jennifer Sparks Harriman

*USA Today* bestselling author **Sherry Thomas** is one of the most acclaimed historical fiction authors writing today, winning the RITA Award two years running and appearing on innumerable "Best of the Year" lists, including those of *Publishers Weekly, Kirkus Reviews, Library Journal*, Dear Author, and All About Romance. Her novels include *A Study in Scarlet Women, A Conspiracy in Belgravia, The Hollow of Fear, The Art of Theft*, and *Murder on Cold Street*, the first five books in the Lady Sherlock series; *My Beautiful Enemy*; and *The Luckiest Lady in London*. She lives in Austin, Texas, with her husband and sons.

CONNECT ONLINE

SherryThomas.com